The
Hollow
Man

A (Transgressive) Novel of Suspense by

G.
Patrick
Huskins

MurderInkPress

THE HOLLOW MAN
Copyright © 2009 by G. Patrick Huskins

First Edition

Library and Archives Canada Cataloguing in Publication

Huskins, G. Patrick, 1963-
The hollow man : a (transgressive) novel of suspense / by G. Patrick Huskins.

ISBN 978-0-9812132-0-0

I. Title.

PS8615.U775H65 2009   C813'.6   C2009-901861-6

1 2 3 4 5 6 7 8 9 10

Manufactured in the United States of America

AUTHOR'S NOTE

"If you can't laugh at others, who can you laugh at?"
Daniel Rourke

The Hollow Man is a work of fiction, part parody of its genre(s), part satire. Any resemblance to actual people, living or dead, is purely coincidental. Any and all references to public figures, living, dead or mostly dead, i.e., Senators Edward M. Kennedy and John F Kerry of Massachusetts, are made within the spirit of satire/parody, as protected by the First Amendment of the U.S Constitution and upheld by numerous Supreme Court rulings safeguarding the latitude of satire/parody as a vital aspect of freedom of speech.

G.P.H

for **GW and The Spense Man**

The Hollow Man

1

Massachusetts Governor Terrence Thornton III's military decorations were on display in a handsome Bakelite frame hanging over the study's colossal Rumford fireplace. During his two tours of duty in Vietnam, he had received the Silver Star, the Bronze Star, the Distinguished Flying Cross, and two Purple Hearts. The governor liked to gaze at these colorful trinkets when he had the good fortune to work from the insulated comfort of home, not out of nostalgia, but as a grim reminder of hard battles fought, and harder lessons learned. After rattling off the cautionary denouement of his latest make-or-break speech, he turned his thoughts from the murky gray of a past half forgotten to the crystalline promise of a future as yet only glimpsed.

"Did you get all that, Donna?"

His assistant's thin, overly red lips were pursed, pencil hovering at the ready over her steno pad.

"Yeah, I got it."

"Not too shabby, huh?"

"Says you."

"What? No shivers down the spine? Your heart didn't go pitter patter?"

A bulimic, bi-polar spinster with a three-pack-a-day nicotine habit and a wanton disregard for protocol, Donna Mathers had been his executive assistant for more than a quarter century. Although they'd had their share of skirmishes over the years, she had served him loyally, and well. For beneath the scowling, makeup-caked exterior was a brilliant strategist with a keen mind. No matter the subject or the stakes, she could always be counted on to 'tell it like it is,' even if that meant bruising his occasionally fragile ego.

"Well?" he pressed.

Like a Mark 7 naval gun traversing, Miss Mathers looked up from the pad and swung her gaze in his direction. "No shivers," she said. "No pitter patter."

"No reaction at all, huh?"

"Aside from tripping my gag reflex near the end? None whatsoever."

"So what's the problem now?"

"It's your allusion to Eliot's *Prufrock*."

"What about it?"

"It makes me want to puke."

"What doesn't?"

Miss Mathers raised her chin slightly. Sent a warning glare screaming over his bow. "Okay, wise ass. It sucks the big one. Is that unambiguous enough for you?"

"Well I like it. It adds a certain sense of-"

"Pompous bullshit?"

"I was going to say panache."

"*Panache?* It's a Democratic fundraiser, Terrence. Have you forgotten the cardinal rule of speech writing?"

"Consider your audience."

Miss Mathers nodded curtly. "Sure the stuffed-shirts from Harvard will get it, or at least have the good sense to pretend to, but the rest of them? No way. Especially the *actors*." She had been engaged to a minor soap opera lothario in the mid-eighties. The relationship had ended badly, and the woman could nurse a grudge to the grave. In the two-plus decades that had passed since the nuptials were axed she hadn't changed her hairstyle, her garish, printed polyester wardrobe, or her opinion of the men and women who chose, as she called it, the profession that dares not speak its name.

"The eternal Footman is-"

"Symbolic of the death that awaits human civilization if we continue to ignore the perils of global warming. *Yada yada yada.* I get it. They won't. They're narcissistic morons." Miss Mathers idly finger-combed her extravagant, bleach-blond mane while she awaited her orders.

"Times have changed, Donna. For some of us, at least." The governor drummed his fingertips on the desktop. "Are you absolutely certain the allusion will be over their heads?"

Miss Mathers chuckled softly. "There's a very good reason why Jeff Spicoli has never led the Vienna Philharmonic in Berlioz's *La Damnation de Faust*, or performed bypass surgery at Johns Hopkins, quadruple or otherwise." She rapped a French manicured nail hard against her temple. "Think about it."

"Sean's a good kid. His heart's in the right place."

"Not that he would know."

The governor closed his eyes, rubbing them absentmindedly while he re-ran the closing stanza through his head. "Okay, okay, you win. Scratch the lines."

With the finesse of Guy Williams' Zorro, Miss Mathers slashed her pencil over the page. "Done. Done. And done."

"Now read it back to me from the top."

"From the top? *Again?*"

The governor smiled patiently. "Humor me," he said. "And with a modicum of feeling this time."

Miss Mathers flipped noisily backward through the spiral-bound pages then began to read in an exaggerated monotone. "The debate on global warming has finally ended. Scientists in every discipline, in every country of the world, have at last reached a consensus. Unfortunately, those of us on the left were right-"

She was interrupted by a psychedelic explosion of color and sound as Captain Planet materialized on the notebook computer sitting open at the governor's right hand. "You've got mail," the cut-rate super hero announced, arms akimbo. "The power is yours. Read it, or delete it."

The e-mail notification software had been presented to the governor on the evening of his inauguration by Ted Turner. Although it annoyed him to no end, his eccentric friend with the gap-toothed grin had become so giddy during its installation, actually tittering until he got the hiccups, that the good governor just couldn't bring himself to banish it to the great cyber beyond.

"Keep reading, Donna."

Miss Mathers responded with a crisp salute. *"Jawohl, herr Kommandant."*

The e-mail, with attachments, had been sent to his private account. The sender's address was unfamiliar. Spam, most likely. Black market Prozac, or HGH. He fingered the curser over to the 'delete' option but paused as the subject line snagged his attention. 'Out of sight, out of mind.' He smiled in spite of himself. *Penile enhancement?* On a lark, he opened it. As he scanned the text, the wainscoted walls of his study began to close in on him, making it difficult to breathe, and there was a stabbing pain in his temples. At the bottom of the page was the child-like rendering of an elephant.

The governor glanced up from the screen. His assistant's mischievous eyes were dancing over her hieroglyphic shorthand as she continued to butcher his eloquent, inspirational call to action, utterly blind to his discomfort. With great trepidation, he clicked on the attachments. There were two. A picture of an old, off-kilter Polaroid, and a muted video clip. He could hear his heartbeat in his head, feel it in his bones, fast and furious, like primitive war drums.

"Terrence?" Miss Mathers said some indeterminate period of time later. "Hello?" She began to wave a hand in the air. *"Hellooo?* Is there anybody home?"

Beads of perspiration popped onto the governor's brow and upper lip, but he dared not wipe them away. He opened his mouth but nothing came out.

"Governor Thornton." There was a new note in her tone, one sharp with worry.

He willed his heart rate out of the danger zone and forced a smile. "The speech is fine, Donna. As usual your input was invaluable."

"Are you alright? You look like you've seen a-"

"One too many late nights on the stump I'm afraid. Nothing to be alarmed about."

"Are you sure? I could call Dr.-"

"I'm fine. Really. I just need a moment or two alone."

Miss Mathers uncrossed her bony legs but hesitated before getting up. He could sense that she wanted to say something more but thankfully, and somewhat uncharacteristically, she bit her tongue.

"Lock the door on your way out," the governor said. "And hold my calls."

"Hold your-"

"Calls, Donna. Hold them all. I'm not here. And you have no idea when I'll be back."

Of all his cherished possessions, Terrence Thornton was most proud of his desk. It was rock-solid, with an exterior lovingly crafted of hand-planed, hand-finished maple. Originally gifted to President Hoover in 1930 by the Furniture Manufacturers Association of Grand Rapids, Michigan, it had been used by Franklin Delano Roosevelt in the Oval Office throughout his exceptional presidency. Although he'd owned the piece for more than a year, the sense of awe and inspiration the first term governor felt each time he rolled his chair between its pedestals had never waned. If all went well with the DNC's nominating convention, and then again with the general election, *President* Thornton would see the desk returned to its rightful place in a little over fourteen months. The only problem was, in the snippet of time that it took for a cheesy cartoon character with a green mullet to blurt 'The power is yours,' his cloudy gray times were no longer a thing of the past.

In the grand second floor study of his Charles Bulfinch designed Federal-style mansion overlooking Boston's Mt. Vernon Street, with the door locked, his calls held, and the numerous state-of-the-art surveillance devices deactivated, the governor stared numbly at the vexatious e-mail. What troubled him most, as a man who valued loyalty above all else, was the fact that it had been sent to his private e-mail account. No more than a handful of his most trusted confidantes were even aware of its existence, which suggested a betrayal close to the heart. He hadn't moved a muscle in the hour and a half since receiving the transmission, and the expected flash of brilliance had yet to manifest itself. Undaunted, he tapped his intercom and called for the advice of a friend.

Seconds later, there was a soft treble knock on his door.

"Come," the governor said.

The lock disengaged and the heavy wooden door creaked open. A muscular, middle-aged black man wearing a blue pinstripe Savile Row suit entered the room and stood at razor-sharp attention. "You wanted to see me, sir." Raymond Sowell was the United States Secret Service agent in charge of his protection detail. They had known each other for more than thirty years and were, as the kids today liked to say, 'brothers from another mother.' "You said it was urgent."

"Close the door. Quickly."

Sowell closed and relocked the door.

"Take a look at this." Thornton spun the notebook computer around to face his visitor. "As to whether it's truly an urgent matter, you're the resident security guru, I'll defer to your judgment."

Sowell read the e-mail. He examined the photo and the video file closely before commenting. "To merely call it urgent is one hell of an understatement, sir."

"It's from *them,* isn't it?"

"From whom, sir?"

"The Republicans. The elephant is their mascot symbol after all."

"Maybe. Maybe not."

"So why the elephant?"

Sowell shrugged.

"Speculate."

"Out of sight, out of mind? The elephant never forgets? I really don't know, sir. Not enough intel to hazard a guess. Yet." He took a small note pad from his pocket and jotted down the sender's e-mail address.

"Don't bother," Thornton said. "After the initial shock wore off I sent a reply laced with some of the more colorful metaphors I remembered from my service days-"

"But it bounced right back to you."

Thornton nodded. "No such address, the error message read."

"If you have no objections, I'm going to follow up on it anyway."

"Unofficially."

"Is there any other way?"

Thornton powered the notebook down and snapped it shut. "What is your assessment?"

The secret service agent smiled wanly. "You certainly cut a fine figure in your day."

"I'll have you know that I still do." Thornton squared his broad shoulders and took a measured breath. "The death threats I can handle, they're to be expected. But this . . . this two-bit shakedown crosses the line." He took another breath. "And I won't pay them a cent. Not a single, solitary cent."

"There's no mention of money in the text, sir."

"Well, I sure as hell won't be dropping out of the race, if that's their intention. I'd rather weather the scandal. Clinton did it."

"That was different, sir."

"Says who?"

"Is any of this being recorded?"

"The room has been secured."

"May I speak frankly?"

"I wouldn't have it any other way."

"There can't be a scandal. Not now. Not with the Iowa caucuses less than three months away. The pollsters, the bloggers, the Las Vegas oddsmakers, are all in agreement. The best hope you have of securing the nomination is to come out of the gate strong."

"But Clinton-"

"Clinton's situation was different. Clinton was different."

"Oh, hell," Thornton said. "Don't you think I know that? The picture, that video, would be viewed as manna by the GOP happy-clappers. But what's the alternative?"

"Did you make a hard copy?"

"Give an old man some credit."

"I'm taking the computer with me," Sowell said, unplugging the device and tucking it under his arm.

"Don't be so melodramatic, Raymond. One key stroke and it's ancient history."

"I'm still taking it."

"Why? What's the big deal?"

"I want to be certain it's gone. One hundred percent certain. You'd be amazed at the information a good forensic tech can extract from a wiped hard drive these days."

"Meaning?"

"When it comes to the matter of your well-being, I prefer to deal in possibility, not probability."

"What do you intend to do?"

"I intend to destroy the computer."

Thornton sighed. "Let me take care of it. I've been hunkered down in this room since five-thirty this morning. The change of scenery, not to mention the exercise, will do me good." He retrieved the notebook computer from his protection head. "As soon as we're done here, I'll cart it down to the gardener's shed and feed it through the chipper. It'll be hothouse mulch inside of ten minutes."

"Good enough."

Thornton thumped his desktop. "Talk about your major hazards and vicissitudes of life. What do you recommend as my course of action?"

"With your permission, I have a plan."

Thornton shook his head. "I'm just looking for advice. This is my problem, not yours. I don't want you involved."

"I won't be involved, at least not directly."

"What do you have in mind?"

"I know someone with the requisite, ah . . . talents for the job."

"Who?"

"You know who I'm talking about."

Thornton's voice descended to a whisper. "You don't mean-"

"I do."

"But he's-"

"Certifiably so."

Thornton lapsed into a lengthy period of silence while he considered the tangled web of his options. Finally, he said, "Do you know what FDR's last written words were?"

Sowell shook his head.

"The only limit to our realization of tomorrow will be our doubts of today. Let us move forward with strong and active faith."

"It's a go then?"

Thornton nodded soberly. "I have faith in you."

"And just for the record, I'm already involved. What affects you, affects me. Especially now. With the presidency in sight."

"Maybe this isn't such a wanton intrusion, after all." Thornton exhaled slowly. "I've always wanted to ask you something but could never quite seem to find an opportune moment."

"You can ask me anything. You always could have."

"Did I do wrong?"

Sowell laid a hand on his shoulder. "What do you think?"

"You've stuck with me through thick and thin."

"And then some."

The pain in his temples had finally begun to subside. He was almost breathing easily again. "Go." Thornton rolled his wheelchair out from behind his desk to escort his friend and protector to the door. "Take care of it before I lose my nerve."

Sowell let out a low chuckle. "The great and powerful Terrence Thornton III questioning his nerve? I don't believe it."

A hitch of a smile appeared on Thornton's face. "I fear that this . . . this unholy mess has the potential to get rather bizarre before it ends."

Sowell paused in the doorway. "Another hell of an understatement, sir."

<u>2</u>

Rimbaud Sullivan nearly creamed his jeans, the hitchhiker looked so hot. It was ten below freezing, in the middle of Butt Munch, New Hampshire, and all she had on was a bloody-murder-red halter top, matching fuck-me-pumps, and a clinging black miniskirt so short he could almost taste her pussy.

City girl, he thought. *Had to be.*

Rimbaud kicked the brake and brought his rusted-out pickup to a skidding halt, extended cab on the narrow, salted sidewalk, ass-end sticking halfway out into the road. He cranked down his window and took a furtive look around. A dark tangle of quivering evergreens lay to the right, the Atlantic Ocean to the left. The moon was full, and the choppy waters shimmered in a gritty, metallic sheen. There were no other vehicles in sight. No houses. No witnesses.

The hitchhiker approached the pickup boldly, walking with an arrogant, long-legged stride. She stopped just outside his grasp and struck an exaggerated hipshot pose. He couldn't help but stare at her plump, thickly lipsticked mouth as she babbled on about her 'top secret recon mission' – whatever the fuck that meant - and how her man's piece-of-crap convertible had left her stranded. Just loving the slutty way she swept her tongue over her teeth, like she wanted to go down on him right there on the road's slushy shoulder. Nothing more than meat, in her own mind and Rimbaud's.

I am goin' to fuck you, whore. I really am.

Weren't they all just meat?

Rimbaud plucked a cigarette from behind his ear and flipped it end over end into his mouth, lighting it with a wooden match that he struck with his thumbnail. He took in a lungful of smoke, and just stared at her for a fierce minute.

Rimbaud dug young cooze and, up close, it was clear that the hitchhiker was in her high school prime, a hard-body, and a real looker. She had platinum-blonde hair, pouty BJ lips, and blank, clueless blue eyes. He let the smoke slip slowly out of his nose.

"So where you headed?"

"Second star to the right, and straight on 'til morning."

"Cut the shit, babe. How far you goin'?"

"As far as you can take me, cutie."

A real looker, but your typical blond. Dumb and dumber all rolled into one. Rimbaud Sullivan wasn't cute. He played pick-up hockey twice a week with the boys from the fish plant and was as chiseled and buffed as a Marvel action figure. His long, luscious hair was strawberry-blonde and his deep-set eyes were startlingly blue. *Cute?* Fuck that. He was beautiful. Irresistible. All he had to do was glance at a broad to open-sesame her legs.

At bedtime, like a teaser for the ultimate reality show, the memories of his conquests would inundate his mind. Night after night, he'd wake in a sweat, the dream still wild and alive in his head as some nameless, faceless whore's press-on nails raked at his flesh, snapping off as she wriggled and bled beneath him, her comically ineffectual screams echoing in his ears.

"The name's Rimbaud," he said coolly.

The hitchhiker chortled. "I take it your mom was a big old Sly Stallone fan."

Rimbaud worked his jaw. "It's pronounced Rom-bow, not Rambo." He flicked his butt at her fuck-me pumps and made her dance in a shower of sparks. "Mama was waitin' tables at a club in Greenwich Village when she got knocked up by some bone-from-the-neck-up college brat. Jerk-off stuck around just long enough to name me before tuckin' tail back to Gay Paree."

The hitchhiker shrugged.

"You gettin' in or what?"

She hustled around to the passenger side and climbed into the cab. He thought he saw a smile flicker on her face as she slammed the door shut, a smile with something pleased in it. He put some vintage Stones in the CD player, which he cranked, a similar smile appearing briefly on his own face.

I am goin' to fuck you up.

Whore.

The hick smelled so stinky-rotten that Earlae had to breathe through her mouth. He was a bony, rat-faced man with the words 'love' and 'hate' tattooed across his knuckles - love on the left hand, hate on the right. He had on a pair of skin-tight jeans, cowboy boots and a threadbare denim jacket over a white wife-beater. His receding blonde hair was pulled back tight on his scalp, hanging to the middle of his spine in a frizzy ponytail. She cracked the window open, letting his stench, not to mention her lingering apprehension, get carried away in the seventy-mile-an-hour slipstream.

"I can't help but notice your heavy breathin'," the hick said, slapping a hand on her knee and giving it a suggestive squeeze. "You feel like partyin' some?"

"Ooh, I love parties."

"I bet you do."

The hick stomped down hard on the brake and muscled the truck into a narrow path hemmed in on both sides by a canopy of fir trees so tall and dense that they completely shut out the moon and the tiny, twinkling stars. The oversize tires crunched and popped along the rutted, frozen earth as the path twisted left, right, left again, and the main road quickly became lost from view. He pulled in deep enough that any screams would never be heard. Several heartbeats later, in an area that reminded Earlae of Winnie the Pooh's magical Hundred Acre Wood, the hick brought the truck to a stop.

"It's not a party," Earlae said, removing her halter top and exposing her distractingly perky C cups, "until somebody gets naked."

"City girl?"

"To the *bone*."

The hick snorted when he laughed. "I knew it," he said. "Knew it soon as I saw ya." He unbuckled his belt and worked his jeans and leopard-print briefs down to his boot-tops.

Earlae nearly giggled when she caught sight of his package. Although fully engorged, it was but a bite-sized morsel, no larger than a Vienna sausage. If truth be told, she had anorexic girlfriends with outtie bellybuttons who were better hung than this guy.

"My goodness," she gushed.

The hick winked at her. "Eighth wonder of the natural world."

Sure it is, Earlae thought. *In La-La-Land.* "So do you want it from behind?" She smacked her lips. "Or do you want a suck?"

He grabbed a breast in response, squeezing her nipple and twisting it like a radio dial until she let loose with a scream inside her head. She felt the tears start at the corners of her eyes and fought to keep them from running down her cheeks.

"Which do you prefer?" she said.

The hick twisted her nipple again. "Don't make no difference to me."

"Stop the presses," Earlae said, cracking the door open. "I just had a super-dee-duper idea."

"Somethin' real fuckin' freaky, I hope."

Earlae arched one eyebrow provocatively. "Let's do it outdoors. Like wild stallions."

He looped an arm over her shoulder and used it to lever her head downward into his swampy smelling crotch. "There's plenty of room right here for what I got in mind."

"Uh-uh."

"Why not?"

"Because doing it outdoors," Earlae said, wrapping her fingers around his itsy-bitsy, teeny wiener, "is such a *huge* turn-on for me, that's why not."

"In case you haven't noticed, it's a goddamned winter wonderland out there."

He closed his eyes like a contented cat as she began sliding her ringed thumb and two fingers up and down his stunted shaft. "By the time I'm through with you," she said, "you won't feel a thing." She released her grip and he opened his eyes. "Scouts honor."

The hick pushed her over backwards and mashed his face into hers, his tongue probing her pursed lips for a way inside her mouth. When she wouldn't let him in, he began to lick her face, circling her closed eyes, her cheeks, her forehead, her ears, covering her in a sticky glaze of spit.

"Outdoors," she said again as she wriggled neatly out from under him and through the open door.

Her stiletto heels poked a trail of tiny holes through the thin crust of snow as she strutted toward a patch of bare ground spotlighted by the truck's high beams. The passenger door was still open and a wicked guitar riff filled the night air as the next track on the disc began to play.

Earlae closed her eyes and let the music into her head, running her hands over her breasts, enjoying their fullness, their porcelain smoothness. She snapped her head backward, and began to grind to the beat, the rhythm of her breath escalating to match that of the music, a rough and raunchy pant.

"You got really hot tits."

Earlae's eyelids fluttered open. The hick, wearing only his boots and the wife-beater, was standing beside the front bumper, his head cocked in the manner of a predator at hunt. He was stroking himself with his right hand, the one with the word 'hate' tattooed on it, while his eyes consumed every inch of her mouth-watering form.

Earlae moved her hands down her chest, caressing her swollen nipples on the way past. She toyed briefly, seductively, with the delicate gold hoop in her bellybutton before easing her fingers beneath the skirt's waistband.

The hick leaned forward, his eyes widening.

"Would you like to see more?"

The offer made his eyes gleam, his eyebrows scaling the heights of his broad forehead. "I'd like that very much."

"Turn around then."

"Huh?"

"Turn all the way around. I've got a Christmas morning sized surprise for you."

"What is it?"

Her fingers ventured deeper into the skirt, and she touched herself. "Silly goose," she said. "It wouldn't be a surprise if I told you what it was."

She teased the slinky skirt over her hips after the hick had turned his back, keeping the silk stockings and the heels, pulling the lovingly sharpened E-Z-Out Knife from the sheath on her garter belt. After she had thumbed the razor-sharp blade open, she sing-songed, "You can turn around now."

Earlae thought the hick's eyes were going to pop from their sockets, and he hadn't even noticed the knife.

"Jesus Christ," he shrieked, "you're a fuckin'-"

"Fucking," Earlae said sharply. "It's all you dirty little boys think about." She laughed, low and deep, like a man, like James Earl Jones might laugh. "Fortunately, it's darn near all I think about, too. So bend over, Rambo."

"It's Rimbaud," he snapped. "And bite me."

He finally took notice of the knife when she jabbed it into his breastbone and a small blossom of blood appeared on the wife-beater. "Take my wallet, my watch. Take my fuckin' pickup for crissake." He began to back slowly away, making a hands-off gesture. "Just leave me some smokes and I swear - I fuckin' swear on my dead mama's soul - I won't breathe a word of this to no one."

Earlae peeled back her foreskin to reveal the skull and crossbones tattoo on the head of her unmentionables.

"See anything you like?"

"Freak," he said, his voice shimmying with rage. "You no good for nothin' faggot freak."

Earlae swiped the blade across the full width of his belly, the skin rolling back from the wound like smirking lips. Blood began to flow instantly, dribbling onto the ground from the matted nest of his pubic hair. In an instant, the look of masculine superiority was gone from his face, replaced by one of bug-eyed fear.

The hick's legs suddenly started churning and he reeled away from her, ricocheting off a limbless tree trunk before entering the dark shelter of the forest. Earlae flicked off her heels, giving chase in her bare feet, heedless of the ice and snow. She was five yards back, and closing fast, when the nose-picker toe of the hick's boot caught an exposed root and he tumbled face-first into a narrow, moonlit pathway.

"Never again," Earlae said through gritted teeth as she loomed over him, casting moon-shadows over the back of his head and on his neck. "Never. Again."

She grasped the hick around the middle and lifted him onto his hands and knees, spreading his hairy, pimpled butt cheeks with her fingers. He started an eerie cow-like lowing in the instant that she entered him.

Quickly building to a thrusting frenzy, Earlae stared out into the dark woods, thinking about how she couldn't wait for this whole messy affair to be done with, her past finally laid to rest so she could settle down to a normal white-bread existence with Bo. Hard to concentrate in the circumstances, however. With the hick's lowing. With the wet sounds her unmentionables were making as they slipped in and out of his hemorrhaging asshole. With Mick Jagger's incessant, nasally lament to his lack of satisfaction. *Tell me about it, Mick.* Hard to imagine that happily-ever-after would ever happen for her.

"Feel good, *Rambo*? Does it feel good?"

The hick shook his head wildly. "Uh-uh."

A resonant thought suddenly intruded in her mind: *Is this what you really want?* She withdrew from his asshole, bent over and stared him in his shiny-wet eyes. Involuntarily, the thought repeated itself aloud, albeit as the faintest of whispers. "Is this what you really want?"

"N . . . n . . . no," the hick said, thinking the question had been meant for him. "N . . . not like this."

"On your knees."

The hick pressed his torso up then turned to face her. Blade at his throat, Earlae slapped her unmentionables - bratwurst-sized - against his pursed lips.

"Open," she said.

He opened his mouth.

"Wider," she said.

Suddenly, the hick went ballistic, uttering a barrage of epithets that combined to form a single, nonsensical sound, like x-rated baby talk. "Hush. Will you just hush up for one second?" She moved the knife over to one of his eyes, actually touching the pupil with its tip. "What do *I . . . shhh, shhh, shhh*, what do *I* want from *you*? Is that what you're trying to ask me?"

His eyes crossed as they attempted to bring the blade into focus. It was a comical, almost Vaudevillian expression, and for one brief moment Earlae considered climbing into the shit-kicker truck and returning to Boston, leaving the hick and his precious 'smokes' to slowly bleed out in the peaceful solitude of the Hundred Acre Wood. "Take a deep breath and calm yourself," she said instead. "I can't understand a word you're saying. Yes or no. Did you just ask me what I want?"

The hick nodded.

Earlae placed the blade back at his throat. "You're a bright guy," she said. "You know what I want."

The stupid hick just stared up at her, not quite getting it yet.

"You know," she said, encouraging him, making the effort to sound pleasant.

Finally, a light bulb snapped on in the dark inner recesses of his hick mind. He scrunched his eyes shut and took the chubby, ruby-red head tentatively into his mouth.

"Aaah."

The warm, wet sensation drove Earlae's free hand to the back of his neck, forcing him to swallow her whole. "Guess you're not so bright after all," she panted as she jerked her hips backward, simultaneously coming on his tear-streaked face - a heart-wrenching, soulless orgasm - and slitting his throat from ear to ear.

3

Tokunbo Shabazz was poised to fire up his latest acquisition, a pre-embargo Bolivar torpedo, when Earlae finally found her way home at ten after two in the morning. He tossed the unlit stick back into his Prometheus Red Madrona Humidor and slammed the lid shut. "Where in hell have you been?" He held his arm aloft and made a show of consulting his eighteen carat, diamond set Piaget Ronde watch. "Do you have any idea what time it is?"

"Don't start with me, Bo," Earlae said, hand on hip, eyes widening and narrowing theatrically as she spoke. "Don't even think about it."

There was an intricate mandala-like stain on the front of her couture top. Tokunbo stomped over for a closer look. He licked his finger and rubbed it over the stain. He shook his head in disgust when it would not go away.

"Is that blood?"

"It's not mine. So forget about it."

Tokunbo ran his hands over his shaven head. "You went out alone. Admit it. You went out without me."

Earlae began to cry. "You work so freakin' much, if I waited for you, I'd never get out. And I would never have found him."

"Found whom?"

"You mentioned his name only once. But I remembered it, and I found him. *All by my lonesome.* He-"

Tokunbo grasped Earlae by the upper arms and gave her a rigorous shake. "Whom did you find?" he said. "Tell me now."

"Stop it, Bo. Stop it this instant." She twisted free of his grip and backed away a step. "You know I can't talk to you when your aura turns black." She backed up another step, then she turned, pirouetting on one spiked Ferragamo heel, and ran toward the master bedroom at the back of the loft.

She moves like a cheetah, Tokunbo thought. *Sleek, sexy, and-*

She cast a coquettish glance over her shoulder as she breezed through the open doorway.

-dangerous.

Blood thumping in his groin, Tokunbo sighed and followed her into the bedroom, just as she knew he would.

Damn her.

He found her straddling their king size, Charles P. Rogers hand-forged iron Campaign Bed, blood-stained top and skirt on the floor, legs spread a shoulder width apart. Benny and Bjorn, Frida and Agnetha, her pet chickens, were perched in an orderly row on top of the mountain of plump white pillows behind her, clucking contentedly. The roosters' black guardian eyes rolled to watch him as he drew nearer to the bed, feathers flaring menacingly. Earlae waggled her beautiful tail.

"No way. Not this time."

"C'mon, Bo. I'm not OCD like you." She made a small space between her index finger and thumb. "You know I have this little bitty impulse control problem." She pulled a sprig of mistletoe out from under a pillow and held it over her pink asshole, which was puckering in anticipation. "C'mon . . ."

Tokunbo absentmindedly began tracing small circles in the pie-shaped tuft of hair located above her pert derriere. "I hate it when you do this," he said. "You know I cannot resist it when you act this way." He traced another couple circles. "When you look this good."

"Make love to me, Bo."

"Not until you tell me what happened."

She flipped the mistletoe onto the floor and sat down on the bed, sinking deep into the hypoallergenic synthetic-down duvet. Her Veronica Lake hairdo was stuck to her face with tears and her mascara was running in black streaks down her salon-bronzed cheeks. She looked like a lost, frightened child to Tokunbo, albeit a highly provocative one.

"Your crappy old car broke down is what happened."

Tokunbo gritted his teeth. "Continue," he said.

"So I stuck out my thumb and this hick picked me up and tried to have his way with me." She brushed her hair from her face and her morning glory eyes hardened. "I had my way with him instead."

"He is dead?"

"Deader than Wacko Jacko's career."

"You murdered him."

"It was a mercy killing."

"How do you feel?"

She shrugged. "Okay, I guess."

"How do you *really* feel?"

Her lips were set in a grim line as she gave the matter pause. "I only feel bad," she said, "that I do feel bad."

"Three things," Tokunbo said.

"Only three this time? Cool."

He let her impertinence slide for the sake of expediency, not to mention his adamantine erection. "First thing, a 1957 Mercedes-Benz 300SL Roadster is a prestige automobile, and not," he made quotation marks in the air with his fingers, "a crappy old car."

Earlae shrugged noncommittally.

"Second thing, the Roadster *is* parked in a safe place."

Earlae nodded vigorously.

"Third thing, I want you to tell me what you did with the dead man's car.".

Earlae giggled. "Hicks drive trucks, silly." She patted the bed beside her and Tokunbo sat down. "Don't worry, Bo. I cleaned up my prints with baby wipes and dumped it near Park Street station." She unzipped his John Varvatos wool-and-cotton trousers and wrapped her fingers around his prick. "No one saw me."

Her nails were painted with the Sally Hansen Teflon Tuff nail color he had selected during a recent jaunt to CambridgeSide Galleria. Although she'd had her heart set on the Black Lights Glitter, he insisted she purchase the Blackberry Wine Frost instead. Blackberry Wine Frost was a classic color, suitable for nearly all occasions, while Black Lights Glitter was quite simply . . .

Quite simply what?

He put an arm around her shoulder. "I was worried, that is all. I am not angry. I could never be angry with you."

Black Lights Glitter was what? He shuddered at the words that sprang to mind.

"I know that," she said.

Tokunbo Shabazz was brilliant and far-traveling, a sophisticated African-American male making the move to bigger and better things. He had transcended the mundane. There was no room for tawdry in his world. Not anymore. No place whatsoever for cheap.

"The next time you feel an impulse, any impulse at all, you shall resist it. Do you understand me? Do I have your word?"

"William Calhoun," Earlae said, promising nothing, jerking him around even as she jerked him off.

The bedroom ceiling was fifteen feet high and two of the walls were banked with windows. The full moon had its pock-marked face pressed to the glass, and an infinite array of imperishable silver eyes were winking salaciously down at him. It felt to Tokunbo like he was on stage with all of creation watching.

"What about Mr. Calhoun?"

"He's the old bitch we snatch next."

Tokunbo smiled for his celestial audience. "On Wednesday nights, William Wallace Calhoun plays house with his disabled wife of thirty-seven years, the former Sarah Michelle Buchanan." He knocked Earlae's hand from his prick, grabbed a fistful of hair, and forced her startled face into the duvet. "From nine until midnight, he watches CNN on his sixty inch, two-tuner, picture-in-picture Sony Grand Wega TV in the master bedroom, downing obscene numbers of Rob Roys, which he mixes himself in the ensuite bar with an inferior blended whiskey." He tongued her asshole, sucked it, lapped at it like a cat attacking a dollop of spilled cream. "While her husband is otherwise occupied upstairs, Sarah reads Barbara Taylor Bradford in the living room, and laments the road not taken." Her sphincter muscle flexed, relaxed, then constricted around his index finger, greedily hauling it deeper inside her. "This coming Wednesday is when we make our move. Not a moment sooner."

Earlae turned to face him, her eyes wide. He extracted his finger from her asshole, and allowed her to suck it clean. Then he stood and unbuckled his Trussardi ostrich-skin belt, his trousers sliding sensuously down his striated, ebony thighs to the imported Italian marble tile floor.

"I daresay you are not the only one who ventures out alone, my dear."

"I want to feel you inside me, Bo. Right now."

Tokunbo made a fist around his prick and choked it hard. "No."

"What?" Her voice was precisely two octaves higher than usual.

"Not until you beg for it. Not until you tell me how completely and how madly you need me."

"You know I need you, Bo. I'd do anything to make you happy. *Anything*."

Tokunbo turned to look out the window, and smiled again.

"We shall see," he said.

4

Daniel Rourke flopped out of bed and cracked open the heavy festoon curtains. As usual, the southern California sunlight was so bright, the multitude of colors so ostentatious, it hurt his eyes to look. Within the meandering stone walls of his palatial oceanfront estate, songbirds crooned, and butterflies fluttered from flower to fragrant flower, as brilliant as the blossoms they kissed. Farther out, along the crescent beach that bordered his property, movie stars, television stars, and the latest cash crop of pre-pubescent super models, sporting thong bathing suits and surgically enhanced bodies, squealed in sweet delight as they frolicked and flirted in the affable Malibu surf. Without a doubt, it was the type of day where thoughts of death had no place, and life ground mercilessly on without Julie St. John.

Even as he stood there, Daniel could feel his essence bleeding away through the gaping hole her death had opened inside him. If it wasn't for the simmering, barely contained animus he held for Paul Watson, Julie's ex-lover and *de facto* executioner, he would probably have ceased to exist a long time ago. He was but a shell now, an empty image of the former man, something his ever-dwindling remains slipped into each morning to make himself exist to the outside world.

After the curtain had fallen from his fingers, he shuffled into the library to squeeze in a few minutes of work between the swells of his melancholy. His first novel, *Vengeance Be Mine*, was ascending the international bestseller lists in paperback, a blockbuster movie deal in the works, and his agent wanted the new manuscript ribbon-wrapped and under her tree in time for Christmas. In spite of the tragedy he had somehow managed to keep churning out the pages. While the creative process wasn't exactly cathartic, it was certainly an easy expression of his current state of mind. When someone pissed him off these days, that person was likely to find him or herself in print with a hollow-point bullet to the brain. The thought of him unloading a clip of Black Talons into the base of Watson's Neanderthal skull made Daniel smile for just a moment.

He was reaching for his portable Dictaphone when he noticed the message waiting indicator blinking in red on the antiquated desktop answering machine.

He punched the listen key.

The first eleven messages were from concerned friends and associates. One after the other, through the use of a different Hallmark card cliché, they implored him to buck up and get on with his life. Mercifully, the twelfth and final message was platitude free. It was from LAPD Detective

Frank Buchanan, Hollywood Division homicide. He hadn't heard from Buchanan since resigning from the DA's Office in mid-May. As usual, the veteran cop didn't mince words. He didn't tell Daniel that he was still young, that Julie was in a better place, or that her death was all part of some divine, unknowable plan. "I need your help," was all that the gravelly, baritone voice on the tape said. "Boston Harbor Hotel. Get your sorry ass here pronto."

Buchanan didn't say what was wrong, but he didn't need to. He said he needed Daniel's help, and that was enough. Daniel owed him for the way he'd fast-tracked and finessed the investigation into Julie's death. Owed him big-time.

December in the People's Republic of Massachusetts? If Buchanan was involved, it meant trouble, and trouble was just the sort of distraction he could use about now. Daniel scooped up the phone and booked his sorry ass on the next flight east.

5

Tokunbo and Earlae were nestled on a Public Garden bench, sipping Starbucks coffee, and watching the Gucci-socialists parade in and out of David Blake's mixed-use, high-rise condominium complex. Tokunbo knew the layout of the newly constructed twenty-seven story bronze and glass structure well. All told, he had spent more than thirty hours online pouring over the architects' blueprints and the various technical reports generated by the fourteen engineering firms involved in its construction. Inside the brassy, but spectacular Empire Tower were one hundred and sixty-two luxury condominium residences, eighty-five thousand square feet of prime office space, two restaurants, and forty-four high-end retail outlets.

"Scrumpdillicious," Earlae said.

Tokunbo took a sip of his own Venti Carmel Macchiato and nodded. "But undeniably fattening," he added.

Earlae lowered the cup from her lips, and affected a pout.

"Not to worry," Tokunbo said. "We shall simply have to expend a few additional calories in the boudoir this evening."

Earlae smiled. "Since you put it that way." She took another, especially noisy, sip.

David Blake was a forty-one year old Notting Hill Brit who had lived in Boston for the better part of a decade. A paparazzi-prized writer, director, and producer of avant-garde, studio-independent films, his last production, *Heracletus Fibbed*, had garnered the Sundance Festival's Dramatic Directing Award. Despite his dashing, matinee idol looks, thick, coal black hair, guillotine-edged jaw line framing a crooked, bad-boy smirk, he had eschewed the limelight early on, opting instead for a career behind the lens. A pop psychologist, former roommate of Blake's had recently opined on *The Larry King Show* that he'd chosen this path to conceal the near-pathological feelings of inadequacy that had plagued him since childhood. Far better concealed, Tokunbo knew, was the fact that David Blake was a sexual predator who preferred the company of tweenage boys to that of the bevy of starlets he was routinely photographed out-and-about with.

"How are you feeling?" Tokunbo said.

"Just ducky," Earlae said. "I won't spaz this time. I really won't. Cross my heart and hope to die. Stick a needle in my-"

"The venting of one's emotions is nothing to be ashamed of," Tokunbo said. "According to Gestalt therapists it is the cornerstone of a healthy psyche."

"Healthy? Are you nuts? Something just seems to snap inside me and I become Linda Blair in *The Exorcist*. You call that healthy?"

"It is referred to as Intermittent Explosive Disorder and I assure you it would be worse if you were to try to keep it bottled up. Infinitely worse. How many times must I tell you? The only hope you have to be free of your past is to get it out of your system. Once and for all."

"You're not ashamed of me then?"

"Not now. Not ever."

"I don't deserve you, Bo. I can't think of a single girlfriend whose man does half the things for them that you do for me."

"Are you ready?" Tokunbo said.

Earlae chug-a-lugged the final few ounces of coffee then burped cutely. "Ready, Freddie."

Tokunbo wiped away her foam mustache with an Earth Friendly, recycled paper napkin, stood, and made a sweeping gesture with his arm. "After you, m'lady."

The bracing New England weather provided the cosmopolitan partners-in-crime with the perfect setting for their daring broad daylight abduction of David Blake. They were wearing matching North Face McMurdo parkas, snorkel hoods raised to cloak their faces from the building's extensive surveillance network. Tight-fitting Concho Snap Deerskin Gloves ensured that no incriminating fingerprints would ever be found. And with the post-Thanksgiving shopping season in full and frenzied swing they were assured the anonymity that only a self-absorbed mob intent on conspicuous consumption could provide.

They crossed Arlington Street, pausing at Earlae's behest to watch a troupe of young, mentally challenged street musicians performing classical music on a series of chrome-plated bicycle horns bolted to an elongated iron rack. Each of the severely malnourished children had bulging, unblinking eyes and shortened arms that terminated in misshapen flipper-like hands. Under the competent but pedestrian direction of their perpetually grinning, tail-coated adult conductor, they would bob in and out, sounding their horns by chomping down hard on the rubber bulbs. In pigeon English a large cardboard sign indicated that they were orphaned brothers from the Darfur region of Sudan and that donations of all denominations were accepted.

"Seven beautiful angels with trumpets," Earlae said.

"They are wonderful," Tokunbo said. "Someday you should swing by and see if they are available to do your show."

"What a neat idea, Bo. They'd fit right in with the Chubby Duck team, wouldn't they? Let's pop back tomorrow and extend them the formal invite. Can we do it, huh? Please, please, please say yes."

Tokunbo looked up and to his left to access the entries in his day planner for the following day. "I have nothing scheduled between two-thirty and three-fifteen," he said. "We can do it then if you like."

"With another round of Starbucks afterward?"

Tokunbo just looked at her.

"Of course, if you're worried we might run short on time we can always skip straight to that whole calorie burning thing. I've heard that the porta-potties nearest to the statue of that tight-assed preacher guy-"

"William Ellery Channing."

"-are really quite romantic this time of year."

"Anytime, anywhere," Tokunbo said.

At the conclusion of Beethoven's masterful adaptation of Friedrich Schiller's *Ode to Joy*, Tokunbo dropped a twenty dollar bill into the dented donation pail and led the way through the tower's grand entrance. The pink marble atrium, complete with backlit waterfall and rare tropical greenery, was five stories tall and lined with mirrors, creating an upscale funhouse atmosphere for the polished horde of shoppers criss-crossing the escalators that connected the potpourri of boutiques in the vertical mall.

"Do not lower your hood until we meet at the rendezvous point," Tokunbo said. "Keep your eyes downcast and do not stray one iota from the route I mapped out for you."

"Sure thing, Bo," Earlae said. "Love ya." And then she broke off to the right.

Tokunbo tracked her with a raptor's gaze as she wove through the horde toward the escalator which led to the mall's lower level. When he was sure that she hadn't been distracted by any of the numerous, boldly advertised sales, Tokunbo went the other way, elevators straight ahead, stairs to the left. He opted for the stairs, descending two at a time, and hustled over to a pair of unmarked swinging metal doors. He pushed through them and headed down a lengthy cinder-block corridor. At the end of the corridor were two gender-designated, wheelchair accessible washrooms, and a dead-bolted service door.

Where the hell are you?

She should have been here by now. God help her if she was in Manolo Blahnik charging another pair of sling-back-

A toilet flushed in the ladies room and scant seconds later Earlae joined him in the corridor.

"Did you wash your hands?" Tokunbo said.

There was a tell-tale pause before Earlae responded. "Yeah," she muttered halfheartedly.

"Take off your gloves."

"What for?"

"Did you forget what I told you about public restrooms?"

"Public restrooms are known breeding grounds for a plethora of germs and bacteria," she said, expertly mimicking his tone of voice and elocution.

Tokunbo took out a travel-size tube of waterless hand sanitizer and waited while Earlae peeled off her gloves. He placed a dollop of the unscented gel in her palm. "Rub it in thoroughly."

"You can be such a nerd sometimes."

"Now put your gloves back on."

"Yes, master."

Tokunbo lowered his hood, took out his nine-piece internet-ordered lock pick set, and turned to face the service door. Thanks to a successful GLAD-initiated ACLU right to privacy lawsuit there were no security cameras in the vicinity of the deliberately well-hidden public restrooms. This, coupled with the fact that the guard wasn't scheduled to patrol the area for another seventeen minutes, meant the odds of their being surprised by unwanted company were exceedingly low. As expected, he picked the deadbolt without interruption and pulled Earlae in after him.

Tokunbo led the way down a short flight of concrete stairs to one of the tenants' three storage vaults. The cavernous space was climate-controlled and reeked of mothballed fashions from decades past. He pressed a button on the wall to call for the freight elevator and when it arrived they hopped in, riding it to the twenty-fourth floor. From there they entered the stairwell sight unseen and climbed the final three flights to the penthouse level.

He opened the Polish Mercor Sa wooden acoustic fire door and listened. He heard no one.

He poked his head out and scanned the full length of the fifteen foot wide, 80% wool, 20% nylon, Dusty Rose carpeted hallway. He saw no one.

"As discussed, we shall proceed using our standard *modus operandi*," Tokunbo said.

Earlae put a hand on her hip and rolled her eyes. "In English, Bo. You know I don't speak a word of pig Latin."

"*Modus operandi* is not- Oh, never mind. We shall follow the same *routine* as at each of the other abductions," Tokunbo said. "We enter the unit. I locate and subdue the target. We spirit him away to the van parked out back."

"Why didn't you just say so in the first place?"

They strode arm-in-arm down the crypt-like hallway as though they were expected guests, casually stopping outside Penthouse Six.

"Not a creature was stirring," Earlae whispered.

"There is no need to whisper, I assure you. The units were constructed to be completely soundproof. You could – How did you phrase it? – morph into Linda Blair here and now, spewing fluids and cursing to your heart's content, and no one would be the wiser."

"Friggin' cool," Earlae shouted.

The lock on the door was typical of most upscale residences, a sorry three-lever affair, more ornamental than functional. A mere forty-five seconds after their arrival on the penthouse level they were standing inside Blake's grand foyer.

The oversized, elegantly appointed unit was truly spectacular. The entry floor was Italian marble. To the right was a walk-in coat closet, to the left a nineteenth century Scandinavian ebonized and gilded wall mirror. Straight ahead, a prairie-like living room with wall-to-wall taupe carpet and a blazing natural gas fireplace. A dozen pieces by famed Bauhaus architect Ludwig Mies van der Rohe, fashioned from stainless steel, plate glass, and ivory colored pigskin, were arranged in intimate conversation patterns over the luxurious carpet. Off the living room, visible through a ten-foot wide pair of etched glass doors, was a library, with Oriental rugs, and natural oak shelves exhibiting a collection, by Tokunbo's estimate, of at least two thousand hardcover volumes.

Blocking Earlae's view of the mirror with his torso, Tokunbo escorted her into the living room and sat her down in one of Mies van der Rohe's iconic Barcelona Chairs.

"Wait here while I locate Blake."

He had taken three steps toward the wide hallway leading to the bedrooms when he stopped. He hadn't intended to, but he couldn't help himself. Removing a glove, he squatted down to stroke the carpet. The fibers were woven, the pile an inch and a half thick, as soft to the touch as freshly whisked cream. "How decadent." He slipped the glove back onto his hand.

Earlae leaned suddenly forward in her chair, and canted her head. "What's that funky noise, Bo?"

Tokunbo raised a hand for silence. A repetitive clanking sound could be heard coming from the far end of the twenty-four hundred square foot residence.

"Stay," he said.

He removed the Bianchi flat sap from his front coat pocket and tracked the sound to the master bedroom suite. The double African mahogany, raised panel doors were closed but unlocked. He smiled as he tested the bone-crunching weight of the sap against his thigh. While a tranquilizer dart fired from a CO2 air pistol was unquestionably a more efficient means of rendering a target unconscious, there remained something to be said for the primal rush of doing it the old fashioned, film noire way.

Easing the door open, Tokunbo slipped stealthily inside, sap palmed and ready.

A thoroughly, arrousingly nude David Blake was kneeling back-to on a blood-spattered canvas drop sheet spread neatly in the center of the spacious, vaulted-ceiling room. He was staring at a glossy magazine that was open on the floor in front of him while repeatedly flogging his lacerated back with a Zangeer, a ritual Shiite Muslim self-torture device that consisted of a series of hand-forged blades attached to a length of chain.

Tokunbo cleared his throat to get the filmmaker's attention.

Blake lowered the Zanjeer, turned, saw the flat sap, and opened his mouth . . . to beg for mercy?

"I've been waiting for you," he said softly.

Strange. "Have you now?"

Blake stood. "One by one, Tokunbo, my mates have gone missing. And I knew that-"

"Knew what, David? What did you know?"

"That it was only a matter of time before you came for me, too."

"Do you really expect me to believe that you were aware of my involvement in this intrigue all along?"

"Hardly. Your involvement comes as quite the surprise given your side business at The Coloss-"

"So what did you mean when you said that you had been waiting for me?"

"I just knew that one day, after all we'd done - all I'd done - an avenging angel would appear."

Tokunbo looked the filmmaker straight in the face. Blake gazed placidly back, unblinking, unflinching. "And that knowledge did not – does not - frighten you?"

Blake motioned with his chin to the magazine. "Look at it," he said.

Tokunbo picked up the glitzy pop-culture rag. It was the latest issue of People. The full color spread featured a sordid, peeping-Tom look at various child stars who had fallen from grace with the onset of puberty. Each was a household name. Two had been nominated for Oscars. No winners, of course.

Blake stood, and tapped the largest, most prominently positioned photograph in the array, leaving a bloody fingerprint on the once-famous, now infamous, tow-headed boy's cheeks.

"I *fucked* him."

The caption beneath the photograph indicated that the unemployed, methamphetamine-addicted actor had recently died from a self-inflicted shotgun wound to the genitals.

"I killed him."

"You drove him to it."

Blake nodded. "There are others, Tokunbo." He closed his eyes and shuddered. "Too many to count."

"You want to stop but you cannot."

Blake nodded again.

"You want to be punished."

Blake gave his head a violent shake. "I thought you understood."

"You *deserve* to be punished."

Blake nodded vigorously. "Look at me."

Tokunbo stroked the filmmaker's cleft chin with his free hand and kissed him gently on the lips. "Too beautiful for words," he said. "On the outside."

Blake frowned. "To atone I must experience their torment."

Tokunbo responded with a lightening-quick series of sap strikes to Blake's elbows, collarbone and knees, dropping him where he stood, as though his bones had been reduced to ash. "I can give you the understanding you desire, reveal to you the face that the eyes you dare not meet in your dreams have glimpsed, the face beneath the exquisite mask you wear."

"I . . . I was also hoping that-"

"And if you desire knowledge of their agony, I can give you that, too."

"On your honor?"

Tokunbo smiled. "I will crucify you."

Tears welled in Blake's eyes, his face reflecting a rapturous joy. "Assist me, Tokunbo. Give me your oath as a gentleman that you'll assist me."

Tokunbo held his hands aloft. "There are some questions that must first be-"

"I'll answer your queries only if you give me your oath. Dispatch me now if you refuse."

The filmmaker's request required little consideration on Tokunbo's part. To put it mildly, he was intrigued.

"I will assist you."

"When? How?"

"Such details are none of your concern." Tokunbo pocketed the sap. "Now get dressed. We will soon be leaving."

A wistful smile flickered on Blake's face as he glanced up at the engraved silver-brass wall clock. Eighteenth century English, if Tokunbo wasn't mistaken. It was nice, but out of touch with the rest of the décor. An heirloom piece, most likely. "Four o'clock," Blake said. "Would it be presumptuous of me to enquire if there's time enough for toast and tea before we depart?" He held up a hand for Tokunbo.

"Afternoon tea," Tokunbo said as he hauled the filmmaker to his feet, "Great Britain's one indisputable contribution to the civilized world. Of course, there is time."

"Where's the lovely Earlae?" Blake said as he hobbled over to his massive wardrobe. "Nearby, I hope."

"As a matter of fact, she is waiting for us out in the-"

Tokunbo charged out of the bedroom at the first sound of breaking glass and toppled furniture. "Let it out, my love," he shouted over the din as he sprinted down the hallway. "Do not be afraid of what you feel. Let it all out."

6

There were no songbirds crooning in the snow-covered parks and beaches of overcast Boston. No butterflies. No blossoms. No half-baked, half-naked celebrities with surgically enhanced bodies frolicking or flirting in the icy surf. Three thousand miles from home, and life still ground mercilessly on without Julie St. John.

Daniel entered the Boston Harbor Hotel suite that Buchanan had procured, and gawked. Needless to say, it wasn't at all what he'd been expecting. The sitting room was elegant yet cozy, decorated in fiery reds, rich creams and buttery yellows. Vases, filled with colorful Roman Candle-bursts of freshly cut wildflowers, were everywhere. The suite had easily cost his friend a week's pay, which made no sense to Daniel. Buchanan's reputation as a skinflint was notorious in the DA's office.

"Somebody's snatched my uncle," the surly detective murmured from the overstuffed L-shaped couch, his Hobbit-like feet resting on the coffee table, the heels of both socks worn clean through.

Frank Buchanan was a long, big-boned man with a red go-to-hell face. He was thirteen years older than Daniel's thirty-five and tipped the scales at two-hundred and thirty pounds, twenty-five pounds heavier than Daniel. His close-set black eyes were the calm in the center of a raging storm.

Daniel dropped his bags and took a seat in a stiff bucket chair facing Buchanan. "Your uncle has bucks," he said.

"Mucho bucks. Used to be the Donald Trump of Boston's Financial District before retiring to his summer home on the outskirts of Portsmouth."

"Virginia?"

"New Hampshire."

"Has there been a ransom demand?"

"Nada."

"How long has it been?"

"Three days."

"If it's not about money, it's personal."

"Agreed."

"And you know what that means."

"Uh-huh."

In the silence that followed Buchanan's reply, a wave of shadow curled into the room through a nearby window. The darkening sky was ominous-looking, with a phalanx of cirrus clouds charging in from the northeast.

"I have a question," Daniel said.

"Charlotte's staying with a cousin in Studio City." Charlotte was Buchanan's adopted daughter, two years old in January. She was an honest-to-goodness miracle who had serendipitously appeared in Buchanan's life during the tail end of a gang-banger murder case he had worked with Daniel. She was his life. "I miss her so much. Phone just doesn't cut it, you know?"

"Actually, I wanted to know why we're shacked up here in Boston when your uncle was abducted in New Hampshire."

"It's just a short hop up the coast."

"And the real reason we're here is . . . ?"

"Okay, okay," Buchanan said. "Truth is some friends in Vice booked the hotel's Girls' Luxury Escape package this weekend. They insisted I take their place when they heard what happened."

"*Gratis?*"

"Yeah."

"Now it makes sense."

"What does?"

"Forget about it."

Buchanan disappeared into one of the bedrooms and came back with his Dopp kit which he placed on the coffee table between them. He unzipped the kit and took out a pair of nail clippers, a roll of hospital tape, scissors, and a two-foot length of surgical tubing with an alligator clip attached to one end.

"What do the cops think?"

Buchanan rolled off his socks and picked up the nail clippers. "Haven't got a clue." He parted his toes one by one, assessing the arc of each nail. When he found one that was out of true he nipped it down, the clippings flying through the air like shrapnel. "They seemed genuinely pissed when I called 'em up asking questions. Wouldn't give me the time of day."

"What do *you* think?"

Buchanan stopped nipping and raised his head above his toes. Snow began to fall behind him, slanting in on the wind which rattled and howled at the windows. "I think you're still fucked up, is what I think."

"I'm okay."

"When was the last time you got a good night's sleep? You look like shit."

"I said I'm okay."

"You feel like talking some?"

"Politics? Religion? Hell, yeah. Space-time and the quantum mechanics of the pre-Big Bang vacuum state? I'll give it a whirl. My life, or lack thereof? No, thank you."

"Talk tó me, man. In case this thing turns serious, I need to know where your head is. Bottom line is all."

"Bottom line, you pull out a bottle of nail polish, I'm out of here. Family or no family."

Buchanan's rough, low voice was a whisper. "Talk to me," he said.

Daniel bit down hard. "All right," he said. "If it'll get you off my back, I'll give you the expurgated, Reader's Digest version. Is that okay with you? Is it?"

Buchanan didn't respond, just waited for him to continue.

Daniel rose and walked slowly across the room. He retrieved Julie's framed photograph from one of his bags. Her face was angled slightly to the right, almost in profile but not quite. Her blonde hair was long and abundant with curls. As corny as it sounded, which was why he'd never voiced the thought aloud, all the light and the color and the joy had bled from his life on the night she died. Most loved ones came back, he knew, like gothic apparitions, haunting the grey matter of those they'd left behind, calling out from the great beyond for fond remembrance.

But not Julie.

When Daniel closed his eyes for some pause and respite, to lose himself in the memories, there was only darkness, an abyss that gaped and beckoned. More and more, he found himself looking at her photograph, as proof that he hadn't imagined it all, proof that once-upon-a-time she really had existed.

He set the frame down on a shelf laden with flowers, pale and wanting beside her, and looked out one of the snow-battered windows. The flakes stuck to the glass briefly before melting and trickling down its length in venous, ever-branching rivulets. Their view from the trendy Rowe's Wharf locale was of the churning, white-capped corridor of Boston's Inner Harbor, and beyond that, barely visible through the encroaching grey wall of storm, the wasp-like comings and goings at Logan International Airport.

"You're right," he said finally, his back to Buchanan. "I'm not sleeping so well these days." He traced a melted snowflake down the window with his index finger. "Every night, every seemingly endless night, I put Sinatra's *Only The Lonely* on repeat, climb into bed, and just lay there. Wishing she was still alive. Wishing we were together again. Knowing all the while it can never be. Wishing I didn't feel like dying with every breath I take." He turned to face Buchanan, choosing his next words carefully. "Otherwise, I'm perfectly . . ."

"Perfectly what?"

"I don't know. Functional? Yeah, that's it"

Buchanan nodded once. "Fine," he said.

"Now I want you to answer my question."

"What do I think? I think something's up. Something big. Something the cops seem hell-bent and determined to keep under wraps."

Daniel sat down on the arm of the couch. "And you wanted me here to . . . ?"

"To help me get to the bottom of things."

"Why me?"

Buchanan scowled. "Fucked up or not - so long as you're not suicidal - you're here 'cos you're the type of guy who can get it up." He pointed the clippers at Daniel's nose. "You're not suicidal, right?"

"Some friends staged an intervention a couple months back. Enrolled me in a twelve-step murder of your soul-mate program."

Buchanan's stormy mien broke into a playful smile. "Twelve step, huh? So where are you now?"

"Not that it's any of your business, but I'm well beyond suicidal. Well beyond feeling anything at all really. The last week or so I've been languishing at step nine."

"Step nine? What's that?"

"The 'I Don't Give a Shit' step." He placed a hand on Buchanan's shoulder. "Don't worry, Frank. We'll find him."

Buchanan looked at Daniel and his smile turned mean and he chuckled. "The way I'm feeling right now," he said, "I kinda hope we don't."

"What exactly are you trying to tell me?"

Buchanan just kept on smiling that mean smile. "That we've shot the shit long enough."

"It seems the local cops aren't the only ones with a hidden agenda."

"In or out?" Buchanan said.

Daniel was silent for a moment, thoughtful. "I don't give a shit."

"That a yes or a no?"

"What else have I got to do?"

"Good. First thing in the morning we're gonna double-team the investigating officer. Get us some answers."

"And this evening?"

"You hungry?"

"Famished."

"Well, today's your lucky day. I picked up a couple pounds of spicy sausage at Quincy Market before you got here. You gimme a minute and I'll fry 'em up."

"This is a Triple-A Four Diamond hotel, Frank. I Googled it on the plane."

"So?"

"In case you haven't noticed, there's no kitchen in the room."

Buchanan pointed to a beat-up, two-burner hotplate plugged into an outlet at the back corner of the room.

"You cheap bastard," Daniel said. "You brought a hotplate onto the airplane, didn't you?"

"In my carry-on with the condiments. You check out the price of room service lately?"

"Sausage, huh?" Daniel said, grinning for the first time in as long as he could remember. "Why is everything phallic with you gay guys?"

"What do you feel like having? Steak, I suppose."

"Now that you mention it, a thick and juicy t-bone would certainly hit the spot."

"Do you have any idea-"

"What steak costs?" Daniel said.

"Well, do you?"

"Not really. I have a service that does all my shopping for me."

"They chew your food for you, too? Wipe your ass the next morning?"

"At five bucks a flush, it's the deal of the century."

"Illegals, right? Doing a job ordinary Americans won't do?"

"*Si*."

"So are you gonna try it, or what? *Semper Fi* Sausage. I learned how to make it in The Corp. Your taste buds'll blow Reveille. I kid you not."

"All right, all right, I'll try it." Daniel glanced down at Buchanan's gnarly, hair-tufted toes. "So long as you wash your hands first."

Buchanan snatched up the tape, scissors and surgical tubing. "I gotta hit the can," he said.

"To wash your hands, I hope."

"Among other things."

"Dare I ask?"

Buchanan shook his head. "If you got the willies watching me give myself a pedicure, my gut reaction would have to be-"

"No."

"Uh-huh."

7

Portsmouth PD was located in a renovated hilltop hospital with a panoramic view of the picturesque New England city. Unlike the many urban ghetto precincts that Daniel had visited over the course of his legal career there was no graffiti on the exterior walls and no bars or chicken wire on any of its street-front windows. He parked the rental car, a late model Chrysler, between a pair of immaculate white cruisers, and he and Buchanan got out. The morning sky was cobalt blue, and the air was cool, incredibly fresh and clean. Aside from a playful pair of seagulls carving figure-eights high overhead, graceful and languid as they flew, the place seemed deserted.

"Emergency evac?" Daniel said.

Buchanan consulted his watch. "Sunday morning in these here parts, folks still go to church."

"The entire population?"

"That's pretty much the way I remember it."

"Must be a sinful bunch," Daniel said.

"If memory serves me."

Inside the station a gargantuan uniformed black man sat reclined behind a tiny metal desk reading the latest edition of Sports Illustrated. A bloated, grey-haired Cassius Marcellus Clay was on the cover. The plaque on the desk read Officer White.

Buchanan flashed his shield. "We're here to see Wagner, Investigative Services."

The officer never looked up from the magazine. "Terry's out." He jerked his spatulate thumb toward an abutting room. "You can cool your heels in there, you want to wait. Shouldn't be no more than twenty minutes."

The waiting room consisted of four stackable banquet chairs and a rectangular pine coffee table with various fluff magazines spread in a poker-hand pattern across its top. A ten foot tall Scotch pine, covered in tinsel, glass balls and blinking, multicolored lights, was set up in the far corner of the windowless room.

As Buchanan sat down his chair pealed along the tiled floor. The shrill, scraping noise caused a molded-plastic, sound-activated Santa Claus to drop from the high ceiling, Ho-Ho-Ho-ing at an ear-piercing volume. Daniel took a shuffle-step to his left, and felt a breeze as Santa narrowly missed cracking him on the noggin.

"Jesus Fucking Christ," Buchanan hissed. "I think I . . . think I shit myself." He wriggled his posterior around on the chair as he assessed the damage. "Naw, I'm good."

Suppressing the urge to grin, Daniel settled into the seat beside

Buchanan, and picked up a magazine. Eventually the laugh track ended and Santa zipped back up to the ceiling. Through the ringing in his ears, Daniel thought he could hear Officer White chuckling in the lobby.

"Ali fan?" Buchanan said softly after observing two full minutes of silence.

"Clay was a Nation of Islam dupe," Daniel said.

"He was a witty, entertaining son-of-a-bitch is what he was," Buchanan said.

"Witty? The man had an IQ of seventy-six. He was a trained parrot. Practically every word that came out of his mouth was put there by Elijah Muhammad."

"Okay, okay, I get it. You don't dig Ali the man. But what about Ali the fighter? Was he or was he not the greatest heavyweight that ever lived?"

"Iron Mike would've kicked his ass."

"Tyson's a punk," Buchanan said.

"He may have ended his career that way," Daniel said. "But in their respective primes, an '88 Tyson against a '66 Clay, I'd lay odds on The Baddest Man on the Planet over The Louisville Lip any night of the week."

Gazing at the scar tissue around Daniel's eyes, Buchanan said, "You used to fight some, didn't you?"

"Back in my reckless youth."

Buchanan's gaze remained focused on the scar tissue.

"What?" Daniel said.

"I just wanna know how a kid from the right side of the tracks ever got involved in a blood sport like boxing?"

"Dad was born and raised in Hell's Kitchen. He was a fighter."

"I thought he was a doctor. Some kind of high class surgeon to the rich and famous."

"A man can't be both?"

Buchanan shrugged.

"Well, dad was both. After setting up his Park Avenue practice, he volunteered his time as a fight doctor. New York. New Jersey. Philadelphia. Big names or nobodies, the cards didn't matter. He lived and breathed the sport, and he let me hang out with him ringside from the time I was old enough to walk." Daniel thumped his chest over his heart. "His love was infectious."

"What was your record?"

"Twenty-one and oh."

"Heavyweight?"

"Light-heavy. I've pumped some iron since my retirement."

"Any good?"

"Golden Gloves."

"State?"

"City."

"Think you could have made it as a pro?"

Daniel thought about it. "Probably," he said.

"What kept you from finding out?"

"Boxing isn't what it used to be. Too many weight classes. Too many sanctioning bodies. Too many paper champions."

"You think it's dead, or just dying?"

"We're all just dying."

"What about MMA? I can't get enough that shit. Watch it on Spike two, three nights a week."

"Me, too. And all the pay-per-views."

"You ever try it?"

"There was this gym in Harlem I frequented in the mid-nineties that dabbled in Brazillian *Jui-Jitsu*. My trainer said I was a natural."

"And?"

"I found my way into the octagon a time or two."

"To see if he was right."

"Yeah."

"How'd you do?"

"Three and oh."

"What made you give it up?"

"School mostly," Daniel said. "Dad offered to bankroll my way through the Ivy Leagues, but I wanted to do it on my own, the same way he had. Academic scholarships, mostly. Part time jobs at night. I figured if I was ever going to make a name for myself as a lawyer, I needed every brain cell I had intact."

"So the fewer blows to the head, the better."

"Exactly."

"That still an issue for you?"

"Is what still an issue?"

"Getting hit in the head?"

"What do you mean?"

"I just wanna know, that's all."

"Know what?"

"That when the shit comes down the pipe, and I have need of your finely honed ass-kicking skills, you're still good to go."

"Oh, I'm definitely good to go. I keep in shape. Workout five, six days a week."

"Any sparring?"

Daniel nodded. "I've been known to tangle with some of the local pros."

"Just to test your metal."

"Yeah."

"Anyone I might've heard of?"

Daniel smiled. "Year before last I had the pleasure and pain of going three brutally intense rounds with Chuck Liddell."

"The man's a fucking animal. How'd that work out for you?"

"I had my nose broken by a boxer in my teens and it used to lean to the right. Chuck-"

"Used to?"

"Chuck straightened it out for me in the second round."

"Looping left hook?"

Daniel nodded. "It rang my bell hard-"

"Did it-"

"But it didn't put me down."

"Hurt?"

"Way too much adrenalin for that."

"You get in any licks?"

"I did okay. Well enough it almost made me regret hanging up the gloves."

"Speaking of regret," Buchanan said. "You ever miss the law?"

Daniel shook his head. "There's only one thing, one person, I miss."

"My offer stands," Buchanan said. "You ever get the itch to hash things out, you know right where to find me."

Daniel said nothing.

"You were a damn good prosecutor."

"It was all a farce."

"You don't believe that."

"I don't? Until Watson's conviction, I'd never seen justice done in a courtroom. Not in the gratifying Old Testament sense. And even Watson's trial was . . ." Daniel searched vainly for the word he wanted.

"Rigged?"

Daniel shrugged. "Justice these days is a politically incorrect concept found only in the pulp fiction aisles. Screw the law. Writing's far more satisfying."

"We all have our demons," Buchanan said. "I know you'll never fully get over what happened with Julie, but I also know that in time you'll learn how to keep it contained at your core. Under control. Manageable."

"That sounds like bitter experience talking."

Buchanan picked up a magazine, opened it in his lap, and began to read.

Their twenty minute wait turned into forty, then sixty minutes. Daniel had thumbed his way through all the old Sports Illustrated and People magazines, and was in the process of picking up a tattered ten year old Cosmo when Terry Wagner walked in. He turned out to be a she, and she had a smile that was quite spectacular.

"If you have the time," Wagner said to Daniel, "there's an excellent article near the back on Toxic Shock Syndrome."

"What's that?" Buchanan said, closing an ancient People magazine with a bikini-clad, jailbait-era photo of the Olsen twins on the cover.

"Nothing you've got to worry about," Daniel said.

Buchanan tossed his magazine onto the coffee table as he stood, and down swooped Santa. Wagner cleared her piece out of reflex, and judging by the look on Buchanan's face, this time he really had gone poopy in his pants.

"If I didn't have to fill out so much goddamned paperwork every time I tossed a little lead," Wagner said, her words measured, severe, "I swear to God, I'd blow that jolly old bastard's head off."

"You know who I am," Buchanan said.

"I know who you are, Detective."

Wagner was tall and slim, and when she took off her cap, shimmering waves of auburn hair rolled onto her shoulders. Although her cheekbones were high and her lips were full, her wide amber eyes said 'don't fuck with me.'

"I want to see the file," Buchanan said.

"As I've told you on the phone, five times already if I'm not mistaken, that would be impossible."

"Nothing's impossible," Daniel said. "Call it a professional courtesy."

"I show you the file and it's my ass. And in case you haven't noticed, I've clocked way too many hours on the treadmill to have this ass chewed off by anyone. Especially my prick of a chief."

Daniel gestured toward Santa whose laughter continued to taunt them. "Is there any way we can go some place a little less distracting?"

"And you are?"

"Daniel Rourke." He extended his hand.

"My lawyer," Buchanan said.

"A writer of fine pulp fiction, actually. And a friend."

"Rourke," she said slowly. "Daniel Rourke. Never heard of you."

"I use a *nom de plume*," Daniel said. "To keep away all the love-struck groupies."

Wagner took an exaggerated look around the room. "It seems to be working."

Her handshake was a silken submission hold. She held Daniel's hand, and his eyes, a heartbeat too long, and he thought, *Hmmm.*

'You're here 'cos you're the type of guy who can get it up.'

"My cubicle is this way," Wagner said as she exited the waiting room.

On the way past Officer White, Buchanan said, "Thanks for the warning, pal."

White shrugged and grinned. His teeth shone. "Ho, ho, ho," he said.

Seated inside Wagner's tiny cubicle, Daniel said, "Did you know that Frank's aunt was supposed to be home the evening his uncle was abducted?"

"She's one lucky lady alright," Wagner said. "If she hadn't been called away, we'd probably be looking for the two of them."

Daniel flashed his thousand watt smile. "I know there are rules in place, but anything you can do for us would be greatly appreciated."

Wagner moved her gaze slowly from Daniel to Buchanan as she considered his words, the gleam of a calculating intelligence evident in her eyes. "With all due respect, there *are* rules, and I have my orders. I'm simply not at liberty to discuss the specifics of an ongoing investigation." She opened a drawer and pulled out a thin manila folder which she slapped down onto the desktop. "Now if you'll excuse me for one moment, I just remembered something that requires my immediate attention."

"Take your time," Daniel said.

Buchanan opened the folder as soon as Wagner was gone. As Daniel had suspected, it was the William Calhoun file. Inside were the handwritten notes of the first officer on the scene, crime scene photos, fact sheets, evidence inventory, serological report, and the typewritten statements taken from interviews with Frank's aunt and the adjoining property owners. The statements were short and to the point. No one had seen anything. No one had heard anything. No one knew anything. There were no suspects or persons of interest. The only item in the file that appeared out of the ordinary was a hastily scrawled scrap of paper stapled to the top left hand corner of the folder's inside cover.

The paper read: Galton, One Center Plaza – Marshall Thomas, Eric Murray, David Blake, George and Marie Taylor.

"You recognize any of the names?" Daniel said.

"David Blake."

"He's a film director of some kind, right?"

"I think so."

"Anyone else ring a bell?"

Buchanan shook his head. "Assuming they're locals, I've been gone from here way too long for that."

"What about the address? One Center Plaza. That's FBI, isn't it?"

Buchanan nodded. "I may just be a dumb-shit cop but I'd bet my pittance of a pension we just found what you hack writers call a clue."

Wagner returned as if on cue and took her seat. She was wearing a shade of lipstick that accentuated her eyes and her hair looked somehow different, like the 'after' shot in a shampoo commercial that promised more bounce and body. Daniel didn't know whether to thank her for her assistance, compliment her, or tell two of his friends about what she had done to her hair. He decided to give the matter some thought.

"Has the scene been released?" Buchanan said.

"It has," Wagner said.

"That's good. 'Cos I'm doing a walk-through as soon as we're done here."

"Before you two go mucking up my crime scene, I want to make sure we're clear on what transpired here today," Wagner said. "What was my official response when asked if you could examine the Calhoun file?"

"You refused my request," Buchanan said.

"Did I, at any time, grant you access to the Calhoun file?"

"No," Buchanan said. "You did not."

"Did I provide you with any information whatsoever regarding the investigation into your uncle's disappearance?"

"No," Buchanan said. "Officially, you stonewalled us."

Wagner's second smile proved that the first was no fluke. Clearly, she was up to something. What it was, Daniel had no idea. What he thought of her, aside from the fact that her follow-up smile was equally spectacular, Daniel also had no idea.

"Just so we're clear," she said.

As mud, Daniel thought.

<u>8</u>

Earlae ducked into her office a few minutes before the start of The Colosseum's Second Annual AIDS Charity Brunch to slip into her latest, fresh from the dry cleaner, vintage Dior find. Merry as a carrousel, she dropped her robe and twirled across the room to the bank of floor-to-ceiling windows, daringly tugging the heavy seaweed-red and -brown drapes open.

"Mirror, Mirror on the wall . . ."

She grinned at the ethereal image reflected in the glass before her. Her cloud-white pashmina and silk bra and panty set had been custom ordered from a hole-in-the-wall boutique in Paris. Her bitchy black heels were Italian. Her hair was styled by a hunky bisexual of Puerto Rican descent.

Three floors below, a raucous mob of pub crawling co-eds spotted her through the glass and gaped as one. Four pretty boys with linebacker shoulders and bulges in their jeans fell to their knees. "We're not worthy," they bellowed drunkenly. "We're not worthy."

"Girlfriend," Earlae chirped, doing the Cleopatra side-to-side thing with her head, "you truly are the fairest one of all."

How deliciously ironic.

She had the narrow hips and full breasts that all men desired, and the face of a goddess - a countenance so beautiful it had once been described in Vogue Italia as blissfully innocent, otherworldly. It just didn't seem possible that anything bad could ever happen to one who looked so fair. And then there were her eyes. Great shimmering mirrors that told no lies.

Earlae met those eyes head on, and beheld the images, the dark and dangerous secrets, reflected therein . . .

***

The little boy regained consciousness in the narrow crawl space behind the furnace. There was a throbbing pain at the base of his skull and he had no feeling in his right arm. Blood was trickling down his forehead from a pulsating gash along his hairline. He must have passed out on a nest of some kind because gigantic bugs, mutant cockroaches maybe, were swarming over his face, burrowing into his nose and ears. He grabbed a wriggling handful that snapped, crackled and popped inside his tiny, tightening fist. After clearing his face, he opened his eyes to a darkness as velvety black as Batman's cape.

He tried to raise himself up to a sitting position, but immediately dropped back down. His head was hurting so much that it made him sick. He puked until there was nothing left inside of him then passed out again.

He wasn't out for long, maybe only a couple of seconds. He opened his eyes once more and lay completely still. His head didn't hurt so much when he didn't try to move, and that helped him to remember.

It wasn't long before the little boy remembered everything: another stupid fight over nothing; the glass bong that the old man, his latest in a long line of out-of-work, perpetually pissed-off step-daddies, had thrown at him; the stunning impact; the lightening flash inside his head; the hail of blows while he was down; more lightening flashes; his crawling away like a kicked dog to hide and heal while the old man slept another bender off.

The cockroaches were everywhere, inside his t-shirt, and his pants, biting him mercilessly. But he didn't dare move. If he moved he was dead meat.

This time the old man hadn't slept much of anything off. He had been in a full-bore rage before the little boy had passed out, and the passage of time had done little to lighten his mood. Above him, the little boy could hear the old man rampaging from room to room, pounding holes in the walls, upending furniture as he searched for his step-son's hiding place.

Despite the summer heat, a heat that had found its way into every crack and crevice of the run-down, story-and-a-half house, the little boy couldn't stop shaking. He scrunched his eyes shut and tried to remember a happier time, a time when he hadn't shook, when he hadn't known fear, only love, and peace, and security. But he couldn't recollect a single such memory.

Life sucks, and then you die.

His best friend Ronnie Cattell had told him that shortly before his death. The little boy had tried to tell him that he was wrong, but he just wouldn't listen. If Ronnie was here right now, he knew exactly what he would say to him.

Life sucks, and then you-

Upstairs, the rampaging stopped, and the silence was overwhelming. He held his breath and listened hard, but all that he could hear was the chittering of the cockroaches in his ears. Nothing at all from above. Then he heard footsteps, echoing down the narrow oilcloth hallway. They came to an abrupt stop outside the basement door.

When another door creaked open, to the bathroom, and immediately closed again, the little boy finally let out his breath. Momentarily, he heard the toilet seat protesting under the old man's gelatinous bulk, followed hard upon by the stormy-weather sounds of one of his self-proclaimed, six times a day, colon cleansing power-dumps.

Now was his chance, he knew.

The little boy shimmied out of the crawl space on his good arm and moved quick as a will-o-the-wisp through the darkness. He started up the stairs. Six steps up, the gaseous rumbling and the splashing came to an end. Seven steps now; eight, nine, ten. The toilet was flushed in the instant that his quivering fingers grasped the doorknob. Fighting the urge to skulk back down the stairs, the little boy kept going.

He was wending a crooked path through the living room, careful to avoid stepping on any of the scattered, ketchup-smeared plates and empty Bud cans, front door in sight, when the bathroom door crashed open.

Instinctively, the little boy dropped to the ground and rolled under the couch. If he was going to get away, he would have to be patient. He knew what would happen if the old man caught him now. Yeah, life sucked, but it also hurt like hell. And it was the pain that frightened him most of all.

As the old man lumbered into the living room, whacking a rolled up copy of the latest *Young Buns* magazine on his leg, the little boy clapped a hand over his mouth in an attempt to quiet his breathing, which was fast and furious. He took a deep breath and let it out slowly. Did it again. Again. Until his telltale breathing slowed.

It was two weeks to the day that his mother had gone out for smokes and tampons and not come back. He swallowed back the lump that was rising in his throat. When he escaped from the hell that was his home he was going to find her, however long it took, and ask the overwhelming question.

Peering through the dusty fringe dangling from the bottom lip of the smelly hand-me-down couch, he watched as the old man, his wrinkled face glistening with sweat, plopped his roly-poly, sweat-suit-clad body into the duct-taped Lay-Z-Boy where he spent the vast majority of his waking hours. Watched as he dropped the magazine onto the floor, picked up the remote and thumbed the TV and VCR on.

After his mother's disappearance, the old man had spent six days and nights editing dozens of his favorite scenes together on one video tape. The greatest story ever told, he liked to say. He watched it a bzillion times a day if he watched it once. He said it his inspiration to go on living.

It started out the way it always did, with a close-up of the writing on the lopsided, grocery store birthday cake.

"Happy twenty-fifth," the old man said.

The camera panned out to capture his mother's beautiful face. She struck a model's pose, lifting her golden tresses from her long, graceful neck, peering suggestively through the strands that had fallen over her piercing blue eyes.

"I love you," she said.

"I . . . I love you, too," the little boy mouthed.

"Make a wish, baby," the old man's off-camera voice said.

His mother pouted her fire-engine-red lips, and blew out the single flickering candle. She trailed her hand through the icing then, one by one, licked her fingers clean, working them slowly between her lips, in and out, in and out.

"Yummy," she said. "Want some?"

"Later, baby, later."

His mother's hand moved down out of the picture. The focus blurred as the camera stalked her wet fingers. They grabbed the hem of her dress, pulling it over her knees, past the garter belt, and higher still.

The camera zoomed in for a better look.

The picture shimmied then sharpened, his mother's juicy, hairless pussy filling the TV screen. In the background, the little boy could hear himself scratching and clawing at the door of the darkened closet where they kept him until he was needed. Under the couch, he pissed himself at just the sound of his terror.

His mother's hand drifted back into the picture, her fingers covered in another gob of icing which she proceeded to smear *all over her*.

"Heh, heh," the old man's voice said. "On second thought-"

The picture jumped to the old man giving head to the boy he called 'The Peckerwood Queer.' When he was through hurting Ronnie for five bucks an hour, and before his crack-head mom came to pick him up, the two boys were usually locked together in the closet. Huddled in the scary darkness Ronnie would whisper stories, fanciful tales of magic and adventure – about a secret world called Orion where kids had wings and flew with eagles. In time his stories had become so real that the walls disappeared and they escaped into the fantasy world he had created. They swooped and soared over an endless city of ruby, emerald and diamond pyramids, perched atop trees so high and mighty they had touched the face of God.

On screen, the old man raised his head, cum and spittle dripping from his trio of chins, and smiled for the camera.

In their minds, they never, ever came back.

"Here it comes," the old man mumbled to himself, all giddy and excited, rocking back and forth in the Lay-Z-Boy, eyes glued to the screen. "Hereitcomeshereitcomeshereit-" He leaned closer to the television as the light flared off his lily-white dentures. He slapped his knee. "Eat your heart out, Robert Redford."

All bruised and battered, Ronnie had that familiar faraway look on his face. He wasn't feeling a thing, the little boy knew. He could tell by his eyes, and by the fish hook of a smile, that his mind, at least, was safe and secure on Orion.

It was the last time the little boy had seen Ronnie. The next morning, over a breakfast of stale Fruit Loops and Dr. Pepper, they'd told him that

Ronnie was dead. They didn't tell him how he'd died. It was probably better that way.

The little boy smiled. Ronnie was gone, beyond the reach of those who'd hurt him. Beyond their reach, but oh so close. In death he had earned his wings for real, and he hadn't flown away at all. The little boy could feel his friend's presence even now, his very own guardian angel watching over him.

The picture jumped to the pretty Indian with the gigantic boobies. A black man in a cowboy hat was fucking her at knife point on the hood of a real boss car. Although the girl was pleading for her life, moans and groans of pleasure had been dubbed in overtop her frenzied cries for mercy.

"You're hurting me," the girl's mouth said.

"Feels so good," the dubbed-in voice purred.

"Same fuckin' thing," the old man grunted as he worked down his sweatpants and began tugging on his cock.

The cowboy was drilling the Indian's pussy so hard that he had to close his eyes to keep out the wash of sweat, his hips moving in a blur like bumblebee wings. The old man loved this part. It always made him laugh.

"Ride 'em, cowboy," the old man shouted a moment later, then laughed until he had a phlegm-filled coughing fit and had to stop.

The cowboy pulled his cock out of the girl's pussy and swung it up to her mouth, forcing it past her lips and down her throat. Then he took his knife and plunged it, handle first, between her legs, working it in as deep as it would go while she choked and gagged on his cock. The cowboy started to moan. There was blood on his hands from his grip on the blade, but he didn't seem to notice, or care.

The hand on the old man's cock was accelerating, his eyes darting this way and that like tadpoles in a jar as he scanned the garbage filled room for the little boy.

When the cowboy started yippy-kie-aying in sweet agony, the old man spun back to the TV. On the edge of his seat, he watched as the cowboy pulled his cock from out of the girl's throat, flipped the knife around and began stabbing her pussy and inner thighs repeatedly, blood spraying out in a trio of bright red geysers.

"Coming, coming," the cowboy screamed as he jerked off over her gigantic blood-stained boobies.

"Watch the paint, Pocahontas," the old man shrieked. "That's a '69 'Cuda. Shit."

The Indian's legs scissored a couple times on the hood of the car, scissored again, twitched spasmodically for a moment, and then lay still.

"Stupid squaw bitch," the old man said.

The camera zoomed in on the girl's face. Her eyes rolled backward in slow motion and disappeared somewhere into the top of her head, only the whites showing. The shot stayed on her dead eyes for several long seconds before fading to black.

The picture on the TV faded back in.

His mother's eyes were rolled backward in her head, whites only, inside a circle of racy blue eye shadow.

"Oh," she said around the cigarette in her mouth. "Feels so good."

The camera panned out, and there *he* was. Out of the closet.

"Faster, goddammit," his mother said. "It's not an ice-cream cone, you stupid fucktard. Lick it harder. Faster."

The little boy on TV raised his wet face up from between her long, shaven legs, teary-eyed, blinking and squinting back the glare of the thousand watt movie light. "My tongue hurts, Mommy. Can I please stop now? Can I go outside and play?"

"Don't stop," his mother panted.

The little boy's gaze pleaded with the camera. "But my tongue hurts."

The old man's arm reached into the picture and pushed the little boy's face back down between his mother's thighs. When he started to wretch, it was the final straw.

With the camera still rolling on the tripod, the old man stormed into the picture, butt fat wobbling, balls dangling to his knees. Except for where it had fallen off the top of his head, his body was covered in a pelt of kinky grey hair.

"Eat your fuckin' mother," he boomed.

The little boy started to cry, on TV, and under the couch, tears and snot streaming down his cheeks in equal measure.

In disgust, his mother kicked him away with a scuffed stiletto heel, took a drag on the cigarette, and said, "Get the faggot outta my sight."

"Ungrateful sissy faggot," the old man said, slapping him hard on the face, once, twice, three times. "I'll teach ya."

"Stretch marks and grief," his mother shouted, cigarette dancing on her lips, hot ash raining down on her perky, gumdrop boobies. "That's all you've ever given me. Sometimes I don't know why I bother."

The old man yanked the little boy into the closet by one bruised, scrawny arm. He briefly mugged for the camera, flicking out his serpentine tongue, before slamming the door shut behind them.

His mother closed her eyes as soon as they were gone and took herself in hand. She was moaning again in no time, drowning out the whimpers and the prayers that echoed from the tiny space where step-daddy number nine was teaching the little boy the facts of life, and what it meant – his words - to be *A Man*.

When the movie was over, the old man belly-bucked himself out of the chair. "Earl," he hollered. "Get the fuck in here. Quit jokin' around."

The little boy wriggled out from under the couch and started running as fast as his shoeless, sockless feet would carry him. He was out the front door before the old man even knew what was happening. The gravel driveway and the broken glass hurt like crazy as he pounded over them. He was still woozy from the beating, but once he heard the old man come barreling through the door after him, he stopped feeling anything but the fear that drove him.

*＊＊

Earlae was running, much the way she had run that crazy night eleven years ago, across the glitzy chrome and neon office, heading toward the door. She had never really enjoyed the things the old man did to her. She always came, but she had never enjoyed them. No way. Not even once.

She wasn't a faggot. Wasn't a faggot.

Wasn't. Wasn't. Wasn't.

<u>9</u>

The Calhoun home was a sprawling, white-shingled Cape perched on a four acre bluff overlooking the wide-open Atlantic Ocean. There were wind- and wave-worn granite rocks on one side of the rectangular property, a stacked fieldstone wall and a thoughtfully managed forest on the other three sides.

"How are you going to handle this?" Daniel said.

Buchanan turned up the collar of his navy pea coat. "I like to start an investigation by taking a preliminary view of the crime scene."

The bare black trees cast skeletal shadows in the half-light of the mid-December morning. As they stood there looking at each other, Daniel noticed that the wind had picked up, as had the chill in the air. Dark clouds were racing toward them from the ocean, skimming over the agitated surface of the water. Another storm was on its way.

"That's not what I meant, Frank."

Buchanan seemed to be working something out in his head. "I spent three, four summers here when I was a kid. I used to love it. Then I hated it. Now I don't know what I feel." He shook his head slowly. "Don't know if I even want to know."

He pointed at some gargantuan oak trees a hundred yards or so from where they were standing. "I used to have a tree fort over there." The fort was nothing more now than a dangling, knotted length of hemp rope and a couple of weather-beaten two-by-fours nailed across the largest branches of the tallest tree. "It was two full stories with a roped observation deck on top. My uncle helped me build it. Sometimes he'd even stay the night with me. We'd light bonfires on the beach, roast marshmallows and hot dogs and shit like that." His smile was there and gone in an instant. "It was Norman Fucking Rockwell, man. Things couldn't have seemed any more perfect."

"Dad and I used to do the hiking and camping thing in Maine every autumn," Daniel said. "Just the men of the house, he'd tell mom as we were loading up the car. They were some of the best times of my life." He laughed. "Mom's too, I suspect. We weren't always the easiest people to live with."

Buchanan nodded but said nothing, still staring at the place where the two-story fort used to be so very long ago, his shoulders squared and set, his face unreadable. As the storm clouds settled overhead, the air turned faintly blue, and large, wet snowflakes began to fall, catching on his hair and eyelashes.

"Any words of advice from the master?"

The question seemed to bring Buchanan back down to earth. "If you can read a crime scene, and most cops can't, you can learn a lot about a perp. Personality. Habits. Lifestyle. You name it." He started trudging along the crushed seashell driveway toward the front of the house. "Use a standard search pattern. Grid, strip, or spiral. It don't matter. Search from the general to the specific. Oh, and be on the lookout for anything that seems contrived. Thanks to shows like CSI, the dirtbags think they know how to throw us seasoned pros off the scent."

"And do they?"

"Not this one."

"Well, I don't watch CSI. Any of them. So give me the Zen of crime scene procedure in *CliffsNotes* form."

"Live behind your eyes. Keep your mind, and your heart, open to all possibilities. No matter how farfetched they may seem."

Daniel grinned. "Wax on, wax off."

"Smirk all you want. The best cops I've known are downright spooky. One look at a crime scene and they just know if something is hinky. Picking up on vibes that no one else is attuned to. Noticing things that would otherwise go unnoticed." He stopped at the front door and peeled away the yellow Mylar ribbon that marked the scene of the crime. "Although the suits at Quantico would never admit it, police work is ten percent textbook, and ninety percent voodoo." He put a key in the lock and pushed the door open.

"Shouldn't we be wearing rubber gloves or something?"

"No need. The scene's already been searched by pros following standard forensic protocol. Besides, our priority is locating my uncle. I don't give a shit if the evidence we find is admissible in court or not."

Buchanan didn't bother to wipe his feet on the jute Welcome mat on his way inside the grand old house. Daniel did. The smell of salt air and antiques was all around them in the humid darkness.

"It's been a while," Buchanan said, groping the wall on either side of the door before locating the switch and snapping on the lights.

"Yowzer," Daniel said. "He really did a number on this place."

The path of destruction led from the back door, where the kidnapper had entered by picking the twin deadbolt locks, over the colorful, furniture strewn rag rugs on the wide pine plank floor, to the broad, carpeted stairway in the central hall.

"He was abducted in the bedroom," Buchanan said. "We might as well start up there."

At the top of the stairs, Daniel said, "Which one?"

Buchanan pointed to one of six closed doors.

Daniel pulled a tissue from his pocket and wrapped it around the doorknob.

"Knob's already been dusted," Buchanan said. "Everything has."

Daniel opened the door. "I know, I know," he said. "You told me."

"So what's with the tissue?"

"Didn't you read the serological report?"

"I might've skimmed it. Why?"

"Traces of semen were found on the bedspread, on the floor of the walk-in closet, on one of the windows, and on this doorknob."

"Homophobe," Buchanan said.

The first thing that Daniel noticed upon entering the bedroom was the vanity mirror. It had been smashed to pieces, with each piece laying reflective side down on the floor. Beyond the broken mirror, in the center of the room between the bed and the pair of heavy wooden dressers, was a blood-spattered Navajo rug. It was on this rug that William Calhoun had been knocked unconscious the Portsmouth PD report had concluded.

A thought nagged at Daniel, but before he could give it due consideration, he noticed something else. When Buchanan had two-stepped around him to check out the toppled wet bar at the back of the room he'd disturbed a cluster of dust-bunnies, sending them scattering in his wake.

"He was hiding under the bed," Daniel blurted.

Buchanan stopped. "Why do you say that?"

"When they yanked him out, the dust-bunnies tagged along for the ride." He pointed to the floor behind Buchanan. "The rest of the room is just too clean to have that much dust drifting around. Under the bed is the only place it could have come from."

Buchanan nodded thoughtfully. "Yeah," he said. "That sounds about right for Uncle Billy."

"I don't have a good feeling about this," Daniel said a moment later.

Horizontal pellets of snow began to batter the divided-light, double-hung windows. A quarter mile out the sea was laced with angry foam.

"What have you got?"

"Just a feeling for now. Nothing I've been able to put a finger on."

"The weather's getting shitty real fast," Buchanan said. "Let's grab the flashlights outta the car, take a look around the grounds while we still can. Maybe something'll click for you out there."

<u>10</u>

Earlae broke through the office's soundproof doors into the sparkle and deluge of The Colosseum, the wildly successful, members-only gentlemen's club that she and Bo owned and operated. Though the rhythmic onslaught of the classic Ghetto Tech mix blaring inside the cavernous, multi-level room shook her body, it paled in comparison to the apocalypse of the heartbeat inside her head.

By all appearances, business was booming.

The evening's theme was Moonlight on the Mediterranean, and the enormous movie screen opposite the main bar was showing the peaceful image of a Mediterranean sunset. The medium-rare sun was just beginning its time-lapsed descent, the white-caps refracting its rays in a rainbow splay of color. Arm in arm, couples swayed to the music, devouring the scenery as well as barkeep Ernesto's notorious 150-proof absinthe concoctions. The large circular dance floor, flanked by two robust olive trees specially imported from Italy for the occasion, was hopping.

By all appearances, the scene was a perfect one, and it very nearly made Earlae hurl.

On the surface everything appeared quite ducky.

Just don't look too closely.

Earlae paused a moment to penetrate the illusion. The second Sunday of each month was Suffragette Day, which meant that drag queens could wet their mustachioed whistles for free. She stood and watched as razor-thin men in tight designer t-shirts jerked and lunged on the strobe-lit dance floor with men wearing thrift shop chiffon dresses and trick-or-treat make-up jobs - their costumes more mockery than homage, a cruel and twisted caricature of womanhood.

I am not at all like you.

On the movie screen the sun dropped below the horizon and a shooting star arced over the rustling olive trees and the bouncy, trouncy, pouncy, liquor-soaked disco queens.

Wasn't. Wasn't. Wasn't.

Earlae charged elbows first through the prideful, frivolous crowd and passed between the bouncers into the elevator, which descended automatically to the basement. The doors rolled open and she headed down the lengthy hallway skirting the fully-booked private function rooms.

In the first room, paid for until midnight at a cost of five hundred dollars per hour, vague shapes glided wraithlike through a mourner's shroud of shadow. "Yoo-hoo," an effete voice called out as she traversed the open doorway. "In here Earlae-Baby. Come and join us."

As her eyes adjusted to the gloom, penetrating yet another carefully crafted illusion, Earlae witnessed a writhing, whispering, moaning mass of bodies on the floor, interconnected in configurations more tormented than sensual, more pained than pleasured. While there was a time she would have naively accepted such an offer, that time had passed.

"No," she said firmly.

The speaker stepped into the light and smiled crookedly up at her. Although she didn't know his name, she had seen him around the club a time or two. He was lean and wiry, as small as a child, his long braided hair hanging down his bare back like a pampered show pony's mane. As he pondered her rejection he began to idly finger his porn star-sized erection which glistened moistly with Vaseline and fecal matter.

"Don't be such a square," he said at last. "It's a real mind-fuck."

"I can't." She crossed her arms. "I won't."

"Your *loss-s-s-s*," the small man said before being hauled roughly but oh-so-willingly back into the fray.

The next three rooms were also occupied, but their doors were closed, their dark secrets unrevealed. In the fifth room, a naked federal appeals court judge was supine on an inclined bench, his arms outstretched, pulled high above his head, wrists secured by leather straps, a greasy rag wadded in his mouth. His elevated legs were spread, strapped securely at the knees and ankles. A dark-skinned man in a turban was kneeling between his legs, sucking him off while five other men, standing in a semi-circle at the lower end of the table, chugged Evian water and pissed buckets onto his purple, panic-stricken face. The judge's head was whipping furiously from side to side as he attempted to avoid the shimmering, criss-crossing streams. The rasp of his panicked breath through his nose was much louder than his screams, which were muffled and gurgling. The man with the turban suddenly stopped sucking and set to work with his hairy hands. The judge's long fingers began opening and closing in anticipation of the payoff, toes curling and uncurling, piss-spattered chest heaving. His eyes caught Earlae's in the split second before he blew his load. Strange eyes. Cold. Like a mannequin's.

Earlae turned and bolted down the last twenty feet of hallway.

Gay? Not gay. Defiled and debauched, perhaps. Certainly not happy.

You no good for nothin' faggot freak.

The hick's words played over and over again through her mind as a catchy little tune sung in the angelic voices of the Vienna Boy's Choir.

Faggots? Hardly. Queers? That's what they were. Every goddamned one of them. Queers. Freaks. Abominations of nature.

Beyond the rooms, under the stairwell to her and Bo's wonderful loft apartment was a locked door, old, short, fashioned of iron-strapped oak. She fumbled for the skeleton key she wore around her neck, twisted it in the lock, and ducked inside.

She could wait no more.

Tonight, in spite of Bo's carefully calculated timeline, the bloodletting would begin, and tomorrow the world would know.

11

The new snow was half an inch deep and still coming down hard. To save time, they decided to split up, with Daniel searching the front of the estate, and Buchanan the back.

In his mind, Daniel divided the allotted terrain into grids of approximately ten feet square. He swept his flashlight methodically over every inch of each grid, making a mental note of anything that appeared out of the ordinary. Proceeding in this manner, he was able to locate two paths that had recently been trampled through the ground-cover leading down from the road on the most isolated corner of the property.

On the first path, Daniel noticed that several saplings had been snapped off at waist height. Although the fractures were recent, he was unable to determine whether they'd been made by the kidnapper on the evening of the abduction or by the police searching the grounds after the fact.

On the second path, after sweeping away the powdery snow with a broken evergreen bough, Daniel noticed a series of small circular holes poked into a rectangular patch of older, crusted snow. Each hole was roughly the diameter of a pencil. There were twenty-one holes in all, and if you extended the line that they traced inward, they led directly to the rear door of the house. He snapped off a series of pictures with his Blackberry, some close-up, some depicting the trail to the door.

"Frank," Daniel shouted. "Check this out."

Standing motionless beneath the row of oaks, Buchanan gave no indication that he had heard him. The aged, knobby trees were teetering on the precipice of a heavily eroded bank, their shallow roots clutching at the rocky soil. Spume from the waves breaking on the rocks below repeatedly spattered Buchanan's back and legs, but he paid the drenching no mind. Something in the tallest tree had captured his attention and wasn't letting it go.

Daniel hurried over, drawing as near to Buchanan as he could without getting wet.

"Frank," he said.

Buchanan attempted a weak smile. Then he shone his light up the trunk into the swaying welter of twisted branches. Numerous divots of the rough corky bark had been scuffed from the trunk and at least three of the higher branches by a clambering shoe.

"Someone's been up there," Daniel said.

"You wanna flip for it?"

"Are you okay, Frank?"

"I asked you if you wanted to flip for it."

"I'll go," Daniel said. "A man your age and girth shouldn't be making like Tarzan."

Buchanan's eyebrows lowered and his eyes narrowed. If looks could maim . . .

In a flash, Daniel scrambled up the tree and out of his brawny friend's reach. Thirty feet up, on one of the sturdy branches with the two-by-fours attached, he found signs of a recent visitor. In a natural depression formed at the intersection of two branches and the trunk, was a stash of cigar butts. The top few looked relatively fresh, while those at the bottom were frozen into the snow-melt that had collected there. All of a sudden, the thought that had nagged at Daniel inside the house became clear. He used a tissue to pick up one of the thick butts. Its familiar gold-colored band was still legible. *Romeo y Julieta*. Churchill. Cuban. Worth a small fortune if it was pre-embargo. He wrapped the butt in the tissue and dropped it in his pocket.

His perch had the guarded feeling of a den, and offered Daniel a sweeping vista of the grounds and the narrow, sway-backed roadway in. They had neglected to turn off the upstairs lights on their way out and the wide dormered windows of the master bedroom were gleaming like the eyes of a jacked deer.

Daniel was shifting his position, getting ready to descend, when a sudden shoving wind struck the tree and he almost toppled backwards off the slippery limbs.

"I throw out my back catching your clumsy, muscle-bound ass," Buchanan shouted up at him, "I'm really gonna be pissed."

Glancing down, Daniel experienced a brief sense of vertigo. "Girly man," he shouted back.

"Fuck you."

"While we're on the subject of getting fucked, we didn't actually find it, you know."

"Find what?"

"The stapled note in the Portsmouth police file. We didn't actually find it."

"How do you figure that?"

"We were *allowed* to find it."

Gazing upward, blinking back the steady barrage of snow, Buchanan appeared to be giving Daniel's words due consideration. "So?" Or maybe not.

"Big difference, don't you think?"

"Didn't anyone ever tell you not to look a gift horse in the mouth?"

"For every cliché, there is an equal and opposite cliché."

"Huh?"

"Does the phrase beware Greeks bearing gifts mean anything to you?"

"Are you suggesting we ignore the information?"

"Not at all. I think we should run with it. See where it leads us. And then . . ."

"And then what?"

Daniel leaned back against the trunk to free up his hands. "The best thing about clichés and phrases is that they can be turned."

"I'm still not following you."

Daniel grabbed the knotted length of rope and held it aloft in a loop. "We play their little game, for now, and if they give us enough of this stuff, we can always use it to hang anyone, friend or foe, who gets in our way."

Buchanan smiled coldly. "I knew you weren't just another pretty face."

When he was safely back on solid ground, Daniel said, "That was where he watched the house from."

"What did you find?" Buchanan said, and Daniel told him. He also told him how he was finally able to put his finger on what had been bothering him inside the house. And then he told him his theory.

"We gotta go," Buchanan said. "My aunt's staying with a friend. Monica Little. Sixty-four. Widowed. They've known each other since they were kids. Same schools. Chased the same boys. A real class act. She lives down the road a ways. In a town named Gloucester."

"Didn't George Clooney shoot a movie there a decade or so back?"

"*The Perfect Storm.* Yeah, that's the place."

12

Clickety-clack.

The garrote wire his captors had attached to his privates was fastened to an iron ring hammered into the ceiling at such a length that he was unable to sit down, unable to twitch more than a muscle without committing the grave and mortal sin of suicide. Upon his arrival in this cell, after being stripped of his clothes and securely tethered, the drag queen had bound his clenched fists with duct tape while the nigger busied himself setting up the A/V equipment.

Clickety-clack.

Such a handsome young lad. Seven, maybe eight years old. Aching and sleepy-eyed, he strained to focus on the precocious tyke. So very handsome. His near-porcelain complexion, his arrestingly dusky eyes, his wet, pouting mouth, just crying out to be violated with extreme prejud-

Clickety-clack.

The sound of the slide projector was loud in the damp, sepulchral room. It was a divine torture. Every dozen or so heartbeats, another sensational snapshot would appear on the screen in front of him. Although, if truth be told, he did have his fav-

Clickety-clack.

Had to keep his head clear. Trying to confuse him, that's what they were doing. Of course, he was wise to their diabolical scheme. Regardless of the sanctimonious, sword-of-vengeance speeches the drag queen was prone to deliver through the bars of his cell he knew exactly what they were up-

Clickety-clack.

Two dozen slides in all. Two dozen candid shots of ripe from the vine, obscenely beautiful boys. He knew them all by heart. Eyes open. Eyes closed. It no longer mattered. And he had a pet name for each and every one of them.

His favorite he called-

Clickety-clack.

The nigger was clearly in charge, and despite the cultured public persona he affected, he remained a product of the ghetto at heart. After a little *bling* money, that's all. Too cocky for his own good, too uppity, the nigger had clearly underestimated him. He was a Harvard man. MBA. *Magna cum laude.* Not some mail-order Masters Degree schmuck. All he had to do was to keep his head clear. Endure their wicked game just a few more-

Clickety-clack.

His favorite was back. Curly red hair. Freckles. Braces on his teeth.

His beauty was ecstasy.

The enigmatic half-smile on the tiny tot's face, exuding an almost feral, preteen sexuality, said it all.

Ecstasy.

What a blessed slut Ecstasy was. He-

Clickety-clack.

He was starving. His stomach was hollow. He hadn't eaten in a day in a half and he could feel himself weakening. Concentrate, he reminded himself for the umpteenth time. If he fell, if he slipped in the slick, malodorous feces mounded at his feet, he would die. And he wasn't ready for death quite yet. Not if he could-

Clickety-clack.

Fellatio. Sodomy. Urolagnia. Coprophilia. They were an imaginative lot. Each boy so very eager to please in his own inimitable fashion. Unlike that gimped-up bunch of losers he'd been diddling of late.

Talk about your bottom-feeders.

Clickety-clack.

Just thinking of food made his mouth water.

Back when they were feeding him, the nigger took great satisfaction in urinating on his gruel. He'd do it in plain sight and then, grinning like a hurdy-gurdy monkey, watch as every steaming mouthful was consumed.

Clickety-clack.

The lust of the eyes mirror the soul, a wise man had once remarked.

He had done nothing to feel guilty about.

He had done nothing wrong.

All one had to do was glance at their beaming, angelic faces, their sticky, lascivious bodies, and he knew . . .

Eyes don't lie. Eyes just don't-

Clickety-clack.

The snare around his privates was burning with the intensity of a Palm Beach sun in July. He closed his eyes and concentrated. To make the faces go away. Make the erection fade. Just to take a breather from the pain.

But the faces and the erection stayed with him.

And the pain? Well, that stayed with him, too.

Clickety-clack.

13

Monica Little lived alone in a nineteenth-century sea captain's house on Pleasant Street in Gloucester's quaint downtown core. The imposing, pumpkin-colored structure was two-and-a-half stories tall with soaring bay windows and a widow's walk. Holiday lights in the shape of candles glowed dimly through the frosted lead-glass panes on either side of the door. Buchanan rang the bell, and Daniel shuffled his feet, doing a Twila Tharp-inspired keeping-warm dance while they waited for a reply.

In due course the door was opened by a tiny black woman with thinning, blue-grey hair and a beaming apple-doll face. "You're little Francis, aren't you? Lordy, yes," she said, gazing straight up at the strapping homicide cop. "I'm Mrs. Little, your aunt's oldest and dearest friend. Do come in."

Daniel caught Buchanan's eye and mouthed, "Francis?"

"Don't go there," Buchanan said.

They stepped into a broad foyer with stairs leading to the upper floors. An arched doorway to the right opened into a spacious sitting room. The house was old-lady rosy, cluttered with overstuffed furniture and age-yellowed photographs of contented men and women in carved gilt-wood frames. Daniel felt something graze his pant leg and looked down to see a brood of cats milling at his feet. He dropped to his haunches and scratched a purring, one-eyed Calico on the head.

"My blessed babies," Mrs. Little said.

"This is my associate, Daniel Rourke," Buchanan said, nodding once toward Daniel. "We need to see Aunt Sarah ASAP."

The old woman made the sign of the cross. "Sarah's in the kitchen, the poor dear." She pointed the way. "Take off your wet things and go right on in. Last door on the left." She padded slowly up the stairs with her cats. "Just holler if you need anything."

Sarah Calhoun was sitting in a Fold 'n' Go wheelchair beside a locomotive-sized wood-burning stove, a knitted shawl covering her lap. She was in her mid-sixties but didn't look a day over ninety. Her uncombed grey hair was shoulder length, and she wore no make-up. Periodically, her hands would twitch and jump involuntarily along the padded vinyl arms of the chair.

"You were supposed to be home that night," Buchanan said.

The old woman maneuvered her chair closer to the stove and raised her palsied hands to the open door, holding them no more than an inch from the sputtering flames. It had to hurt like hell, but she never once flinched.

"Weren't you?" Buchanan pressed.

"William and I spent every Wednesday evening together. It was the only time our schedules permitted. You're right, I should have been there," she said, her voice filled with more regret than words could speak. "Maybe that monster wouldn't have come if I'd been home." She lowered her hands from the fire and wedged them under her inert legs. "Or maybe I could've stopped him."

Looking at Frank's aunt, listening to her, Daniel felt an almost visceral tug. She reminded him so much of his mother, Juliana Rourke, in the final days before cancer had taken her life that it made his heart ache. Had Sarah Calhoun been home that night, she wouldn't have hid under the bed, he knew. She would have fought to the bitter end. The same way his mother had.

"They expected you to be there."

"No!"

"They wanted you, too."

"There's been no ransom demand. The police in Portsmouth said it was a random act of violence. Chief Russo told me that himself."

"Frank's right, Mrs. Calhoun," Daniel said. "They came for the two of you."

"But the police said-"

Buchanan tilted his aunt's chin up with his fingers. "I *am* the police," he said. "And I'm telling you now it wasn't random." He knelt down in front of his aunt so that his eyes were level with hers. He slipped her hands out from under her legs and squeezed them tightly in his own to quiet their tremors. "Daniel and I just came from the house. We found some things the locals missed."

"What things?"

"For starters, we found the place where the perp hid while he watched you."

"Surveilled you," Daniel said.

"What does he mean, Francis?"

"The perp watched the house for quite some time before he struck. He knew your routine. He knew Uncle Billy would be home that night. And he expected you to be there, too. I know you, Aunt Sarah. You're a creature of habit. You should have been there."

"But I wasn't," she said. "I got called to the hospital after Monica had another of her spells. But you knew that already. I told you the whole story on the phone." She fixed Buchanan with her gaze. "So tell me what else you found. Tell me now."

"There were cigar butts snuffed in the branches of a tree with an unobstructed view into the house," Daniel interjected. "More than a dozen."

"The old oak," Sarah Calhoun said.

Buchanan nodded. "Big ones."

"Churchills," Daniel said. "Seven inches long. Forty-seven ring gauge."

"And they were smoked down to the band," Buchanan said. "I don't know about you, but I've been hustled at enough poker nights to know it takes a good long while to smoke a stogie that size all the way down. So whoever was in that tree was there for a long, long time."

"Also," Daniel said, "some butts were noticeably older than others. Which suggests that he was there on more than one occasion. Surveilling you. It also suggests that he meant to abduct you both."

"I want you to split for LA immediately," Buchanan said. "You can stay at my place until we wrap this thing up. It's not the Taj Mahal but at least it's-"

"Impossible."

"You're not listening to me," Buchanan said. "It's not safe for you here. He may decide to come back for you."

The old woman jerked her hands from Buchanan's grasp. "I can't leave William. I can't." She crossed her arms defiantly. "And I won't."

The sound of Christmas music sifted into the room from somewhere upstairs. Nat King Cole was singing *Have Yourself a Merry Little Christmas.* Sure, Daniel thought. Seventeen sleeps and counting.

"Aunt Sarah, please. Listen to reason."

There was an angry, frustrated look in her eyes. "William never left me. No matter how sick I became, no matter how ornery, he stayed with me. He stayed when I began to wet the bed like a baby. Stayed when I could no longer . . . no longer please him."

"But-"

"I won't go," she said firmly. "And you can't make me."

Buchanan exhaled loudly. "Okay," he said. "But I want you to bunk with Mrs. Little until I tell you otherwise. You do not leave this house. And you do not go back to Portsmouth for any reason."

She began to shake her head. "But it's my home."

"You can't go back there."

"I'll stay on one condition."

They stared at each other for a long moment. It was Buchanan's turn to speak and the old woman patiently waited him out.

"Name it," he finally said.

"Find my husband."

Buchanan looked at Aunt Sarah long and hard. "I promised you I'd find him when you called me out here," he said, "and I always keep my promises."

Sarah Calhoun's mouth formed a sad, crumpled smile. "I know you do," she said. "I love you, Francis. I'm so glad you're home."

Buchanan buried his head in her shoulder and hugged her tightly.

"I missed you, too," he said.

14

Earlae studied the psychotic old bitch through the bars of his cage in utter disbelief. Although the images were intended as a perverse, albeit poetic, means of torture, she could tell by the beatific look on his face, by his glorious, shuddering pole of an erection, that he viewed them as anything but. What manner of man takes pleasure in the exploitation and dehumanization of children? she wondered. Standing her ground, she watched him watching them, her anger growing exponentially as she gathered her resolve, momentarily filling the vast empty space inside her.

The old bitch's cold, bloodshot eyes tracked lazily over to her as she threw open the deadbolt and entered his cell.

"Do you want to live?" She did not raise her voice. She was much angrier than that.

His gaze deserted her and returned to the tortured, haunted souls on the projection screen. "This *is* living," he said. "*Amore regge senza legge.*"

"What did you say?"

His parched lips cracked into a patronizing smile. "Love rules without rules," he said.

Evil incarnate, that's what they were. Living, breathing ghouls from the bowels of Hell. She placed the tip of her index finger on the wire, exerting enough force to whiten his yellowed, parchment-like skin.

"Now see here," he sputtered. "I am only going to say this once. I demand that you release me immed-"

"Quiet," Earlae said, crouching down. She could feel the tension on the line increase as he attempted to retreat from her, his erection melting in her mouth. *Like budda.*

"What's the matter? Too old and decrepit for your tastes?"

"Let's cut the off-off-Broadway theatrics and get down to brass tacks. Name your price." The old bitch winked. "If you've got a pulse, you've got a price. Am I right or am I right?"

Earlae chuckled, and the old bitch winked a second time. "I thought so," he said.

She stood straight, shoulders back. Stopped chuckling and began to laugh wholeheartedly. She laughed until a river of tears rushed down her face, until she was left gasping for breath and the old bitch's smile had turned upside down.

"Don't be stupid. I can pay any amount you want."

Still, Earlae continued to laugh.

The old bitch clenched his eyes shut and pressed his bound fists to his ears. "Just name your price, goddammit."

"Ha, ha, ha . . ."

"Silence," he commanded.

"I don't want your stupid money," Earlae hissed.

He opened his eyes. "I am not a man without influence. I have powerful friends. I can give you whatever it is you want."

"Oh, really?"

"Whatever. You. Want."

"Beg for my forgiveness then. Like you mean it. Nothing too off-off-Broadway, of course."

"That's it? No money? No favors? Nothing?"

Earlae paused to emphasize what she was about to say. "Fall to your knees and beg for my forgiveness. It's all that I want . . . all that I need from you."

"You deranged little queer. I am *not* going to feel bad simply because you're telling me to. I refuse to be persecuted. Especially by the likes of you. *Why?* Because I did nothing wrong. *Nothing.* Look at their faces, goddammit. Just look at their shiny happy faces. Then look into your own heart." His voice fell to a hoarse, staccato whisper. "You experienced firsthand the madness, the frenzy, the ecstasy of man-boy love, and you enjoyed it. Even if you won't admit it aloud, or in the whispered confessional of your midnight mind, you know that I'm right."

Earlae did what was asked of her. She turned to the screen and took a good hard look into their faces, feeling every wound that would never heal, and she apologized silently to every kid for whom she hadn't acted in time to save.

"You're wrong," she said.

Finally, her anger reached the flashpoint, erupting like an unstoppable force of nature. She began to rake the old bitch's body with her nails, his screams of pain rivaling those of her own. When the strength in her arms was thoroughly spent, her throat red-raw and burning, she swept his wading-bird legs out from under him.

The old bitch dropped onto his ass with a wet smacking sound, blood popping out the hole beneath his gut in spurts, his cock still attached to the piano wire and penduluming in front of his only briefly startled face.

"Dammit," he muttered.

For a moment he tried to plug the hole with his useless hands, but he soon grew too weak to do even that. With his remaining strength, he wriggled up against the stone block wall and leveled his gaze at the screen, grinning maniacally, seemingly oblivious to the menstrual-like flow of blood from between his legs, and to the severed cock still swinging to and fro in front of him. With monumental effort he raised one trembling arm, gesturing toward the screen.

Earlae turned to look at what had caught his eye. It was a slide showing a frail red-headed boy being buggered by a barrel-chested man wearing a rubber Halloween mask in the likeness of JFK.

"See that one? That one makes my dick hard."

And then he was dead.

Earlae looked down at the old bitch, and began to laugh again. Initially, her reaction seemed fine, natural even. Until she realized she was powerless to make the laughter stop. She was losing control, she feared, losing control of everything that had ever mattered to her. She was crying now, and laughing, and staring at the corpse on the floor as though it contained an answer, a truth, which might bring an end to the insanity. But the old bitch just lay there in silent repose, his empty eyes unchanged by death, still gazing adoringly at the profane images that continued to appear on the screen every seven seconds like clockwork. Something told her that a scalding-hot dip in the tub, to wash the blood from her hands, the meat from under her nails, and a nice glass of California Chardonnay would make the haunting laughter stop.

Unfortunately, they wouldn't.

<u>15</u>

The storm blew its wad by eleven AM, and what had started out as an ugly morning gave way to a glorious, sunshiny afternoon. Slip-sliding toward Boston on a lane one snow plough-blade wide, Daniel at the wheel, Buchanan riding shotgun, they were making excellent time. Before leaving Monica Little's house, after a belt-loosening feast of honey-glazed ham, mashed potatoes and homemade pumpkin pie, Buchanan had managed to track down a Special Agent in the FBI's Boston Field Office named Barry Galton and cajole their way into a four o'clock meeting. About what? They had no idea. Their carefully laid plan was to play it by ear.

At precisely two minutes to four, Daniel wheeled the car into a metered space outside the sweeping, curved façade of One Center Plaza and braked sharply.

"Galton's busting his hump on a Sunday," Buchanan said. "What's that tell you?"

"Could be another case entirely," Daniel said. "It is the FBI we're talking about. Under-worked they're not."

"And if it's not another case?"

"Then you were right."

"About it being something big."

"And under the radar."

"Which we could work to our advantage."

"Exactly what I was thinking."

After signing in at the visitor's desk, a thin, leathery-looking security guard with a drinker's nose led them across the lobby's highly polished terrazzo floor to a wide bank of elevators. He unlocked one of the doors and punched the requisite call button. "Someone'll meet you topside," he mumbled.

The doors closed then reopened in the amount of time it took Daniel to blink, revealing a trim, pistol-packing brunette in her early thirties who identified herself as Special Agent Sloan. She led them through a rat's maze of hallways to a meeting room with bare, industrial green walls, and then left. Aside from a rectangular oak table with six matching chairs, the room was empty.

Two male agents arrived within seconds of Sloan's departure. The first, who genially introduced himself as Leonard Farmer, was young, and well-dressed, with a decidedly Machiavellian smile. A series of thin white scars criss-crossed the left side of his face. He wore round gold-rimmed glasses and his thick, black hair was slicked straight back. A diamond stud earring glistened in his right ear. The other agent, introduced by Farmer as

Barry Galton, was a decade or two older. He had a salt and pepper Frankie Avalon hairdo and was wearing a rumpled navy blazer, white oxford shirt with a button-down collar, no tie. His five o'clock shadow was so thick that it appeared blue under the florescent lights. Unlike his partner, he wasn't smiling.

"Start talking," Galton said. "Wong's all-you-can-eat buffet started at four, so you got about five minutes before I boot your asses outta here."

"We're looking into the disappearance of William Calhoun," Buchanan said.

"That's Portsmouth's headache," Galton said. "A simple missing person case. Nothing I gotta worry about. Four and a half minutes."

"I haven't been in town long," Daniel said, "but there seems to be more to Mr. Calhoun's disappearance than people are letting on."

Galton smirked and glanced over at his partner. Farmer's mouth was still smiling, but his eyes were scared. "I assure you," Farmer said, "if there's anything at all we can-"

"Thomas," Daniel said.

"Excuse me," Farmer said, the smile wavering only slightly. He reached up and began to fiddle with his earring.

"Thomas," Daniel said again. "Murray. Blake. Taylor. The mister and the little missus."

"I don't know what you're talking about," Farmer said, still smiling and fiddling.

Daniel slowly moved his gaze from Farmer to Galton. Galton was the hard case, but he was also the go-to guy. If they were going to get anywhere with their investigation, they would need his blessing. Galton met Daniel's eyes and never once blinked.

"Yeah," Daniel said. "You do."

"What do you want from us exactly?" Galton said.

"Show us what you got," Buchanan said. "It's all we want."

"Oh, is that all?" Galton said in a loud and belligerent tone. "How about I tell you what I want instead? I've been pulling double duty for a week and a half on account of some new strain of open-border flu that's been working its way through our ranks. What I want is to get the hell out of here, get stuffed on multiple platefuls of Mr. Wong's wonderful chow, and fall asleep beside my old lady watching *Law and Order* reruns on A & E. What *you* want doesn't enter into things. I don't give a flying fuck what *you* want."

Farmer clapped his hands sharply, like you would at a misbehaving puppy. "Watch your potty mouth, Special Agent," he said. "Such blatantly offensive language is against bureau policy and I could write you up for it."

"Fuck you, too," Galton said.

"Listen to me," Daniel said. "All we have right now is a list with a couple names on it. When Frank and I start digging, I suspect we're going to quickly find more, and a lot of people are going to start asking a whole lot of questions. Especially the press. Is that also what you want? To be gang-raped by the media?"

Farmer laughed. He looked over at Galton as if to say, Laugh too. Galton, however, couldn't even conjure up a smile.

"Back when I was prosecuting scumbags in Los Angeles, I worked my fair share of high profile cases," Daniel said. "Do you want to know what I loved most about them? It was that whole fifteen minutes of fame thing. Spinning the facts to a sea of cameras then tuning in to the news to watch my reasonably telegenic mug smirking up and down the TV dial. NBC. CNN. Fox. Univision. I've got primo contacts at them all. I'll dial the DA right now if you want to check out my background."

Galton turned to Buchanan. "Now your background I know," he said. "I had your jacket faxed to me after you called. Your Lieutenant said you're a regular pit bull. Said once you sink your teeth into something you don't let go 'til it's cleared. But she also said you're not here in any official capacity."

"So?"

"So why should the FBI show you squat?"

"He's family, and I-"

"Isn't that awful," Farmer said, breaking in to offer empty empathy in accordance with some bullshit policy or other. "Simply awful." He would in all likelihood go far in today's Bureau.

"I have reason to believe that they also wanted my aunt." Buchanan took an aggressive step into Galton's personal space. "Something that'll only happen over my dead body."

Galton sneered. "And that loose-cannon attitude is why we can't allow you access to our files." He poked a stubby finger hard into Buchanan's chest to drive home his point. "You're too goddamned close to the case. Too involved. Too emotional. You'd only fuck it up. Get us all in deep shit."

"Agent Galton," Farmer said. "One more time with such language and I really will report you to the-"

"We've got one," Special Agent Sloane said, pounding twice on the door jamb to get their attention.

Galton and Farmer exchanged looks.

"Dead or alive?" Galton said.

Sloane responded with a somber shake of her head. "Boston PD's already secured the scene. Their initial report is not good."

Galton and Buchanan were now engaged in a full-fledged schoolyard stare-down. Thankfully, Galton was the first to blink. "Okay," he said at last. "Show me what you got. I like what I see I'll consider spreading the wealth."

<u>16</u>

The loft was shrouded in darkness but Earlae was home. Tokunbo could hear the mystical strains of Albinoni's *Adagio in G Minor* wafting out from the bedroom, where she was doubtlessly, not to mention anxiously, awaiting his arrival. According to plan, tweaked ever so slightly after their captive's premature execution, Tokunbo had spent the better part of the afternoon with nitrile gloves and a surgical blade prepping the corpse for its public unveiling. Needless to say, his creation was pure genius, with an aesthetic both imminent and evocative. He couldn't wait to see the bombastic, bold-faced headlines in all the morning papers.

Tokunbo edged the bedroom door open and stole a peek inside. While the mussed-up bed was empty, candlelight, faint and beckoning, flickered through the arched doorway leading to their ensuite bathroom. He removed his lizard-skin Dolce & Gabbana ankle boots and tip-toed across the spacious room.

The bathroom was positively sylvan, a veritable oasis of one-of-a-kind orchids that he'd genetically tweaked to compliment the space. Their blossoms, radiating with every imaginable tincture, were inordinately huge, their scent achingly sweet. He unbuttoned his Prada stretch-silk shirt and caressed his nipples as he admired the tanned calf draped demurely over the side of the eight-person, deep-basin Jacuzzi tub.

The work on the old man's corpse had provided him with an unexpected rush of euphoria and he remained in a heightened state of arousal. He couldn't wait to join Earlae in the ardent water, couldn't wait to touch her, nibble every silken inch of her rose petal flesh.

But first . . .

Tokunbo stole to the kitchen for a bottle of bubbly. When he had last spoken to Earlae, on the phone late in the morning, she'd sounded happier than he had ever heard her. In fact, throughout their brief conversation she'd been unable to contain her mirth, giggling like a tickled toddler. It was an excellent sign, he knew. For the first time in their nearly three wonderful years together, he seemed to be getting through to her. A celebration was most definitely in order.

He chose a properly chilled magnum of champagne from his extensive collection of grape from around the globe. Tattinger Cuvee Brut Blanc de Blancs Millesime, 1986. With its tempting aromas of citrus, fresh mint, and a freshly-picked posy of wild flowers, it seemed the perfect choice for the occasion. The only choice, really. A wisp of a smile touched his lips. The fact that the vintage possessed an almost shameless freshness was but an added bonus.

"Sorry, I'm late," he said, mincing through the arched doorway the same way William Powell had done it countless times in the classic *Thin Man* series of motion pictures.

The still corked magnum and Riedel Vinum glasses disintegrated as they struck the genuine pre-Mexican revolution terra cotta floor tiles.

"I'm right here," he shouted as he vaulted into the tub. "Hang on, baby. Just hang on."

Head lolled back, organically-grown Dosakai cucumber slices on her eyes, the love of his life was marinating in a blush-colored pool of blood.

Tokunbo couldn't recall Myrna Loy ever having slashed her wrist. Not even in *Song of the Thin Man*, the most harrowing adventure of RKO's classic six part series.

No! he thought. *No! No! No!*

RKO . . . ?

Not RKO.

It was MGM.

<u>17</u>

Daniel leaped from the police launch as it butted the gravel beach on the windward side of Georges Island, a thirty-nine acre drumlin located seven miles from downtown Boston. On the choppy boat ride over Galton had given them the run-down on the island. Originally used for military purposes, from the mid-eighteen hundreds until shortly after the second world war, it was now a popular tourist destination in the spring and summer months. On the hillock above them the silhouetted gun emplacements of historic Fort Warren were visible through the swirling, ethereal fog. They were empty now, like the rest of the island, without a single witness to the crime. The area had been cordoned off with yellow Mylar ribbon. Portable lights blazed every ten feet along the fluttering perimeter. A dozen feet away a female cop sat back-to on a slick black rock near the beach, head between her knees, alternately weeping and retching. Daniel, Buchanan, Galton and Farmer stepped over the ribbon and gave their names to the five-foot-nothing pocket-cop with the clip-boarded crime scene attendance list. He had a queasy look on his face that said he wished he was sitting on a rock with his head between his knees, too.

Daniel was the first member of the group to reach the body. Prior to Julie's death such a sight would have caused him to regurgitate his honey-glazed ham lunch; now he felt no such inclination.

Buchanan was the next to arrive. His friend stared hard at the body for a moment, saying nothing. His nose was slightly red from the cold and his breath steamed around his inscrutable face.

Daniel said, "Is it . . . ?"

Buchanan shook his head. "It's not him."

The fingernail gouged corpse was draped doggie-style over a weather-distressed park bench at such an angle that it effectively mooned all ships entering the city's bustling harbor. An incision had been made around the anus, the bluish-grey lariat of intestines pulled through the hole and coiled around the throat. The penis had been sheared off at the pubic bone and was nowhere to be seen.

"Have they ID'd the body?" Daniel said to a cop hovering nearby and chomping on a wad of grape-scented bubblegum. He was a big, round kid with red hair and a freckled, wise-guy face. The badge on his uniform said his name was Tucker McNally.

"It's Eric Murray," McNally said, affecting the cavalier attitude of a latch-key kid raised on violent TV and ultra-violent video games. "Or should I say it *was* Eric Murray." He smacked his gum. "Ever see anything that looked quite like that, sir?"

"Not since dinner last night," Daniel said. "*Semper fi* sausage wasn't it, Frank?"

"From here on in, we're dining at Meritage," Buchanan said with a low growl, referring to their hotel's highly rated in-house restaurant. "Your treat."

Daniel looked at McNally. "Any sign of the penis?"

"No, sir," McNally said. "The way I figure it, whoever whacked him kept it as a trophy."

"Now that's fucked up," Galton said.

"Weirdest case of asphyxiophilia I've ever seen," Buchanan said, "and I've walked the Sunset beat."

Daniel and Galton chuckled, and so did McNally.

"This isn't about sex," Farmer hissed. "Rape is never about sex."

"I disagree," Daniel said. "The public display of the body, its pose in a popular sexual position, the mutilation of the genitalia, all tell me that sex is exactly what it's about."

"No way," Farmer said with a shake of his head.

"The brain is man's most powerful sexual organ," Daniel said. "If that's screwed up, really screwed up, what do you think the sex is going to look like?"

Buchanan, Galton, and McNally nodded thoughtfully, while Farmer continued to shake his head. The effete, unabashedly PC agent struck Daniel as the type of man who was prone to confuse the way things ought to be with the way they really were. Farmer just didn't get it, and in all likelihood he never would.

"Okay, hotshots," Galton said. "It's time to put up or shut up."

Buchanan stepped forward. "Someone gimme a pen."

"Cough it up," Galton said to Farmer.

Somewhat reluctantly, Farmer handed Buchanan a flashy gold fountain pen.

Buchanan removed the cap, tucked his tie into his shirt, and stepped over to Murray's bare backside.

"What's he doing?" Farmer said.

With the nib of the pen, Buchanan lifted a flap of skin from around the wound.

"Aw, man," Farmer whined. "That's a fourteen carat Waterman. My mom gave it to me for my high school graduation."

"Flashlight," Buchanan said.

Galton shouldered his way past Farmer and shone the beam of his keychain penlight into the hole.

"Something's in there," Galton said.

"Ten to one," McNally said, "it isn't granny's Christmas stuffing."

Buchanan looked at Galton, who indicated with a nod that he could proceed. It only took Buchanan a moment to fish the object out.

"What is it?" McNally said, edging closer.

"It's a note," Galton said. "Ribbon wrapped around Murray's severed squeaky toy."

McNally blew a bubble and popped it loudly. "What's it say?"

Buchanan tossed the pen to Farmer, who fumbled the catch, then put on his gloves. Very carefully, he opened the moist, thrice-folded paper.

"Out of sight, out of mind."

Galton hollered for an evidence tech who promptly deposited the penis and the note in separate glassine evidence bags.

"Nice work," Galton said. "You got anything else for me?"

"There are two men at work here," Daniel said immediately. "One is the cool, calculating mind, and the other is the frenetic, emotional mind."

"Hair, fiber and fluid analysis point to a single perp," Galton said.

"There are two of them," Daniel said. "And you can bet that what they're doing here is meant to be some kind of message."

"To who?" Galton said.

Daniel shrugged.

"Any bright ideas on what that message might be?" Galton said.

Daniel shrugged again. "Some fucked up message to the masses? A warning? Graffiti of the flesh? I don't know. At this stage, without looking at your files, I couldn't even hazard a guess."

"You're a lunatic," Farmer said.

"Quite possibly," Daniel said. "But I'm also right."

"You can back this two-man theory up?" Galton said.

Daniel nodded.

"Call me first thing in the morning," Galton said. "We'll discuss things then."

"No way," Farmer said to Galton. "There is no way I'm going to play sloppy seconds to these two yahoos." He grabbed Galton by the arm and pulled him aside, speaking in a whisper loud enough for everyone in the vicinity to hear. "I don't want any outsiders messing around with our case, Barry. I'll fight you on this if I have to. Call in every favor the powers-that-be owe me. And you know they owe me plenty."

Galton fixed his cold, black eyes on Farmer's grip on his arm, which released almost immediately. "Listen up, Assface, and listen good. If you don't get the fuck outta my sight right now, I'm gonna take the baton from young McNally's utility belt and beat you to a pink mist. You hear me?"

While Farmer struggled with bared teeth to come up with an appropriate, policy-sanctioned reply, Galton turned his back and started walking, leading Daniel and Buchanan back aboard the idling launch.

"Assface?" Daniel said as the launch surged away from the island.

"His face got messed up during a freak hog-petting accident at a PETA 'Meet Your Meat' campaign about five years back," Galton said.

"You're joking," Daniel said.

Galton chuckled. "According to the doctor the best match for the graft was the skin on his-"

"Bottom," Daniel said.

"Exactly."

"Makes sense to me," Buchanan said.

Galton nodded. "What doesn't make sense is the useless little shine'll probably make Special Agent in Charge in a couple, three years. The politicos and the community organizers just can't seem to get enough of his nonsense."

"You gonna take any heat on this?" Buchanan said.

Galton scratched a moment at the Velcro-like whiskers on his chin. Then he turned and looked back at Farmer, who was standing alone on the edge of the beach, watching them leave, growing steadily smaller, more insignificant, as the distance between them increased.

"Nothing I can't handle," he said.

<u>18</u>

Tokunbo flicked away the cucumber slices. Earlae's pupils were vast, completely crowding out the irises. Aghast, he watched as her wide eyes swept frantically back and forth, looking through him at sights that only she could see, sights that no civilized person should ever have to see.

"*Alive . . . !*" he whispered.

Her breathing was irregular and her pulse was weak, but she was alive. He removed his shirt, tore out a strip of cloth, and bound it tightly around the wound.

She felt as light as a Victorian lace-angel in his arms as he whisked her into the bedroom, softly nuzzling her cheek along the way, kicking at the cursed chickens that always seemed to appear underfoot at precisely the wrong moment. He placed her gently down on their bed and covered her with the Kansas Lily patchwork quilt that he had hand sewn for her on the occasion of their second anniversary. Her face, ghostly pale in contrast to the indigo blue theme of the quilt, was a study in tragedy.

His heart seized to look at her this way.

Tokunbo knew all about her sordid past, and how much she had suffered to become so beautiful. And he understood. Anything for Earlae Horowitz. Their relationship was truly symbiotic. She was the pilot fish to his Great White. He had always felt alienated from the world before meeting her, knowing sex, and sexual-opportunism, but never love. She was his first. His one and only.

Tokunbo reached down and removed a strand of hair from underneath her collagen-plumped lips. For the first time her gaze settled on him and he saw a spark of recognition. Then she closed her eyes and laid so still that for one terrifying moment he thought she had expired. Thankfully, she was only sleeping.

After stitching the inch-long, partial thickness wound closed, he removed his sodden Versace worsted wool trousers - ruined now - and slipped under the quilt against her, whispering sweet nonsense in her ear, trying to talk her into coming back to the place where someone loved her best of all. She began to revive approximately three hours later when he spoke of buying Southfork, the splendid homestead from the TV show *Dallas*, and keeping the decor seventies kitsch. It was her all-time favorite show and she watched it religiously in syndication. She considered Sue-Ellen Ewing a goddess, the pinnacle of the female species.

"I thought I had lost you this time," he said.

Earlae muttered something that Tokunbo could not hear. He bent closer. "If I was one of them, a genuine bouncing baby girl, maybe he'd have left me alone. Maybe he would have left mom and me both alone. Maybe he wouldn't have hurt me so. Maybe mom would've . . .

"Maybe."

"Do not worry," Tokunbo said. "We shall get them all. You have my word on that. Every last one of them."

"Really?"

"Soon it will all be polka dots and moonbeams."

"Polka dots and moonbeams?"

"Forever and ever."

Earlae raised a hand in the air. "Pinky swear?"

They locked fingers and gently tugged.

"I swear," Tokunbo said.

Earlae coughed weakly. "I don't feel so good, Bo. It's like there's a mean old prickly porcupine in my throat. I . . . I think I'm going to be-"

"Hush little baby," Tokunbo said. "It is time to rest."

"Cuddle with me, Bo."

And he did.

19

"Wake up, Lazy-Bones," Tokunbo heard Earlae say as she gently rocked him awake. "Time to rise and shine."

Tokunbo opened his eyes. During the night she had changed into her Elise Aucouturier silk chiffon baby-doll nightie. The negligee was made of a pink, ultra-sheer material that gave the illusion of perpetual motion. Except for a distinct lack of color in her face, she looked none the worse for wear, her beauty as intoxicating as ever.

While Tokunbo sat up in bed, stretching out the kinks, Earlae crossed the room and threw open the curtains that hung in billowy folds across the broad wall of Pozzi Wood Windows. She drew a gigantic happy face in the condensation on the inside of one window, turned, and fixed Tokunbo with a smile equally as grand.

"Isn't it just a splendid hot-chocolaty-morning?"

"Come here," he said, and she did.

Tokunbo searched Earlae's eyes for signs of remorse. Finding none, he fixed his attention on her recently mended wrist. "What happened?"

Earlae began to cry. Tokunbo waited, letting the question hang. Finally, she broke away from him and leaned back on the bed so that she could hug her drawn up knees.

"You know how it is."

"No," Tokunbo said. "I do not."

Earlae leaned forward and her voice became a girlish chirp. "Yeah, you do." She canted her head. "It was TTOTM again."

"TTOTM?"

"That time of the month? You know. The curse? The bitch is back? Code red?"

"Enough," Tokunbo commanded. "You said things would be different once we set my plan in motion." He shifted his position and put his arm around her. "Are things not different now?"

Earlae said nothing. Instead, she cast her eyes downward and began lightly stroking his thigh with her index finger.

"What if I had not arrived home when I did?"

"You're always there for me."

"And what if one day I am not?"

The tone of her voice was wistful as she spoke. "If it wasn't for you, I'd have been dead a long time ago. Life terrifies me, it always has, but you make it bearable. More than bearable, actually." She climbed on top of him and slid sensually against him until he was fully, almost painfully turgid. "I don't doubt things, myself especially, when I'm with you." He took in some air. He smelled freshly harvested Muscat grapes in her hair, nutmeg on her skin. "The only reason I've been able to carry on, day after day after day, is because of my faith in you. And the knowledge that no matter how bad things may get you'll always come lippity-lop to my rescue."

Tokunbo ran his hands up her bare legs and gave her taut, cellulite-free buttocks a tweak. "Do you know what I am going to buy you the instant that my plans are realized?"

"What, Bo? What are you going to buy me?"

"Tell me what you desire more than anything else in the world?"

"In the whole wide world, Bo?"

He nodded.

She touched his face lightly, suggestively.

"Aside from me," Tokunbo said.

Earlae rolled her eyes up and to one side, thinking.

"You know," Tokunbo said, urging her on.

She tipped her head, looking at him from the corner of her eyes. "Good golly Miss Molly, you don't mean . . . ?"

Tokunbo nodded. "I do," he said. "Your very own vagi-"

She hushed him with a finger to his lips. "Don't say it aloud," she said, her eyes dancing as she considered the possibility. "A wish won't come true if you say it aloud."

"I have been in touch with a very nice, very competent gender reassignment surgeon in Mexico, and as soon as we are through here, I shall schedule the procedure."

"You're the greatest, Bo."

"Kiss me," Tokunbo said.

"I don't have to ask for it?"

Tokunbo shook his head.

"Beg for it?"

"Not today."

"I'll tell you what," Earlae said as she somersaulted out of bed. "Give me two shakes of a lamb's tail to go potty, and I'll do a whole lot more than give you a smooch."

"What about the papers? I thought that you wanted to dash out first thing and pick up all the morning papers for your scrapbook?"

"Hmm," Earlae said, moving her hands up and down as though they were scales, "making carnal, drunken monkey love or perusing the funny pages?"

Tokunbo laughed. "Whatever are you getting at Miss Horowitz?"

"Just give me a minute to clean out the pipes, my tall, dark chocolate prince, and I'll show you exactly what I'm getting at."

<u>20</u>

Galton and Farmer were exchanging heated words inside the meeting room with the bare industrial green walls when Daniel and Buchanan arrived bright and early the next morning. Their body language was as animated as their tone and all conversation ceased the instant they noticed they had company. Farmer did not look pleased, and Galton looked much the way he did the day before. Rumpled navy blazer. A blue sheen of five o'clock shadow, at eight o'clock in the morning. Angry as hell. On the oak table were four, inch-thick file folders and four VHS video tapes. A thirty-two inch Sony television and a Toshiba VCR sat on a rolling stand in one corner of the room.

"It's all here," Galton said. "Everything we got. Gimme a shout when you're done."

"Rest assured," Farmer said, pointing first at Daniel and then at Buchanan, "I'll be keeping my eye on the two of you."

"I'm sure they feel safer already." Galton rolled his eyes and made a small circular motion at his temple with an index finger. "You guy's need anything before we leave you to it? Tea? Coffee? A soda pop?"

"We're fine," Buchanan said.

"Just peachy keen," Daniel said.

Alone with the door closed, Buchanan said, "Let's do this chronologically. Pull a chair over and we'll comb the files line by line."

They began with the file on Marshall Thomas, the first of the group to be reported missing. They read the notes made by the first BPD officer on the scene, the crime scene attendance list, the interview summaries, BPD and FBI, and the various tech reports. Only when they were done with the paper file did they view the videotaped crime scene evidence. They repeated this process for the Murray, Blake and Taylor files and were finished in a little under six hours.

Like the Portsmouth case, there were no witnesses to any of the Boston abductions. Except for the DNA fingerprinting they were awaiting on the semen deposits found at the Murray, Blake and Taylor crime scenes - useless without a sample to match it against - there was no hard evidence establishing the abductor's identity, and no tangible leads.

Murray's preliminary autopsy report indicated that trace amounts of limestone and granite dust had been found in the hairline at the nape of the neck, and it was the coroner's opinion that the incision around the anus had been made with near-surgical precision. There were no fingerprints or other identifying marks on either the note or the body.

The various front page accounts of the murder were strictly by the numbers, expressing indignant outrage, while offering a near-canonization of the man.

"Any thoughts?" Buchanan said.

"Murray sounds a little too good to be true."

"Anything else?"

"No press clippings," Daniel said, fanning through one of the files. "Aside from the various write-ups on Murray's murder, there were no stories whatsoever regarding any of the other abductions."

"What about this?" Buchanan opened the Blake file and pulled out a magazine called East Coast Entrepreneur. It featured a three page profile of the filmmaker. On the first page was a glossy photograph of Blake in happier times, sitting on the porch of a rustic cabin with a glass of port and an electronic notebook, presumably at work on his next screenplay.

"It's a fluff piece," Daniel said. "There's no mention of his disappearance. Probably written before it all went down."

Buchanan closed the magazine and looked at the date on the cover. "October edition," he said. "Galton must be a magician to be keeping this from the press."

"He must have struck some kind of deal," Daniel said.

"What about patterns?" Buchanan said. "You see anything?"

"Similar backgrounds," Daniel said. "White. Elderly. Affluent. Active in a variety of feel-good, do-nothing charities. Active politically. On the surface, they're all pillars of the community. Philanthropists of the first order."

Buchanan frowned. "All of 'em just a little too good to be true," he said.

"You scratch beneath the surface everyone's got something to hide."

"By all accounts they're swimming in coin, yet there hasn't been a single ransom demand."

"Which is what we suspected from the start," Daniel said. "Whatever's going on here has nothing in the world to do with money."

                                    ***

"So convince me there are two of them," Galton said.

"First," Daniel said, "I want to know what's not in the files."

"Pretty much everything we got is in there," Galton said.

"I thought you guys had a hard-on for profiles," Daniel said.

"BSU's reviewed the profiling inputs," Galton said. "Late last night they forwarded a preliminary decision process model and crime assessment. It's with the big guy right now. I've seen it though."

"What's it say?" Buchanan said.

"Not much. It's kinda flimsy."

"Let's hear it anyway," Buchanan said.

Farmer cleared his throat. "The UNSUB is an organized offender. He-"

"Organized?" Daniel said. "There's no way those crime scenes were the work of an organized man."

"For any number of reasons an organized offender might create a disorganized crime scene," Farmer said. "He may have been under the influence of drugs or alcohol, for example. Or it may have been a crime of passion."

"Continue," Daniel said.

"He is an organized offender with average to above average intelligence. White male. Mid-twenties to mid-thirties. Reasonably attractive. Well-read. Follows crime in the media. Inconsistent childhood discipline. That's really about it. For now."

"Question," Daniel said.

"Shoot," Farmer said.

"On the subject of profiling," Daniel said. "How come Muslims weren't specifically targeted post-9/11 at our nation's airports?"

Farmer made a sour face. "That would be *racial* profiling, Mr. Rourke. And in case your moral compass is on the fritz, it's not only wrong, it's downright offensive."

"Why is it then every time you guys release a profile of a serial killer, he's white? Isn't that racial profiling?"

Farmer looked almost smug. "It's no such thing, Mr. Rourke."

"What is it then?"

Farmer issued a long sigh. "Common sense, Mr. Rourke. Through years of research, conducting exhaustive interviews and pouring over detailed questionnaires, the hardworking men and women at VICAP have determined that the average serial killer is, among other things, white and male."

"Like John Allen Mohammad and John Lee Malvo?" Daniel said.

"I didn't say that all serial killers were white." Farmer looked quickly back and forth between Galton and Buchanan. "Did anyone in the room hear me say that?"

"Okay," Daniel continued, "What about Wayne Williams, the Zebra Killers, Carlton Gray, Elton Jackson, George Russell?"

"Or Mohammed Adam Omar," Buchanan chimed in. "Alton Coleman-"

"Maury Travis, Coral Eugene Watts, Henry Louis Wallace," Galton added.

"And don't forget my man Chester Dewayne Turner," Buchanan said. "I busted my hump on that twisted prick's task force for more'n a year. DNA linked him to at least thirteen murders, including an unborn kid."

"Are you aware," Daniel said, "that the average black man is twice as likely to be a serial killer as the average white man?"

"That's simply not true," Farmer said.

"Is, too. Look it up, you don't believe me."

"Okay, okay," Farmer said. "As Galton's already told you, the profile is in the preliminary stage only."

"Back to my earlier 9/11 question," Daniel said. "Not all Muslims are terrorists, but virtually all modern day terrorists are Muslims, so why don't-"

"Because, Mr. Rourke, we don't wish to offend-"

"*Terrorists?* You profile serial killers based on the fact that a mere percentage of them are white, yet you refuse to profile terrorists despite knowing full well they are all Muslim, and all because you don't wish to offend anyone? Frankly, I'm offended."

Farmer shook his head. "The politics of race relations in America is a-"

"Despicable, dirty business," Daniel said.

"If you're just about through race-baiting my overly PC partner," Galton said. "It's your turn to impress me with the matter at hand." He flicked his fingers at Daniel, making a 'gimme' gesture. "Whattaya got?"

"We'll start with the body on Georges Island," Daniel said. "What'd you notice?"

"I guess the first thing I noticed was the scratches. You'd have to be Stevie Wonder to miss those."

"Or Ronnie Milsap," Daniel said, jerking a thumb in Farmer's direction. "We wouldn't want to offend anyone."

Farmer scowled.

"You know what I mean," Galton said.

Daniel nodded.

"The next thing was the absence of blood. Assuming Murray was sliced and diced some place else, there should still have been at least some blood present."

"What does that tell you?" Daniel said.

"Someone cleaned him up after he was butchered."

"Surely, the snowfall before the body was discovered would have washed the blood from the body," Farmer said.

"Some of it," Daniel said. "Maybe even most of it. But traces would still have been found where the skin folds in on itself, at the knees, for example, and the elbows and arm pits. Yet the autopsy report says there was none."

"I suppose," Farmer said.

"Tell me what you noticed about the cut around the anus," Daniel said.

"It's clean, precise," Galton said.

"Exactly," Daniel said. "There were no trial cuts. Whoever did it had balls of steel. He knew what he wanted done and he acted without hesitation."

"I still don't see where you're heading with all this," Galton said.

"Tell me now what you noticed about the crime scenes," Daniel said. "Maybe it'll start making sense then."

Galton and Farmer said nothing.

"They're escalating," Buchanan said, priming the pump.

"I did notice that," Galton said. "They're getting wilder, crazier, with each abduction."

"I noticed you used the word 'they' just now," Daniel said.

Galton smiled. "Slip of the tongue, wise guy."

"You're actually starting to fall for this psycho's line of BS," Farmer said. "I don't believe it."

Daniel ignored Farmer's outburst and continued to look at Galton. "You happen to notice the smashed mirrors at any of the crime scenes?"

"I did. Every piece shiny side down. Although I have to admit, it doesn't make much sense to me."

"It only makes sense if you accept the fact that there are two of them. The flipping of the mirrors is about maintaining control."

"Forgive me if I still don't get it," Galton said.

"The fingernail gouges on Murray's torso, the havoc wreaked at the crime scenes, including the smashed mirrors, the cum shots on the doors and the walls and the ceilings were all the work of the emotional mind. This man is raging, and his rage is growing."

"Okay," Galton said.

"Now try to picture this same man making the cut around Eric Murray's anus, which the coroner described as near-surgical in its precision, after he just finished scratching the body all to hell with his nails like some kind of wild animal. Can you picture him giving the blood-slicked body a bubble bath? Or dropping to his hands and knees and flipping over the hundreds of pieces of the mirror that he'd smashed only seconds earlier while in a fit of blind rage? Can you picture him with the patience to spend the countless hours staking out the homes of the men and women he had chosen for abduction?"

"No," Galton said. "I guess I can't."

"Ask yourself how you would view these apparent inconsistencies if there were two of them, if the second man had a head as cool as the first had a head that was hot."

"Then it would make sense," Galton said.

"Exactly," Daniel said.

Farmer stood up so quickly that his chair toppled over backward. Except for the scars on his cheek, which remained paper white, his face was scarlet. "This is nothing but supposition," he shouted. "Pure and unadulterated bullshit."

"Did he just say bullshit?" Daniel said.

"He did," Galton said.

"Isn't that kind of boorish slang forbidden by Bureau policy?" Daniel said.

Galton leaned back in his chair and clasped his hands behind his head. He stared poker-faced at Farmer for a moment without speaking.

"I do believe it is," he said.

"As his superior are you going to write him up for it?" Daniel said.

"I'm certainly going to mull it over."

When Daniel, Buchanan and Galton couldn't maintain their poker faces any longer and burst into laughter, Farmer stormed from the room, muttering various threats under his breath.

"That was mean," Galton said, thumbing the tears from his eyes, "but it felt fucking fantastic."

"If you can't laugh at others," Daniel said, "who can you laugh at?"

"In case I haven't mentioned it yet," Galton said, "you've convinced me."

"We're in?" Buchanan said.

"So long as the flow of information goes both ways."

Buchanan nodded. "First thing I need you to do is call the next of kin. Let 'em know we'll be stopping by to view the crime scenes, maybe ask a question or two."

"Done," Galton said. "Anything else?"

Daniel dropped a wad of tissue on the desk and opened it to reveal the cigar butt. "We found this in the tree where Mr. Cool surveilled the Calhoun estate. How much do you want to bet the DNA on the cigar won't match that of the cum shots?"

"I'll see if I can't put a rush on it," Galton said. "In the meantime, I want you guys to do something for me."

"Just name it," Buchanan said.

"Whatever you learn, you share with me, and only with me."

Buchanan looked at Daniel, who nodded.

"Deal," Buchanan said.

21

". . . forty-five, forty-six, forty-seven," Tokunbo said, counting the press of Boston Common beggars surrounding Earlae near the park's ornate cast-bronze Brewer Fountain.

Appalled, he pressed his ambergris-softened palms against his eyes and turned his thoughts inward. City officials had invested tens of millions of dollars the previous fiscal year establishing a host of new and innovative programs for the homeless of Boston. After the programs went largely ignored, a blue ribbon commission was established to determine their real-world desires and to make recommendations on how best to provide for them. Six months and seven-point-seven million dollars later they committed their findings to paper. According to the two page, seven paragraph report the homeless community's desires - in no particular order - consisted of obscene amounts of illicit narcotics, budget-priced alcohol and a never-ending supply of tobacco. Needless to say the report was quickly and quietly buried. Unfortunately, four months earlier, while combing Tokunbo's drawers for something sexy for him to wear to one of the many annual AIDS benefits they attended each month, Earlae exhumed a copy. Since that time, she insisted on spending one hour the second Tuesday of each month tossing menthol cigarettes to the local beggars. She had chosen a popular menthol brand for its alleged breath freshening ability. Tokunbo lowered his hands from his eyes.

He watched in fascinated revulsion as Earlae grabbed a fistful of cigarettes from the bread bag and tossed them over the heads of the larger, more aggressive beggars to the smaller, sickly ones waiting on the outer fringe of the herd.

Earlae blew out a cloud of steam and smiled at Tokunbo. She was dressed in a faux-leopardskin jacket and thigh-high patent leather boots with six-inch heels. "Do you know what this weather reminds me of?"

"I have no idea," Tokunbo said. "Forty-eight, forty-nine . . ."

The air was ice-cold and still. The snow had stopped falling sometime in the early morning and the streets were not yet plowed. Sunlight reflecting off the pristine drifts made Tokunbo squint.

"It reminds me of-

"Whoopsy daisy," Earlae exclaimed as she slipped in a pool of slush, her arms wind-milling briefly before she caught her balance. "Where was I? Oh, yeah. It reminds me of vodka that has been left overnight in the freezer. You know how that first delicious sip tastes?"

Tokunbo nodded. "Fifty."

A beggar with permanently crossed eyes and no teeth motioned for everyone to look at him. He took a drag on his lumpy, hand-rolled cigarette then blew a series of small, smoke-filled bubbles from the mucus in his nose. The bubbles, being lighter than the air, floated lazily skyward. Everyone applauded and Earlae rewarded him with the final few menthols.

On the way to the newsstand, finally, Earlae said, "Do you think we made the front page?"

"But of course," Tokunbo said.

They were halfway there when beggar number fifty-one, a mutt, neither black nor white, short-haired and rail thin, wrapped in a urine-stained Scooby Doo comforter, came shambling over with a look of dull-eyed determination on his face, a grubby, thumbless hand extended. The man had a meaty slaughterhouse stink that hung over him like a pall. He looked so pitiful to Tokunbo that it was all he could do not to stomp the life out of him.

"Please," the man said, slurring his words, "I haven't eaten in three days."

"If only I had your willpower," Earlae said.

"You would be a perfect size three for sure," Tokunbo said.

Earlae looked at Tokunbo with her eyes narrowed. "I *am* a perfect size three."

He was about to confess that he was only teasing when the beggar, agitated for some unknown reason, made a move to strike her. Tokunbo quickly interceded, snatching the beggar's matchstick arm and twisting it around behind his humped back.

The beggar let out a squeal of pain. "You're breakin' my arm, bro."

Tokunbo cast the beggar to the ground and kicked him hard in the ribs. He reminded Tokunbo of Aristotle's Natural Man, a slave to his addictions, savage and soulless. "I am *not* your brother," Tokunbo hissed. "I am *nothing* like you."

"C'mon, let's go," Earlae said.

"You do not have to be out here," Tokunbo said to the beggar, ignoring Earlae's continued pleas to move on. "There are soup kitchens and shelters for creatures like you. The government wants to help. All you have to do is give up this illusion of freedom you have and let us take care of you." Pupils vast over glassy farm-animal eyes, the beggar just stared at him. Tokunbo was unable to look at him without an expression of disgust twisting his face. "I should never have to see, let alone interact with, the likes of you."

Beggar number fifty-two materialized from out of a shadowed doorway and staggered blindly into the slippery road raising a cacophony of horn blasts and curses.

Tokunbo raised his voice to a hoarse shout. "Any of you."

"C'mon, Bo," Earlae said. "Let's go." She hooked her arm in his and

Tokunbo grudgingly let her tug him away.

They reached the newsstand two minutes and six beggars later. As it turned out, they had indeed made the front page. The Boston Globe's bold headline was typical. It read: Thrice Honored Citizen Murdered. The article made no mention of the note or any of the artful mutilations which he had so painstakingly crafted. Obviously taken from a distance with a telephoto lens, the grainy, centerpiece photograph showed a group of witless police officers milling uncertainly around Eric Murray's mostly concealed corpse.

"Dinner out this evening?" Tokunbo said. "I was thinking Thai."

"That would be nice," Earlae said, her eyes downcast. "Shooting wraps at four-thirty."

Three seagulls swooped down from the sky and started snapping at each other in a fight to be the first to reach a sticky scrap of pastry that had fallen on the sidewalk outside a Starbucks that Tokunbo couldn't recall being there a week ago. A female beggar - number fifty-nine - wearing a white wedding dress and a '70's-era gold-sparkle motorcycle helmet shoved her shopping cart at the birds and snatched up the scrap as they soared to safety. "Greedy gull bastards," she yodeled into the sky at their shrinking silhouettes, shaking her swollen, frost-bitten fist in the air. With her feral eyes sweeping the sidewalk for more fallen goodies, she swallowed the scrap then rounded the corner with her cart.

"Are you okay?" Tokunbo said.

"Next time we won't make the same mistake, will we?"

They stopped at the intersection of Washington and West Streets to wait for the light. On the other side of the crosswalk, a Salvation Army Santa Claus was jangling his bell in earnest.

Tokunbo placed both hands on Earlae's face, careful not to disturb the makeup he'd applied before they left the loft, and gently kissed her pink button nose. "We will not," he said. "The next time I shall call the press instead of the police."

The light changed, and they crossed the intersection. Tokunbo stopped beside Santa, drew a hundred dollar bill from his Fendi jacquard fabric wallet, folded it lengthwise then held it over the red donation pail. Santa was stereotypically white, his cheeks rosy with something other than the cold. "Is this what you want?"

"God bless you," Santa said.

"Happy Kwanza," Tokunbo said, the bill still gripped tightly in his hand.

"Merry Christmas," Santa said, smiling.

"Christmas is the white man's holiday." Tokunbo wiggled the bill in front of Santa's bloodshot eyes. "Happy Kwanza. Say it."

"It's Santa Claus, Bo. Give him the money."

"Not until he says it."

"But Bo-"

"Say it," Tokunbo hissed.

Santa's smile faded, and there was a long pause while he glared at Tokunbo with the familiar unwavering hate-filled smile. Behind his eyes could be read the thought, *Fucking nigger*.

Tokunbo slipped the bill back into his wallet, turned and started walking.

"I thought so," he said.

22

Eunice Thomas was waiting for Daniel and Buchanan in a late-model Mercedes coupe outside the wrought-iron gates of her father's rambling suburban estate. She slipped gracefully out of the idling car and approached them with a wary smile, hopeful and doubtful at once. She had shoulder length, nut-brown hair and was wearing a fitted black suit and plain white blouse, open at the neck. Her skirt was short but tasteful. Daniel noticed that her legs were quite nice. He also noticed that the PTZ video surveillance cameras mounted on the high red brick wall on either side of the gates, initially scanning back and forth along the street, had surreptitiously tracked to their position.

"Frank Buchanan." Buchanan extended his big hand and Eunice Thomas took it. "My partner's Daniel Rourke."

"Nice to meet you," Daniel said.

"I haven't been here since well before that night," she said.

"You don't live here then, Miss Thomas?" Buchanan said.

"No, I don't. And, please, call me Eunice. My father was . . . is . . ." She turned away from Buchanan then looked quickly, almost self-consciously back to him. "He lives an insulated life. Although I'm sure he loves me in his own way, he and I aren't especially close." She handed Buchanan an infrared remote and a pair of house keys on a leather fob. "Unless you have need of me inside, I'd prefer to wait for you in my car."

Buchanan activated the remote and the gates swung open. "You mind if we walk in?" he said to Daniel.

"Not at all," Daniel said.

"I could use the exercise." Buchanan grabbed hold of his midsection and gave it a jiggle. "This whole Meritage meal deal we got going is really starting to pack on the pounds."

***

Marshall Thomas lived in a nine-bedroom Georgian Colonial mansion situated on several park-like acres in Weston, perhaps the toniest of Boston's numerous tony suburbs. The way inside was through a wide, moss-green, raised-panel door with a brass kick-plate. There was a large iron knocker in the center of the door in the shape of a fist gripping a polished brass ring. According to the police report, there was no sign that the front door, or any of the other doors or windows, had ever been picked or jimmied. Buchanan slipped the key into the lock and turned it.

Behind the mansion's magnificent façade was an elegantly tiled foyer that opened into a grand hallway. Straight ahead, twin stairways curled up to the second floor. Inside, the air was cool, delicately scented with orange oil wood polish. With the door closed it was as if the outside world had ceased to exist. The only sound came from the husky, six-foot-tall grandfather clock standing sentinel in the pink, gold and cocoa-brown sitting room to the left of the foyer. Through the twin Palladian windows at the far end of the room the snow-blanketed lawn swept downward in a series of snowy tiers.

According to the file, Marshall Thomas was sixty-two years old and Chairman of the Massachusetts Human Rights Commission. He was divorced, with one daughter, Eunice Thomas, thirty-six years old, and single. He was active in a number of high-profile, civil rights-oriented charities, both domestic and international, and had coached the same peewee hockey team for the past twenty-one years.

They began their search on the main floor, meticulously working their way to the upper levels. Every room was filled with heavy nineteenth-century furniture, every wall filled with gallery-quality artwork. Everything matched. Everything glistened. Everything gleamed. Nothing appeared out of place.

On the third floor, they turned right and headed down a fifteen-foot wide corridor lined with bookshelves that ended in a pair of carved oak doors. The heavy doors opened without a whimper of protest.

The study walls were crimson and trimmed with dark, mahogany wainscoting. The velvet drapes matched the walls perfectly and were tied back with braided gold-colored ropes. Mounted on the opposite wall was a 108-inch Sharp Electronics LCD TV. A massive Halcro Logic MC50 home theatre amplification system was flush-mounted into the wall and numerous JMlab speakers or varying size and design were indiscreetly arranged around the room. A leather eggplant-colored couch with brass studs was positioned directly in front of the TV. On the end table next to the couch was a programmable remote control, capable of full visual access to the mansion's numerous surveillance cameras, and a half-empty box of tissues. There were no CDs or DVDs visible anywhere in the room.

Behind the couch was an Italian Rococo writing desk, inlaid with precious woods and ivory, and a complementary period chair with painted leather upholstery. The desk had two framed photographs on the right-hand corner. The first photograph showed Thomas shaking hands with Massachusetts Governor Terrence Thornton. Thomas was a physically imposing man of six-four or -five, whose eyes appeared dark and dangerous even though he was smiling broadly. The second photograph was an on-ice shot of Thomas' most recent crop of Gretsky wannabes.

After two hours of poking and prodding into all the requisite nooks and crannies, including the basement, Daniel and Buchanan were satisfied that neither the police nor the FBI had missed anything of value. Unlike at the Calhoun house and in the videos they'd seen of the Murray, Blake and Taylor crime scenes, there were no signs of a struggle.

"It's almost as if he went with his captors willingly," Daniel said. "And he doesn't strike me as the type who'd do that. He looks like a guy who would've fought them fist and boot."

"Unlike Uncle Billy," Buchanan said.

"That's not what I meant, Frank."

"Maybe Thomas isn't a part of all this," Buchanan said. "Maybe he just fucked off to some place warm for the winter without bothering to tell anyone. He definitely looks like a guy who'd do that."

"His disappearance smells bad," Daniel said. "He's mixed up in this somehow. I just hope it doesn't take his disemboweled corpse turning up on some nearby island to prove it."

"If what we've assumed so far is right, that the emotional mind is escalating," Buchanan said, "then I'm inclined to agree with you."

<u>23</u>

Although Chubby Duck was a closed set, Tokunbo could come and go as he pleased. Having carnal knowledge of the star of Public Broadcasting's third-rated children's show did have its perks. Earlae was in full Mallard costume when he arrived, leading the children in a song about a Black Widow spider named Shawanda that had been born with only seven legs.

". . . we love you just the saaaaame," the kids sang as the band gave the catchy tune a big Duke Ellington-style finish, complete with a flourish of brass and a clash of cymbals.

"Cut, cut, cut," Timothy Frears, the WASP director, hollered. "Goddammit, cut."

Earlae pulled off her painted paper Mache bill. "What is it this time, Timmy?"

"It's Oscar Fucking Mayer again," the director said. "He's not moving his mouth."

'Oscar Fucking Mayer' was a catastrophically deformed child of indeterminate age who had been flown in for the show from a remote village in Somalia on an O1 Entertainers Visa. He had been born with no arms or legs, and could neither hear nor speak. If you fingered the base of his stump he would move his mouth like a fish out of water so that the voice of one of the behind-the-scenes, non-handicapped, Caucasoid children could later be dubbed in as his own. Sadly, there wasn't an aspect of the boy's physiognomy that hadn't been tainted during his formation in the womb, with the sole and undeniable exception of his eyes. When he had first arrived in Massachusetts it used to give Tokunbo the willies the way he just stared at everyone with a melancholic hopefulness shining in his beautiful, flint-colored eyes. Tokunbo knew, of course, what had transpired since then, and he understood why the boy no longer looked at people in quite the same way.

"His name is Edogiawarie, and he's my little buddy," Earlae said. "You call him Oscar Mayer one more time and you can pack up your toys and go home. *Permanently.*"

"This show is a goddamned joke. I don't know why you brought that dumb bastard here."

"Because Chubby Duck is representative of American society as a whole. Weren't you listening to the song about the spider with seven legs? It's only the central theme of the show." She spoke with her hands and her eyes as much as with her mouth. Every word was dramatized. "We love everybody. It doesn't matter who or what you are. Just take a look around you."

The director laughed. "You're kidding, right?"

Tokunbo cast his gaze around the set, a Fauvist interpretation of a marsh, ignorant of design, composition and color. All the on-camera children were either African-American or of South Asian descent and possessed of a multitude of crippling infirmities.

"If you can't see the big picture, maybe you shouldn't be a part of the Chubby Duck team."

"When you're right, you're right." The director snatched up his Hugo Boss worsted-wool overcoat. "Representative of America?" he shouted on his way out the door. "Give me a fucking break. Oscar Fucking Mayer's from North Fucking Africa, for fuck sake."

Earlae marched over to Tokunbo. "I can't believe how many Cro-Magnons there still are in this day and age." She began to fan her hands in the air over her head. "So much negative energy. Shoo! Shoo!"

"Kumbaya, my love," Tokunbo said. "Just take a deep breath. Find your Ch'i."

"Did you hear what he called poor Edogiawarie?"

"He is gone. Permanently. So do not worry. I will find someone with the necessary vision to take the reins. Mark my words, Chubby Duck will be off public television and on one of the big-three networks in time for sweeps week."

"Honest Injun, Bo?"

"Indigenous person," Tokunbo said.

"Honest indigenous person, Bo?"

Tokunbo nodded.

Earlae threw her arms around his neck and held him tight. "You're too good to me," she said.

"What's up, duck? When you called you said you had something special in mind for tonight."

Earlae rolled her eyes and turned her head shyly into her shoulder. "I've been a bad widdle girl," she said.

Tokunbo reached behind her and gave her tail feathers a tug. "That is fine by me," he said. "Since, if you will pardon the cliché, I know how good you can be when you are bad."

Earlae put her lips to his ear and whispered, "Remember how you made me promise that I was to never tell another living soul about what we're doing?"

"Please tell me you did not."

"Okay," Earlae said. "I didn't."

"But you did."

"Yeah, I did."

Already the muscles were knotting in his neck. "No," he said.

"Yeah," she said.

Tokunbo could feel the tension migrating upward through the base of his skull to take hold in his temples. "Whom did you tell?"

She put her lips back to his ear. "He'll keep our secret. He just wants to have a bit of fun with one or two of the old bitches before we punish 'em. A little harmless fun, Bo. That's all."

"*Whom did you tell?*"

Earlae smiled.

"Not Lloyd," Tokunbo said. "I would rather you have told Patrick Reagan, Boy Scout FBI Special Agent-in-Charge than Lloyd Mathis. The Feds I can handle."

"Ace won't make a peep."

"Lloyd? Not make a peep? Have you gone mad?"

<u>24</u>

Eunice Thomas pulled her sedan alongside Daniel and Buchanan as they hiked back along the twisting boxwood-lined driveway. The window hissed down. She smiled hopefully up at Buchanan as he returned the house keys and the infrared remote.

"Did you discover anything of interest?"

Daniel and Buchanan shrugged in unison.

A small vertical wrinkle appeared on her brow as she frowned. "I always had the feeling that I was somehow a disappointment to him, that what he'd really wanted was a son." The wrinkle disappeared. "Nevertheless, I do love him, and I pray that you find him soon."

"Can we call you if we think of any pertinent follow-up questions?" Buchanan said.

She reached into her purse and pulled out a pen and paper and scribbled something down. "My number."

Buchanan pocketed the paper.

"You will call me, won't you, Frank?"

"Of course, Miss Thomas . . . Eunice."

Eunice Thomas nodded once then drove away.

"Not too shabby," Buchanan said as her sedan cruised almost silently through the gates and disappeared from sight around a bend in the private road.

"Nice set of pins for a broad named Eunice," Daniel said, grinning.

"So I noticed." Buchanan started walking toward their car, then stopped, turned and looked at Daniel. "Funny thing that, isn't it?"

***

A trio of black SUVs with heavily tinted windows sat idling next to Daniel's rental. Their doors opened as he and Buchanan drew near, disgorging six somber men in dark suits who took up strategic positions along the boulevard. A seventh man, black, athletic-looking, strode briskly over to them. "Ray Sowell," he said. "The man wants to have a word with you."

"We got a choice?" Buchanan said.

Sowell placed his hands on his hips, parting his jacket to reveal a large handgun in a quick release shoulder holster. "You do not."

"Since you put it that way," Daniel said.

"You're Rourke, aren't you? Daniel Rourke? The writer?"

"Love-struck groupie?" Daniel said.

"I read your book, man. Couldn't put it down. Kept me up 'til three in the morning." Sowell grinned wickedly. "The ending was especially satisfying."

"I abhor gray," Daniel said.

Sowell grinned again. "You and me both."

"I thought you wrote under some funky, foreign-sounding name," Buchanan said to Daniel.

"He does," Sowell said.

"Then how did you . . . ?"

"It's my job to know things, Mr. Buchanan. And I'm good at my job."

Good? Something about the man's bearing told Daniel that he was being more than modest.

Sowell mumbled something into his wireless collar mike and a sliding door split the side of the nearest SUV. A man with iron-grey hair over a cinder block jaw appeared in a wheelchair and was gently lowered to the ground on a hydraulic platform. Even if he hadn't been a news junkie, Daniel would have recognized the Massachusetts governor. Since announcing his desire to seek the presidency, he was seemingly everywhere. Late Night. The Daily Show. BET. The View. Everywhere. He rolled his chair over to Daniel and Buchanan and stuck out his hand. It was large and well-callused with fat blue veins like garden hoses. His grip was relentless. "Terrence Thornton," he said.

"Governor Thornton," Buchanan said. "It's an honor, sir."

"I assure you, Mr. Buchanan, that the honor is entirely mine."

"What can we do for you?" Daniel said.

"Marshall Thomas and I go a long way back, Mr. Rourke. So when my contacts at the Bureau informed me that there was an extremely capable third party enquiring into his whereabouts, I thought it only prudent to meet with them, and offer my assistance."

"Any help would be muchly appreciated, sir," Buchanan said.

"Excellent," the governor said. "My name opens a great many doors in this town, and you've got my permission to drop it as you see fit."

"What a lucky coincidence, sir," Buchanan said, "our running into you like this."

"It wasn't a coincidence," Daniel said.

"What do you mean?"

"They've been watching us on the estate's video network from the moment we arrived."

The governor smiled. "Guilty as charged," he said. "Before Raymond here joined the Secret Service, he was CIA, with surveillance being just one of his many formidable talents. If push came to shove, the man could coax sound and video out of a toaster oven with nothing more than chewing gum and a pencil."

"Piece of cake," Sowell said.

"According to the FBI file," Daniel said, "the security network was down briefly for routine maintenance on the night that Thomas disappeared."

"I had Raymond pay a visit to the security company the next morning. Just to make sure the timing was on the up and up. He can be very persuasive."

"And was it?"

"It was."

"But . . ."

"Just like you, Mr. Rourke, I have a suspicious mind. I also do not believe in coincidence."

"So you think he was abducted."

"I do."

"Mr. Thomas was your campaign manager."

"That is correct."

"Until he was fired."

"That is also correct."

"You fired him."

"I did."

"Personally."

"Yes."

"Why?"

"We had a disagreement."

"A disagreement, I presume, that is unrelated to his disappearance."

"I certainly hope so."

"What did it concern?"

"It was a disagreement of a personal nature, Mr. Rourke, and that's all I'm prepared to say on the matter. I do not betray the confidence of my friends."

Sowell put a hand over his ear and nodded to the voice in his head. "Time to go, sir," he said.

The governor turned to Buchanan. "If you can spare an hour tomorrow, I'd really enjoy the pleasure of your company. I've been working on something special I think you might find interesting. Mr. Rourke, too."

"We'll make the time," Buchanan said.

"Raymond will e-mail the specifics to your suite."

"Thank you, sir."

"You won't be disappointed."

<u>25</u>

Earlae led Tokunbo by the hand through the automatic Wal-Mart doors. They were trailing a young African-American couple with twin toddlers. The twins were identical, pint-sized Nubian princesses with pigtails and purple, fur-lined snowsuits. It was two weeks before Christmas and while the surly hordes of shoppers, carrying armloads of parcels, jostled and cursed each other on the way to the clotted check out aisles, holiday music played softly over the PA system. The current selection was *Hark! The Herald Angels Sing*, as interpreted on the East Indian harmonium.

"Ace won't say a word," Earlae said for what must have been the hundredth time. "I'm telling you, he knows how to keep his lips zipped."

Tokunbo stopped and shot Earlae a deadpan look.

"You know what I mean," Earlae said.

Lloyd 'Ace' Mathis was still on duty when they arrived, greeting the customers as they entered the store. He had on a pair of Velcro Spiderman sneakers, tight black slacks three inches too short, white shirt and a blue vinyl Wal-Mart vest. The outline of his PSP was visible in his front pants pocket. The name tag on his vest was covered by a piece of masking tape with the word 'Ace' scrawled on it in black marker. He was a small man with narrow, hunched shoulders and his eyes were perpetually squinting and blinking. He smiled broadly as the African-American family approached his position.

"Welcome to Wal-Mart."

He got down on his haunches and tweaked the twins' chubby cheeks.

"What sweet little-

"PORCH MONKEYS," he hollered.

The mother and the twins were in tears and the father had his hands wrapped around the little man's throat by the time Tokunbo reached him. Lloyd looked confused and terrified and feral. He was rapidly patting the man on the buttocks with his index finger and singing the theme song from *The Beverly Hillbillies* in a gargling, off-key voice.

Tokunbo grabbed the man's hand and lifted it forcefully from Lloyd's throat.

"He meant no harm, sir."

Incredulous, the man turned toward Tokunbo. He was a tall, handsome man with a soul patch and Jamaican jerk spice breath. "No harm? Did you hear what he called my kids?" Like a sour note in a symphony, his mispronunciation of the word 'kids' caused Tokunbo to wince.

The man wheeled around to face Lloyd. "And will you stop touching me, you dirty perv."

Lloyd looked at the man and in a serious tone said, "*So they loaded up the truck and they moved to Beverly. Hills that is. Swimming pools. Movie-*"

"He has Tourette's Syndrome," Tokunbo said. "He can't always control what he says. He sings the songs and taps out the rhythm with his finger to distract his mind. As fantastic as it may seem, it really does help. And he really did mean your children no harm."

The look of anger on the man's face faded somewhat. "It's too bad he's sick and all, but I'm still going to have it out with his manager. Someone like that shouldn't be on the sales floor. He should be taking stock on holidays, or mopping up the aisles after hours. An incident like this could scar a kid for life."

Tokunbo winced again. "The word is kid. K-id. Kid. Not *keed*," he offered helpfully.

The man's eyes swiveled back and forth between Tokunbo and Lloyd as though he couldn't decide which one was crazier.

"Apologize," Tokunbo said to Lloyd.

Lloyd's jaw was rapidly clenching and unclenching as he resisted the impulse to scream out.

"Now," Tokunbo said.

Lloyd extended his hand.

The man hesitated only briefly before accepting the handshake.

"I'm s . . . s . . . sorry," Lloyd said.

"Sure you are," the man said before leaving to join his family inside the store.

"Have you been taking your medication?" Tokunbo said.

Lloyd's brow furrowed and his Adam's apple began to pulse. Then he began to whistle the theme song from *The Andy Griffith Show*, and his Adam's apple slowly settled to rest.

"I'd say that's probably a no," Earlae said.

"Listen to me," Tokunbo said, taking a firm grip on Lloyd's shoulders and looking him in the eye. "If you do not take your medication, I cannot help you. You will lose this job. Unfortunately, your episodes frighten people, and frightening people is not a part of the job description of store greeter."

Tokunbo saw tears at the corners of Lloyd's eyes. "I forgot, that's all. It won't happen again." Lloyd touched his nose. His fingers came away red.

"It had better not," Tokunbo said. "I have placed my reputation on the line for you."

Lloyd dabbed at the blood with a large hankie that he pulled from his back pants pocket. "I get off in five minutes, guys. So wait up." He giggled maniacally. "I can't believe the cool stuff you're into. It's like we're starring in our own RPG."

"Rated 'M' for Mature," Earlae interjected.

"Tonight's going to be way wicked cool," Ace said.

Tokunbo shook his head. "And you cannot say anything about it. Ever. To anyone. Do you understand, Lloyd?"

"They call me Ace." Lloyd pocketed the hankie and made a move to pat Tokunbo on the buttocks but Tokunbo neatly deflected his touch. The little man patted his own buttocks instead. "You can trust me, Tokunbo. You know I won't say nothing."

"You had better not," Tokunbo said. "And in case you are wondering, I should know something about that other job by tomorrow afternoon."

Earlae clapped her hands rapidly together. "Oh, goody gumdrops," she said. "Is Ace really going to get the store Santa Claus gig?"

"Well, he was the only employee who applied for the position after that nice Ugandan lesbian checked into detox. Provided he takes his medication, and doesn't have any more incidents like the one this evening, it certainly appears promising. As I am sure you are both aware, his employers cannot discriminate against him based on his medical condition."

"Or sexual orientation," Lloyd chimed happily in, before turning to greet the next wave of customers with a raucous, off-color version of the theme song from *The Brady Bunch*.

"Wow," Earlae said. "That Mike Brady sure sounds like our kind of people."

Although Tokunbo tried hard not to, he couldn't help but crack a smile.

26

Daniel drove, and Buchanan navigated, barking out the Google directions forwarded to them by Raymond Sowell. It wasn't long after passing a bullet hole pocked sign welcoming them to Roxbury that they entered the community labeled on the map as Grove Hall. To Daniel's mind, Grove Hall resembled Beirut, circa 1975, complete with block after block of crumbling tenements, and a roadway littered with the burned out husks of stripped cars, several of which were still smoldering.

"Makes Compton look like Pacific Palisades," Buchanan said as he crumpled the map into a ball and tossed it into the back seat.

In the distance staccato bursts of small arms fire could be heard.

"I was thinking more along the lines of Beirut," Daniel said.

"Six of one, a half-dozen of the-"

Daniel braked sharply to allow a skeletal jaywalker passage. The man was in his late-fifties, with a matted grey Sideshow Bob hairdo. His rheumy, hate-filled eyes caught on Daniel, and he deliberately slowed to a snail's pace. Buchanan reached over and blasted the horn. Without human expression the jaywalker reached across his body with his right hand and pulled something out of the drooping waistband of his jeans.

"Gun," Buchanan hollered. "Reverse, reverse."

"Screw that," Daniel snarled.

With a half-smile etched on his face, he dropped the hammer, aiming straight for the ghetto-trash son-of-a-bitch in a stuttering squeal of rubber. The jaywalker bobbed and pivoted then quasi-cartwheeled to the curb, the fish-tailing car missing him by the narrowest of margins.

"Fuck that was close," Buchanan exclaimed a few seconds later. "Too close. How'd you know the worthless sack-of-shit would get outta the way in time? I had him pegged as too stoned, too gimped up to be anywhere near that nimble."

"I didn't know," Daniel said.

"You what?"

"It was him or us." Daniel glanced over at Buchanan and the half-smile returned. "I chose him."

In the rearview mirror, Daniel watched as the jaywalker lurched to his feet. He gave his ratty head a shake then limped into the shadows between two boarded-up, fire-bombed beauty shops, one named after Cleopatra, the other Nefertiti.

"So long as I'm not suicidal, you said."

"Fucked up or not. I remember."

They concluded their journey in silence, arriving at their Humboldt Avenue destination a few moments later. Daniel eased into a vacant space behind Thornton's motorcade outside the graffiti-covered William Craft Elementary School. With Buchanan close on his heels, Daniel edged past a gangsta wanna-be hawking tiny baggies of weed to a pod of overweight pre-teens waving crumpled dollar bills in their fists.

"You take out the full insurance pack on the rental?" Buchanan said.

"As Billie Holiday used to sing: One never knows, does one?"

"That a yes?"

"Zero deductible, baby."

They nodded at the pair of Secret Service agents standing outside the main entrance and entered the school.

Daniel was shocked to note that there was even more graffiti inside the school than out, depicting enough anti-white propaganda to keep a rapper at the top of the 'urban' charts for millennia. As they stepped into the narrow locker-lined hallway, they were immediately greeted by a second pair of agents and ushered over to Thornton and Sowell, who were in the process of wrapping up the ten cent tour with the school's principal, an overly curvaceous woman with cornrow braids and large gold hoop earrings named Maxine Massiah-Jackson.

"As I'm sure you are aware, Governor Thornton, William Craft is a Read First school and our primary goal is to have reading on level by grade three," Massiah-Jackson said.

"And are you meeting that goal?"

"Not even close," Massiah-Jackson said. "But we are working with Harvard University as a member of their ASPIRE program. Oh, and we've also implemented what is known at William Craft as Open Circle Time."

"Open Circle Time? What is that precisely?"

"It's an intensive series of lectures given by various leaders of the black community with the stated goal of teaching the children about their glorious roots as kin to the kings and queens of ancient Egypt."

"Truly inspirational," Thornton said.

"Its purpose is to instill in them a racial pride that will endure to their dying breath."

"It really does take a village, doesn't it?"

Massiah-Jackson smiled graciously.

"It cannot be denied that some pretty amazing things are in the works at your wonderful little school," Thornton said. "You certainly deserve kudos for all that you have accomplished in your brief tenure here."

"Why, thank you, Governor," Massiah-Jackson said. "But if anyone deserves kudos, it is you. Come and let us conclude your visit in Miss Burke's grade five classroom, so that you may make the announcement personally. I can hardly wait for you to witness the children's boundless expressions of joy."

<u>27</u>

Massiah-Jackson escorted her guests into a classroom filled with eerily vacant faces, seating them at a rickety table at the head of the class next to the teacher's knife-scarred, cigarette-burned desk. "You may proceed with the roll call," she said to the young, obviously well-medicated, white teacher.

Miss Burke pulled out a pad of paper from her middle desk drawer and began to read aloud the names printed upon it. "Kavarious, Quivander, Creshonda, Kentorious, Lakeytsia . . ."

Not a single student deigned to respond. They just stared blankly ahead. Daniel was taken aback at how old their tiny eyes were. Not cold, or cruel. Just numb. Too beaten to show life, let alone joy, boundless or otherwise.

". . . Tezaree, Franktreka, Dywoine, Shareatha, Bashawn, Pimpin' Brown . . ."

"Those poor bastards don't stand a chance," Daniel whispered to Buchanan.

"Shhh," Massiah-Jackson said, prompting a titter from a chubby, gap-toothed girl at the front of the class. Daniel winked at the girl, who winked right back at him.

". . . Charenesia, Tontanisha, Qsahhahhrah, Drameco, Shantanna, Chatavia, Shaquandro, Latrice."

Miss Burke returned the pad to her desk. "Mostly present and accounted for," she said.

Massiah-Jackson stood. "Wonderful," she said. "As I'm sure you're all aware Bashawn Waters lost his baby brother, Tamarcus, in a tragic drive-by shooting yesterday."

The students continued to stare blankly ahead, completely unaffected by her words.

"Tragic," she intoned again. "So I thought it only fitting that you all should be the first to hear the good news. In this regard, I have invited an esteemed member of our community, and our most generous benefactor, to reveal it to you personally. I am referring, of course, to Massachusetts Governor Terrence Thornton III. Before he takes the floor I would be remiss if I didn't give you just a taste of his background."

Again she was met with the students' near-catatonic stares.

"Unlike the majority of you, Governor Thornton was born into one of the oldest and wealthiest families in the nation."

"The majority?" Daniel whispered to Buchanan. "Unlike them all."

"Shhh," Massiah-Jackson said again.

Daniel made a locking motion over his lips.

"Despite his privileged background, and unlike so many others of his race and class, he chose to go to war for his country when called, a hero in every sense of the word. He rose quickly to the rank of Captain and, thanks to his fearless nature, became one of the most decorated navy pilots of the era. Tragically, he was held as a prisoner of war for more than two years after being shot down in his A-4 Skyhawk over Vietnam in 1971. During his confinement he was routinely tortured, his feet and legs burned and beaten to the point that he forever lost the ability to walk."

One of the kids at the back of the class put his finger in his cheek and made a loud popping sound

"When he returned home following his rescue by American troops he could have wallowed in pity and fallen completely to pieces, but he didn't. Instead, he helped himself by helping others. Using his own money, he established a foundation in Boston called Peace Brother, working with disadvantaged youth in several communities, including our own. When the hometown program had proven itself an unqualified success, he rolled them out in other troubled urban centers, including Chicago, Houston, St. Louis and Los Angeles."

Another loud cheek pop broke the principal's overly dramatic pause.

"I present to you now," Massiah-Jackson said, clapping furiously, "Governor Terrence Thornton III."

Thornton maneuvered his wheelchair to the center of the class and made eye contact with each and every one of the students before speaking. "First thing's first. I'm no hero. The mere fact that I was careless enough to get shot down by an ill-equipped enemy force suggests, to me at least, quite the opposite."

"Word," Cheek Popper said.

Thornton laughed merrily.

"And to set the record straight, Ms. Jackson-"

"That's Massiah-Jackson," the principal said. "With a hyphen. Like African *hyphen* American.

"To set the record straight, Ms. Massiah-Jackson, I wallowed in pity for quite some time following my return stateside. I was also twisted by anger, and hatred, and I did some things that I am quite ashamed of. In point of fact, the disintegration of my character reached a stage where I could no longer stand the sight of my own face." Thornton swept his arm over the audience. "I recognize some of what I saw then in the faces before me now, which is why I travel to schools like William Craft. I consider it my mission, my calling if you will, to preach the power of hope, and of choice, to the disadvantaged children of this wonderfully diverse land."

Massiah-Jackson launched into another overly generous round of applause.

"In the opening paragraph of our great nation's Declaration of Independence, Thomas Jefferson wrote the immortal phrase 'all men are created equal.'" He paused to let the full import of the words sink in. "Its meaning is quite simple. At birth we are both equal and empty, a blank slate for our life to be written upon." He walked over to Cheek Popper. "How does this help you? Quite simply, if you *choose* to be great, you *will* be great." He began to point at various children around the room as he continued. "Doctor. Lawyer. Scientist. Commander-in-Chief. Whatever you decide." He chuckled as if from some private joke. "The power is yours."

"A brilliant insight," Massiah-Jackson gushed. "Simply brilliant."

The governor chuckled again. "You can thank Captain Planet for that last bit." Then, to the students, he said, "Now if it's heroes you children want to meet today, let me introduce to you now two *bona fide* members of that most exclusive club."

Thornton gestured toward Sowell. "Raymond, come over here, please."

The secret service agent settled into an at-ease stance next to his charge.

"Raymond Sowell graduated *magna cum laude* from Harvard University in 1984 and immediately thereafter took up service to his country, as a Navy Seal, and as an operative with the CIA. Currently, he's a senior agent with the U.S. Secret Service."

"That don't make him no hero," a skinny boy in a skullcap interjected.

"No, it does not," Thornton said. "What makes him a hero is the journey he undertook more than thirty years ago, a journey of enlightenment that took him to where he is today."

"Where he start from?" Skullcap said.

Several of the children were now leaning forward in their seats. Thornton was in his element, Daniel saw. Though he hadn't thought it possible, the governor now held the students' rapt and undivided attention.

"He grew up in a foster home a stone's throw from this very room."

"He from our hood?" a girl at the back of the room said.

Thornton nodded. "Castlegate Road."

"I got a cousin deals dope there," another girl said. "Drives a Chrysler 300 with chrome spinners, ya'll."

"When I first met Raymond he was thirteen years old and a member of the Castlegate Road Gang. Let me tell you, he was one bad apple. Bruises and all. But it wasn't long after he showed up at the Peace Brothers safe house and took an active role in the program that he began to make the choices that would turn his life around."

All but the most hard-core of the group began to nod their approval of his words.

"I present to you now my protector, my ally, my best friend forever, Raymond Sowell," Thornton said.

Sowell nodded at the governor then looked out at the children. "Who wants to hear a secret?"

The children nodded as one.

Sowell walked to the blackboard and picked up a piece of chalk. He drew a horizontal, bow-shaped line on the board."

"Does anyone know what this figure represents?"

Skullcap hollered, "A big old bitch's titty?"

The class chortled.

"Anyone else?"

An obese boy at the back of the room put up his hand.

"Yes," Sowell said.

"The shape of the pile of green I'm gonna make as the number one power forward in the NBA."

The class chortled even louder.

Sowell smiled. "Actually, it's a visual representation of a normal distribution, commonly referred to as . . ."

Daniel turned to Buchanan and mouthed, "The bell curve."

"Anyone? Anyone at all? No one? Okay. The answer is the bell curve."

"That ain't no secret," Gap Tooth said, whipping her head away. "That's book learnin' shit. Don't be nothin' I got to know."

Sowell looked at the governor. "Not to be disrespectful, sir, but my interpretation of Jefferson's words is quite a bit different than yours."

"Oh?"

"I believe what Jefferson meant to say is that we are all equal in rights, despite being unequal in just about every other way."

"And this relates to your secret how?"

"We can't all be Tiger Woods, or LeBron James, or Albert Einstein, or-"

"Al Einstein," Obese said. "Who he play for? The Sonics?"

"It's just not possible. And all the hopes and wishes and prayers in the world won't change that simple fact." Sowell turned back to the blackboard. "Every skill, every talent that we possess can be plotted on this curve. A person with average talent falls in the middle, at the thickest part of the curve, while those with the least fall to the left."

"So?" Obese said.

"Let's use the ability to consistently hit the three point shot as an example." He made a line through the farthest edge of the curve on the right-hand side. "This is Reggie Miller." He made another line at the opposite edge of the curve. "This is me."

The class burst into laughter.

"When I was a kid I also dreamed of playing in the NBA. Shooting guard for the Celtics. I never did. Do you see why?"

"Hell, yeah," Obese said. "'Cos you down on the loser left wit' my cousin Prince Obadu."

"This doesn't mean that you all can't have a valued place in society. You can. The key, *the secret*, to finding it is to discover what your own skills and talents are, and develop them to their fullest. If you do that you'll not only succeed in life, you'll find infinite happiness."

"And if we don't?" Obese said.

"If you don't, you won't."

Massiah-Jackson didn't look pleased. "But as visible minorities we must deal with the constant-"

"The smallest minority on earth is the individual. Ayn Rand said that, and truer words were never spoken. We are all minorities, Ms. Massiah-Jackson. In one form or another, we all suffer discrimination. We can either get over it, or we can let the anger and the bitterness color our lives for the worse. I chose to ignore the ignorance of others early on. And I chose to do only such things as would enrich my life, and by extension the lives of those around me."

Evidently Massiah-Jackson's authority at William Craft Elementary was rarely, if ever challenged. A heavy silence descended over the room. It was uncomfortable to say the least, and only broken when the girl at the back of the room shouted, "He from our hood," and the other children erupted in cheers and whistles and India-rubber 4/4 beat handclaps.

When the rhythmic ruckus had finally abated, Thornton interjected, "The second hero I want to introduce to you is Detective Frank Buchanan, LAPD."

Buchanan appeared genuinely surprised by the introduction, though less than surprised at the reaction of the children, who were booing loudly and tossing balled up sheets of paper at him. He grinned and waved.

"Five-O's in the house," Gap Tooth shouted.

"Lil' beeyotch," Skullcap said.

Thornton silenced the class with a single raised finger. "Detective Buchanan has worked as a volunteer at the Los Angeles chapter of Peace Brother for more than a decade and has rescued countless souls from a life of crime. In my book that makes him a hero and a man worthy of our respect. Please stand and say a few words, Detective."

Decidedly green at the gills, Buchanan moved front and center, stumbling over an untied shoelace in the process. His hands were shaking. He was sweating profusely. His eyes were glued to the floor. "Stay in school," he said. "And just say no."

"No to what, fool?" Skullcap said.

"To drugs."

"What about booze?" Skullcap said, smirking. "Booze okay?"

"No."

Buchanan turned and headed back to his seat.

"That all you got to say to us, hero man?" Skullcap said.

"You want more?"

"You got more?"

"Yeah."

"Lay it on me."

Buchanan coughed into his fist and stole a glance over at Daniel who nodded encouragingly. Buchanan mumbled something to his shoes that was mostly inaudible.

"Whatchoo say?" Skullcap said.

"I said always wear a rubber."

"Fuck you, motherfucker," Skullcap said. "'Cos that ain't the way I roll."

"You ain't wearin' no glove," Gap Tooth sang, "you ain't getting' no love."

"Crazy ho," Skullcap said. "Love got nothin' to do wit' it."

"If I'm a ho then the next time we lay down you payin' for the privilege. Gonna gimme what I'm worth, too."

"Anyone got change for a nickel?" Skullcap said with a laugh that sounded like sped up coughing. Obese leaned over in his chair and the two boys bumped fists.

Sowell spoke into his collar mike, walked over to the door, and whispered to one of the other agents. Daniel guessed that the visit was about to wrap up.

"Take my word for it," Thornton continued. "These men are heroes. I am simply a man who cares and who, by a most fortunate accident of birth, has enough money to make good news happen."

"Quit wit' the bullshit," Skullcap said. "What's this big news you all been goin' on about?"

Thornton turned to the principal. "A man who appreciates the bottom line. Excellent." He redirected his attention to the students. "The good news is that I have donated sufficient funds to your school to finance the addition of a state-of-the-art music wing and to refurbish that rather lumpy basketball court you have out back." He winked at Skullcap. "No bullshit."

Wild cheers erupted around the room and two tiny girls rushed Thornton, giving him a big, heart-melting hug.

"The formal announcement takes place tomorrow," Thornton concluded. "I expect each and every one of you to be there. Refreshments will be served afterward. All you can eat."

"Hey, Mother Theresa," Daniel said, knocking Buchanan with his elbow, "You never told me you'd rescued countless souls from a life of crime."

"Only one I'd swear an oath to," Buchanan said.

Massiah-Jackson spun to face them.

"I know, I know," Daniel said. "Shhh."

28

When Daniel suggested they return to the hotel for dinner following their fruitless searches of the Murray and Taylor residences, Buchanan, having grown accustomed to the wonderful cuisine at Meritage, especially the Ostrich and Vermont pheasant, readily agreed. The Rowes Wharf eatery was hopping when they arrived at half-past six and they were directed to the sparkling black granite bar to await a table.

"What is it with you and Thornton?" Daniel said.

"What do you mean?" Buchanan said.

"You act like a lovesick teen every time he comes near. If I was the jealous type, I might take it personally."

"I may not have saved as many souls at Peace Brother as Governor Thornton said I did, but I've damned sure made a difference in a good many lives. The program works. It's a real good thing in a real bad place. And if it wasn't for the obscene amounts of time and dough the governor pumps into it year in, year out it wouldn't even exist. He's a great man. I respect him. End of story." Buchanan grabbed a fistful of the cashew and cranberry raisin mix in a large bowl on the bar top and tossed them into his gaping maw. "You know I could ask you the same question."

"What is it with me and the governor?"

Open-mouthed, Buchanan began to munch. "You were a real prick yesterday. Interrogating him like he was some common street thug."

"This above all: to thine own self be true."

"Once an asshole always an asshole?"

"I thought I was a prick?" Daniel said.

"Prick, asshole," Buchanan said. "You know what I mean."

Daniel nodded.

"Out with it," Buchanan said. "What is it about the guy that gets under your skin?"

"He's a politician."

"That's it?"

"That's it."

"So he's a politician. So what?"

"Two plus two."

"Huh?"

"Answer me. Two plus two equals . . . ?"

"Four."

"Wrong. It's six."

"No, it's not."

"It is."

"Man, I can't wait 'til we're through with the east coast and I don't have to listen to your non-stop, *non sequitur* nonsense twenty-four hours a day."

"Humor me. I'm trying to make a point."

"What? That you're a moron."

"We're at an impasse. I say it equals six; you say it equals four. What do we do about it?"

"Nothing. I'm right. You're still a moron."

"You're thinking like a person with common sense. Think like a politician."

Buchanan shrugged.

"What are politicians best at?"

Buchanan shrugged again.

"Reaching compromise positions."

"Meaning."

"Two plus two equals five."

"That's idiotic."

"Agreed. Hence my disdain for politics and politicians. When right is right, there's simply no room for compromise."

"C'mon, there's got to be more to it than that."

"The art of compromise or my feelings for Thornton?"

"Thornton."

Daniel nodded. "I'm a news junkie. Always have been, always will be. I've followed the stump speeches, the candidates' debates, Republican and Democrat, and Thornton's nothing special. Just another run-of-the-mill Massachusetts liberal."

"Define Massachusetts liberal."

"Smug. Possessing a self-adoring sense of oneself as a social redeemer. A mortal enemy of things as they are. The America that you and I grew up with."

"Jesus," Buchanan said. "You're worse off than I thought."

Despite the caveat about politics, religion and polite conversation, Daniel was about to defend his thesis, using all manner of fact and figure, when their pretty, blond hostess issued a polite cough behind them. "Your table is ready."

She took them to an intimate niche for two with a twinkling water view. "Your waiter's name is Juan Carlos, and he'll be with you in just one minute."

True to her word, Juan Carlos arrived exactly sixty seconds later. Buchanan broke with tradition, ordering the Kobe beef, while Daniel opted to sample the Nantucket scallops. Daniel asked Juan Carlos to surprise them with the choice of wine. This added responsibility seemed to please him greatly.

"He did impress me today though," Daniel said.

"Who did?"

"Thornton. Didn't you notice anything out of the ordinary about his visit to the school?"

Buchanan laughed. "You mean the names of those kids? Talk about being branded for life."

"Not that. Something else."

"Must've missed it."

"There wasn't a single member of the fourth estate present," Daniel said.

"So?"

"Thornton's a dark horse candidate gearing up for the biggest race of his life. His visit was a public relations wet-dream. Images of those sweet little girls clutching onto him like that would have been worth a couple points in the polls."

"Easy," Buchanan said.

"So what's the poop?"

"I never met the guy before yesterday, but I have several buddies at Peace Brother who are tight with him. The governor meant what he said today. He really does see his charity work as a mission. Reporters would've only cheapened the moment. Corny as it sounds, he loves those kids."

"Although I hate to admit it, I kind of got that vibe myself."

"So he's not *all* bad."

"And Charles Manson jammed with The Beach Boys."

Buchanan grinned mischievously. "I can tell him then, he gets the nod from the Dems, your vote's a lock?"

"Hardly. Now if Raymond Sowell were to run . . ."

"Apple and tree," Buchanan said. "Word has it the governor raised him from a pup."

"Nature trumps nurture," Daniel said. "Ideologically, they're polar opposites."

"You think so?"

"Not everyone can be Einstein? Hopes, wishes, and Head Start be damned. That took guts to say. People like Thornton believe us commoners are far too fragile to hear such truths. I promise you, if a teacher had said it, he'd have been burned at the stake for heresy. And the good governor would have been first in line with a match to light the-"

"Here's Juan Carlos with the wine," Buchanan said.

<u>29</u>

David Blake lived in Penthouse Six in the newly constructed Empire Tower overlooking Boston's coveted Public Garden. On their way inside Daniel and Buchanan had to bulldoze their way through a group of runaways huddled in front of the doorway smoking skunk-scented weed and drinking convenience store coffee from doubled-up paper cups.

"Blow you right here for twenty bucks," one kid about twelve or thirteen years old said to Daniel, his voice not even changed yet. He had on a quilted Michelin Man jacket and an off-kilter Orlando Magic toque. "Or you can take me inside where it's toasty warm and I'll shower you in brown for ten."

Daniel worked his jaw, teeth gnashing, biting back the urge to respond. In the elevator ride up to Blake's penthouse unit, he launched a Muay Thai elbow into the brushed aluminum door, denting it.

"Did you hear what that little cocksucker said to me?"

Buchanan nodded.

"I thought you guys had gaydar? Do I look like a puffy bunny to you?"

"No offense, but you're a pretty boy. The kid just assumed you were queer."

Daniel shot the door another elbow. "Well, it gave me the heebie-jeebies."

"Because he thought you were a queer or because he was jail-bait?"

The elevator doors slid open and they stepped out.

"I've got to be honest, Frank. My first reaction was to lay him out cold." Daniel started down the hallway, but stopped short after only a couple steps. "I'm well aware of your, ah . . . sexual orientation, Frank. And don't get me wrong, I like you. Hell, after everything we've been through, you're probably my closest friend. But I'm just not comfortable with this whole 'every day's a pride parade' PC crap that seems to be sweeping the land."

"And you think I am?"

Daniel shrugged. "A part of me can't help but believe it's wrong. Maybe it's the time and the place I grew up talking, but it's just that every gay man I've ever met has had . . ."

Buchanan grabbed Daniel by the elbow. "Had what?"

"Honestly, I don't know what to call it. It's like something happened in their formative years that made them turn out that way, some form of early trauma, and their being gay is no more than a symptom of that trauma."

"Whatever happened to nature trumps nurture?"

"You're talking about a gay gene?" Daniel said.

"Yeah."

"I just don't see it."

"Why not?"

"How could a gene for hereditary homosexuality avoid extinction? It just wouldn't make sense in the grand scheme of things." Daniel grinned as the anger began to ebb. "Unless you guys have secretly mastered asexual reproduction, the limp-wristed gene wouldn't survive natural selection."

Buchanan nodded soberly. "Number six," he said.

***

David Blake was a critically acclaimed writer/producer/director of independent, arthouse-style films. He was an only child, had no children of his own, and had never been married or engaged. According to his medical history, he was a died-in-the-wool Vegan who spent at least two months a year in various hospitals for numerous dietary deficiencies.

The gilt-framed mirror in the grand foyer was on the floor and leaning against the coat closet door. The hook that had held the mirror to the wall was still attached to the picture hanging wire on its back. Buchanan turned it around. There was a perfect imprint of a smallish fist in its center. According to the notes in the FBI file, the mirror had been found face down on the closet floor. DNA testing on the blood traces found on several of the edges of the shattered glass matched to a ninety-eight-point-nine percent certainty the DNA in the multiple semen deposits found at the scene, as well as the deposits found at the Gaines and Buchanan crime scenes.

"He punched the mirror, it shattered, but held mostly together," Buchanan said. "He must have ripped it from the wall because he could still see himself. The control freak you mentioned was probably the one who stashed it in the closet."

The living room was huge but sparsely decorated. The furniture, arranged in three separate clusters, was made of tubular steel and creepy, flesh-colored leather, like something the Nazis might have made if they hadn't been obsessed with lamp shades. The stark white walls were vacant, except for one, which was covered with posters showcasing movies with self-consciously pompous titles that Daniel had never heard of. Each one had Blake's name attached in one capacity or other. The odd-poster-out depicted someone dressed in a duck costume holding what appeared to be a three-foot-long sausage.

Buchanan leaned in and squinted at the poster.

"The sausage has eyes," he said.

"Teeth, too," Daniel said. "It's smiling."

"Surreal, isn't it?"

Daniel pointed to the PBS logo on the poster's bottom corner.

"That explains it," Buchanan said.

Beyond the living room and the library was a stainless steel and granite kitchen large enough to accommodate the officers and crew of the USS Ronald Reagan. Tugging open the massive refrigerator doors, Buchanan said, "You read what that sick fuck did to Blake's soy milk?"

"He urinated in it."

"The sick fuck."

"Have you ever tried soy milk?"

Buchanan made a face and nodded. "If you ask me, the piss probably improved the taste."

"It couldn't have made it any worse."

"That's for damn sure."

The master bedroom had a killer view of the Public Garden, from the winding bows of its pathways to its willow-lined lagoon. Blake's unmade bed was tucked behind a painted screen showing a group of cherubs dancing beside a stream in an idyllic wood, its pillow-top mattress mottled with stains whose origins Daniel didn't even want to begin to contemplate.

"Judging by the condition of his bed," Daniel said, "maybe it was Blake who sullied the soy milk. The guy doesn't seem too particular about the places he let it rip."

"When you gotta go, you gotta go," Buchanan said.

Against the wall perpendicular to the bed was a large black lacquered armoire. Daniel opened it and was immediately met with the tart scent of copper. On the shelves next to the neatly pressed and folded designer togs were numerous implements of self-torture and self-mutilation. The pooled blood on the bottom of the armoire had dried to a rusty brown.

"It seems the golden boy has a tarnished side."

Buchanan poked his head in for a peek. "Don't you all?"

The second bedroom had been converted into a home office. On the two inch thick, pickled oak pedestal desk was the latest Apple computer, and Canon's top-of-the-line color laser printer. In the oversized drawers, three on a side, were several thousand eight-by-ten-inch sheets of photographic quality paper, and a Leica M8 camera.

Buchanan thumbed the camera on, and fiddled with it for a moment. "Nothing in the memory," he said.

"What do you mean?"

"Where've you been living the last couple years?"

"In a seventy-five hundred square foot Malibu Beach house. Pardon my ignorance."

"Digital cameras store the data, the picture, on a microchip. You can view the pictures on the unit or, if you want a hard copy, you can sync it to the computer and use the printer."

"I'm a 35mm film guy myself," Daniel said. "Have my own darkroom and everything. So where'd you learn all this newfangled stuff?"

"I took a turn through vice in the mid-nineties," Buchanan said. "Before digital cameras went mainstream they were quite popular with peds. Cops nabbed you taking overly candid snaps of kids, you could make them go bye-bye with the touch of a button. No evidence. No conviction. You know how that old tune goes. Plus where the picture was digital, it could be instantly transmitted via the web to broad-minded folk the world over."

"If your knowledge extends to personal computers," Daniel said, "perhaps we can sneak a peek at the type of photography that turned Blake's crank."

Buchanan cracked his interlaced fingers loudly in front of his chest. "No sweat. It was a requirement in vice that we keep up on the latest trends in computers and the web." He turned on the computer and scrolled through the various directories. "It's been wiped. Not so much as a game of Solitaire."

"I don't recall this particular fact being mentioned in the FBI file, do you?"

"I do not," Buchanan said.

"Seeing as how you're the resident computer dufus, why don't you pay a visit to Galton tomorrow and get his take on the omission."

"And you?"

"While you're feeling Galton out, I'll swing by Thomas's workplace. If he really did know his abductors, it's as good a place as any to start."

***

The kid with the Orlando Magic hat made loud kissy-face noises at Daniel as he and Buchanan exited the high rise. They got in the rental car. Daniel cranked the engine, put the heater on high, and the CD player on low. The year was 1966 and Sinatra was at The Sands with Count Basie and his wonderful band and in fine form. As *The Chairman of the Board* belted out *My Kind of Town*, a group of young blacks, dressed in G-Unit warm-up suits, moon-boot sized running shoes and do-rags, paused in front of a white stucco wall. There were five of them, all male, approximately the same age as the runaway who'd offered to shit on him for the price of a pair of sport socks. The tallest kid looked quickly up and down the street, then whipped a spray can from out of his pocket and let the paint fly.

"I've known four homosexuals in my life," Daniel said.

"And?"

"Two are dead."

"AIDS?"

"What else?"

"Were you close?"

"Close enough that I cried when they died," Daniel said. "And I don't cry."

"Never?"

"When mom and dad died, and Julie, of course. And then there's that scene in *Field of Dreams*, the one where Kevin Costner plays catch with his dad. It gets me every time."

"You and me both. Now what about the other two?"

"The third, one of my law school roomies, tested HIV positive six months ago."

"Damn," Buchanan said. "And the last guy?"

"I don't know," Daniel said, looking hard at Buchanan. "You've never broached the subject."

Buchanan was silent for a while. "I'm no big-time, big-bucks writer like you," he finally said, "but there's this line by Hemingway that's always stuck in my head. I don't remember how it goes exactly, whether it's something he wrote, or something he belched out one night on a Key West bender."

Daniel craned his neck to get a look at what the tall kid was working on, but couldn't see around the others, who were shielding him with their bodies in case an errant squad car should happen by.

"So what's the line?"

"What's right is what feels good afterwards." Buchanan blew out some air. "In ten years I can count the number of times I've had sex on one hand. The last time, it finally hits me. If having sex was something I had to get shit-faced to do, maybe it was something I didn't really want to be doing."

"You don't like sex?"

"Not the kind I'd been having. Heat of the moment, it felt good, even great. But afterwards? Hemingway was right. The morning after my last drunken tumble, I felt so low, low sick, it was all I could do to keep from eating my .38 for breakfast."

The tall kid pocketed the spray can and disappeared around the corner with his posse. His finished work read:

> *If you cain't bear no crosses,*
> *You cain't wear no crown.*

"I've had friends who caught the bug and died, too," Buchanan said. "It's rough, man. Something you don't ever get used to. I get tested every year, and every year I come back clean, several of my other friends don't. Every year I lose a couple more."

<u>30</u>

The only light inside Marshall Thomas's cell came through a small barred window set high in the door, casting a jaundiced checkerboard pattern on the concrete floor. Last night, with Bo accompanying them, they'd just looked. Tonight, with Bo busy at the club, they were going to get up close and personal.

"Stay behind me, Ace," Earlae said.

She was wearing a chic-chic black leather bodysuit that fit like a second skin. From the moment she'd zipped it on at the boutique, leaving just a peep-show of cleavage, she'd felt invincible, like a modern-day Emma Peel, a sexy, sassy, kick-ass bitch. She'd selected black so that it wouldn't show the blood.

"Where is he?" Ace said, peering cautiously around the murky room. "I don't see nothing."

"He's here. I can smell him."

"I'm scared," Ace said.

"Don't be. He's nothing more than a creepy old bitch whose end has finally come."

This time Earlae was prepared. With Murray, she had expected him to beg for his life, if not her forgiveness, and was thrown for a loop when he hadn't. What had bothered her most was the way he'd spoken to her, like she was still a helpless child, scolding her with the tone of his voice, and with his eyes, as much as with his words. It was as if he had stolen a glimpse into her soul, and he *knew*. Knew how emotionally fragile she was. Knew exactly what it would take to destroy her. But she had survived their encounter. Learned from it. Grown stronger? She would see.

"Come out, come out, wherever you are."

The heavy chain around Marshall Thomas's ankle clanked over the floor as he materialized from the shadows at the farthest corner of the room. Except for the gold crucifix around his neck, and the soiled adult diaper he had been wearing beneath his Brookes Brothers suit on the evening of his abduction, he was naked. Earlae hadn't seen him since his abduction and was shocked by his appearance. Three weeks of bread-and-water captivity had certainly taken its toll. He was so much smaller than she remembered - all frail-looking and shriveled, like an autumn leaf just waiting for a puff of wind to blow it away.

"It wasn't me," he gasped.

He took a plodding step closer.

"You've got to believe me."

Earlae had no idea what he meant. Obviously, he was delirious.

Thomas moved a couple of steps closer, until the chain around his ankle grew taut to the wall. "You've got to convince Tokunbo it wasn't me. I'd never tell. Never." His voice was no more than a rasp. "But I know who would." He placed his hands over his face and began to blubber. "Help me, Earlae. Please."

She walked regally over to him.

"Why should I?"

Thomas lowered his hands from his face and straightened to his full and imposing height. He looked down at her. In an instant, the illusion of frailty was broken. He smiled.

Earlae realized what was happening too late.

"Oh, crap," she said, turning to run.

He snared her around the waist before she could retreat a single step, crushing her in against him and dragging her into his lair of shadows. Head snug against his chest she could hear the beating of his heart.

Thumpa . . . Thumpa . . . Thumpa . . .

It was a confident heartbeat.

Thumpa . . . Thumpa . . . Thumpa . . .

The heartbeat of a man without a worry in the world.

"No one fucks with Marshall Thomas. No one."

He stopped and set her down, his arms still wrapped tightly around her.

"The key," he said. "Give it to me."

"I don't have it."

"Where is it?"

"Bo has it. He has them all."

"Ah," Thomas said. "And where might my trusted friend and associate be?"

"I . . . I don't know."

"Then we wait. Sooner or later he'll come looking for his prize possession. That's all you are to him, you know. And when he does-" He sniffed the top of her head and sighed. "It's been awhile."

Thomas began to grind his cock into her. She could feel it rigid against her butt. Through his supersaturated diaper and her sexy, sassy kick-ass bodysuit, she could feel it, feel its impatient throbbing.

Thumpa . . . Thumpa . . . Thumpa . . .

Just like his heartbeat.

Thumpa . . . Thumpa . . . Thumpa . . .

Implacable. Inescapable.

"What's the matter?" His words were hot splashes on her neck. "You know you want it." He slipped his hand between their bodies to touch himself. "C'mon," he said. "Tell Uncle Tommy how much you want it."

When she didn't respond, he clamped a forearm around her throat to hold her in place while he unzipped her to the crotch with his free hand.

"Help . . . me," Earlae managed to croak at Ace, who was cowering in the doorway.

Her friend took a tentative step forward, his face a twitching mask of terror.

"Boo," Thomas shouted, prompting Ace to scamper back to the relative safety of the doorway.

Thomas laughed. "Wait right there, little man," he said. "I'll get to you in a moment."

Earlae turned her head and sank her teeth deep into the hairy meat on Thomas's shoulder. He hollered, momentarily loosening the lock on her throat. Bending at the waist for leverage, she launched her head backward, smashing it into his face. He hollered a second time then slumped to the floor. She spun around, kicking at him, striking him once in his crotch, hard, then a second time, even harder.

"I am not helpless, do you hear me?"

With a roar, Thomas lunged at her. She tried to hopscotch around his flailing hands, but he got lucky and caught hold of her heel and the next thing she knew she was reeling over backwards. She landed flat on her back, the breath bounced from her body.

Thomas's eyes were like empty black holes as he stared balefully down at her. "Not helpless? You?" He began to peel away the bodysuit. "They just don't come any more helpless. Here," he lowered his voice menacingly, "let me show you what I mean."

Earlae's chance to escape came when Thomas raised his middle up high enough to extract his cock from the reeking, sewage-filled diaper. She slithered out from beneath him. He swiped at her legs as she scrambled toward the outer range of his chain. Her fingers closed over the splintered door jamb just as he caught her by the heel. He jerked her backwards, and a spear-tipped, two foot length of the jamb snapped off in her hand.

He struck her with a short, hard punch to the side of her face.

"Drop it," he commanded. "Drop it."

White spots danced before her eyes.

He punched her again, and she let go of the broken jamb.

Softly humming Bach's *Passion According to St. Matthew*, one of Bo's favorite pieces, Thomas climbed on top of her, using his great weight to pin her face-first to the floor. Shifting his body slightly, he clamped her arms to her sides with his hands and forced her legs apart with one knee. She struggled to get out from under him, bucking, wrenching, twisting this way and that, but he didn't budge an inch. He was just too strong.

The cold crucifix knocked against the flesh between her shoulder blades with each vicious thrust of his hips. Thomas was right, she thought. She really was helpless. A large part of her wanted to surrender, let him kill her and be done with it. It would all be so easy.

A shudder passed through Thomas's body. Then, moaning loudly, he withdrew from inside her, and she felt his sticky seed spurting onto her back.

It would all be so easy if it weren't for the pain. Eleven years later and it was still the pain she feared most of all.

"Ace . . . !" she said. "Please . . . !"

From the periphery of her vision she caught a blur of motion, and then-

Thomas stiffened above her.

She craned her neck to the right and aimed her sight upward. Thomas was staring down at her, a puzzled look on his face, the broken jamb embedded in his side. He opened his mouth and blood gushed out like a liquid scream, filling her own screaming mouth.

Had to get out, Earlae suddenly knew. Had to get out before she lost it again. She started for the door, pulling Ace after her.

"No," Ace said, jerking his arm from her grip.

"Let's go."

Ace's squinty eyes fixed on her. "Not yet," he said.

***

All alone, Earlae splashed through the narrow, serpentine corridors, heedless of direction. She ran until her legs gave out and she tumbled to the ground, hopelessly lost.

"Earlae? Are you there?" Ace's tentative voice whispered from around a corner a long time later.

"I'm over here."

Ace's hunched form slipped into the light. His shirt was off and his jeans were open at the fly, his off-kilter erection pointing the way to heaven. His bony chest shone with sweat and blood. He smiled down at her uncertainly, looking for her approval.

"He's dead."

Earlae just stared at him. She could still taste the blood, thick on her tongue and in her throat, but mostly in her head. "Whatever happened, he deserved worse," was all that she could think to say.

Ace's smile broadened. "He got worse, Earlae. Believe me, he did."

"My God, Ace. What did you do?"

"Let's just say it was the most fun I've had since the release of Halo 3. What a rush." He levered his erection into his jeans and zipped up. "Can

we do it again tomorrow, Earlae? Please? Same bat time, same bat channel?"

"I don't know," Earlae said, running her fingers through her hair and tearing at the wet, ropy strands. "I don't know how much longer I can do this."

She was tired, and she was sick at heart. She hated the killing and that she was party to it. Believing that it was necessary, even righteous, did little to make it any more palatable. She would have to have a long chat with Bo when she got home. He would know what to do. He always knew.

Ace tapped her on the shoulder.

"You want to know what the coolest thing about tonight was?"

"What, Ace? What could possibly be cool about what happened tonight?"

"I didn't tic once, Earlae. My nose didn't bleed. I didn't cuss, didn't tap no one's ass, and I didn't sing a theme song from a single friggin'- aw, shit-"

"What is it, Ace? What's wrong?"

"*Come and knock on our door. We'll be waiting for you. Where the kisses are hers and hers and . . .*"

***

The bloody-steak smell of death hung heavy in the air outside Marshall Thomas's cell.

"Sweet Georgia Brown," Tokunbo exclaimed as he strolled through the open door.

Marshall was sprawled in the center of the room. He was missing his head and his left arm, and the fingers on his right hand had been gnawed down to the bone. EMINEM RULES was written in fiendishly dripping bile on the shadowy wall opposite the door. He did a rather jaunty shuffle, ball, change around what looked to be a heart - half-eaten - and followed the scattered trail of severed toes to find Marshall's lipless, toothless head gaping at him from a cavity in the stone wall behind the door.

"It looks as if there will have to be a change of plan, old friend." With the gloved fingers of his right hand he gently closed Marshall's eyes. "There is simply not enough of you left for me to work with."

Tokunbo had always known that Lloyd Mathis was a little off, but after bearing witness to the fruits of his rage, he knew that he would have to re-evaluate that assessment.

Eminem Rules?

A white rapper rules?

Lloyd wasn't just *off*. He was legally, clinically, unequivocally insane.

Marshall's cell, like all the others, had been wired by an associate for sight and sound. Tokunbo couldn't wait to kick back at The Malloy penthouse with a snifter of Cognac and watch the carnage in full HD. He wondered if his special guest had watched it live. He would have to ask him.

But first thing's first.

Tokunbo left poor Marshall to the final judgment of his pissant cucasoid god and rounded the corner to prepare the next victim for discovery.

<u>31</u>

The receptionist inside the Massachusetts Human Rights Commission was eighteen or nineteen years old, Samoan, and pleasantly plump, even by Samoan standards. She was wearing a royal-blue- and white-hibiscus muumuu that reached all the way down to a pair of blue rubber flip-flops. Her toenails were French manicured.

"If you'll please have a seat in the waiting area," she said, "I'll alert Mr. Shabazz that you're here."

Daniel said, "And Mr. Shabazz is . . . ?"

"Acting Director of the MHRC."

The receptionist picked up a stack of files and headed toward a pair of doors to the left of her desk, evidencing a surprising amount of hip sway for a woman of her girth.

"I thought you were here to prevent sexual harassment in the workplace," Daniel said, "not incite it."

The receptionist placed a dimpled hand over her mouth and giggled sweetly.

Twenty-five minutes later, an overly intense black man, mid- to late-forties, with a shaved head stalked into the waiting area. He was appropriately dressed for the office in standard business/casual 'fight-the-power' attire, charcoal pants, neatly pressed, a pair of black suede shoes, freshly brushed, and a violently colored dashiki. It was a look that somehow suited him. No stranger to either fighting or violence, he had a nose shaped like a sweet potato and obscene amounts of scar tissue around both of his dark liquid eyes.

"Mr. Rourke," he said. "I am Tokunbo Shabazz. How may I be of assistance?"

Daniel held out his hand, but the Acting Director just stared at it. "If I could have a few minutes of your time, in private, I'd be happy to tell you."

The acting director's shark-like eyes flicked back and forth, up and down, picking apart Daniel's face, his hair, his jacket, his pants and shoes. "Fine," he said at last. "We shall speak in my office."

The plaque on the door said Marshall Thomas, Director. The office was medium-sized with a decent cityscape view. There was child-like art on the walls, sub-Saharan folk pieces mostly, and the small bookcase in the corner was full of books with the words 'racism', 'rage' and 'revenge' featured prominently in their titles. The Koran and a dog-eared copy of Wallace Fard Muhammad's *The Supreme Wisdom* sat on a wooden pedestal in the corner opposite the windows. His desk consisted of two concrete pedestals supporting an inch-thick, rose-colored glass work surface.

Shabazz took a seat behind the desk and steepled his long fingers. The diamond solitaire on his pinky was at least three carats in size. On the wall behind him, sandwiched between framed portraits of Louis Farrakhan and Tupac Shakur in saintly, backlit poses, was a Masters degree in African Studies from Columbia Pacific University granted to one Fillip Walter Dixon, and a dry-mounted letter of recognition addressed to Tokunbo Shabazz from the ACLU's first openly gay, first Hispanic Executive Director.

"I'm looking into the disappearance of Marshall Thomas."

"I thought I had answered all your questions already." Shabazz unsteepled his fingers and leaned forward in his chair, impaling Daniel with his eyes. "Wait just one minute." His tone was sharp, impatient, each syllable chiseling like an ice pick. "The FBI has full jurisdiction over this matter, does it not?"

"It does."

"Please show me your credentials."

"I'm working with the Bureau as an outside consultant. I used to be a special prosecutor with the Los Angeles District Attorney's Office. I have experience in this type of case and was asked to-"

Shabazz made a tell-it-to-the-hand gesture. "No credentials? I presume then you would not mind if I sought confirmation of your claim before speaking with you."

"I have a contact at the bureau you can call. His name is Barry Gal-"

"If you do not mind, Mr. Rourke, it just so happens that I have a close personal relationship with one of the special agents assigned to the case. I shall speak with him. To get it straight from the horse's mouth as it were." He picked up the phone and pecked out some numbers. "Leonard Farmer, please. Yes, I will hold."

"Horse's mouth? Don't you mean horse's ass?"

"Leonard is horribly and permanently scarred," Shabazz said. "If your comment is in any way related to his tragic accident and subsequent, excruciating graft operations then I am afraid I shall have no choice but to terminate this meeting. I do not converse with persons insensitive to the plight of others."

"I wish I had that luxury," Daniel said. "But I have a job to do. And for the record, my comment related not to his appearance, but to his character."

"I really do not - Leonard? Hello, sir. Tokunbo Shabazz. Yes, thank you. We are all fine over here. All things considered." Shabazz nodded several times quickly. "I have one Daniel Rourke sitting across the desk from me. He claims to be-" Shabazz launched into another series of rapid nods.

"Yes. Yes, I see. Yes. I thank you for your time."

Shabazz looked at Daniel. The muscles in his jaw tensed, relaxed, and tensed again. "Whilst Special Agent Farmer has confirmed your claim, I feel compelled to advise you that there is a definite reciprocity of ill will."

"Once again, I'm here to look into Marshall Thomas's disappearance, not to make friends."

"I do not believe you have to worry about the latter matter at this office," Shabazz said. "And as to the former, I have already told the authorities all that I know. Frankly, I do not see how I can be of any further assistance."

"Sometimes, when a case has stalled, all it requires to start it moving again is someone taking a poke at it from a fresh perspective."

"And you are that perspective?"

Daniel smiled. "Certainly, I've been called fresh on more occasions than I care to remember."

Shabazz sniffed. "I am sure that there many individuals in this world who think of you as a riotously funny man. Fortunately, I am not one of them."

"So you're the exception that proves the rule," Daniel said. "Now what can you tell me about Mr. Thomas?"

"Marshall was a great person," Shabazz said.

"Any enemies that you know of?"

"He was a person of the people."

"A person of the people? How absurd. Is that a yes or a no?"

"He had no enemies. The people adored him."

Shabazz noticed Daniel's eyes pass over the degree on the wall behind him. "Dixon was my slave name," he said.

"You're Sudanese?"

"Now why would you ask such a thing?"

"Because it's the only country I'm aware of where slavery is still practiced."

"You know what I meant by my comment."

"Obviously not," Daniel said. "But that's neither here nor there. How would you categorize Mr. Thomas' worldview? His politics?"

"Marshall cared deeply for the common person. He was a person of integrity, a champion for the rights of those who face discrimination on a daily basis."

"Finally," Daniel said, "a voice for the much maligned heterosexual white male."

Shabazz scowled. "If it wasn't for Marshall Thomas, racial preferences would have been left for dead in Massachusetts a long time ago."

"And that's a good thing?"

"No, Mr. Rourke, that's a great thing. After all, what is the alternative?"

"Letting people succeed, or fail, based entirely on merit would be a pretty decent start."

Shabazz's eyes narrowed. "Marshall believed it was incumbent upon government to take a proactive role in the war against discrimination."

"But that makes no sense. Affirmative action-"

"Diversity," Shabazz said.

"You and I both know that so-called diversity programs are nothing more than affirmative action in drag," Daniel said. "They breed animosity between the very groups they seek to bring together. And they perpetuate the age old stereotype of certain racial and/or ethnic groups as not being bright enough, or motivated enough, to succeed without Big Brother's help."

Shabazz said nothing, seething in a barely contained rage.

"Although he screwed just about everything else up, George W. Bush got it right when he referred to the underlying rationale of such programs as 'the soft bigotry of low expectations.'"

Shabazz's hands clenched into fists. "Pardon my French, Mr. Rourke, but that is nothing more than right-wing bullshit propaganda."

"Is it? Let's take a look at your current situation. If you're ever made full-fledged director of this office, there will undoubtedly be those who'll claim that the only reason you got the job is because you are-"

"I am what?"

"Black."

Shabazz made a loud sucking sound through his front teeth. "African-American," he said. "And I assure you that *when* I am made director, it will be based entirely upon my qualifications, and without regard to the color of my skin."

"Maybe you're right. But thanks to affirmative action – excuse me, *diversity* - we'll never know for sure." Daniel stood. "Will we?"

Shabazz stormed out from behind his desk until he was standing toe to toe with Daniel. The anger Daniel felt emanating from the Acting Director was palpable.

Although Daniel smiled broadly as he spoke, there wasn't so much as a trace of humor in his voice. He placed his hand on the Koran. "So is it really true that Islam is the religion of peace and tolerance?"

"I'm afraid that I was wrong in my earlier assessment of you," Shabazz said. "You are not merely insensitive. You, Mr. Rourke, are a Nazi."

"You may want to check the history books on that one, Mr. Dixon," Daniel said.

"How so?"

"Hitler was a socialist," Daniel said, motioning with his chin to the dry-mounted letter of recognition. "Like you and your ACLU brownshirt pals."

For a long time Shabazz was silent. "I believe this meeting is over," he finally said. "Good day, Mr. Rourke." His diamond pinky ring caught the overhead lights and flashed in a kaleidoscope of colors as he pointed the way to the door.

32

Buchanan slid his Post-It Note flagged copy of the Blake file over the desk at Galton. "Other than a token appearance on the inventory sheet," he said, "there's no mention of the computer. That strikes me as-"

"An unfortunate oversight?" Galton said.

"Negligent," Buchanan said.

Galton had his familiar navy blazer off and hanging on a hook on the back of his office door. The cuffs were rolled back on his badly wrinkled, white cotton-polyester-blend shirt. His pungent cologne was of the ship on the bottle variety. "My understanding is that the computer was a fairly recent purchase. There was nothing on it relevant to Blake's disappearance." He leaned back in his chair and clasped his hands behind his head. "In fact, there wasn't a single active file on the hard drive."

"There were no files," Buchanan said, "because they'd all been deleted."

There were two photographs in a hinged frame on Galton's gun-metal grey Barney Miller-style desk. One was of a rotund, stern-looking woman wearing a risqué teal dress that showed cleavage all the way down to her deep-dish navel. The other was of an English bulldog with sagging jowls and crooked yellow teeth. Galton reached over and turned the frame a couple degrees toward him before speaking. "Wow," he said in a low monotone voice. "You think there was something on it we weren't supposed to see?"

"Odds are fifty-fifty," Buchanan said.

"How do you figure that?"

"The information deleted was either relevant to the investigation or it was not. I don't know about you, but I've followed up leads on cases with odds a helluva lot skimpier than that."

"Now this bugs the shit out of me," Galton said in the same monotone voice. "If you're right about this, someone on the team may have either knowingly destroyed evidence or covered up the fact that evidence had been destroyed."

Buchanan felt his insides tighten like a fist. He didn't like what he was hearing. He glanced down at the photographs while he contemplated how best to handle things with Galton from here on in.

"In case you're wondering," Galton said with a smirk, "the old lady's on the left."

Buchanan smiled in spite of himself. "Is there any way you can get an expert to autopsy the system, to see if they can't resurrect any of the deleted files?"

"There's a good man over at MIT I could call. You know, to keep it out of the loop."

"Good idea," Buchanan said.

"And just remember," Galton said, "you find anything, you talk to me, and only to me." He waited for Buchanan's nod. "While we're waiting on the hard drive, is there anything else I can do or get for you?"

"I want the names of everyone who had access to Blake's computer. And a copy of their personnel files."

"Shouldn't be a problem."

"Oh, yeah, and any pre-employment background checks you got," Buchanan said. "I want those, too."

"You'll have everything I can get my hands on by tomorrow evening," Galton said.

Buchanan gestured toward the photograph of the woman with the droopy boobs. "So what's her name?"

"Spike."

"I meant your wife."

Galton laughed. "So did I. It was a pet name from back in her wild youth that just kinda stuck. The mutt's name is Penny." He gazed adoringly down at the photos. "Cute, isn't she?"

Buchanan didn't know which of his ladies Galton was referring to, so he exercised his right to remain silent.

<u>33</u>

"Something's definitely up with Galton," Buchanan said as he stomped out of the bathroom wearing a maroon velour bath robe, his pale ham hock calves visible above his mismatched socks, one gray, one black. He motored over to the window, and looked out.

"What do you mean?" Daniel said.

"When I raised the matter of the deleted computer files, he never batted an eye. Real cool like, he says, 'now this bugs the shit outta me.' You believe that? As a cop, he may be Beantown's answer to San Fran's Dirty Harry Callahan, but when it comes to acting, he's no Clint Eastwood."

"What does he suspect?" Daniel said.

"Dunno. Although I did get the distinct impression he believes that someone's dirty as dog shit in the investigation."

"Who? Did he say?"

Buchanan shook his head. "A cop, a fed, I don't know. I don't think he has any direct evidence. Just a feeling. A hunch. I will say, however, that he doesn't trust Farmer."

"Would you trust Farmer with your back?"

"No way. The guy's a reg spouting, bureaucrat sleezeball."

"So Galton's been whoring us all along," Daniel said.

"Big time," Buchanan said.

"It makes sense when you think about it," Daniel said. "Someone close at hand is working both sides of the street, you don't know who you can trust, who better on the case than a couple of outsiders with impeccable credentials and a personal interest in seeing things wrapped up."

Buchanan grunted in the affirmative.

"Does this change anything for you?"

Buchanan shook his head.

Daniel drifted in beside his friend, watching a small MBTA commuter ferry bobbing futilely over the harbor's choppy grey waters.

"Not even your opinion of Galton?"

As he waited for a reply, Daniel continued to watch the infinitesimal progress of the ferry.

"He's a sly one alright," Buchanan finally said. "We could use a guy like that on the LAPD. What about you? How did you make out today?"

Daniel shrugged. "Honestly, I don't know."

Buchanan ducked back into the bathroom. "Good cop or bad?" he shouted.

"What do you think?"

"Total asshole cop'd be my guess."

"I wanted to see if I could ruffle the guy's feather boa enough to get him to blurt something out he might have held back in earlier interviews. A lot of people, even the good ones, get nervous when dealing with cops and clam up. It's human nature. I don't know about you, but it's been my experience that if you get a guy pissed enough, you can sometimes loosen his lips."

Buchanan came into the room carrying his Dopp kit. "Couldn't quite make out that last part. What did you say?"

"I said I acted like an asshole because you can sometimes get people to open up if you piss them off enough."

Buchanan unzipped the kit and extracted the two-foot length of surgical tubing with the alligator clip. "Did it work?"

"Not really. But it was more fun than a barrel of monkeys."

"What's he like? Thomas's replacement."

"His name's Tokunbo Shabazz. He's queer, but he's no cream puff. If I hadn't left when I did, he would've taken a poke at me."

"You don't think he's involved in any of this, do you?"

The ferry was still bobbing up and down on the waves without really getting anywhere. It reminded Daniel of the progress that they were making on the case. Hell, it reminded him of his own existence. He turned away from the window and took a seat on the couch.

"I don't know."

"What do you know?"

"That I took an immediate disliking to the guy. He spoke of Marshall Thomas like he was a saint, but he'd already moved the poor man's furniture out of the office. And what was worse, he kept referring to him in the past tense, like he was already dead. Like maybe he knew something we didn't."

Buchanan reached into the shaving kit and extracted the scissors and surgical tape.

"Although I suspect I'm going to regret it, my curiosity's getting the better of me," Daniel said. "What precisely do you do with that stuff every night?"

"I'll show you if you want, but this is some serious shit. The last thing I need is you laughing at me."

The telephone began to ring.

"I won't laugh," Daniel said.

"Just remember," Buchanan said. "You asked for it."

His roommate dropped his robe just as Daniel picked up the receiver, and he wasn't wearing any underwear.

"Jesus Christ," Daniel exclaimed.

"You may want to have your Caller ID checked," a familiar female voice said.

"Officer Wagner," Daniel said. "How nice to hear from you again." He swiveled his body on the couch, facing away from Buchanan, who was in the shameless process of beating-off no more than two feet away from him.

"Unfortunately, this is a business call," Terry said. "Off the record, of course."

"Sure, sure," Daniel said. "What's up?"

"What's up is I got hauled into the Chief's office today and given the third degree about your involvement in the Calhoun case. He wanted to know what I'd told you, and whether I showed you the file. His fear is that I somehow compromised an especially sensitive investigation by providing you with certain need-to-know information."

Buchanan moved back into his line of sight and began to wrap surgical tape around his erection where the foreskin met the shaft. "Just give me a couple seconds to get soft." He closed his eyes and began to softly chant the name Hillary Rodham Clinton.

"Are you still there?" Terry said.

With each utterance of the former First Lady's name, Buchanan's erection shrank that much more.

"I'm still here," Daniel said, closing his eyes. "What did you tell them?"

"The truth," Terry said. "That I told you nothing. That you were advised there could be no access to the Calhoun file during the active phase of the case."

"So why all the flack? It makes no sense. The FBI has granted us full access to their investigation. Hell, they've done everything short of deputizing us."

"What would you say if I told you that it was someone from the Bureau who called my Chief and instigated the whole brouhaha. A Special Agent by the name of-"

"Leonard Farmer," Daniel said.

"That's right. And he's on a witch hunt. He doesn't like the two of you very much. You especially. He said you've been stepping on some rather important toes."

Buchanan tapped Daniel on his shoulder to get his attention. Daniel turned and watched as he attached the surgical tubing to the ring of tape. When he was done, he squatted and fastened the other end, the one with the alligator clip, to his black sock.

"What did Galton have to say about it?"

The pause was neither long nor dramatic, but it was enough to confirm Daniel's hunch.

"What do you mean?"

"Barry Galton," Daniel said. "Farmer's rumpled partner. You've been in cahoots with him all along, haven't you?"

This time the silence was both long and dramatic.

"Whose idea was it to let us bully our way into the investigation? Yours, or his? And here I was thinking it was my thousand watt smile that got us a peek at the file."

"The smile certainly made it a guilty pleasure," Terry said. "When did you figure it out?"

When Buchanan stood, the tension from the surgical tubing stretched the foreskin over the head. It hurt to look at and caused Daniel to cross his legs in reflex. "I was uncomfortable with the way you handled things from the start. Leaving the room with the file unattended? I haven't seen that particular move since *Magnum, P.I.* went off the air. Then, when we waltzed into FBI headquarters and straight into their case, it all seemed just a little too pat for my liking. But, hey, we wanted in and we were in, right?"

"Kettle's boiling, Rourke. I've got to go. You two watch your backs, you hear?"

"Terry?"

"Yes, Daniel?"

"Thanks for the warning."

"While we're on the subject of warnings," Terry said. "The next time I call, it might not be for business."

She hung up before Daniel could respond. He couldn't put what he felt into words. All he knew for certain was that whatever it was he was feeling, beneath the hazy veneer of guilt, it wasn't entirely bad.

He set the receiver down and glared up at his sheepishly grinning roommate.

"It's a foreskin restoration device," Buchanan said. "Designed is to undo the tragedy of male genital mutilation." His grin widened. "A few more months and it'll be fully restored to its former glory and I'll be-"

"Former glory? It's a dick, Frank, not a Picasso."

Buchanan's grin vanished. He took a step closer. A little too close for comfort given his current state of dress. "But you-"

"Get that thing away from me."

"You promised-"

"Not to laugh," Daniel said. "Does it look like I'm laughing to you, Frank? Does it?"

34

By the time Tokunbo had been congratulated by each and every one of the three hundred and fifty-four Social Register guests, he was positively aglow. As a vocal advocate for GLAPA, The Gay and Lesbian Adoptive Parents Association, he had wisely been placed in charge of organizing their annual fundraiser for charity. The white tie affair had been booked nine months in advance at the prestigious Sterling Cliffs Country Cub in Plymouth, Massachusetts, a converted thirty-two room, seventeen fireplace mansion, built on one-hundred sprawling acres. With a single phone call, Tokunbo had been able to procure the club's facilities at a rather sizable discount. Although the evening was young, the event had already proven itself an unqualified success, generating more than two hundred and twenty thousand dollars at last count. This year the event had particular meaning for Tokunbo. Thanks to his tireless lobbying for GLAPA, every penny raised was earmarked for his favorite charity, the Planned Parenthood League of Boston, so that they might continue their mission of offering abortion services in a safe and non-judgmental environment.

"This music blows," Earlae said.

In keeping with the decorum of an Ultra-formal function, Tokunbo had engaged the services of a world-renowned Seattle-based string quartet. Beethoven. Debussy. Kernis. Mendelssohn. Shostakovich. Their repertoire was as eclectic as their technical command was masterful. Thus far they had exceeded even his lofty expectations. Currently they were charging full speed ahead through the relentless finale of Schubert's *Death and the Maiden Quartet*.

"Unfortunately Fergie was otherwise engaged," Tokunbo said.

"Bummer," Earlae said.

Although the fourth movement's emotional coda promised major-mode triumph only to snatch it ruthlessly away, Tokunbo refused to allow the parallel of her ignorance of the Viennese classical school to diminish one iota his own well-deserved moment of triumph.

When the final, weeping note had faded to oblivion, very nearly bringing a tear to his eye, Tokunbo whispered to Earlae, "Give me your hand, you beautiful shape!"

Earlae smiled, interlacing her slender fingers with his own.

"I desire a moment alone with you," he said.

"I was wondering when you were going to make your move. I'm horny as a goat. Been that way since we got here."

After collecting their overcoats, classic double-breasted Burberry for him, funky Balenciaga for Earlae, Tokunbo led the way along the Italian marble walkway to exit through the mansion's glittering stained glass *porte-cochere*. Arm-in-arm they traversed the snow-sifted gardens to a gazebo perched on the two hundred foot cliff overlooking Cape Cod Bay. The brisk cloudless night offered a romantic view of the ocean and beaches stretching from Plymouth, to the Cape Cod Canal, and all the way to Provincetown.

Earlae closed her eyes and raised her face provocatively to his. But instead of taking her in his arms and tasting her lips, Tokunbo did the unexpected, saying, "I do not want any more such incidents."

Earlae's eyes popped open. "Excuse me?"

"What happened the other day with Marshall Thomas was inexcusable."

"He tried to kill me. And if wasn't for Ace he'd have done it, too."

"You entered his cell. You deliberately provoked him."

"I did not," Earlae began. "I only-"

"I believe I had made it crystal clear after you dispatched Eric Murray without my consent," Tokunbo said. "You may look at our little critters through the bars of their cages, but you may not touch them."

"I was only trying to-"

"I know what you were trying to do, but you are simply too delicate a creature. I conduct the inquisitions, not you. And those remaining in confinement shall not be put down until after I have heard a credible confession to the sin. Fortunately, I had finished interrogating both Mr. Murray and Mr. Thomas prior to your rather disrespectful interventions."

"Disrespectful? They're monsters and they-"

"Disrespectful to me," Tokunbo said

"But you told me I had to get it out. Had to get it all out. Told me I wouldn't be free of my past until-"

Bo shoved her hard. She stumbled backwards into the Gazebo. Then he spun her around and bent her over the waist-height, whitewashed rail. "You are not to initiate direct contact without me. For any reason. Do you understand?"

"Yeah. It won't happen again."

Hiking up her overcoat and her beaded ivory House of Dior gown, he said. "Unless I am-"

"There with me. I get it, Bo." She whimpered as he pushed himself into her, roughly, and bone dry. "I'm not stupid."

Through gritted teeth, he said, "Then stop acting that way."

<u>35</u>

Daniel unpacked his Dictaphone shortly after Buchanan had ducked out for a conciliatory six-pack. He was hoping to finish work on the final chapter of his sophomore novel while he had a rare moment alone. He had just made the opening paragraph sing when the door to their suite slammed open, the silhouette of an extremely large man framed inside the broad opening. "Knock, knock," the stranger said as he swaggered into the room.

The man was fat with a ruddy outdoor face and a red mullet. He had on a pair of baggy tie-dyed sweatpants and fingerless gloves. The bulge inside his black, satin-finish jacket indicated that he was armed.

"If you're Rourke. I'm here to give you a-"

"Finally," Daniel said, affecting a lisp. "The escort service said you'd be here an hour ago."

"Hey, fuck you, pal," the fat man said.

"That's generally what one pays a man-whore to do." Daniel dropped the lisp. "Of course, I could always fuck you up, you don't tell me what you're doing barging into my room like this."

"I heard you were a comedian," the fat man said. "A regular laugh riot, I was told."

"You hear the one about the fat pig with the relief-pitcher haircut and the tiny dick who walks into a bar with a-"

"You shut your fucking yap, I can deliver my message and split."

Daniel remained seated at the desk, which meant that the fat man would have to speak a little louder to be heard from across the room.

"What's the message?"

"The message is you and your pal got no business looking into the disappearance of Boston's *crème de la creme*. You keep sticking your noses where they don't belong and something bad is gonna happen. From here on in you let the experts handle things. Unnerstand?"

"Yeah," Daniel said, his voice flat. "I understand."

The fat man slapped his fist into his palm. "I was kinda hoping you wouldn't get it so quick. Kinda hoping I could raise a little pain on your wise ass before you and your pal split Dodge."

Daniel looked at him dead-eyed. "Maybe later," he said. "Maybe later I'll show you what I've got."

"What you got? You got shit."

On the way out the door the fat man knocked Julie's picture from the shelf and ground his boot heel into it, shattering the glass and shredding the glossy photographic paper to confetti.

Daniel picked up the phone and punched out the numbers to

Buchanan's cell. "Frank," he said. "Where the hell are you?"

"In the lobby. I got Guinness for you - I don't know how you drink that sludge - and some Sam Adams specialty brew for me. It was a little on the pricey side but the girl at the shop said it-"

"You should see an abnormally large man getting off the elevator any second. Red hair. Used to work out a long time ago, but he's let it turn to flab."

"Walks like he's got a fire hydrant shoved up his ass?"

"That's the guy."

"What's the deal?"

"The deal is we were just asked by the men-in-blue to butt out."

"The dumb fuck actually identified himself as a cop?"

"He didn't have to. He felt too much like street heat to be anything but. Follow him, Frank. Find out where he goes, then swing by and pick me up."

"You got something in mind?"

"Oh, yeah," Daniel said. "I've got something in mind."

"He just jumped into an old TA double-parked out front. I gotta split," Buchanan said, and the line went dead.

<u>36</u>

Daniel and Buchanan were on their way to the fat man's house when they were sidetracked by a phone call from Galton. There had been another abduction. Much to Daniel's chagrin, the fat man would have to wait.

The latest victim lived on Washington Street in what politicians coyly refer to as high-density housing. Galton was waiting for them in the hallway when the elevator doors groaned open on the vertical ghetto's run-down fourth floor. He pointed down the hall. "Second door on the left. Just past the largest mound of human feces."

"The one the kid in diapers is playing with?" Buchanan said.

"That's a dog turd. I meant the next mound down. The one with little bits of red and green in it."

Hop scotching the numerous, irregularly spaced deposits of human and animal waste, they followed Galton to a door with a sign that said *Caution, Attack Rats!*

As soon as Daniel entered the reeking, garbage-strewn apartment he sensed that something wasn't right. Everything that hadn't been nailed or bolted down had been completely and utterly destroyed, including a large wall mirror. The broken pieces of the mirror lay where they had fallen, some face-down, some face-up.

"Looks like he just had the place feng-shuied," Daniel said.

"What's that?" Galton said.

Farmer lowered the silk paisley handkerchief that he had been holding over his mouth and nose. "It's the ancient Chinese art of harmonic placement," he said. "And as a long-time practitioner I feel compelled to caution you, Mr. Rourke, that I do not find your offhand remark in any way humorous."

"Birds of a feather," Daniel said. "You and your friend Shabazz both."

"So who was he?" Buchanan said.

"Ira Banks," Galton said.

"He doesn't fit the profile," Daniel said.

Galton nodded. "The guy's a three-time loser. Never had more than two welfare checks to rub together in any of his fifty-six years."

"Strange," Buchanan said.

Galton held out a plastic evidence bag. "You wanna see strange," he said. "Check this out."

Inside the bag was a pair of grey pigtails braided with eagle feathers and thick rubber bands, the kind used by the post office. The roots and the bloody plugs of flesh still attached to the individual hairs suggested that the braids had been forcibly ripped from the scalp.

"We found 'em on the kitchen floor in front of the fridge."

Buchanan moved his face up close to the bag. "Something's squirming around in there. All kinds of somethings actually. What the hell are they?"

"Head lice," Galton said.

"Now that's just fucking gross," Buchanan said.

"Aside from the victim not fitting the profile," Daniel said. "The MO's also different this time around."

"How so?" Galton said.

"The difference," Daniel said, "is that there was only one perp."

"The broken mirror," Buchanan said. "Some of the pieces are sitting shiny side up."

Daniel nodded. "The calming influence of the cool and calculating mind is missing."

"No wonder the place looks the way it does," Galton said. "Only the nut job put in an appearance this time."

"The gentleman behind this is obviously ill," Farmer said, his words muffled slightly by the handkerchief. "He's in need of immediate psychiatric care not insults. Who knows? It may have been such cruel and taunting remarks that turned him into what he is."

Galton shot Farmer the bird then turned toward the short hallway to the bedroom. "Nikki," he shouted. "Get your pretty little butt out here."

Nikki Sommers was a twenty-something evidence tech with a tight, gymnast's body, unabashedly artificial breasts, and very blond, very teased hair. She had on high-heel boots, skin-tight leather pants and a top short enough to show off her pierced bellybutton.

"Barry Galton." She feinted a grab at his crotch and chuckled when he flinched. "How's the hammer hanging?"

"We catch you on a hot date, or what?"

"Naw," she said. "I always look this good." She glanced over at Daniel. "You just never know who's gonna show up at one of these things."

"What can you tell me about what really went on here?"

"The Indian was-"

"Native-American," Farmer said sharply.

Nikki rolled her cornflower blue eyes. "The Indian was in bed, probably sleeping one off, when the perp surprised him with a blow to the head. It fucked him up royally, but it didn't put him down."

"What do you mean?" Galton said.

"Get this," Nikki said. "The guy gets cracked on the head with an imitation brass table lamp, rolls out of bed and heads to the kitchen for a little hair of the dog."

"What are you The Amazing Fucking Kreskin?" Galton said.

"Blood spatter doesn't lie," she said. "The trail weaves from the bedroom to the kitchen, ending at the fridge."

"I mean how did you know he was going for booze?"

"Follow me."

Nikki pushed open the door to the kitchen, which whimpered like a wounded animal. Inside the narrow rectangular room, she tugged the refrigerator door open. "Take a look. Seventy-seven bottles of Bud brand firewater." She began opening the kitchen cupboards. "No food. Check it out. Not a single morsel." Behind each door cartons of cigarettes were stacked three high and three deep.

"Could be he's a terrorist," Daniel said with a grin. "There's enough tobacco here to take out an entire city block with secondhand smoke."

"Black market?" Buchanan said.

"That'd be my guess," Galton said. "The guy was into everything else."

Farmer's phone rang. "I have to take this," he said. "I'll be in the hall if you need me."

"Sure," Galton said. "Come running when we holler."

"That was where his braids were ripped off," Nikki said. "See the smears on the floor over there in front of the fridge?" She pointed to a large brownish-red stain on the orange oilcloth floor. "Judging by the jumble of prints in the blood, he was still alive when it all went down. It looks like our boy wrestled him down, put a size eight boot on his face for leverage then used both arms to yank 'em off."

"Ouch," Galton said.

Nikki turned to Daniel, adjusted her breasts for maximum loft then cooed, "Fuck me if I'm wrong, but is your name Koresh?"

"You're barking up the wrong tree with that one," Galton said. "He's more likely to be checking out the way my pimply old butt wiggles than yours, if you get my drift."

"The guy's a queer?" Nikki looked hard at Daniel. "Figures."

"If you'll pardon the pun, Galton," Daniel said, "you've really got to get your background checks straight."

"What are you talking about?"

Buchanan held up his hand and waggled his fingertips. "The queer's over here."

"No fucking way," Galton said.

Daniel stuck out his hand and Nikki took it.

"My name's Daniel," he said. "Daniel Koresh."

Nikki shrugged. "You win some, you lose some," she said.

37

Buchanan parked two doors down from the fat man's house and killed the headlights. The fat man lived a two gallon commute from the city in a vinyl-sided back-split with attached garage on a cul-de-sac of virtually identical homes. His car, a black Smokey and the Bandit-era Trans Am, was parked in the snow-blown asphalt driveway behind a late-model, four-door Honda Civic.

Buchanan said, "What do you have in mind?"

"I'm sick of all the goddamned secrets and lies and half-truths," Daniel said.

Buchanan seemed to take his time choosing his words. "I know exactly what you mean."

Daniel was reaching for the door handle when he was restrained by his friend's iron grip. "I remember what went down in LA last year," Buchanan said. "You don't have anything too medieval in mind, I hope."

"This guy could be the loose thread we've been looking for," Daniel said.

"How do you figure that?"

"Ask yourself why someone would go through the bother of sending a slugger to threaten us?"

"Could be we crossed the line," Buchanan said. "Farmer's right. We've been treading on some serious toes since we got here. Law enforcement types are a touchy, territorial bunch. How will it look if we solve this thing before they do?"

"Could be you're right," Daniel said. "But what if you're wrong? What if the real reason this guy showed up at our hotel is the same reason Galton and Wagner decided to deal us in?"

"Dirty cops," Buchanan said.

"That, my friend, is one of two things I hope to settle here tonight."

"What's the other thing?"

Daniel's gloves fit like a second skin and an anxious puff of laughter escaped his lips as he curled them one, then the other, into familiar fists.

***

Daniel brushed a peephole in the frost on the rear window of the Civic and peered inside. An infant's booster seat was strapped in the back. The fat man did not live alone. He had a family. And that was exactly what Daniel had been counting on.

He walked calmly to the end of the driveway then continued around to the door at the back of the garage. Although the next house over was less than fifteen feet away, it was completely dark, like the fat man's house. He tried the doorknob. Locked.

Undaunted, he slid his lock pick kit from out of his coat pocket. He removed his gloves and inserted the pick and tension tool into the sturdy deadbolt lock and immediately went to work on the pins in the cylinder. He'd learned the proper technique of working a lock from a particularly talented pick man during the course of a B&E he'd defended his first year out of law school. Something to fall back on, he figured, if the whole writing thing didn't pan out.

A minute passed.

He looked over his shoulder. The windows in the house next door remained dark. He began to feel the buzz in his stomach, the eagerness. He couldn't wait to see how the night would play itself out.

Three more minutes passed.

His fingers were growing numb from the cold. In another minute they would be useless.

Finally, there was a click. He stretched his gloves back onto his hands, and slipped inside the fat man's house.

Enough ambient light from the street slipped through the sheer curtains that he had no problem navigating the homey living room. He took a seat in a yellow floral-pattern couch and turned on the TV with a USS Enterprise-shaped remote control.

It wasn't long before the fat man, 9mm in hand, flicked on the lights and found Daniel watching a Jerry Springer re-run. He was wearing a pair of black silk pajama bottoms and no shirt.

Daniel had been wrong. He wasn't really fat at all. His build was somewhere between Mr. Olympia and a Budweiser draught horse. His chest and arms, a spider-work of veins and stretch marks, were so massive that they bordered on the grotesque.

The big man's eyes hardened as recognition set in. "What the fuck? You wise bastard."

"Just thought I'd pop by and say hello," Daniel said.

"Why I oughta-"

"Who is it, Bobby?" a frightened female voice called out from the back of the house. "Who are you talking to? Is everything okay?"

"Everything's fine, Muffins. Just a buddy looking for some place warm to sleep one off."

"Clean blankets are in the linen closet." There was no longer even a hint of fear in the woman's voice. "Extra pillows, too." Apparently drunken men popping by for a late night sleepover was nothing new to her.

"The fuck are you doing here?" His voice was a hoarse whisper.

Daniel switched on his Dictaphone and set it down on a coffee table. The big man's voice from his visit to their Boston Harbor suite was crystal clear.

When the recorded exchange had ended, Daniel said, "The original is in a safe place with instructions that it be made public if anything untoward should ever happen to me." It really wasn't, but the big man had no way of knowing that.

"And you expect this to stop me from blowing your fucking head off? You broke into my goddamned house."

"Shoot me and you'll be charged with murder inside a minute of the tape surfacing." Daniel stood. "So take a load off while I tell you the facts of life."

The big man sat down.

"First off, you threaten me again I'll turn your suburban dream life into a nightmare. You have a wife and a kid. I have no one. My fiancé was murdered last year. My parents are dead. I'm willing to bet you're a man who cares about a great many things. Me? I don't give a shit about anything. And that includes whether I live or die. You, therefore, are vulnerable. I am not."

"You threatening my kid?"

"You say so much as boo to me again and I guarantee you'll find that out."

"What do you want from me?"

"Your name to start with."

"Robert."

"Robert what?"

"Crudup."

"I bet they call you Big Bobby downtown."

The man said nothing.

"Am I right? Do they call you Big Bobby?"

The man nodded.

"Okay, Big Bobby. Who sent you to the hotel?"

The pause before he answered was a little too long for Daniel's liking. "No one sent me. It just pissed me off, two outsiders blowing into town like they were the shit. Like us local Joes couldn't get the job done."

"You're lying," Daniel said. "How much do you weigh?"

"What?"

"I asked how much you weigh."

"I dunno, man. Two-eighty-five, two-ninety. What's that got to do with the price of crack in Funkytown."

"Who sent you?"

"No one sent me. Honest. I wouldn't lie to you."

Daniel pried the 9mm out of Big Bobby's fingers, and held it before his wide eyes for maybe a minute before he spoke again. "Sure you would. Now who sent you?"

Big Bobby got to his feet. "No one sent me."

Daniel looked up at him, and said, "How tall are you?"

"What the fuck? Are you fucking nuts?"

"Six-six? Six-seven?"

"I'm six-foot-eight."

"One more time, Big Bobby. Who sent you?"

"No one, man." His voice became a panicked whisper. "I'm telling you. No. One. Sent. Me."

Daniel checked the ejection slide to verify that there was a round in the chamber. Then he turned and headed up the photo-lined stairs toward the bedrooms at the back of the house.

Big Bobby grabbed Daniel's leg. He started to cry, tears rolling down his cheeks in waves. "I . . . I can't." Spit bubbled out of the corners of his mouth. His nose ran. "I . . . I . . . can't say a word. Honest. They'll . . . they'll kill my kid."

Daniel's face was expressionless. No more than a foot from his shoulder was a photo of a little girl riding on her father's back. She was maybe three years old, and a real darling. The doting father was Big Bobby. "And you don't think I will?"

"No," he said. "I . . . I think you'd do me in a heartbeat, maybe even get off on it. But I don't think you have it in you to do my little girl. She's only four . . . years . . . old."

"Dammit," Daniel said.

"Thank you," Big Bobby said. "Thank you."

"Answer me this then," Daniel said. "Is it a cop? Are the cops in any way involved?"

Big Bobby took a series of furtive glances around the empty room then shook his head. "It's not the cops," he whispered. "Not the cops."

After setting the safety on the single-action pistol, Daniel headed back down to the living room and placed it on the coffee table beside the USS Enterprise.

"You still want me to show you what I got?"

Big Bobby nodded, snuffled, and nodded again. "I want that very much," he said.

"I bet you do," Daniel said.

38

Tokunbo placed a Victorian silver-plated tray with foliate border on the George IV mahogany tea table and took a seat opposite David Blake. There was a loaf of rustic, whole-wheat olive bread on the tray, a pair of ogee bowl wine glasses, and a bottle of earthy Italian Sangiovese.

"The last supper?" Blake said.

"Not yet."

"When?"

"Soon."

"You have treated me well, Tokunbo. Better than I expected, or deserved."

The interior of David Blake's lofty cell looked like something straight out of the pages of House & Garden magazine, complete with all the creature comforts: a carved chestnut bed with four hundred thread count Egyptian cotton sheets, a buttery-soft Astoria leather couch, plasma TV, and an eighteenth century wardrobe crammed with the latest Italian fashions. Far from being a jailbird in a gilded cage, Blake was free to come and go as he pleased. He could have flown the coop at any time, but he hadn't. He could have freed the other captives, saving at least four lives in the process, but he hadn't done that either.

"And do you know why I have treated you this way?" Tokunbo said.

"To fan the flames of my guilt," Blake said.

"To an inferno," Tokunbo said.

"Well, it's working. If this goes on much longer I fear I'll spontaneously combust."

Tokunbo dusted a few stray crumbs from his Valentino sweater. "Did you happen to catch the uproar in Marshall's cell the other night?"

"I've never heard anyone scream like that. The sounds he made weren't of this world."

"Earlae assured me that Marshall was dead when Lloyd-"

"He was dead. Or close to it. I was referring to the sounds that strange little rat-faced lad was making."

"He is insane."

"Me, you, him," Blake said. "Each in his own special way."

<u>39</u>

Daniel, Buchanan and Big Bobby Crudup crossed Chenowith Street and entered a narrow trail leading into the thick, dark woods. Big Bobby appeared ready for all out war in his urban commando outfit, a woodland camouflage field jacket, matching cargo pants and black Special Forces Boots. Ten paces in, he extracted a flashlight from one of his many pockets and switched it on. In the glimmer of its LED beam, shadows crouched in pools amid the tangle of heavy brush and close-set trunks, playing tricks on the eyes, and making for treacherous footing. They walked in single file, with Big Bobby leading, winding their way through a maze of forested hills and ravines.

"No matter what happens," Daniel said to Buchanan. "This stays between me and Officer Crudup."

"Is he involved?"

"He can't tell us anything."

"You offer him protection?"

"It wouldn't have made a difference."

"We should at least try."

"He has a daughter, Frank. Just a little older than Charlotte. You've seen what they're capable of. You know what they'd do to her."

"But-"

"He's not going to talk."

"So what the fuck are we doing out here, in the middle of the goddamned woods, in the middle of the goddamned night?"

"What we're doing," Daniel said, "stays between me and Officer Crudup."

"Whatever you say," Buchanan said.

"I mean it, Frank. No reports to Galton or anyone else. And no interference."

A quarter mile later they emerged onto the basketball court of a small high school. The area was deserted, silent save for the shrill cries of the rapacious wind. As they reached center court, a pair of motion activated lights mounted on the roof of the school blinked on.

"Fuck me," Buchanan muttered as Big Bobby shrugged out of his field jacket. Beneath the jacket he was wearing a blue BPD t-shirt with the sleeves cut off. He folded the jacket and walked it over to Buchanan.

"This won't take long," he said.

Too juiced to remain in one place, Daniel began pacing, moving like a ghetto Pit Bull on a chain, kicking up chips of crusted snow each time he changed direction. He hadn't been so seized by an emotion, any emotion, since the night of Julie's death. He could feel the darkness receding as the simmering hostility flared to a white-hot rage.

Big Bobby moved in front of Daniel, stopping him in his tracks, and spat on the ground between them. "You got shit," he said.

Daniel made a bring-it-on motion with his hands.

Big Bobby drew back his sledgehammer fist and let it fly. Daniel took it high on the cheek, turning his head with the blow to divert most of its power. He staggered back a step and dropped to one knee. Behind him, Buchanan gasped. Daniel took the mandatory eight-count then rose calmly to his feet.

"We'll see about that," Daniel said.

Head down, chin tucked into his chest, Big Bobby charged. Daniel spun to one side, landing a reverse side kick on his backside as he rumbled past, sending him sprawling to the ground.

Big Bobby scrambled to his feet, red-faced. "You're a fuckin' dead-"

Daniel danced in, cracked him with a stiff left jab on the nose, and danced back out. Blood started down both of the big man's nostrils.

Big Bobby charged again, his right arm scything around in a giant roundhouse blow. Daniel sidestepped the punch and shot out another jab that snapped his head back, opening a fish hook-shaped gash on his brow. Big Bobby threw another roundhouse right. Daniel moved straight back, feeling a whoosh of air as the follow-up left narrowly missed his head. He stepped back in and hit Big Bobby with a hook to the cheek.

Big Bobby reached out and grabbed Daniel's sweater. Pulling him in against his massive chest, he began to squeeze. As strong as he looked, the reality was that he was even stronger. No matter how hard Daniel struggled, he could not break free. On the verge of blacking out, galaxies whirling about his head, Daniel decided to abandon the Marquis of Queensbury rules and go street on the big man's ass. He pressed his thumbs deep into the other's eye sockets.

Big Bobby let out a yelp of pain. Shifting his grip, he hoisted Daniel over his head then sent him spiraling to the ground.

Daniel landed flat on his back. He sucked in some air. A dozen feet away, his huge hands clenching and unclenching at his sides, a faint smile appeared on Big Bobby's battered, blood-streaked face.

"Get up," Buchanan shouted.

Big Bobby took a running leap. Daniel rolled and a size sixteen boot narrowly missed his head. Big Bobby leaped again. Daniel rolled twice more, pushed with his hands and levered himself upright. He feinted with a straight right that caused the big man to flinch, and then caught him with the real deal, a left uppercut thrown from the knees. Big Bobby grunted loudly, and spit out his two front teeth. Lucky for him, Christmas was just around the corner.

Circling to his left, Daniel began hitting the big man on both eyes with lights-out rights. Big Bobby's left eye was completely closed, and the right eye was closing fast. His barrel chest heaved. He threw a desperation left hook. It was weak, slow. Daniel caught his wrist and ducked nimbly underneath. Using his shoulder as a fulcrum, he yanked down hard. The elbow joint dislocated with a sickening crunch, and ligaments popped. Daniel released the arm and moved back outside, letting his fists fly.

Big Bobby's legs buckled following a Ray Robinson inspired flurry to the head and he pitched face-first onto the ground. On his hands and knees, he vomited blood. Then, with what had to be sheer strength of will, he wobbled to his feet, taking a series of small, staggering steps before finding his equilibrium. His left arm was completely useless, just dangling at his side.

"You destroyed her picture," Daniel said.

Big Bobby looked at him with his one functioning eye, but without comprehension.

Daniel said, "I've got shit?"

Big Bobby spat between them. "You got shit," he said, though with significantly less conviction than before.

In what could only be described as a physical exorcism, pulse in the stratosphere, Daniel launched an all out assault of left hooks and Muay Thai elbows on Big Bobby's right eye, closing it completely, leaving him blind. Then he punched him in the stomach, in the groin, spun him around and punched him in the kidneys and on the back of the neck. Finally, Big Bobby's will was exhausted. He collapsed into an inert heap at the home team's free-throw line.

But Daniel wasn't done.

He stomped down hard on the hand that Big Bobby had used to topple Julie's picture. Over and over he stomped. Then he stomped on the foot that Big Bobby had used to turn it to trash. He heard a sharp cracking sound as the ankle bone gave way.

"Stop it. You're killing him."

Daniel heard Buchanan's voice ringing in his head. Then he felt Buchanan's arms encircle him, dragging him roughly away.

"It was all I had to remember her by," Daniel shouted.

Big Bobby Crudup lay motionless on the ground, the blood-spattered snow trampled for several yards in all directions around him. The white-hot rage was gone. Daniel's head was a roiling cloud of fragmented recollections and jumbled emotions. He closed his eyes and strained to fix his imagination on her face, but the darkness had returned, and he saw nothing.

She was gone, he knew. Her face forever lost to his memory.

For a moment, Daniel stood tall. Then, slowly, languidly, he slumped to his knees.

With an air of detachment, pulse coming back under control, he watched as Buchanan approached Big Bobby, who still wasn't moving. His legs were splayed and one of his ankles was seriously askew. He watched as Buchanan removed a glove and placed two fingers to the big artery in his neck. For a moment, nothing. Then Buchanan looked over at Daniel and nodded.

After calling for an ambulance on the phone he'd found in one of Big Bobby's pockets, Buchanan said, "What the fuck was that?"

Tasting salt, Daniel realized that he was crying. He thumbed the tears from his eyes.

"Step number ten," he said.

<u>40</u>

Tokunbo ascended the ornate cast-iron stairway and activated the intercom to announce his arrival. While he waited to be buzzed inside he cast an appraising glance around the trendy, gentrified neighborhood. Leonard Farmer leased a monk's space in an historic brownstone walkup on Newbury Street in Boston's Back Bay. Newbury Street was only minimally pretentious, with some of the best boutiques and cafes on the east coast. An apt reflection of the ambitious Special Agent's id, he decided. The door buzzed and Tokunbo entered the brownstone.

Leonard met him in the high-ceilinged, wainscoted hallway wearing a dazzling Indigo blue silk kimono. The tightly-belted lingerie was thigh-length, and certainly accentuated the positive, the Special Agent's trim hips and fine sprinter's legs. He greeted Tokunbo with a manner of embrace usually reserved for the nearest and dearest of friends.

"Thank you for agreeing to see me on such short notice," Tokunbo said.

Although it was his first visit to Leonard's home, the décor was exactly as Tokunbo had imagined. Brazen colors on the walls and in the richly symbolic patterns of the Lesghi and Akstafa rugs. A harmonious, eclectic approach to design. What he had accomplished on a civil servant's subsistence-level salary was nothing short of miraculous.

"You like?" Leonard said.

"The Post-Modern movement suits you well."

"Who am I to make judgments?" Leonard said. "As in my dealings with other peoples and cultures, neither do I discriminate when it comes to the various schools of design. I embrace the merits of all styles and periods."

"Well said, Leonard."

The special agent made a courtly gesture toward the Victorian walnut-framed parlor sofa. "I shan't be a moment," he said as he swished across the room, pushing through the saloon-style doors into the adjacent galley kitchen.

Tokunbo sat down on the firm, horse-hair stuffed seat and immediately felt a covetous twinge. The sofa was wonderful, mid-nineteenth-century, with pierced scrolling foliate surround, and delicate yet surprisingly sturdy cabriole legs. It was book-ended by an equally wonderful pair of beech pedestal tables in the style of Emile Jacques Ruhlman, French Deco, early nineteen-twenties.

Leonard returned in short order with a pair of Riedel red wine glasses on a silver-plated service tray. "I picked up a Depardon Fleurie that came highly recommended by a former lover at Justice," he said. "Like you, he's something of a connoisseur." He took a seat on the sofa beside Tokunbo, their thighs brushing. "I hope you won't be disappointed."

Tokunbo swirled the aromatic nectar around in the large Burgundy-style glass before testing its nose. Satisfied, he took the requisite multi-decibel slurp and then swished it thoroughly around in his mouth.

"You like?" Leonard said.

"A masterpiece of violets and ginger and Turkish-delight impishness," Tokunbo said.

Grinning at the compliment, Leonard took a sip from his own glass. "Turkish-delight impishness?" He made a loud smacking sound with his lips. "More casual seduction, I'd have to say."

"Do you know why I requested this meeting?" Tokunbo said.

"I do," Leonard said. "The sentiments expressed by the boorish Mr. Rourke were inexcusable."

"In my professional opinion they were racist and Islamophobic to say the least." Tokunbo set his glass down on the table and made piercing eye contact with Leonard. "If such comments were ever to be made publicly, in jest or otherwise, I shudder to think of the consequences to the Federal Bureau of Investigation's hard-won reputation as a civil rights champion."

"It would be set back by years."

"Decades," Tokunbo said. "Have you a recommendation as to how we should proceed with this matter?"

"A complaint to the Special-Agent-in-Charge would only fall on deaf ears. Now if we were to approach Washington directly . . ."

"Are you suggesting that we contact the Director personally with our concerns?"

"The Bureau and the Republican administration can ill afford another barrage of negative press coverage heading into an election year."

"The hypocrites," Tokunbo said.

Leonard scrunched his eyes shut and lowered his head, looking up after a brief moment of contemplation. "Prepare a notarized transcript of your conversation with Mr. Rourke," he said. "I will forward it under cover of a letter setting out my own concerns with respect to Mr. Rourke and Mr. Buchanan's involvement in this most delicate investigation."

Tokunbo took another sip of wine.

"Excellent," he said.

<u>41</u>

The sound of the telephone rescued Daniel from the suffocating, hateful blackness of his unquiet slumber. He sat bolt upright in bed, rigid and sweating profusely, sucking in huge gulps of air. The luminous red numbers of the nightstand clock read three-twenty in the morning. He fumbled the receiver to his ear.

"Daniel Rourke," he said.

"We got two more. They-"

"Galton?"

"Yeah."

Daniel blinked and tried to orient himself in the darkness. He tossed the wet sheets aside, his heart still pounding, and rolled to his feet. From the bedroom on the far side of the suite, he could hear Buchanan's blissfully ignorant snores.

"Who?"

"George and Marie Taylor."

"How bad?"

He heard Galton take a deep breath and let it out. "Not on the phone."

"Where then? When?"

"I want you and Frank out front of the hotel in two minutes. Ride's on its way as we speak."

***

According to their driver, a chatty, heavyset cop of indeterminate gender named Burke, the crime scene was located inside the decommissioned Charlestown Navy Yard on the spar deck of Old Ironsides, the USS Constitution. As they careened over Charlestown Bridge, top hat flashing, Daniel caught sight of the towering, spot-lighted masts of the mighty ship. No more than a death-defying minute after crossing the bridge, Burke dropped the car into low and kicked the brakes, screeching to a halt on Constitution Road nearest the dock. As they climbed out of the cruiser, Daniel counted five squad cars, two meat wagons, and more than a dozen media trucks parked along the shoulder.

"So much for Galton's discreet investigation," Buchanan mumbled through a long, drawn-out yawn.

Burke escorted Daniel and Buchanan through the scrum of reporters jockeying for position on the long, roped walkway beside the ship. The uniformed cop guarding the entrance nodded a greeting at Burke but otherwise stood his ground.

"They're okay," Burke said.

The cop moved aside.

They found Galton on the upper deck. He was standing over the bodies, scratching his thoughts into a small notebook. The wind whistled an anxious tune while they waited for Galton to finish, and sleet began to fall, small pellets that stung like birdshot. The lights of the city blurred then disappeared completely behind a shimmering lamp lit curtain of white. When he was done scratching, Galton pocketed the notebook then curtly dismissed Burke.

"Kinda gives me the creeps," Buchanan said.

Galton nodded. "It's just not natural for a broad to have a goatee," he said.

Buchanan looked at Galton. "I wasn't talking about Officer Burke." He gestured toward the bodies.

"Oh," Galton said.

George Taylor's corpse was rectally impaled on a small-bore cannon, a clown's smile painted on his face with a creamy, show biz-style makeup. A few feet away, Marie Taylor was sitting cross-legged on a red and white gingham picnic spread that had been stapled to the wood latticework of the main hatch. Her eyes had been plucked from her head, her eyelids peeled back to the hairline. She was dressed in a flowing Daisy Buchanan gown with matching sun hat. The hat was fastened to her skull with four Phillips Hex Head screws. At first glance she appeared to be gazing in wide-eyed adoration at her gaily frolicking husband.

"Fucking clowns," Buchanan said. "I hate 'em. Used to scare the shit outta me as a kid."

"At least we know we're not dealing with the master criminal type," Galton said.

"How's that?" Buchanan said.

"It doesn't take a Mensa IQ to know that the clown is supposed to go inside the cannon." He started with the familiar self-defense smile but was stopped mid-expression by the flash of a nearby camera.

They turned in time to see a male reporter with spiky razor-cut hair standing on the starboard cat-headed anchor boom and peering at them over the ship's bulwarks. Somehow he had scaled the side of the ship to capture the money shot. "Who are these two men Special Agent Galton? And what is their involvement in this case?"

"I want this scene secured," Galton roared. "Now."

"Ten bucks says he's NYT," Daniel said.

"You're on," Galton said.

As soon as a uniformed officer had hauled the reporter over the bulwarks and began to forcibly escort him from the ship, Daniel could hear the tired old freedom of the press bullshit threats being hurled at Galton. An elderly couple, married for forty-seven years with three children and five grandchildren, had been butchered, their corpses violated, and the prick with the hundred dollar haircut had the gall to bitch about his rights being violated. What about the Taylor's rights? What about the rights of the family and friends who would suffer as their loved-ones' corpses were paraded to the world as ghoulish front page fodder?

What could a person have done to deserve such a fate? Daniel wondered. He squatted down in front of the nearest body. George Taylor had died in extreme agony. That much was certain. Behind the insipid painted-on smile, his face was still contorted by his final ghastly scream. The pain he had felt in the final moments of his life was undeniable. His mouth was wide-open and his tongue, colored blue, protruded slightly. The silent scream rang in Daniel's ear. He looked quickly away. He just had to.

"Was there a note?" Daniel said.

Galton handed him a laser printed note inside a clear plastic evidence folder. There was a large hole in the center of the paper. Before Daniel could ask about the origin of the hole, Galton spoke again. "It was stuck to the old lady's chest with a hand-carved ivory dildo," he said. "M.E. says it pierced her heart."

"Hand-carved ivory, huh?" Buchanan said. "You the resident dildo expert, or what?"

"M.E.'s a broad," Galton said. "And she's longtime single."

"Gotcha," Buchanan said.

Although some of the letters were smeared, Daniel was able to read it. "Out of sight, out of mind," he said.

"Same as the note stashed inside Murray's asshole," Buchanan said.

Galton rubbed his temples with his thumbs. "I want you two to go back to your hotel and order up a couple pots of strong coffee. I'll get there as soon as I can and we'll brainstorm. All night long if we have to." He turned his glacially cold gaze toward Daniel and Buchanan, his teeth bared. "This shit has gotta stop."

42

"Before I forget," Galton said as he entered their suite, "you were bang on about there being two perps."

"The cigar," Daniel said.

Galton tossed a thick accordion folder onto the coffee table. "DNA in the saliva didn't match the cum-shots."

"You test it for race?" Daniel said.

Galton shook his head.

"Why not? LAPD used it on a serial rape case I worked a few years back. Six UCLA girls raped and beaten to within an inch of their lives. No witnesses. Plenty of DNA evidence though. But thanks to the profile you guys prepared, the cops spent a month been looking for the stereotypical white guy. When public pressure got too much for them they ran a test called DNAWitness and it turned out the rapist wasn't white at all. Not even close. The guy they should have been looking for was eighty-five percent sub-Saharan, twelve percent European and three percent Native American."

"They get the prick?"

"It turned out they had his DNA on file from an earlier conviction – rape, of course - and they picked him up the same afternoon the results came back."

"Nice," Galton said.

"Not really. Had they run the test right away they would have spared five girls the trauma."

"VICAP is standing by their profile."

"Why guess when you can know?"

"Why do you think?"

Daniel made a face. "So how'd Farmer handle the news? The fact that I was right."

"He called it beginner's luck. But I could tell he was pissed."

"Pissed that he hadn't caught it first."

"Yeah."

"Speaking of Farmer," Daniel said. "Where is the sanctimonious little twerp?"

Galton shrugged. "He was paged four hours ago. Same as me."

"I kind of missed his antics back at the ship," Daniel said. "Comic relief goes a long way in a case like this."

"That much he's good for."

"Okay, okay, so there are two of them," Buchanan said. "We've confirmed it. And judging by recent events there appears to be a widening rift between them."

"So you guy's still think Mr. Cool is losing control of his partner," Galton said.

"Why else would the crazy fuck do the last snatch solo?" Buchanan said.

"It certainly appears crazy," Daniel said.

"You believe there's a method to the madness," Galton said.

"Let's start with the bodies," Daniel said.

"They were on display," Buchanan said. "Arranged like an Andrew Lloyd Webber adaptation of *American Psycho*."

"Meant to be seen," Galton said.

Daniel stood and began to pace the room. "The notes read 'Out of Sight, Out of Mind,' yet the killers prominently display the bodies. Meaning for them to be found. Hoping they will cause a media sensation."

"In sight, in mind," Buchanan said.

"Makes sense," Galton said. "This time it was the press, not the cops, who were tipped. An editor from the Globe called BPD two full minutes after their guy was *en route*."

"So what they're trying to say, their message, is here for us to see," Daniel said, looking at the multi-angle photos of the three murder victims. "All we have to do is open our eyes."

"There are definitely sexual overtones," Galton said. "You think our guy's some kind of super perv?"

"More than likely," Daniel said. "But his appetites are only incidental. It wouldn't explain the notes, would it?" Even as he spoke the words the answer appeared as a wraith on the shadowy fringe of Daniel's mind. But each time he tried to bring it into focus, it would drift just out of sight.

"No," Galton said. "I guess it wouldn't."

When Daniel couldn't quite shake the feeling that he was onto something, he decided to change the subject, to let his brain toy with the problem on a subconscious level. "What do you have on Banks?" he said. "He's the wild card in all this. I suspect the fact that he doesn't fit the profile will tell us more about the case than anything else."

Galton pulled three stapled sets of documents from the folder. "His rap sheet." He handed one copy each to Daniel and Buchanan. "In and out of the joint since the age of fifteen. Arrested and convicted for robbery, theft, pimping, pornography - kiddie stuff mostly - rape, kidnapping, money laundering. You name it and he's tried it at least once."

"Any connections to the missing men? Known associates?"

"Nothing yet. But we're working on it."

"You'll let us know as soon as you hear anything?" Daniel said.

Galton nodded. "Oh, and before I forget," he said to Daniel, "you wanna tell me what happened?"

"What do you mean?"

"The black eye, the bruises on your knuckles. What the hell happened?"

"I was assaulted."

"You report it to the proper authorities?"

Daniel jerked a thumb at Buchanan, who suddenly didn't look so hot, with a complexion approaching the spooky, blanched potato whiteness of a post-Thriller Michael Jackson. "Yeah, he said. "I told a cop."

Galton removed another, albeit thicker, set of documents from the folder. "I've got copies of the personnel records you asked for. Everyone who had contact with Blake's computer is in here, from the first BPD officer on the scene all the way along the chain of evidence to me and Farmer." Galton gave Daniel the dead-man's stare. "The first officer on the scene was one Robert Crudup."

Daniel said nothing.

"Funny thing is Officer Crudup never showed up for work today."

"What's so funny about that?" Daniel said.

"What's funny is he claims he was assaulted, too. The guy's apparently a real mess, but he refuses to name names, or press charges. You wouldn't know anything about that would you?"

"Crudup, Crudup," Daniel said. "Doesn't ring a bell."

"Sure it doesn't," Galton said. "Just let me know if you stumble across anything that's not on the level with this guy. If he's involved, or if anyone else in these documents is involved, I wanna take him down personally, hard, and permanently."

"Will do," Daniel said.

When Galton was gone, Daniel said, "You look like you've seen a spook. What's up?"

"Not a spook," Buchanan said. "More a demon from the past." He snatched up his coat from the back of the couch and put it on. "In the morning I'm gonna give you the low-down on Uncle Billy."

Daniel motioned toward the clock on the wall. "It's morning now," he said.

"Not just yet," Buchanan said. "There's something I gotta do first." He looked at Daniel without seeing him, his eyes focused somewhere else. "Someone I gotta see."

"It's about the case, isn't it?" Daniel said.

"Yeah it is," Buchanan said. Then he practically sprinted out the door.

<u>**43**</u>

At precisely seven forty-five in the morning Daniel was roused from his bed by a roly-poly Hispanic police sergeant and escorted to FBI headquarters for an emergency meeting with The Big Kahuna. The sergeant led Daniel to an office with wide double doors then walked away without so much as a throwaway *hasta la vista*. Daniel knocked once before stepping inside. Galton, Farmer, and two men Daniel didn't know, one white, one black, were sitting on high-back leather chairs around a large mahogany desk. A copy of the New York Times sat folded in half on the desktop in front of them. Farmer had the look of a cat that had eaten a roost of canaries. That look, coupled with the uncharacteristically calm expression on Galton's face, left Daniel feeling decidedly uneasy.

One of the men Daniel didn't know, the white one, moved around from behind the desk and gripped Daniel's hand tightly. "Patrick Reagan," he said. "Special Agent in Charge. Good of you to come so quickly."

The Boston Field Office head exuded intensity. He was bald and broad-shouldered, with large, square hands that looked as though he had actually worked for a living before taking up the desk. He reminded Daniel of District Attorney Charles Burley, his old boss back in Los Angeles, a hard-ass, no bullshit kind of guy, who took a long time to get to know, but to know him was to love him.

"Daniel Rourke. And it's not a problem, sir."

"Where's Detective Buchanan?"

Daniel shrugged.

"Have a seat," Reagan said.

"If it's all the same to you, I think I'll stand."

"Suit yourself."

"So what's up?" Daniel said.

The black man cleared his throat. "My name is Antwan Patton and I am here on behalf of the USDOJCRS." Daniel's blank stare caused the man to unfurl the lengthy acronym. "The United States Department of Justice, Community Relations Service."

"Oh-oh," Daniel said. "The PC Police. Someone's in deep doodoo."

Patton made a loud hissing noise through his amply gapped front teeth. "PC Police," he said with more than a measure of disdain. "The USDOJCRS is the Federal government's peacemaker for community conflicts and tensions arising from differences of race, color, ethnicity, religion and national origin. It was established by the Civil Rights Act of 1964 to assist State and local governments, private and public organizations, and community groups with resolving racial and ethnic tensions. In a nutshell, it uses impartial mediation practices and conflict resolution procedures to resolve problems and restore stability."

"Wow," Daniel said. "I bet you can't say that three times fast."

"I am not here as a foil for your childish banter," Patton said. "I'm here in response to a formal written complaint alleging that you uttered racist and anti-Islamic slurs."

"You're joking."

"I do not joke about such serious allegations."

"I assume you're speaking of my meeting with Shabazz."

"Mr. Shabazz. I am, Mr. Rourke."

"During that meeting I debated the concept of affirmative action with a willing participant, and made an offhand remark referring to Islam as the religion of peace and tolerance."

"It was the mocking tone with which you uttered the remark that was deemed offensive."

"May I be frank with you, Mr. Patton?"

"Please."

"The truth is your office is nothing more than a glorified make work project for a small group of untalented, underachieving loudmouths. I much prefer the way men and women of common sense worked your mandate in the good old days."

"Lynchings, Mr. Rourke?"

"Sticks and stones, Mr. Patton."

"Enough," Reagan said.

"This has all been wonderfully surreal," Daniel said, starting for the door. "But if there's nothing else . . ."

"As a matter of fact," Farmer said, "there is something else." He snatched the paper from the table and tossed it at Daniel.

"Who are these two men?" Daniel said, echoing the bold-faced front page query. The accompanying photograph showed Daniel and Buchanan looking down at George and Marie Taylor's mutilated corpses. The caption beneath the photograph gave their names and listed their status as unaccredited outsiders working with the FBI: Frank Buchanan, an LAPD cop on leave from his duties, and Daniel Rourke, an author of risqué crime fiction who had exited the Los Angeles District Attorney's office under highly questionable circumstances. The tone of the article was critical of their involvement in the investigation.

"What do you have to say for yourself?" Farmer said.

Daniel looked at Galton and held out his hand. "I was right about the reporter with the fancy haircut."

Galton plucked a pair of fives from his wallet and passed them to Daniel. "A bet's a bet," he said.

"Do you realize how this makes the administration of justice in Massachusetts look?" Farmer said.

"Like the good guys are doing everything possible to bring the bad guys to justice," Daniel said. "That's how it looks to me."

"Not to the Chairman and Publisher of the New York Times, it doesn't."

"At the risk of sounding impertinent," Daniel said, "who gives a damn what he, she or it thinks."

"It?" Farmer said. "Now you really are being impertinent."

"There was a rather pithy article in The American Conservative a few years back that featured a workplace diversity survey that the New York Times had distributed to its employees. Under the gender category they listed three choices: male, female, and transgender – otherwise known to the vast majority of the populace as-"

"An it," Galton said.

When an indignant Patton started to open his mouth, Daniel said, "Just add it to the list."

"To return to the issue at hand," Farmer said. "What the Chairman and Publisher of the nation's most influential newspaper thinks does, in fact, matter."

"Bullshit," Daniel said. "Our involvement makes perfect sense. Interested parties working together for the common goal of justice."

"What you see as cooperation," Farmer said, "we see as interference."

"Toe-may-toe, toe-maw-toe," Daniel started.

"And I'm calling the whole thing off," Reagan broke in. "I must admit, Mr. Rourke, that I was initially opposed to your involvement in this investigation. But Galton here was an effective advocate of your cause, and against my better judgment, I relented. In light of today's headline, however, and the scorching heat I'm now taking from the higher-ups in DC, it's a decision I've come to regret dearly."

"I told you so," Farmer muttered to Galton.

Reagan gave Farmer the thousand yard stare. "Let me say straight out that the CSR complaint is bullshit. It's got no teeth and it goes no further than this room. The headline, however, concerns me. Traitor paper or not, it makes my office look like a bunch of bush-leaguers, enlisting aid not from other law enforcement agencies, but from private citizens. Although we have done nothing wrong, the article raises an appearance of impropriety." He took a deep breath and let it out slowly. "As of this moment you are officially out of the loop. Any paperwork that you have received from the Bureau will be returned to my attention forthwith. Have I made my position clear?"

"Am I free to leave?"

"You are, Mr. Rourke. And please convey the gist of this meeting to Mr. Buchanan, as well as my deepest sympathy."

Daniel paused in the doorway, turning back to face Reagan. "Before I leave I have two questions for Detective Farmer," he said.

"Two questions? I see no problem with that," Reagan said. "Do you Special Agent?" And everyone in the room knew by the force of his words that Farmer had no choice but to consent.

Farmer shook his head slowly. "Of course not." Through clenched teeth, he added, "*Sir.*"

Daniel made eye contact with Farmer. "Where were you last night? In Washington, perhaps? Setting this whole farce in motion?" Farmer's red face provided Daniel with ample confirmation of his hunch.

"Unlike you and your partner in crime I play by the rules," Farmer said. "They exist to ensure that no person's constitutional rights are violated for any reason, especially for such antiquated notions of justice that you and your type seem to so desperately cling to. No one is above the law, Mr. Rourke. No one."

"And your second question?" Reagan said.

"When you have the sniffles, Special Agent Farmer, and reach for something to blow your nose, which do you prefer, Kleenex or Charmin?"

Galton laughed, and the Special Agent in Charge maybe even snickered a little.

"Get the hell out of my sight, you insensitive bastard," Farmer roared.

"Temper, temper," Reagan said, a ghost of a smile still on his lips.

Yeah, under different circumstances, Daniel could definitely get to like the man.

44

Daniel and Buchanan settled into an empty booth of a greasy spoon on Salem Street in Boston's predominantly Italian North End. Buchanan didn't appear ready to talk and Daniel reluctantly chose not to press the matter. The Detroit-born, Massachusetts-based frontrunner for the Republican nomination was scheduled for a nine o'clock photo op a stone's throw away at The Paul Revere House and the usual Looney Tunes were out in protest, wailing for substance, forcing the morning rush hour traffic to a bitter standstill. Daniel watched from his window seat as a group of angry marchers passed by chanting rhymey-dimey pro-choice and anti-death penalty rhetoric in the same breath, oblivious to the irony of their positions. Next came a group of camo-clad peaceniks who halted the protest to kick the collective asses of the boisterous environmentalists behind them whom they felt were generating just a little too much noise pollution. All the while Buchanan said nothing, and Daniel continued to bite his tongue.

Their haggard waitress, wearing white leather duty shoes and black support hose, eventually limped over and aborted the pregnant silence between them by announcing in a loud put-upon tone that the special of the day was a heaping platter of home fries, bacon and sausage, served with a side order of buttered toast. The badge on her uniform read Faith.

"Death by breakfast," Daniel said. "I'll pass."

Buchanan made a peace sign. "Two coffees," he said.

The waitress reached deep into the stiff, bottle-blonde hair piled three-stories high on her head and extracted a pencil. "Anything else, Mr. Rockefeller?"

"No," Buchanan said. "Thank you."

She scratched their order into a small notepad and limped back the way she had come.

Daniel kept glancing at Buchanan, waiting, until finally he said, "Sometimes it's best to spit it out. Once you get a little momentum going, it's easy."

"You feel like spilling your guts about Julie first, Dr. Phil? Just to show me how it's done."

"Touché," Daniel said.

"Sometimes it helps to talk things through," Buchanan said, "and sometimes it doesn't. I didn't come home last night because I went to see Aunt Sarah. I told her everything. And for your information, it wasn't easy, and it didn't get any easier once I'd started. It also didn't help things any. If I didn't think it was relevant to the investigation, I'd have never brought it up in the first place."

"What is it, Frank?"

"Look, I don't want you judging me is all."

"I won't judge you," Daniel said.

Buchanan chuckled. "You've been doing it since you got here. Why should I believe you're gonna stop anytime soon?"

Daniel said nothing. He decided to give the matter some serious thought before responding.

Finally, Buchanan shrugged. "My uncle was a twisted bastard," he said. "I mean, not always. After my folks died he was great. Until that fucked-up Saturday night in my tree fort out back of the house that he-"

Faith suddenly appeared at their table with two mugs of coffee and a plate of dairy creamers. She slammed their order down and left without saying a word.

Motionless on his side of the cracked Formica tabletop, Daniel waited as Buchanan stirred generous portions of cream and sugar into his coffee. His hands were big and thick, his fingernails chewed down to the quick.

"We were in the Portsmouth house on vacation. I'd just finished grade six and it was the perfect summer day. It started with a kiss. I . . . I knew it was wrong, but I thought-

"Shit, I don't know what I thought. He was my new dad, right? When it went beyond a kiss, that's when I knew it was fucked up. I was only twelve, but I knew. Still, a part of me couldn't help but think that maybe I'd asked for it. Deserved it even."

Buchanan took a sip of coffee but his eyes never left Daniel's. Daniel had to will himself not to look away from the fear and confusion in his friend's face.

"Do you know what's worse?"

Daniel shook his head. He really didn't know. What could possibly be worse?

"There's still a piece of me feels that way even now." He took another sip of coffee. "He was a twisted bastard, all right.

"Aunt Sarah was sick even then. The MS had just been diagnosed and she wasn't coping real well. I couldn't tell her. He was all that she had and she needed him. So I decided it was best for all concerned if I just . . . just disappeared. I figured if I was the root of the problem and I left, maybe the problem would resolve itself. Maybe he'd straighten out with me gone. Return his attention to Aunt Sarah. She needed him more than she ever needed me."

"Jesus, Frank."

"We all have our demons, right? Well, Uncle Billy was mine. And here I am trying to rescue his sorry excuse for an ass."

"Have you seen him since?"

Buchanan shook his head. "I confronted him over the phone shortly after joining the force. At first he denied anything had even happened. He only admitted it after I threatened to go public. He said he'd made a terrible mistake, and that it'd kill Aunt Sarah if the sins of the past were ever to be dredged up. He swore he'd gone for counseling and that it had never happened again."

"Did you believe him?"

"You've prosecuted your fair share of baby rapers," Buchanan said. "What do you think?"

"Pedophilia has the highest rate of recidivism of any crime. Abusers don't stop. They just move on to their next victim. They cannot be rehabilitated. There is no known cure. Only death will stop them."

"Uh-huh."

Finally, Daniel was able to make the connection that had eluded him during their meeting with Galton the previous night. "It all makes a warped kind of sense," he said. "Now."

"Fucking obvious, isn't it?"

"But we're going to need proof. Suspicions aren't enough. Not with this class of people. No one would believe us."

"What do you recommend?"

"Packing our things and heading back to sunny California."

"Believe me, there's nothing more I'd like to do. But I gave my word to Aunt Sarah."

"Then we head back to the crime scenes. We learned bubkes the first time around because we were looking for evidence to establish the abductors' identities. This time we'll be looking for evidence of the abductees' dirty little secrets."

"But we've been shut out of the investigation," Buchanan said.

"It's still a free country," Daniel said. "They can't stop us, say, from socializing with one of the victims' daughters. And if she should decide to let us into her father's house . . ."

Buchanan lowered his eyes.

"You're blushing, Frank. You're actually blushing."

"Okay, okay," Buchanan said. "You get off my back, I'll give her a call."

Daniel smiled. "And what we talked about just now? It goes to the grave."

"Thanks, pal."

45

"So how did it go?" Daniel said, tapping on the walls of Marshall Thomas's walk-in closet.

"How'd what go?" Buchanan said, stepping into the immense suit-lined room.

"You're blushing again."

"We have a date, okay? Things cool down some we're going out for coffee and cheesecake."

Daniel began to sing, "Frank and Eunice up in a tree, K-I-S-S-I-N-G. First comes love then comes-"

Daniel never got to mention the 'M' word, because at precisely that moment he felt Buchanan's 9mm being pressed into his palm.

"I want you to hold onto this for me," Buchanan said.

"What for?"

"Because if you don't there's a fairly decent chance I'll end up shooting you with it. That's what for."

Grinning broadly, Daniel tucked the sleek Sig-Sauer into the waistband of his jeans. "'Nuff said."

"You find anything?" Buchanan said.

"No false walls. No secret compartments. Nothing. You?"

"Sweet dick all. What next, Einstein?"

"Study," Daniel said.

Marshall Thomas's study housed a large desk, leather couch, and a home theatre system that retailed for only a few thousand more than a starter home in the 'burbs. The room was decorated with wainscoted walls of darkly stained mahogany, polished brass wall sconces and a museum-quality collection of antiques. With the drapes tied back, the pair of large bay windows offered a sweeping vista of the broad back lawn. Although it was only three in the afternoon, the sun was nowhere to be seen and the sky was the color of dull chrome.

"Doesn't it strike you as odd," Daniel said, "that the man has a state-of-the-art TV, stereo and High-Def DVD player, yet there are no movies to be found anywhere in the house?"

"Unless they're the type of flicks he doesn't want anybody to see," Buchanan said.

"Exactly what I was thinking," Daniel said.

Dusk was edging into night by the time they located Thomas's private stash. One of the wainscoted panels was hinged and when tricked open revealed a half-dozen home-made DVDs and an envelope bound by several elastic bands. One of the brittle bands snapped and skittered across the room as Daniel slid out a stack of Polaroids. Daniel held up the first photo.

"I need a drink," Buchanan said.

He crossed the room to the wet bar, poured two fingers of Jack Daniel's, which he downed, then immediately poured another two.

"You want a slug?"

Daniel shook his head. "I'm putting on the DVDs."

To the mirror behind the bar, Buchanan said, "Why the fuck not?"

Daniel popped the first disc into the player and settled into the big comfy couch to watch the show. Buchanan set his drink down on the side table next to the remote control and the box of tissues and took a seat beside him.

The first scene had obviously been downloaded from the internet and featured several small Asian boys being violated and degraded in a variety of ways by several small Asian men. Throughout the assault the infinitely gentle, infinitely suffering children made faint kitten sounds. Although the strange mewing in and of itself was negligible, it nonetheless drove itself into Daniel's brain like a sonic spike.

When one of the men finished desecrating his child he tossed him to the floor, gave the camera the thumbs-up, and exited stage left. Leaning against an unmade, fold-away cot in the center of the room, hands laced over his knees, the boy stopped mewing and began to rock gently back and forth, sobbing softly to himself. A slow-moving, bed-headed man with pimples on his shoulders loped into the scene with one hand over his eyes and a buck-toothed grin on his face. The man spread his fingers, peered through the cracks at the sobbing boy, and giggled. Catching sight of the man, the boy scrambled up and over the cot like a crab, backing toward the wall, smearing a trail of red on the rumpled sheets. Still giggling, the man with the buck teeth and the shoulder pimples followed him.

Daniel reached over Buchanan, snatched up the remote control and punched forward scan. It was the only way he could stomach watching any more of the disc, and even then just barely. He tried to find the appropriate word to describe what he was witnessing, but couldn't come up with a single candidate, couldn't come up with a word that came close. He doubted such a word even existed. The only thing he didn't doubt was that Eric Murray and George and Marie Taylor, as gruesome as their murders had been, hadn't got what they deserved at all.

"They deserved worse," Buchanan whispered, as if he had been eavesdropping on Daniel's thoughts.

"You sure you don't want to just pack it up and head home?"

"I told you I made a promise to Aunt Sarah."

"She still wants him found?"

"Didn't tell me she didn't."

"Too bad."

"Yeah."

When they had scanned their way through the last of the discs, Daniel turned to Buchanan. "What you said at the diner about me judging you, you were right."

Buchanan's jaw tightened. "Go on."

"Although I can't begin to understand what you suffered through as a child, you are without a doubt the most honorable man I have ever known, and I am proud to call you my friend."

Buchanan reached over and touched Daniel on the arm. "Ditto," he said.

Unlike the DVDs, the seventeen photographs inside the envelope were not of small, frightened Asian boys. For the most part they were of small, frightened New England boys. Several of them still had on their skates and their hockey jerseys as they orally gratified their coach inside the Home Team's locker room. The final photograph in the stack was the most revealing. It depicted a group of naked men watching several severely handicapped, dark-skinned children in various states of undress. David Blake was in the group, brandishing a video camera. Ira Banks was also there, beer and a cigarette in one hand, half-mast erection in the other. The identities of the other four men, however, could not be ascertained. Two were facing away from the camera and the heads of the other two, the men closest to the camera, were cropped at the shoulders.

Buchanan pointed to one of the closest men. He had skinny legs and a protruding belly covered with irregular tufts of grey hair. "You can't see his face," he said, "but that's Uncle Billy."

"Okay," Daniel said, "I think we know the why of it, now we need to find out the who. Any ideas on where we go from here?"

"You think you're up for a little undercover work?"

"What do you have in mind?"

Buchanan grinned wickedly. "Two weeks to Christmas," he said. "I think it's high time we got into the holiday spirit and donned-"

"Our gay apparel," Daniel said.

<u>46</u>

Daniel couldn't locate a public parking space close to Governor Thornton's Mt. Vernon Street address. According to the dog-eared tourist brochure that Buchanan was prone to leave beside their toilet, Beacon Hill had been designed more than two centuries earlier to satisfy an old Puritan dilemma, being both a part of, and apart from, the surrounding metropolis. Despite the passage of time, precious little had changed. Resident parking permits were a posted requirement, and given the platoon of testosterone-jacked, uber-lesbian meter maids scouring the curbs for non-resident violators, Daniel decided that the odds of being ticketed and/or towed and/or castrated were just too high. He aimed his car toward the nearest exit, beeped twice at a meter maid who bore more than a passing resemblance to 80's wrestling phenom Randy 'Macho Man' Savage, and headed north.

Several minutes later, Daniel found an empty meter, and he and Buchanan set out. Luckily, it was a perfect day for a hike. The sky was cobalt blue, and the quiescent air was brisk without being biting. Three blocks south the din of the modern city began to fade as they re-entered Beacon Hill, a quiet, affluent community of red brick and cobblestone, secret gardens, brick sidewalks, and gas-lit streets.

"Let's cut through there," Daniel said, pointing toward a tasteful, hand-painted sign that read Louisburg Square.

The Square was a small rectangle of yellow grass and leafless trees surrounded by a cobblestone plaza and gently rippling bow-front townhouses. They were almost through the park when the door to one of the townhouses blew open and John Kerry came charging out in a hooded, hoop-skirt length parka. In his hands was a box kite printed in the likeness of the American flag. Several reporters followed him out the door, cameras rolling.

The dour-faced senator slid to a stop between the statues of Aristide the Just and Christopher Columbus then proceeded to make a droning, on-air statement. Almost as soon as he had begun, however, he was interrupted by Teresa Heinz-Kerry. She was standing on the steps of their home in a rather smart navy pantsuit, waving a pair of gloves over her head. "John Forbes Kerry," she cawed, "you get back here this instant. You'll catch your death."

A glum, slump-shouldered Kerry headed back home for his gloves.

"Isn't it a little late in the year for kites?" Buchanan said.

"A day late and a dollar short," Daniel said. "As usual."

Exiting the park, they turned left onto Mt. Vernon, heading toward Thornton's imposing, Federal-style mansion. The red brick façade consisted of four bays with recessed arches on the first floor, and three bays with engaged Corinthian pilasters on the second and third floors. The roof was hipped with jet-black slate shingles.

"It kind of suits the old Brahmin," Daniel said.

"The old what?" Buchanan said.

"Do you think he'll see us?"

"Anytime, anywhere, the governor promised. He'll see us."

Daniel puckered his lips and made a loud kissy-face sound.

Upon passing through the mansion's grand front entrance, they were wanded by a multicultural trio of secret service agents. Buchanan checked his piece, and one of the agents (Laotian?) escorted the duo up the broad, carpeted stairway to the second floor. The governor's personal secretary, a Miss Mathers, was perched behind an Edwardian writing desk on the marble tiled landing. She had a Farrah Fawcett hairdo and a shade of blush on her cheeks that reminded Daniel of the swollen rump of a Mandrill he'd once seen at the San Diego Zoo. Her meager, painted lips were pursed and totally devoid of smile lines. She was the governor's gate keeper and it was a role she obviously relished.

"Do you have an appointment?" she rasped in a voice ravaged by years of cigarette smoking.

"We do not," Daniel said.

"Buchanan and Rourke," Buchanan said. "Tell the governor we're here. He said we had an open invite."

The secretary picked up the phone and had words with Thornton. "In the future I suggest you make an appointment," she said as she slammed the receiver down. "No appointment, no meeting."

"Is he going see us or not?" Daniel said.

He took the full force of Miss Mathers' dagger-death stare without wincing. "The governor will see you. This time." She pointed to her left with a nicotine stained index finger. "He's through that door."

Buchanan scraped his shoes on a hedgehog-shaped boot brush before entering the governor's inner sanctum. Daniel did not. The study was burgundy, with plenty of darkly stained trim, and a burgundy leather couch and chairs. The governor was seated behind a desk the size of a battleship, with his secret service protection head, Raymond Sowell, standing close by. They were watching a wall-mounted LCD television and laughing uproariously.

"Have you . . . you fellows seen this yet?" Thornton said.

One of the local news channels was running a live feed from Louisburg Square. On screen, the gangly six-foot-four inch senator was galloping up and down the park, dragging the limp kite behind him. Periodically, he would leap awkwardly into the air as if that motion would somehow carry the kite aloft.

"We caught the first act on the way here," Daniel said.

Tears were streaming down the governor's face, and he had to take several deep breaths before he could speak again. "He's not . . . not even seeking . . . the nomination this time around. So what's with the . . . the photo-op?"

"Probably angling for the VP slot," Daniel said.

"He sends any . . . any feelers my way, you know what I'm going to tell him?"

Although Buchanan was shaking his head, grinning in anticipation, Daniel knew exactly what was coming next.

"To go fly a kite," the governor said.

"Chris Rock couldn't have come up with that one," Daniel said.

Thornton swiped the tears from his eyes. "He's windsurfed for the press, snowboarded, played tennis and electric guitar. All badly, of course. But this . . . this one takes the cake. It makes him look even wackier than that time he was photographed in that . . . that bunny suit at the Kennedy Space Center. You guys remember that one?"

"If you ask me," Daniel said, "those early '70's pics with Hanoi Jane were worse."

"Turn . . . it . . . off," the governor said to Sowell. "Can't breathe. Can't . . . take it . . . anymore."

Sowell flicked the television off.

The governor lowered his head and took several deep breaths. When he looked up again he was all business. "Now what can I do for you?"

Daniel looked askance at Sowell.

"Raymond and I have no secrets," the governor said. "You may speak candidly."

"I want to know why you fired Marshall Thomas. No 'private matter between friends' bullshit this time."

Thornton grew red in the face. "I've told you all that I-"

"No more bullshit," Daniel said.

"Why now?" Sowell said.

"Some new evidence has come to light," Buchanan said.

The governor shook his head. "I told Raymond you two were sharp." He glanced at Sowell. "Didn't I tell you that?"

Daniel took a step closer to Thornton. "So you knew all along and you said nothing?"

"I received an anonymous e-mail a month or so back. There were pictures, and a ghastly home movie. Dear God, they were just children, innocent children."

"The governor thought it was a crude attempt at blackmail," Sowell said.

"Was it?"

"It took some time, but I managed to trace the e-mail back to Thomas himself. And it wasn't blackmail at all. He was file-sharing with some of his internet chat room buddies and the governor's private e-mail address was inadvertently included."

"You went to the police?" Daniel said.

"Governor Thornton wanted to. He wanted the whole sordid thing to be made public. But I talked him out of it."

"Now why would you do that?"

Sowell looked over at Thornton with narrowed eyes. "The governor's done a lot of good for a lot of people. No matter how it trickled down, the scandal would have tainted him. Killed him politically."

Daniel had the sense that there was more to it than that but let it go. For the moment. "So you had him fire Thomas instead," he said.

The governor nodded. "I agreed not to go public if he sought professional help."

"And did he?" Buchanan said.

"I set up an appointment with the finest psychiatrist in the state. Raymond kept tabs on him. He never missed a session."

"Until his disappearance," Daniel said.

"Correct," Sowell said.

"Why didn't you inform the cops about the e-mail after he disappeared?" Buchanan said.

"Because," Thornton said, "we had no reason to believe that his disappearance was in any way connected to his, uh . . . orientation."

"Orientation?" Daniel said.

"You know what I meant."

"What if I were to tell you we now have evidence which strongly suggests that his disappearance was, in fact, connected?" Daniel said.

The governor appeared only momentarily startled. "What have you discovered?"

"Evidence," Daniel said.

"What sort of evidence?"

Daniel said nothing, and motioned for Buchanan to do the same. It was an old lawyer trick. Stay silent long enough, and the witness would invariably start talking again. Elaborating. Filling the uncomfortable silence. But Thornton did not bite right away. At least not with words.

Eventually, the governor bowed his head.

In shame, Daniel thought. On a hunch, he said, "But you knew that already, didn't you?"

Thornton nodded somberly. "I put two and two together when that Native American fellow went missing. He was a pornographer, you know. A lousy child pornographer."

"You're going to have to go to the feds, sir," Buchanan said. "There's no choice anymore. You're going to have to tell them everything."

"Once again," Sowell said, "we're one step ahead of you."

"How so?" Daniel said.

"As soon as we suspected Thomas's taste for human veal was tied to his abduction, the governor and I paid an off-the-books, after hours visit to the FBI."

"Galton never mentioned it," Daniel said.

Sowell smirked. "That's hardly surprising, seeing as how you've been ousted from the investigation."

"And there's been no mention of it in the press," Buchanan said.

"The Special Agent in Charge and I go way back," Sowell said. "For the sake of the families of the missing men and women, he's agreed to exercise the utmost discretion when it comes to the nature of the information that gets released for public consumption."

"There's no reason that the innocent should suffer along with the guilty," the governor added. "I have it on good authority that you've made quite the impression on Eunice Thomas, Frank. Surely you cannot fault us for the way in which the press is being managed."

"She is an amazing lady," Buchanan said.

"Now what did you find?" the governor said.

Daniel smiled. "We just put the evidence together like you did," he said. "Two plus two equals four, right?"

"And if you were to find any direct evidence . . . ?" the governor said.

"Of course, we'd turn it over to the proper authorities." *Eventually.*

"Which would be a whole lot easier to do if we were allowed back into the FBI's case," Buchanan said.

The governor raised his hands. "If it was up to me," he said, "you'd not only be in, you'd be running the show. But it's not. It's Washington's decision." He smiled his on the campaign trail smile. "Now if you were to ask me again in thirteen or fourteen months . . ."

"Is that all for today?" Sowell said.

Buchanan looked at Daniel, who nodded. "That's it," he said.

Daniel ran his hand over the top of the governor's desk. "Nice," he said.

"It's okay," Thornton said.

47

Galton was pacing holes in the carpet outside their Boston Harbor suite when Daniel and Buchanan returned from Beacon Hill.

"What's up?" Buchanan said.

"I wanted you to hear the news from me," Galton said.

"It's my uncle," Buchanan said. "You've found-"

"Inside," Galton said.

Daniel key-carded the door and the trio entered the suite. They left their coats and their shoes on. No one made a move to sit down. Galton closed the door.

"Out with it," Buchanan said.

"It's not your uncle," Galton said.

All the color drained from Buchanan's face. "Hell, no," he gasped.

"Monica Little contacted Gloucester PD approximately thirty minutes ago," Galton said. "She said she'd come home from the bank to find her front door open, wide open, your aunt gone."

"Maybe she snuck out for a snack or something. It's still early."

Galton shook his head. "Her upended wheelchair was discovered by a patrol officer in the sitting room. And there was something else-"

"Out with it," Buchanan said. "What else did they find?"

"They left a note."

"What's it say?"

"That you and Daniel are to head for home on the first available flight."

"And if we don't?"

"Note says she'll be dead by morning."

"Let's go," Buchanan said. "I wanna view the crime scene."

"You know I would if I could," Galton said. "But you're out of the case."

"That's bullshit," Buchanan said. "You know what's going on here. You know the real reason we're out."

"Yeah, I know the reason. But it changes nothing."

"Then take a hike. I want to be alone."

"Sure, I'll go. But as soon as I hear anything, anything at all, I'll be in touch." With a lingering sympathetic look back, Galton left the suite, closing the door quietly behind him.

"Your call, Frank," Daniel said.

"It's all my fault. Those bastards must have tailed me last night."

"Which means they're watching us."

"Yeah."

"And they wouldn't be watching us unless we were doing something right."

"Yeah."

"What do you want to do?"

"Exactly what they want us to do. Catch the first flight outta town."

"And then?"

"We double back. Follow through with our original plan."

"If we play our cards right this could actually work to our favor."

"Agreed," Buchanan said.

"Do you mind if we make a quick pit stop on the way back?"

"Quick being the operative word," Buchanan said.

Daniel nodded. "When you spoke to me about confronting your demons, it started me thinking."

"About what?"

"That maybe it's time I confronted one of my own."

"Which is?"

"Julie's past for a start," Daniel said. "Her mother lives just outside Chicago."

"I'll book American Airlines, Los Angeles via O'Hare. It'll be easy enough to shake a tail in that mad house on the off chance they put someone on us. You can exorcise Mama St. John while I exercise your plastic picking up our undercover duds."

<u>48</u>

Pamela St. John lived in a Colonial-style MacMansion on the outskirts of a small, upwardly mobile community west of Chicago. The home was isolated, set deep into the thick, landscaped lot, out of sight of the neighbors. Crescents of snow had gathered in the corners of the shuttered windows and a beckoning orange-red glow flickered through the panes. It was the type of place that realtor's referred to as a doll house. The name on the mailbox said Goldman. Daniel rang the bell.

"May I help you?"

The woman who opened the door nearly stopped his heart. She was wearing a man's white cotton dress shirt, and nothing else that he could see. Her legs were long and tanned, and her thighs were firm looking. Although he knew Pamela St. John to be forty-five years old, forty-six in February, she could easily pass for a nipped, tucked and Botoxed thirty. She was exquisite, the mirror image of her daughter. Her painted lips were full, their achingly familiar curves parted in a warm, welcoming smile.

"I'm Daniel Rourke."

She stoked her smile considerably. "What a lovely surprise," she said. "Do come in."

The living room was paneled in knotty pine and the high ceiling was beamed. There was a half-empty wine glass and a bottle of domestic Sauvignon Blanc on the coffee table in front of the floral-pattern couch. New Age treacle oozed from expertly camouflaged speakers, and scented candles burned from seemingly every level surface in the room.

"I was about to have a glass of wine and a bubble bath, if you'd care to join me." She held a dainty hand up to her mouth and giggled. "For some wine, I mean."

Daniel shook his head. He heard a noise coming from a room with an open door along the hallway to the back of the house. The silhouette of a man's hairy leg was visible on top of a king-sized canopy bed.

"Mr. Goldman?" Daniel said.

"A new friend. Mr. Goldman and I are separated."

According to Julie, Pamela St. John was a predator. She said her mother had been married so many times that if she hyphenated the surnames of all her unfortunate hubbies her name would read like a Joyce novel. A Baptist by birth, she had converted to Judaism because, as she'd bragged to her daughter, it's where the shekels were.

Pamela St. John picked up the glass and took a sip. "We were so different, she and I. She was such a needy, clingy girl, while I was always the fun one, the winged free spirit." She twirled on her toes and sloshed some wine onto the rug. "She never understood how very different we were. Never understood that I needed my space. Time alone to work on my poetry. Time with my man to fulfill my needs."

She fixed Daniel with a glance, paralyzing him.

"You look like a man who understands such things, a man who knows how to fulfill a woman's needs." She bit her lower lip gently. "So what do you think?"

"About what?" Daniel said.

She drained her glass and set it down on the coffee table.

"About this," she said.

She slipped her fingers between the buttons of his shirt, pulled him into her, and kissed him fiercely. One of her legs was wrapped around his back and he could feel her pubic bone riding up the length his thigh. She began to moan loudly into his mouth which he had opened out of reflex. Her tongue was sweet with five-dollar-a-bottle wine.

Daniel's mind was reeling as the floodgates opened and he was inundated with a torrent of repressed emotions. He felt hate. He felt love. He felt lust. He felt guilt. He felt unmitigated joy. He felt pity. He felt like punching her lights out. He felt like throwing her to the floor, climbing on top of her, and just pretending.

Instead, he shook his head. Pushed her away.

Almost immediately, her eyes began to fill. She reached for a tissue from a nearby end table and dabbed at the tears to keep her mascara from running.

"I wanted to be there. I really did."

She was talking about Julie's funeral. It had been held in Los Angeles and Daniel had wired her five thousand dollars to cover the expense of the trip. But she hadn't come. Hadn't called. Hadn't returned the money, either. Probably blew it all on scented candles and Yanni discs.

"The more I tried to find my own space, the tighter the poor little thing would cling."

She picked up the bottle to pour another round but found it empty. Undaunted, she shook the last few drops into her glass and downed them.

"It was," she scrunched up her face as she searched for the right word, "sad."

Ironically, she was right. It really was-

"Sad," he said.

"Hold me, Daniel."

Without warning, she careened into him. He put his arms around her and gently patted her back while she sobbed uncontrollably. Eventually, her upper body stopped heaving and she made this nifty slight-of-butt motion, shifting her position almost imperceptibly such that he was no longer comforting her but rather embracing her. One hand began to stroke his penis, which remained shamefully hard. She raised her face and stared him in the eyes.

"Fuck me," she said.

"No. But thanks for asking."

"You think you're better than me, but you're not. I know your type." She took a step backward and unbuttoned her shirt. "And I know exactly what you want."

Aside from the Star of David medallion around her neck, the shirt was indeed all that she was wearing. Her breasts were too high and too perfect to be her own, but that didn't make them any less fantastic to look at.

"Fuck me," she said again.

"I don't want to."

"Yeah, you do," she said, her hand back on his penis. "I can feel it."

"What do you expect from me? I'm a guy."

"What's that supposed to mean?"

"I find an empty parking space in rush hour, I get a woody. I'm a guy, you know? It's nothing personal."

Suddenly, there were tears streaming down her cheeks, washing away the thick mask of her makeup, exposing the crow's feet and the frown lines and a myriad other imperfections that Daniel hadn't noticed before. It was as if she was aging before his very eyes.

She bent over the couch and began fumbling in her purse. When she straightened up there was an unlighted cigarette in her mouth. "You stand here acting all high and mighty, like it's somehow my fault she died the way she did." The cigarette bobbed up and down as she spoke. "But do you know what?"

Daniel said nothing. He didn't really want to know, but he suspected she was going to tell him anyway.

"If you had you met us both in our primes, she wouldn't have stood a chance." She fumbled in her purse some more and came up with a lighter and in two quick flicks had her cigarette going. "You wouldn't have looked twice at the little ice princess."

Pamela St. John lifted a small plastic plaque from the wall above the couch and slapped it into Daniel's hands. Although the script was faded with age, it remained legible.

Grinning triumphantly, she said, "Read it."

"I did."

"Out loud, stupid."

"Mother of the Year."

"Julie gave me that the Christmas before she went to live with her born-again psycho of a grandmother." She shook her head. "Everything I did for her, everything I taught her, it was never enough. I was Mother of the Fucking Year, and she was an ungrateful bitch."

"Whatever gets you through the night," Daniel said.

"She was an ungrateful bitch, and you're a son-of-a-bitch. You deserved each other. Now get the fuck out of my house before I wake Jaim and have him throw your candy ass out."

Daniel looked hard at Pamela St. John, a cruel, crumbling caricature of the woman he loved, nodded a polite goodbye, and walked calmly from the house.

<u>49</u>

Their return flight touched down in Boston shortly before 10PM, one hour and twenty minutes behind schedule. Daniel was tired and cranky, and more than a little pissed with Buchanan. While in Chicago, during a momentary lapse of judgment following his visit with Mommie Dearest, he had let his friend talk him into altering his appearance as an aid to their going undercover. On Daniel's dime, and at considerable expense, Buchanan had purchased an extensive wardrobe of leather, silk and rubber. Then, at the airport beauty salon, they'd had their hair cut and dyed by a lisping, razor-wielding eunuch named Mr. Alex. Daniel's itchy new do was strawberry-blond while Buchanan's was pomegranate-red.

Standing curbside outside Logan's arrivals terminal, surrounded by a mob of dour dark-skinned strangers, listening to a dozen conversations, none of them in English, Daniel said, "Any idea where we're going to spend the night? Obviously, we can't go back to the Boston Harbor."

"Let's head downtown," Buchanan said. "Find some outta-the-way, glitz and glitter free, shit-hole that doesn't ask too many questions."

Buchanan waived off a veritable parade of stretch limos and freshly waxed taxis, hopping into the first gypsy cab death-trap that rumbled past. Given their circumstances it was the safest way to travel, he explained *en route*. Unlicensed owner/operator. No dispatch. No paper trial. Like being invisible.

***

The Rex Hotel was situated on the western border of Balkanized Chinatown in a part of the city that had thus far managed to evade the insidious, color-coordinated blight of urban renewal. Dark buildings, storefronts mostly, with freshly skinned ducks hanging in the windows, huddled together beyond the reach of the flickering sodium vapor streetlights. There was no glitz in this ethnic black- and blue-collar neighborhood and the only glitter that Daniel could see was on the frost-bitten cleavages of the mangy hookers trolling its filth-ridden sidewalks. A strip club called The Poontang Palace was located directly across the street from the hotel and a live recording of John Mellencamp singing *Dance Naked* could be heard reverberating through its poorly-insulated walls.

"If the average American's appreciation of multiculturalism is really as great as guys like Thornton and Farmer would have us believe," Daniel said, "ask yourself, why are there no slaughtered cows hanging in

McDonalds' windows?"

"Don't you mean worms?" Buchanan said. "I seem to remember reading somewhere that their burgers are made with worms."

"Cows. Worms. Just think of the upside."

Buchanan made a face. "There'd be an upside?"

"Our nation's obesity epidemic would be cured overnight."

Inside, the hotel had a registration desk, a dented Coke machine with electrical tape over the coin slot, and a small sitting area complete with an off-kilter Charlie Brown Christmas tree. Beside the tree a well-dressed black man with his pants around his ankles was schmoozing on a cell phone while a septuagenarian whore of Asian descent bobbed stiffly away. To the left of the sitting area a worn, Astroturf-clad staircase wound up to the bedrooms.

"Shit-hole is an understatement," Daniel said.

"Perfect, isn't it?" Buchanan said.

"Let's hurry up and register," Daniel said, unbuttoning his coat and heading for the desk. "I want to grab a shower, see if I can't wash some of this crap out of my hair before we paint the town pink."

The desk clerk was sprawled in a folding metal chair, head back, eyes closed. There was a transistor radio tuned to a grunge station on a low, cluttered shelf beside him. Buchanan thumped the bell on the desktop but the clerk never flinched. Daniel reached over and killed the radio. The clerk blinked a couple of times, made fleeting eye contact with Daniel then slowly sat up. He was in his mid-twenties with thinning, prematurely grey hair and a dozen silver studs in each ear.

"Two rooms," Daniel said. "Connected, preferably."

"No can do," the clerk said. "Only one room available in the entire joint. It ain't the Presidential Suite, but the sheets are clean." He smirked. "Clean being a relative term in this part of town. Got two queens in it, you don't mind sharing."

Daniel looked at Buchanan. He nodded.

"I'll tell you what," Daniel said. "Adios the queens and you can light up the no vacancy sign."

The clerk's brow furrowed as he pondered Daniel's words, then he chuckled, shot Daniel with his thumb and forefinger, and said, "Gotcha." He opened a drawer and pulled out a tattered spiral bound book and a pencil. "Man says I gotta get your names."

"Jesse Jackson," Daniel said.

"Al Sharpton," Buchanan said.

The clerk did not ask for their IDs and did not seem at all concerned when none were offered. Daniel paid a month's rent in advance in cash. The clerk counted the stack of crisp, new bills twice before wadding them into the hip pocket of his low-rise jeans.

"I wonder if you can help us out with some info," Buchanan said. "We're new in town and-"

"You want some twat sent up to the room." This time he shot Buchanan. "No problemo."

"Not quite," Buchanan said. "What we're interested in is heading out on the town for a little drinking, a little dancing, a little-"

"I hear you." The clerk smirked again. "And I know all the happenin' spots. You like 'em black, white, yellow, red, fat, thin, amputee, mentally retarded, I know right where to send you."

"What if we're into the same-sex scene?" Buchanan said. "The younger the better, if you get my drift. You still know right where to send us?"

The clerk never batted an eye. "Sure, I know those spots, too. Different strokes, right?"

"Let's start with the nearest establishment," Daniel said. "What's it called and how do we get there?"

"That'd be A Bird in the Hand. Out the door and turn right, another right at Mr. Wu's Pu-Pu Pagoda, then follow the techno-shit music to the lilac-colored doors." He chuckled. "You can't miss it."

Their thirty-dollar-a-night room was two flights up and looked out on the street. The walls were a patchwork of flaking colors, and the outer edges of the ceiling were covered with a slick mossy film that reeked of wet dog. The lumpy, queen-sized mattresses resembled giant potato chips, misshapen, sagging in the middle, curled up on the edges. The bedspreads did not match the sheets and the pillowcases did not match either the bedspreads or the sheets. The cast iron beds, one black, one gold-glitter, were separated by a narrow curtained window and a radiator that had apparently been set on broil the previous winter and forgotten.

"It's so hot in here the room is sweating," Daniel said.

"I've been in worse," Buchanan said.

"I've seen your apartment."

"What's that supposed to mean?"

"It means I believe you."

Buchanan shrugged. "Take your time in the can." He flopped onto the nearest bed with his shoes on. "I'm gonna try and catch up on some shut-eye."

Inside the bathroom, Daniel stripped down and took a long, cool shower. Afterwards, while shaving, he noticed that the blotch of purple on his cheekbone had faded considerably from the day before. He leaned closer to the mirror. The blood had almost completely cleared from around the cornea of his right eye. It was a face that a mother could almost recognize. He folded his clothes, threw on his robe, and after five solid minutes of shouting and shaking and kicking the bed, he woke Buchanan.

"Take a cold shower," Daniel said. "It'll perk you up."

Buchanan yawned and stretched, his joints creaking and popping, then squinted at his watch.

"We've got time," Daniel said.

While Buchanan was in the shower, belting out an off-key rendition of the early seventies AM radio hit *Daddy Don't You Walk So Fast*, Daniel slithered into a pair of black leather pants and a flaming-red silk shirt. The pants were so tight that he couldn't bend his knees, forcing him to do a zombie shuffle over to the small, dust-covered television. He turned it on, casting a grey rectangle of light over the room. He flicked through the channels until he found CNN, shuffled over to his bed, and settled in to wait for Buchanan. Twenty minutes later, Buchanan strolled out in a towel, gazed appraisingly at Daniel, and smiled.

"Almost perfect," he said.

"Almost? I hope you're not suggesting that I could possibly get any fruitier looking?"

Buchanan undid the buttons of Daniel's shirt all the way down to his navel. "You betcha," he said. Then he put on his own leather pants and a robin's egg blue silk shirt, which he also left unbuttoned to the navel.

The desk clerk lifted his head off the desktop as they shuffled into the lobby. "Couldn't see it before," he said. "But I sure as hell can see it now."

"Our room's a little on the toasty side," Buchanan said. "You think you can turn the heat down before we get back?"

"Sure thing," the clerk said, lowering his head back down to the desktop, eyelids fluttering closed. "I'll get right on it."

Soft feathery snowflakes began to drift down from the low belly of the sky as they exited the hotel. The strippers on the other side of the cardboard box lined street were between sets and Daniel could hear the telltale thumping of techno music in the distance.

"Right turn, Clyde," Daniel said, and started walking.

No more than a dozen steps out Buchanan stumbled on an empty wine bottle and lurched into Daniel.

"Follow the hooker spoor," Daniel said after he had righted his friend. "It'll be safer for us both."

"Hooker what?"

"Unless you want to take another spill just stick to the trails the hookers have worn in the garbage," Daniel said.

Shortly after taking the second right at Mr. Wu's, a red-headed hooker with forearm crutches wobbled out of an alley onto the sidewalk in front of them on knobby, coltishly awkward legs. She had neglected to lower her skirt after doing the dirty deed and Daniel and Buchanan couldn't help but gawk at the plumes of steam that were rising from her unkempt, semen-spattered bush.

"Now there's something you don't see every day," Buchanan said.

"A pro with polio?" Daniel said.

"Naw, man. A pussy that's been fucked so hard it smokes."

"Speak for yourself," Daniel said.

<u>50</u>

Buchanan paused before the glossy lilac-colored doors of A Bird in the Hand. "It's all right," he said in a treacly, albeit patronizing, tone of voice. "There's nothing to be afraid of."

"I'm not afraid," Daniel snapped. "It's just that I've never been to one of these places before."

"Tell you what," Buchanan said. "For as long as we're undercover, you're my bitch. Anyone wants to mess with you they gotta get through me."

"Why can't you be my bitch? Let me be the one who gets to bust the heads."

Buchanan laughed. "Because," he said, "you're too pretty not to be the bitch."

Daniel nodded. It made sense. Sort of. "Does the Zen master have any new words of wisdom to impart?"

"Keep your eyes and ears open, and your asshole puckered."

***

The clientele was exclusively male, doe-eyed college kids and young upwardly mobile professionals, dirty dancing on a Studio 54 inspired lighted panel floor. Taking Buchanan's advice literally, his butt cheeks clenched tightly together, Daniel sidled over to the bar for a shot of liquid courage. The bartender was a short, wiggly man in a white Armani Exchange tank top, his skinny arms tricked out from wrist to shoulder with x-rated jailhouse tattoos. Daniel was about to order a full measure of single malt scotch when Buchanan beat him to the punch.

"Gimme a Bud," Buchanan said.

"And for your luscious friend?"

"Pink Lady Fizz," Buchanan said.

"I'll have a scotch," Daniel said. "Cask Strength Laphroaig if you've got it."

"Don't you want to pass?" Buchanan said.

"I thought that was what this ridiculous looking outfit was for."

"It isn't working." Buchanan did a double-take over Daniel's shoulder. "Then again-"

"Then again what?"

"Maybe it is."

The man approaching Daniel was of medium-height, slight build, with a golden brown tan. His strawberry blonde hair was thick and smoothed straight back. He was wearing a black silk double-breasted suit, white shirt buttoned to the top, no tie. His right leg was noticeably shorter than the left causing him to walk with a pronounced though graceful limp. Buchanan spun conveniently away upon his arrival to make idle chit-chat with the bartender.

The man with the limp looked Daniel up and down a half dozen times, moving only his eyes. "My name is Marcello Valenzano," he said, smiling crookedly, "and you, dear sir, are the choicest cut of meat I've seen all night."

"Jesse Jackson," Daniel said.

The man shimmied in uncomfortably close.

"Frank!"

"In a minute," Buchanan said without turning.

"You're invading my space, Mr. Valenzano."

"Invade," Valenzano said, his crooked smile widening. "To enter for conquest and plunder." He reached around and squeezed Daniel's still tightly clenched butt. "How apropos, Jesse."

Daniel took in a long breath and let it out slowly. He wanted to lay the pervert out cold, but couldn't. He was undercover, and he was trying to pass. He considered slapping him on the cheek, or maybe pinching him, or scratching his eyes out, but ultimately decided to hold Buchanan to his word and let him be the one to fight for his honor. He did, however, lift the man's heavily lotioned hand from his butt.

"Listen to me," Daniel said slowly, enunciating his words carefully. "I gave up sodomy for lent. I'm not that way. Not anymore."

The bartender placed a Collins glass filled with a milky, bubble gum-colored liquid on the bar in front of Daniel.

"Your Pink Lady Fizz, sir."

Valenzano winked. "Sure, you're not," he said.

When Buchanan finally turned around, Daniel couldn't help but notice that his usually dead eyes were bright with amused pleasure.

"Blow," Buchanan said. "The pop tart's with me."

Valenzano took a quick step backward and eyed Buchanan like he was a walking case of the clap. The sudden movement knocked a shock of hair loose from above his right eye which he fingered back into place with a practiced economy of motion.

"Are you gonna blow already," Buchanan said, "or do I gotta beat you into a coma?"

Although Buchanan was smiling, he was a large, and he carried himself with the arrogance of someone who could kill a man a dozen different ways without breaking a sweat. Valenzano took only a moment to size up the situation and determine that he was out of his league. He hooked his fingers into claws and made a loud cat-like hissing sound at Buchanan.

Then, as he limped gracefully, pridefully away, he half-turned and shot a saucy parting glance at Daniel, shouting loudly for all to hear, "You know what they say, sweetie. Tight buns, asshole like an old gym sock."

"Pop Tart?" Daniel said.

"If the pump fits," Buchanan said.

For the next hour, Daniel stayed close to Buchanan as they prowled though every corner and crevice of the flashy, multilevel club. Although Daniel made a mental note of everything he had seen and heard over the course of the evening, he had neither seen nor heard anything that would lead him to believe that they were hot, or even lukewarm, on the killer's trail.

"Looks like we struck out tonight," Daniel said.

Buchanan waggled his eyebrows. "Just so the evening's not a total bust," he said, "you wanna go for a twirl?"

Daniel took a firm grim on Buchanan's shoulders, holding him at arm's length. "In order to avoid any possible misunderstanding given our current living arrangements, I'm putting you on notice. You whip out your dick in my presence one more time and I swear by all that is holy I will tear it off with my bare hands and pitch your screaming carcass out the window."

Grinning, Buchanan hooked his fingers into claws and said, "Pfffffft."

51

After brushing his teeth and attaching his foreskin reclamation contraption, Buchanan climbed into the gold-glitter bed and proceeded to thrash around on top of the rumpled sheets for the next twenty minutes. "Lazy motherfucker didn't lower the heat," he mumbled.

"Who didn't do what?" Daniel said.

"Tomorrow morning, bright and early, I'm gonna have a chat with our clerk."

"About what?"

"He turns down the heat, or else."

"Or else . . . ?"

"I'm taking my shirt off."

"A threat he'll, no doubt, appreciate." Daniel grinned. "Did you catch the look on his face when he saw us in our undercover duds?"

"I mean I'm taking it off right now. I'm too fucking hot."

"No," Daniel said, "you're not."

Between Daniel and Buchanan, the radiator rattled and hissed and the temperature in the room notched another couple degrees higher.

"Yes, I am," Buchanan said.

"Oh, no, you're not."

Daniel opened the curtain. The window was old and warped and painted shut. He put his legs and his shoulders into the effort but the sash wouldn't budge. Across the street The Poontang Palace's neon signage announced in a throbbing rainbow splay of colors that *Live Nude Girls Girls Girls* were in residence. Snow was still falling and the hookers were still out in force.

"Do you want to give me a hand?"

Buchanan's face held no expression. His black eyes were bottomless. "I'm not gonna ravage you in your sleep if that's what's worrying you. Hell, I don't even find you attractive." He looked down at Daniel's arm, at the tight tee shirt that swelled over his vascular biceps. "Not really."

"Jesus Christ, Frank. Take the shirt off."

Buchanan pulled the sweat-soaked shirt over his head, tossed it onto the floor with the rest of his dirty laundry, and settled back down.

But sleep wouldn't come, for either of them. Instead of staring at the ceiling, watching the moss glow in the gloom, Daniel rolled over on the narrow cot, trying to drift into some kind of mind-numbing limbo. Buchanan, however, was restless. He was tossing and turning and blowing tight sighs, like a spoiled kid gearing up for a Category 5 tantrum. Irritating as hell.

"If you're still hot why don't you help me with the window?" Daniel said.

Buchanan exhaled loudly then grudgingly rolled out of bed. It was a struggle, but working together they were able to raise the sash three glorious inches. They lingered between the beds for a moment, just enjoying the nippy breeze. The neon lights from the strip club intermittently lacquered Buchanan's face and chest red and yellow and blue. For no apparent reason, he began to laugh.

"What's so funny?" Daniel said.

"That strip clubs feel the need to advertise the fact that the broads they showcase are of the living and breathing variety."

"I don't know how many peelers you've seen," Daniel said, "but sometimes it's a little hard to tell."

"I just think it's funny, that's all."

"You want to know what's funnier?"

Buchanan nodded.

"What's funnier is they'd probably double their profit if they featured cadavers instead."

"Buck-naked ones," Buchanan said.

"Yeah."

"Now that's fucked up."

"But true."

Daniel was just nodding off when the hookers finally started to score. Through the paper-thin walls arose the eerie sounds of their psychopathological coitus. From the room nearest to Buchanan a man could he heard, complete with expletives, telling his 'dirty little whore' that he knew precisely what she wanted and how, in graphic and libertine detail, he was the one to give it to her. Above them, stiletto heels tap-danced over the oilcloth floor, a whip cracked and a man cried out in pain then begged for more, which he promptly got. In the room next to Daniel, a headboard thumped irrythmically against the wall. The gloom and the temperature and the noise were like a thick soup inside the tiny room. Daniel felt like he was drowning in it.

"You awake, Frank?"

"Who can sleep with all this freaky shit going on around us?"

"Hey, Frank?"

"Whaddya want this time?"

"Something you mentioned the other day has really been eating me up."

"About the case?"

"Not really."

A minute passed. The man in the room nearest to Buchanan began shrieking at his hooker who responded with a series of inaudible whimpers.

"What is it? Tell me."

The man slapped the hooker several times and she yelped in pain.

"Tell me now."

Daniel leaped out of bed. "In a minute," he said.

The door to the yelping hooker's room was unlocked. Daniel opened it and stepped inside with Buchanan close behind him. Between the doorway and the bed was a painted chair with a tailor-made suit and overcoat combo draped neatly over it. The hooker, Cambodian, or maybe Laotian, and no more than eighteen or nineteen years old, was propped against the wall and gripping the edge of the mattress tightly with her claw-like hands. She was an APL amputee, missing both of her legs below the hip. Her pelvis was hovering a good foot off the bed, rotating wildly around the John's fist which was buried in her anus up to his glinting watchband. Her breasts were a fiery red from where the John was bitch-slapping them with his free hand.

The skewered pelvic rotations slowed as the hooker caught sight of the intruders. Her eyes narrowed menacingly. "This ain't no goddamned peep show," she cried out in a heavily accented voice. "Fifty bucks you wanna watch. Cash money. Fifty bucks each."

The John was good-looking, mid-thirties, with a fully waxed, swimmer's physique. "Would you mind waiting outside 'til I'm through, guys?" With a wet, suctiony sound, he turned his fist inside the hooker's anus and glanced down at his diamond-studded watch face. "I've still got another twelve minutes left." He gave the hooker's tits another smack.

"Give 'er," Daniel said.

"Fuckin' sicko perverts," the hooker shrieked through the closed door after they had gone.

Back in their room, and back on their beds, Daniel said, "You mentioned a while ago that you didn't find me attractive and I just want to know what's up with that?"

"*What?*"

"You asked me a moment ago what was eating me up."

"You're fucking with me, aren't you?"

"I eat right. I work out. I'm a snappy dresser. So what's the problem?"

Buchanan's chuckle was pure evil. "The problem, *big boy*, is that you're a walking ruckus. Not the sort who'd just give it up to the likes of me. I'd have to take it. Knock you down to the ground and hold you there. It'd be worth it though. For both of us. *Mmmm-mmmm good.* I gotta tell you. There's no finer feeling in the world than one man piercing another man's tight virgin assho-"

"Okay, okay," Daniel said, covering his ears with his hands. "You were right. I was just messing with you. So shut the hell up."

Buchanan's chuckle escalated into full-bore laughter. "Hey, dick-wad," he said. "You're not the only one with a sense of humor."

"I know that, Frank, and I'm sorry."

Buchanan sat up and shrugged, his expression dead serious. "Truth is I've never been all that comfortable with the homo lifestyle myself. Which is why I work so goddamned hard. No time for a personal life and all that other jazz."

"Don't answer if you don't want to, but I've always been curious. What exactly runs through your mind when you come face-to-face with an interesting, intelligent, funny, sexy lady? Haven't you ever had the urge to just . . . ?"

"To just what?"

"Hump her to a pulp."

Upstairs, the whip cracked and the man, his spirit finally broken, began to bawl like a newborn.

"Sure I do," Buchanan said. "But I worry that - Jesus, I can't believe I'm telling you this - I worry that I won't be able to function. And I'm scared, too. Scared shitless that what Uncle Billy did to me as a kid fucked me up for good with women."

Daniel began to think out loud. "So you've been stretching your . . . your foreskin as a . . . ."

"A what?"

"I'm not sure how to phrase it exactly. A symbolic rebirth? A second chance at being . . . normal? Does that make any sense to you?"

Buchanan was quiet for a beat. "I never really thought of it like that, but yeah, I guess it does."

Daniel rolled onto his back and stared up at the ceiling. "My own past kind of left me with a similar fear," he said.

"How so?"

"Up until last year I'd never had a relationship that lasted more than a couple months, and I'd never gone more than a week without plunging into the next one."

"Dick first, I bet."

"Crude, but accurate."

"That's not so unusual. For a young, hunky studmuffin like yourself."

Daniel turned his head and made eye contact with Buchanan. "Not unusual? I guess not. But healthy?" The man in the room beside Daniel moaned loudly as he came and the headboard finally settled to rest. "Julie showed me that it was actually possible to feel love, real love, and have a normal, healthy relationship. Like the one I grew up with. Like mom and dad had."

Buchanan grunted his understanding. "While we're on the subject of Julie," he said. "How did your visit with her mom go?"

"She's easily the most self-absorbed, self-deluded person I've ever met, and I've never loved Julie more than I do at this moment."

"Because she could grow up around that - despite that - and become the person she did."

"She inherited her mom's looks, but the meat and potatoes of her character she got from her dad."

"He's dead, right?"

"Car accident. Shortly after she was born."

"It's tough for a kid to lose a parent."

"Like you, she got through it okay. She lived life on her own terms, and she died the same way. I'd always known why she made the choice she did, intellectually, at least, but I'd never really accepted it."

"Emotionally."

Daniel nodded.

"Until now."

Daniel nodded again.

"You about ready to move on then?"

Daniel considered the question carefully before answering. "Maybe it's time," he said. "Time I turned my boat against the current and started paddling like hell."

"Whatchu talkin' 'bout, Willis?"

Daniel smiled. "Am I ready to move on? I've certainly been mulling the possibility."

"With a certain Portsmouth cop and her buns of steel?"

"I wouldn't know about that. Her buns, I mean."

"Pure poetry," Buchanan said. "Take a gander the next time you see her, you don't believe me."

"What about you and Miss Thomas with the nice pins?"

"Maybe we're both ready."

Daniel turned and stared at Buchanan. "In a way it's almost too bad."

"What do you mean?"

"Nothing. Forget I said anything."

"It's too late now. So spit it out."

"Well," Daniel said, "if you really must know-"

"I do."

"I . . . I couldn't help but notice . . ."

"Notice what?"

"That for a man in the twilight of his life your pecs are exquisite. Quite pleasing to the eye."

The pillow struck Daniel squarely in the face, and the rolling thunder of Buchanan's laughter drowned out every other sound in the hotel.

<u>52</u>

Daniel and Buchanan spent the following night cruising gay bars with cutesy names and even cuter Smart Cars and M&M-colored Japanese hybrids double parked out front. Despite enduring four and a half hours of catty slumber-party gossip over mind-numbing dance music, they had discovered no clues to Sarah Calhoun's whereabouts, and no clues to the identity of her captors. Despite the efficacy of their disguises, it seemed time to re-think their approach to the investigation.

"How many people would you say live here?" Daniel said, his hands stuffed into his coat pockets, his shoulders hunched against the cold.

"Boston?" Buchanan said.

"Yeah."

"City or metro?"

"City," Daniel said. "Five, six hundred thousand?"

"Sounds about right," Buchanan said. "Why?"

"Doesn't there seem to be just a few too many gay bars for a city this size?"

"We're here, we're queer," Buchanan said.

On the way back to The Rex Hotel, they took a shortcut through a graveyard called the Old Granary Burying Ground. It was a veritable who's who of the Revolutionary War-era, and Daniel couldn't help but feel humbled. Samuel Adams. John Hancock. James Otis. Robert Treat Paine. Paul Revere. Patriots who had dedicated their lives to their country, so that those who followed would enjoy liberty, and the freedom to live as they chose.

The wind had picked up considerably in the five minutes since they'd departed The Fruit Basket, whistling and howling as it tore through the cluttered field of silhouetted crosses and helter-skelter headstones. As they rounded a corner the howling of the wind was immediately overwhelmed by a long, drawn-out wail reverberating the length and breadth of the graveyard. Although it sounded like a plaintive cry from a single voice, Daniel was able to discern that it was actually an incomprehensible Babel of many voices, male and female, young and old. His eyes swept the murky darkness as they moved cautiously along the center of the pathway.

Almost immediately, indistinct forms, hunched and tattered, appeared along the visible perimeter of the snow-speckled gloom. They were everywhere, all around them, and too numerous to count. Daniel looked at Buchanan, who indicated with a short nod that he also saw them.

Abruptly a massive form materialized from the murk in front of them and forced them to a halt. It was a wino, male, morbidly obese, wearing a white, badly stained bathrobe over a pair of green hospital scrubs. His eyes were covered by a milky film and his ruddy face was speckled with weeping sores. One hand was extended, the other clutching the wilted bouquets that he had liberated from the gravesites. Although he looked to be well into his sixties, Daniel guessed he was probably closer to half that age.

"Mad abbots," the wino mumbled as he pressed a bouquet to Daniel's arms.

"Excuse me?" Daniel said.

The wino belched once, twice, a third time then mumbled, "Mad abbots," again.

"Let's scoot," Buchanan said.

As Daniel brought his wallet into view the wail from the surrounding gloom rose in pitch and the hunched forms edged closer.

"Don't do it," Buchanan said.

"I don't mind," Daniel said.

He extracted a five dollar bill which was promptly snatched from his grip. The wino began to giggle uncontrollably. He held the bill up close to his face, scrutinized it, and stopped giggling. He shrieked, "mad abbots," and something else that Daniel could not make out. Then he made a clumsy grab for Daniel's wallet.

Daniel parried the wino's hand. "I don't understand what you're saying."

"He wants more money," Buchanan said.

"I gathered as much."

"No," Buchanan said. "That's what he's actually saying. Among other things."

"What other things?"

"You don't want to know."

"The only thing I've been able to make out is 'mad abbots.' An abbot is something like a priest, isn't it? Or a monk of some kind?"

"He's out of cigarettes," Buchanan said. "What he's actually saying is 'I'm outta butts.' Says he can't buy a single carton of smokes with what you've given him. Says five bucks is an insult to his dignity."

"I thought he was hungry," Daniel said.

"The man weighs four hundred pounds," Buchanan said. "An empty stomach woulda been my last guess."

The wino coughed and spat something that looked like a first trimester fetus onto the ground at Daniel's feet. "Hung-gree," he said. Tears began to spill down his cheeks and his nose began to run.

"Hung-gree," the voices in the gloom wailed. One by one the others began to shuffle closer, closing in on them in the manner of a wolf pack approaching cornered prey, their bare, frostbitten hands outstretched. "So hung-gree."

Daniel saw Buchanan starting to open his mouth and he cut him off sharply. "You say I told you so and I'm going to-"

"What I was actually gonna say," Buchanan said, plowing shoulder first through the pack, "is let's get the fuck outta here."

They had just found their way clear of the pack when they heard what sounded to be the trash-talking preliminary to a drunken brawl. They slowed to a walking pace. In the center of the graveyard, on the opposite side of a massive spot-lit obelisk marking the resting place of Ben Franklin's parents, a man was hurling epithets at the moon. No brawl was in the offing. In fact, the man was completely alone. He was small and stoop-shouldered and had on a pair of red vinyl pants under a tight vinyl bomber jacket with padded shoulders and an overabundance of zippers. His face was an asymmetrical white oval inside his turned up collar and low-slung coonskin cap.·

"Retard?" Buchanan said.

"Tourettes syndrome by the sound of it," Daniel said. "Look at the way he keeps twitching and snapping his head back with each syllable he utters."

With the shit-licking, cum-guzzling spic of a moon thoroughly castigated, Tourettes exited the graveyard and walked stiffly south along Tremont Street toward Chinatown.

· "What do you say?" Daniel said. "He is wearing tighter pants than the ones we've got on."

"Not to mention he's going our way."

Daniel and Buchanan fell in silently behind him.

Two blocks later, Tourettes turned down a barricaded side street. Buchanan stopped Daniel. "Let's give him some room. The street's deserted. We don't wanna spook the little fella, having him thinking we're muggers, or worse." They gave the man a thirty second head start before rounding the corner. Wooden boxes covered all the street lights and several buildings were wrapped from the ground floor to the roof with a heavy plastic cover. No parked or abandoned cars were anywhere to be seen.

"What the hell's going on here?" Buchanan said.

"I haven't got a clue," Daniel said.

Fifty yards ahead of them, Tourettes stooped to pet a stray cat. Buchanan pulled Daniel into the recessed doorway of a large, ornate building with boarded-up doors and windows.

"What a shame," Daniel muttered.

"What is?" Buchanan said.

"This used to be a grand hotel. The Malloy. The notice on the wall here says it's scheduled for demolition in a couple days. The test activation is tomorrow morning."

"Demolished for what?"

"It doesn't say," Daniel said.

"Another parking lot probably."

Daniel rubbed his hand over the hand-carved, Rosetta Marble door surround, beautifully detailed with embossed grape floral pillars, and twelve-foot-high capitals. "It must really have been something in its day. I'm surprised they didn't opt for renovation. It would have made a sweet condo complex."

"That's why there were so many bums hovering in the cemetery," Buchanan said. "The city must have kicked the squatters out to allow the workers in. If you ask me the real shame is it woulda made an even sweeter homeless shelter."

Daniel pulled out his Blackberry.

"What are you doing?"

"Dialing 911. With any luck the ambulance'll get here before your bleeding heart does you in."

Buchanan tugged on Daniel's arm. "He's moving again. C'mon."

A minute later Tourettes hopped another set of barricades, and turned left onto Lagrange Street, heading toward a nightclub with no line-up at the door and no name displayed anywhere on its windowless facade. The bouncers, a pair of beefy black men with shaved heads and matching silver down-filled jackets, let him pass unchallenged.

"Looks deserted. You still want to check it out?" Daniel said.

Buchanan shrugged. "Why the hell not? We strike out again we can always grab an order of suicide wings and a couple pints of draught. Better than roasting our chestnuts at the Rex."

***

One of the bouncers put a gloved hand to Buchanan's chest, and said, "Private club, dawg. You're gonna have to take it some place else you wanna get any male-tail tonight."

"Get your fucking mitt off me," Buchanan said. He looked at each bouncer carefully, making alpha-male eye contact.

"C'mon, Frank, let's go," Daniel said.

"Let's let 'em in, Thang," the other bouncer said. "I've got a feeling the merry men'll go buck wild for that other one. Maybe slip us a bonus for lettin' him in."

Thang glanced obliquely over at Daniel. "I think maybe you're right, Custis." He unclipped the red velvet rope and opened the door. "Gentlemen," he said.

Daniel caught Thang gazing poignantly at his butt on the way past. Thang noticed he'd been busted and shrugged unapologetically. "Oh, yeah," he said, "The skinny white boys are gonna have a high old time with that one."

Custis high-fived Thang and said to Daniel, "Don't do nothin' I wouldn't do."

"Nigga," Thang said, "there ain't nothin' you won't do. Least ways nothin' I ever heard tell of."

"Word," Custis said, putting out his hand for a low five, which he got, then enthusiastically returned.

<u>53</u>

Daniel and Buchanan stepped into a massive concourse of towering rainforest flora, pump-driven waterfalls and effete couples making out on the numerous, discreetly positioned, hellishly red, leather couches. The entrance into the actual nightclub was on the other side of an orchid covered bridge built over a babbling, Koi-infested brook which bisected the rectangular, open-concept room. From the cover of a cluster of aromatic fronds, they watched as Tourettes crossed the bridge and passed through a pair of soundproof doors with the words 'The Colosseum' set in large backlit marble letters above them. They waited a moment then trailed him inside.

The doors opened into a circular hallway lit with sputtering gas-lit torches. The outer wall was frescoed and depicted well-endowed brutes in white togas making music and war and love with other, similarly attired, equally well-endowed brutes. Inside the outer wall was a ring of plaster columns and arches opening into three descending circular tiers of tables surrounding a circular dance floor. In the center of the dance floor a fire raged inside a hand-forged iron bowl that was a full four feet in diameter. The bowl was supported a dozen feet off the ground by an ornate wrought-iron stand.

Tourettes disappeared inside an elevator door that appeared to be a part of the intricate artwork on the outer wall. The door was guarded by two Mr. Universe types wearing gladiator outfits complete with distressed leather armor and helmets made of bronze. The gladiators looked at each other after the small, twitching man had passed, shook their heads, and snickered.

Deking and dodging through the crowd, Daniel noticed a bar beside the dance floor and headed toward it. He expected Buchanan to follow him down but he didn't. The pulsing music was so loud down below that conversation was only possible by shouting into your neighbor's ear. Like an aural lobotomy, the music consisted of one insipid track blending into another, each sharing the same dull thumping beat. At the bar, Daniel ordered a Guinness. The bartender, a Tom Cruise look-alike with long black hair and silver hoop earrings, handed Daniel a frosted glass of the cascading brown stout and moved on to the next customer. Leaning casually against the bar, Daniel swallowed a cool mouthful and took a casual look around.

The dance floor was a swarm of chicken bone-slim pretty boys wearing tight designer brand tanks and t-shirts. A strobe light pulsed down from on high and billowing clouds of smoke rose from a series of vents built into the floor, enveloping their whirling forms up to their bronzed bony chests.

Beside Daniel, a hirsute colossus with a beer keg belly, wearing leather chaps and cowboy boots, no shirt, no boxers or briefs, tossed back a Miller Lite and started putting the moves on Tom Cruise. One after the other the man in the chaps screamed his most perverted pick-up lines at Tom, who did his level best to humor the man without actually encouraging him. When the man realized it was *Mission Impossible*, he hurled the beer bottle into the garbage can at the end of the bar and turned to leave.

All of a sudden someone killed the music and everyone in the bar stopped dancing and flirting and sipping their slushy drinks to glare over at the man, who glared menacingly back at as many of them as he could.

The crowd pounced as one before the man knew what was happening. In seconds, several dozen queens, snarling and spitting, were hanging off his bulky butch form as he swiped and swatted and kicked and stomped at them. His face was a fiery red and rivulets of sweat streamed down his undulating cheeks and jowls. The man was big and he was mean, but he wasn't in shape, and big and mean, Daniel knew, could only get a man so far.

Strobe light still pulsing, he lurched a couple steps onto the dance floor in what appeared to be slow motion before he was overwhelmed by the sheer weight of the masses, disappearing from view beneath the smoke, his hand clutching helplessly at the air for one brief moment before also disappearing.

After a full twenty minutes of hissy-fit brutality the two gladiators entered the fray to drag the man's inert, profusely bleeding form up the stairs. The gladiators had just passed through the archway closest to the main door when Tom Cruise swaggered out from behind the bar and retrieved the beer bottle that the man had thrown into the garbage can. He walked the bottle two steps over to the blue recycling bin and placed it reverently inside. The pulsing music began again and the crowd carried on as if nothing out of the ordinary had happened.

"That's him," Buchanan shouted over the music, grabbing Daniel roughly from behind and spinning him around.

"Jesus Christ, Frank. Did you see that?"

"Fucking environmentalists," Buchanan said. "Now take a look at what I found." He pointed toward a huge man in a wheelchair on the uppermost tier, his arm around a man with a blonde ponytail and drawn on eyebrows that made him appear to be in a constant state of shock and awe. Although both of the huge man's eyes were blackened, his face swollen and criss-crossed with stitches, Daniel had no trouble recognizing Big Bobby Crudup.

"Bada bing," Buchanan shouted in Daniel's ear. "We're getting close. I can feel it in my bones."

"Let's go," Daniel shouted back. "The longer we're here, the greater the chance someone will see through these Clark Kent disguises we're wearing."

"You think we should stake this place out after hours tonight?"

"I'm bagged. Let's head back to the hotel and get a good night's sleep. Tomorrow morning we'll find out who owns this little shop of horrors, and decide where we go from there."

<u>54</u>

The checker cab turned onto Boylston Street and stopped in front of the Renaissance Revival palace known as the Boston Public Library. Daniel paid their sullen, non-English speaking driver and ran to catch up to Buchanan who was just passing through the building's triple-arched main entrance.

Inside the pink marble vestibule, Daniel said, "Which way?"

Buchanan shrugged. "What's that noise? This is a library right? People reading books and shit?"

Beyond the low, broad entrance hall could be heard the sound of raised voices, masculine, guttural, agitated.

"Didn't you ask for directions when you called about the computers this morning? This place is massive."

"I figured we'd ask once we got here."

Daniel approached a portly, middle-aged guard. "We're looking for the public internet access area," he said.

"That'd be the Washington Room," the guard said. "Second floor."

"What's all the commotion?" Buchanan said. "New Harry Potter book?"

The guard made a sour face. "A couple dozen rag-heads showed up about an hour ago. They're protesting some dusty old paintings in the Sargent gallery. Triumph of Religion, I think they're called."

"You serious?" Daniel said.

"As cancer of the balls," the guard said. "They claim they discriminate against moose-limbs 'cos they glorify our red, white and blue religion, and not their own. The paintings have been in this building for more'n a hundred years, and they're demanding we remove 'em, or give equal space to Osama, or Hadji, or whoever the fuck their prophet guy is."

"Mohammad," Daniel said.

"Same difference."

"Have the cops been notified?" Buchanan said.

The guard shook his head. "Word came from the groundhogs to let 'em be."

"Groundhogs?" Daniel said.

"Management. You know the type, afraid of their own shadows."

"They told you to do nothing? Even if they disrupt the other patrons?"

The guard nodded his head. "No cops," he said. "Unless they start blowin' shit up, we're not to say so much as boo to 'em."

Daniel offered the man his hand, and they shook. "Thanks again," he said.

"Don't mention it."

Daniel and Buchanan elbowed their way through the angry bearded mob clotted on the grand staircase. At the top of the stairs they located a second, equally pissed off security guard who pointed the way to the computers. Inside the Washington Room they signed up to use the last available computer and Buchanan took a seat at the desk.

Daniel passed Buchanan a slip of paper with the municipal address of The Colosseum printed on it. "You know what we're looking for?"

"The name of the club's owner."

"And you're sure you can find it here?"

"You know what you're doing, you can find anything online. And I do mean anything."

Buchanan located the information they'd come for in five minutes flat. Daniel took control of the mouse and slowly scrolled through the pages. The Colosseum property consisted of a total of four interconnected buildings, he learned. The buildings had been purchased one at a time from various owners during a six month period a little over three years ago.

Buchanan slammed a fist into the palm of his hand. "So who's the unlucky bastard?"

"The owner is a numbered corporation," Daniel said.

"That's it?"

"That's it."

Buchanan ran his finger down a series of names on the screen. "What about these guys? Any of their names mean anything to you?"

Daniel shook his head. "They're corporate officers, president, vice-president, treasurer, secretary, the men and women who have the authority to bind the corporation by contract or deed. Lawyers, probably, from the local firm that set up the corporation."

"Is this gonna be a problem?" Buchanan said.

"Massachusetts isn't a tax haven," Daniel said.

"And this helps us how?"

"There are strict rules in place obligating full disclosure."

"Which means?"

"Which means that all corporations must publicly list its directors and shareholders at a central registry."

Buchanan threw up his hands. "Which is where precisely?"

"If you're as good with a computer as you think you are, another quick jaunt down the information highway should do the trick."

Twenty minutes later Buchanan back-doored the corporate records.

Daniel leaned in for a closer look at the screen. "The company was

established three and a half years ago and all registration fees are current."
Daniel grabbed the mouse again and scrolled to the next page. "The plot
thickens."

"What did you find?" Buchanan said.

Daniel pointed to the line that had caught his attention.

"The owner of The Colosseum is one F. W. Dixon," Buchanan said.
"So?"

***

Galton answered his cell on the first ring.

"Do you know anything about a nightclub called The Colosseum?"
Daniel said.

Galton chuckled. "So how's the weather in sunny California?"

"Eerily similar to that of Boston, I suspect. So how about it?"

"I've heard of it."

"And?"

"What do you need?"

"Whatever you've heard."

"Can you call me back in a bit? I gotta take a walk, gotta go some
place where the walls don't have quite so many ears."

"Farmer?"

"Yeah."

"Talk to you in five," Daniel said.

"Better make it thirty," Galton said. "I gotta crap like the dickens."

"Wong's again?"

"Yeah."

"Thirty minutes it is."

"Coffee?" Buchanan said.

"Sure."

Back out on Boylston, Daniel hailed a cab, and after assuring the
Muslim driver that they weren't in possession of any form of alcohol,
including wine gums or rye bread, he reluctantly agreed to take them to the
waterfront. They quickly located a coffee shop with a primo view of the
harbor and ducked inside. Daniel ordered a dark-roasted Panamanian blend
with a splash of low fat milk. Buchanan ordered a small decaf with cream
and three tablespoons of refined sugar. They never said a word after taking
their seats, just watched as a lopsided container ship with Communist China
markings was bullied toward Conley Terminal by a rubber-wrapped tug a
fraction of its size. When the requisite period of time had elapsed, Daniel
flipped his phone open and punched redial.

"Officially, The Colosseum is a private gentleman's club," Galton said. "Unofficially, it's rumored to be home to some real perverse goings on." He paused. "I know BPD has had someone inside with the liquor licensing guys on several occasions. Once they even managed to get a search warrant. But each time they've come up empty-handed. It's almost as if-"

"They knew the heat was coming," Daniel said.

"Exactly," Galton said.

"Can I ask you a question?" Daniel said.

"Shoot."

"You're one of the top Feds in the state yet you have all these trivial facts floating around in your head concerning what appears to be nothing more than a routine vice investigation."

"You said you had a question," Galton said.

"My question is why?"

"I used to be Boston vice before joining the federales," Galton said. "I still got buddies on the force. They ask me for advice, I give it. If I only worked my own cases I'd spend most of the time on my ass, sitting on it and watching it grow wider with all the cream filled donuts I'd have to eat to while the time away. So I help when I'm asked, and most of the time it happens to be vice related."

"Do you know anything about the club's owner?"

"Not really," Galton said. "I know vice sent a cadet over to the Suffolk Registry of Deeds once to run a title search, but she came up with zip. If I'm not mistaken, some company with a name that reads like a credit card number owns it."

"That's all they found?"

"It wasn't exactly a high-priority investigation if you get my drift, based on unsubstantiated rumors concerning certain well-connected segments of Boston's fairy community and all. Besides we're not all fucking lawyers - thank God. Last I heard that's as far as it went."

"Luckily, I happen to be a lawyer," Daniel said, "and this morning I pierced the corporate veil and came up with a name."

"Anyone we know?"

"How does the name F. W. Dixon grab you?"

After a moment of thoughtful silence, Galton said, "I heard of him. Wrote the Hardy Boy books didn't he?"

"Different guy."

"Then I never heard of him."

"Sure you have."

"You want I should sit some vice buddies on the club?"

"Don't," Daniel said. "There's a very good reason the cops never turned anything up."

"A rat," Galton said.

"A decidedly large one," Daniel said.

55

Daniel was hunched over a table on the lower tier of The Colosseum, waiting for Buchanan to return from the washroom and recollecting a passage written more than three hundred years earlier by the English poet John Dryden.

There is pleasure sure,
In being mad, which none but the madmen know!

The mood inside the club was decidedly festive. According to the blitzkrieg of announcements over the PA system, the witching hour marked the opening round of the First Annual Butt-Darts for Charity Tournament. The master of ceremonies, an elderly queen with white flyaway eyebrows and a waxed Rip Taylor moustache, was warming up the standing room only audience with a straight-bashing stand-up routine that had them rolling in the aisles.

"The bouncers are still pulling sentry duty," Buchanan said as he dropped into the seat beside Daniel. "How much you wanna bet something's back there Shabazz doesn't want anyone to see?"

Daniel coughed to signal Buchanan to zip it. Their flirty waiter, Raoul, was on his way back to the table.

"Have you decided yet?" the waiter said.

Daniel flipped his menu over to the Butch side. "I believe we'll have the Filet Mignon dinner," he said. "But I have a question first."

"An excellent choice, Mr. Jackson. And what is your question?"

"What does Old Maid refer to?"

"It's management's little attempt at humor, sir. The meat is cooked to a grey-brown throughout."

"Well-done."

"That's right."

"So Menstrual would mean . . . ?"

"Bloodier than a Peckinpah frame."

"Medium rare," Daniel said. "For both of us."

"What I would have chosen myself," the waiter said. "Were I not a vegan."

"May I ask another question?"

"You can ask me anything." He fluttered his eyelids with an intensity that threatened to blow the menus from the table. "And I do mean anything."

"The elevator those two muscle-heads are guarding, where does it lead?"

The waiter glanced around to see who was listening before he answered. "To the special rooms, sir."

"Special rooms?"

"Rooms for rent."

"Like a hotel?"

"Hardly. They're rented by the hour, if you get my drift, and for a king's ransom. Available only to the owner's favored guests."

"Why all the security?"

"That's mostly for the owner. He lives back there you know."

"What's his place like?"

"I've never been. None of the hired help have. Although I've heard from some of the chattier members that it's really quite wonderful. Is that all, Mr. Jackson?"

"Yes, Raoul. Thank you."

Daniel leaned over the table as soon as their waiter had bustled out of earshot. "The security could be strictly for show," he said. "Shabazz is the type of guy who values appearance above all else. Style over substance. The way he dresses. The way he talks. Could be he forgot to color co-ordinate the butt plugs with the titty clips and simply wants the *faux pas* kept under wraps."

"Won't know until we get back there," Buchanan said.

"Gentlemen and gentlemen," the MC said, "may I have your attention. For those of you who don't know me, my name is Caligula, and I'll be your host for this evening's festivities." He paused to laugh. "But seriously, folks. I'm Morgan Raye-Mann and it is my honor to say:

"LET THE GAMES BEGIN."

The spotlights above the dance floor razzmatazzed over the multitudes before zeroing in on the uppermost archway on the opposite side of the club. When nothing immediately happened the MC started clapping in a four-four beat and motioned for the audience to do the same. The last time Daniel had heard a ruckus this loud had been twenty years earlier when a sell-out crowd at MSG was attempting to coax a second encore from The Dead.

After five minutes of thunderous applause, a man decked out in full Roman centurion attire came charging through the archway on a chariot harnessed to a pair of male bodybuilders wearing skin-tight black rubber suits and long white horsehair wigs. Scattering rose petals in his wake, he guided the chariot down the winding series of wheelchair ramps onto the dance floor then brought his spirited stallions to a halt. Placing a hand to his brow to shield the glare of the lights from his eyes, the centurion gazed theatrically back up the way he had come.

Daniel's eyes followed the spotlights as they once again pinpointed the curtained archway. Trumpets sounded and a group of five naked men strolled into the light. In single file they followed the rose petal path to the center of the dance floor. The men were numbered from one to five on the small of their backs.

"Assume the position," the MC said.

Moving their legs a shoulder width apart, the men bowed deeply at the waist, their hands gripping the wrought-iron stand that supported the flaming bowl. The centurion stepped down from his chariot, carrying a steel bucket and a stiff-bristled brush. He dipped the brush into the bucket then proceeded to slop several coats of a glistening oil-like solution into the crack of each man's ass. When he was done, he climbed back aboard his chariot and galloped away to the wild cheers of the adoring crowd.

"Think they'd move aside for my shield?"

"What?" Daniel said, unable to keep his mind on business, unable to concentrate on anything other than what he was seeing but not quite believing.

"The bouncers stationed at the elevator to Shabazz' lair," Buchanan said. "Do you think they'd move aside if I badged them?"

Daniel looked at Buchanan. "Your shield's LAPD. If they can read, were through. We don't want to tip our hand, announcing our presence prematurely. Remember, we're still *persona non grata*. We only have one shot to find your aunt, Frank, and I don't want to waste it."

"Doesn't mean we don't take chances," Buchanan said.

"May we have the contestants please," the MC said.

Five beams separated from the main cluster of spotlights, which remained targeted on the numbered men, and raced along each of the five flights of stairs leading up from the dance floor. At the top of each flight stood a naked, blindfolded man with an erection. Each man was covered from head to toe in a different color of paint: red, yellow, green, orange and purple. They were all on the waifish side with the exception of purple, who was at least a hundred-and-fifty pounds overweight. Behind each man stood another man wearing a white toga and holding an ostrich feather and a large wooden paddle. Periodically the men in the togas would tickle the contestants' genitals with the feathers to keep them turgid.

A drum roll sounded.

"Ready," the MC said.

The men in the togas raised their paddles to the heavens.

"Set," the MC continued.

The naked men placed their hands on their hips and thrust their pelvises forward, leaning over backward like they were about to do the limbo.

"GO!"

The men in the togas smacked their paddles down onto the backsides of the contestants and, to the quirky strains of Quincy Jones' *Soul Bossa*

Nova, they were off.

"The purple one looks like one of those Teletubbies," Daniel said. "You know the one I mean, from the kids show on PBS. The one rumored to be queer."

"Tinky Winky," Buchanan said.

Daniel looked at Buchanan but never said a word.

"What's your problem?" Buchanan said. "I watch it with Charlotte. She fucking adores 'em."

"Sure she does," Daniel said.

Four of the contestants, Red, Yellow, Green and Orange, went straight for the stairs, while the fifth, Tinky Winky, taking tiny Geisha girl steps, headed down the pathway of wheelchair ramps, using the feel of the rose petals on the soles of his feet for guidance.

"Any ideas on how we're going to get inside?" Buchanan said.

Red, the fleetest of foot, had reached the dance floor and was approaching the man with the number two stenciled on his back. His sense of direction was impeccable and his erection appeared to be approaching its target at precisely the right altitude. The crowd cheered and Number Two spread his legs another couple inches to brace for impact.

"I've been tossing something around in my head," Daniel said.

Red was within a yard of reaching his goal when one of his feet met with some drips of the oil-like solution and flew out from under him. His head bounced once on the terra cotta tiled floor and then he lay still. The crowd booed and hissed.

"Care to enlighten your old buddy?" Buchanan said.

The next two contestants, Orange and Green, stepped onto the dance floor at precisely the same moment, milling about its surface without apparent purpose or destination. The other contestant who had taken the stairs, Yellow, never made it to the bottom as his erection had found the open mouth of one of the spectators and, judging by the look on his face, seemed quite content to remain where he was. All the while Tinky Winky continued to descend slowly along the ramps, approximately three quarters of the way down now.

Daniel stood. "Watch and learn," he said.

He slipped into an empty space at the dance floor bar beside a man standing back-to and watching the show, a Corona with a lemon wedge in one hand, a slender cigarette in the other, neck pistoning in and out to the beat of the music. He had on a cognac-colored Valentino blazer, black t-shirt and faded jeans. The heel on his right Doc Marten was two inches higher than the heel on his left. Daniel glanced back at Buchanan who was sitting there and looking rather confused. Daniel gave his friend a hearty thumbs-up sign.

Tinky Winky had just reached the floor and was following the rose petals to the man with the number four stenciled on his back when Daniel said to the man beside him, "Do you live here often?"

Marcello Valenzano turned and raped Daniel with his heavily lidded, reptilian eyes. As recognition set in his eyes widened, his expression cycling between confusion and fear. On the dance floor Green and Orange were unsuccessfully attempting to penetrate each other in the instant that Tinky Winky simultaneously collided with and penetrated Number Four who let out a girlish squeal of delight.

"Where's your butchy friend?"

Daniel made a point of looking all around. "I don't see him. Do you see him?"

The answer seemed to calm the man somewhat. "What do you want?" He set his drink down and crossed his arms.

Daniel leaned against the bar and accidentally on purpose knocked the Corona over with his elbow. As Valenzano lunged to right the bottle, Daniel used his foot to switch the recycling bin with the garbage can. "I guess I want to apologize for the way I handled things at A Bird in the Hand the other night."

Valenzano snuffed out his cigarette. "I'm listening."

Eyes closed, foam dripping from his wide-open mouth, Tinky Winky was fucking Number Four's ass hard. Daniel averted his gaze and ran Sinatra's *All I Need Is The Girl* loudly through his head in an effort to keep a grip on his sanity.

"After you grabbed my ass, I must admit, my first instinct was to take you by the throat and choke the life from your scrawny, gimped-up body."

"And now?"

With smiley pleasant overtones in his voice Daniel leaned in close to Valenzano and said, "I'm thinking I should have trusted my instincts."

"You, sir, are an uncouth ass."

Daniel made a palms-up gesture. "Tell me something I don't know."

Valenzano picked up his beer bottle and unwittingly pitched it into the garbage can. Almost immediately the music and the buggery stopped, and a pair of powerful spotlights fixed him in their unforgiving glare. Valenzano appeared completely at a loss until he glanced down and saw what had happened.

"It wasn't me," he whined. "Honest, it wasn't. Didn't you see what happened? It really wasn't me." He pointed to the empty space where Daniel had been. "It was *him*."

Buchanan's eyes crinkled with amusement upon Daniel's return to their ringside table. "You're such an ass," he said.

"So I've heard."

<u>56</u>

Leonard Farmer hopped off the jostling, curry-scented MBTA bus at the corner of Boylston and Dalton Streets and jogged the remaining distance to the Boston Sheraton Hotel, site of the Massachusetts Democratic Party's $2,500.00 a plate fundraising dinner. He caught the elevator to the second floor and joined in the slow-moving queue outside the Back Bay Ballroom behind Sean Penn, Leonardo DiCaprio, and several dozen bearded Harvard professor types. At the head of the line, a guard with high cheek bones and a great hair cut was reconciling a guest's photo ID against the computerized attendance list.

"I thought you were brilliant in Mystery River," Leonard whispered to Mr. Penn, who just glared at him over a surprisingly narrow shoulder.

Leonard reached out to touch the hem of the Academy Award winning actor's garment, a funky yellow and shocking pink blazer.

"D&G?" he said.

A second guard materialized at Leonard's side and pointed to a large brass placard mounted on the wall.

"Don't touch the celebrities, sir," he said.

"I *am* sorry," Leonard said. "I didn't see the sign. It won't happen again."

Although presidential hopeful Governor Terrence Thornton was the evening's keynote speaker, the Funny Girl herself had been tapped to make an appearance via satellite from her bluff top Malibu home. The 8:30 PM EST dinner hour had been stipulated by the vivacious diva so that she might be lit to full splendor by the golden rays of the setting west coast sun. Needless to say the room was abuzz with speculation over which designer she had chosen to clothe her. While an out-of-this-world House of Dior creation was the odds-on favorite, Leonard let it be known to all who would listen that she would be wearing a one-off Herrera number.

With a glass of DeLoach Vinyards OFS Chardonnay in hand, Leonard located his assigned seat in the deepest and darkest corner of the room and instantly melted into a heated discussion on the merits of radical environmental activism with several disheveled, but surprisingly eloquent, Greenpeace activists, and a wild-eyed, surprisingly ineloquent former *St. Elsewhere* actor named Ed Something-Or-Other, Jr..

At precisely 4:55 PM Pacific Time the overhead lights were dimmed and the velvet-voiced songstress appeared onscreen in a demure midnight-blue Jean-Paul Gaultier dress. Draped over a lovely Victorian settee, she began with a flourish of blown kisses before launching into a tearful soliloquy, broken only by sustained periods of applause and two costume changes (a beaded Giorgio Armani gown with diamond-studded tiara followed by a sexy *pinot noir*-red Carolina Herrera gown), wherein she praised Muslims the world over for their continued tolerance and civility in the face of American intolerance and incivility. Thirty minutes later, following a surprise endorsement of Governor Thornton's presidential bid, the lights were raised and dinner was served by a sprightly flock of red-breasted waiters.

To Leonard's delight, the menu was vegetarian. Spiced honeybush tea, fresh coconut water, garden salad with Italian herbal vinaigrette, and vegan Tur-kee drizzled with a tangy portabella mushroom gravy. Unfortunately, the delicious, fur-people-friendly meal was almost ruined by Something-Or-Other, Jr., who began an invective-laced anti-big business tirade with the appetizer that lasted through to the after dinner aperitif, unceasing even when his mouth was crammed full with food.

All conversation was mercifully halted when the chairperson for the Massachusetts Democratic Party, an Hispanic female, took the dais and introduced Governor Thornton in Spanish. Against a backdrop of alternating American and Mexican flags, the governor took the microphone firmly in hand and delivered what was billed in numerous pre-event press releases as a common sense policy address on energy conservation. During his twenty-five minute speech, the charismatic gentleman shared his vision of a sustainable, eco-friendly lifestyle, which included everything from high tech solar panels to low tech compost piles. He spoke passionately and eloquently on the need for ordinary citizens to grow their own fruits and vegetables and to limit daily travel to bicycles or public transportation. With respect to lengthier, cross-country sojourns his thoughtful recommendations included the use of AmTrak passenger trains, which he assured the audience was far more environmentally benign than petroleum guzzling airplanes. By the governor's estimation he could make America energy self-sufficient before the end of his second term as president. The standing ovation at the conclusion of his speech was as lengthy as it was thunderous, dwarfing even the one awarded to Babs when she had reappeared on-screen in the slinky, low-cut Herrera masterpiece.

The waiter had just topped up his spiced honeybush tea when Leonard spotted Tokunbo through the gaily chattering crowd, one of several luminaries holding court with Governor Thornton. Leonard wanted to pop by and say hello to his friend, maybe get in a word or two with the man of the hour, but a decidedly tipsy Something-Or-Other, Jr. was off on another of his tangents, bemoaning the insidious nature of hybrid-electric transitional vehicles, which he believed to be a last-ditch effort by the petroleum industry to keep their hands in the pocketbooks of average Americans. Magnetism was the wave of the future, he ranted to everyone with whom he was unlucky enough to make eye contact. By the time Leonard was finally able to ditch the overzealous, out of work actor, Tokunbo was nowhere to be seen.

Leonard approached a squat lesbian attorney whom he knew from his work with the bureau. She was wearing a smart navy-blue pinstriped suit, and tan faux-leather brogue oxford shoes. "Hello, Anne," he said. "You're looking ship-shape as usual."

"As are you," the attorney said.

"I do my best."

"I noticed that they stuck you at the children's table. Tough luck."

Leonard leaned in close to the woman. "I really can't complain, since I didn't shell out a single penny for the invite."

The attorney made a fist and smacked it against her palm. "Would've made no difference to me. Two hours sitting at a table with that clown, let me tell you, I'd have done a hell of a lot more than complain."

Leonard chuckled. "Now that I would gladly have paid twenty-five hundred to see."

"Have you met my most recent life-partner?" She motioned toward a bony blond in a matching pinstriped suit who was engaged in a bawdy, laughter-ridden conversation with Whoopi Goldberg and a red-faced, visibly swaying Ted Kennedy.

"I can't say I've had the pleasure."

"Kelly," the attorney bellowed. "Haul your can over here. I've got someone I want you to meet."

The woman excused herself from the actress/comedian and the long-time senator, gave Anne a quick peck on the cheek, and took Leonard's hand.

"Leonard Farmer, Kelly Halston," Anne said. "Leonard is a special agent with the FBI."

Kelly jerked her hand away and took a quick backward step.

"Not to worry," Anne said. "He's one of us, I assure you."

"Pleased to meet you, Mr. Farmer," Kelly mumbled, seemingly unconvinced by her lover's endorsement.

"Have you seen Tokunbo Shabazz?" Leonard said. "He was here just a moment ago. I wanted to say a quick hello before I called it a night."

Anne shook her head. "Sorry," she said.

"Last I saw he was heading toward the oppressor's room with Governor Thornton," Kelly said. "Couldn't have been more than a minute ago."

"Oppressor's room?" Leonard said.

"Lesbian feminist humor," Anne said. "She meant the men's room."

"Well it was great to see you again," Leonard said as he broke away from the pair. "Keep up the good fight."

"To my dying, gin-soaked breath," Anne said.

<u>57</u>

Daniel and Buchanan slipped into the elevator while the bouncers were otherwise occupied with kicking Valenzano to the curb. They descended automatically and in a matter of seconds the door whisked open to reveal what appeared to be the basement of an adjoining building. The room was cavernous, two full stories tall and approximately eighty feet in length. There were six doors on either side of a narrow hallway on the ground level and six doors on the second level which was accessible by a full length balcony with circular cast-iron staircases at either end. Seven of the doors were open and lights were burning in three of the rooms.

"Is the hair on the back of your neck standing at attention?" Buchanan said.

"For about an hour now," Daniel said.

Hanging on the wall beside the nearest of the lighted rooms was a framed poster that read *Diversity: It Includes Us All*. Inside the room two pot-bellied middle-aged men were getting it on. One man was frantically masturbating and straddling the other, who was noisily chowing down on his asshole.

"I'm going, I'm going," the man on top said in a breathy falsetto voice.

"Do it, Father Larry. Do it now," the man on the bottom said gruffly.

"Father Larry doesn't know if he's coming or going," Daniel said.

"Oh, he knows all right," Buchanan said.

Like driving past a car wreck, Daniel couldn't look away. What he was witnessing here, in private, and for a princely sum, was worse than what he'd seen at the butt darts tournament. Much worse. This wasn't being done for laughs, or for the entertainment and applause of others; it was purely for personal pleasure.

"Going . . . going now," Father Larry said. Then, grunting and straining, he lowered his bulk and began gyrating his hips, smearing his feces over the other man's face before sliding down his chest and settling on his erection, which he promptly rode for all that he was worth.

Daniel turned his back and walked away.

"Man's greatest inhumanity to man," he said.

Buchanan's silence spoke volumes.

"Sorry, Frank," Daniel said.

"That isn't me," Buchanan said through clenched teeth. "That was never me."

***

The stairwell into Shabazz' apartment was located at the end of the hallway. Although the glistening, streak-free stainless steel door at the top of the stairs was locked, Buchanan was able to pick his way past the deadbolt in maybe a quarter of the time it would've taken Daniel. He cracked open the door, took a look inside and immediately let out a long, low whistle.

"What is it?" Daniel said.

"His living room is bigger than my yard. Front and back."

The ceilings were lofty and the walls were banked with windows draped completely in rich ecclesiastical purple. There were African war masks and ornamented shields and spears on the walls and expensive-looking Persian carpets scattered thoughtfully over the bleached oak floor. Against the far end of the room was a twenty foot long by twelve foot high working replica of the Trevi Fountain, complete with Corinthian columns, horses and, in the likeness of Shabazz himself, Neptune, the Roman god of the sea.

"I'll check the bedrooms," Buchanan said. "You start with the kitchen and work your way out."

Daniel had thoroughly searched the kitchen and the half-bath and was opening the red lacquered humidor on the living room coffee table when he heard Buchanan scream, heard his footsteps pounding out from the farthest bedroom, heard a high-pitched, feral sound that he didn't recognize. He looked up in time to see his friend fending off the attack of a frenzied fighting cock. The cock was scratching and pecking at Buchanan's legs, occasionally flapping up to make a series of slashes at his face with its talons, driving him ever backwards toward the door. Two hens and a second cock, feathers flared aggressively, were standing in the bedroom's doorway, clucking their approval.

"She's not here," Buchanan said. "Let's beat it."

***

In the basement, tucked behind the stairwell to Shabazz' apartment was a closed door that Daniel hadn't noticed on the way up. He was reaching for the handle to take a look inside when the door was opened from the other side and a beautiful young woman came drifting up a set of hammered stone steps. She was wearing a long, diaphanous black dress with spaghetti straps, black panties, black stockings and garter belt and black high heels with no back. Her face and arms had the glow of good health and her teeth were snow white. Her nipples were assertive without being rude.

"Well, well," she said to Daniel, "aren't you the handsome one."

"You're not so bad yourself."

"My name is Earlae, and I run this juke joint."

"Jesse Jackson," Daniel said.

She put a hand to Daniel's chest and rubbed it back and forth over his pectorals. "If it's all the same with you, I'll just call you the Incredibly Handsome Hulk."

"Works for me," Daniel said.

Behind the young woman's back Buchanan caught Daniel's eyes and made a gagging motion by sticking his fingers in his mouth.

"Well, it does," Daniel said.

"May I ask how you got back here?" Earlae said.

"We just kinda snuck in for a peek when the hired help wasn't looking," Daniel said.

"You've been a very naughty boy," she said to Daniel. She bit her lower lip gently. "Perhaps a good spanking would teach you a lesson."

"I don't know if I'd go that far," Daniel said.

"Perhaps we can discuss how far you would go over an inhibition lowering nip of Cognac. My treat, of course."

Daniel shrugged at Buchanan in a what-can-you-do fashion, and followed her back to the elevator.

Back inside the club, Earlae's hips began to swish and sway. "I just love to dance," she said, her lips brushing softly against Daniel's ear. "Do you remember the Macarena?" She held out her hand and Daniel took it.

"Macarena?" Daniel said.

Earlae snapped her fingers and the Macarena song was immediately phased into the mix. "I'd love to," she said, and led him onto the dance floor. "I know it's kitschy, but it's my all time favorite tune."

Standing flat-footed, Daniel said, "Kitschy? That's the understatement of the century."

"I'll tell you what," Earlae said, still moving to the music. "Name a tune that puts you in the mood and I'll have the DJ spin it for you."

Daniel leaned in and whispered in her ear.

Earlae laughed. "I'll be right back."

The Chicken Dance Song was in full swing by the time she returned and Daniel was squatting and flapping around the dance floor while everyone else in the club, Buchanan included, looked on in slack-jawed amazement.

***

On the modest walk back to their dingy hotel, Daniel said, "Shabazz is Mr. Cool."

"How do you know?"

Daniel reached into his pocket and pulled out a cigar, which he passed to Buchanan.

"Romeo and Juliet. Like the ones out back in my tree in Portsmouth. Where'd you find it?"

"In a trashy-looking humidor in Shabazz's living room," Daniel said.

"Here I am the so-called professional, and I not only find nothing, I get chased out of the bedroom shitter by a chicken with a bad attitude."

Daniel chuckled at the memory. "You notice anything strange about the bathroom?"

"Not really," Buchanan said. "Why?"

"There was no mirror in the one I searched. There was a toilet, and a sink, but no mirror."

"Come to think of it, I don't recall seeing one in the master bath either."

"And none on any of the walls. No reflective surfaces anywhere. Even the drapes were all closed tightly-"

"Preventing a reflection in the glass," Buchanan said. "We got 'em."

"We've got one of them. What we need to find out now is the name of Shabazz' partner, and where they've got Aunt Sarah stashed. It obviously isn't at the club."

Buchanan laughed. "One mystery down, one to go."

"What do you mean?"

"Considering you just tripped the light fantastic with Shabazz's partner in crime, all we need to do is rescue Aunt Sarah."

"But Shabazz' partner is a-"

"A chick with a dick."

"No way," Daniel said.

"You get a load of the fuck-me pumps he was wearing?"

"She," Daniel said. "And I most certainly did."

"Gimme your phone."

"Why?"

"Just do it."

Daniel passed his Blackberry to Buchanan and watched him thumb through the menu.

"You remember these?" Buchanan turned the phone. On screen were the holes in the snow that he'd photographed outside the Calhoun home. Twenty-three pencil-thin holes that traced a path straight to the back door.

"Her stiletto heels made the holes," Daniel said.

Buchanan smiled. "His stiletto heels."

"If you ever breathe a word of my dancing with a-"

"Chick with a dick," Buchanan said.

"I'm serious, Frank. You tell anyone, and I'll-"

"Okay, okay," Buchanan said. "So it's *Let's Make a Deal* time You keep that whole screaming retreat from a chicken incident under wraps and I swear to God, I'll never tell another living soul about what a sweet couple the two of you made."

Daniel held out his hand and they shook on it.

"Deal," he said.

<u>58</u>

The hallway to the men's room was blocked by a phalanx of ethnically diverse, v-shaped secret service agents. They remained firmly rooted in place as Leonard approached, refusing him passage.

"I apologize for the inconvenience, sir," an Asian agent said, his slicked back hair as smooth as a raven's wing, "but this restroom is temporarily unavailable. If it's an emergency situation, however, I'd be glad to point you in the direction of the nearest alternate accommodation."

Beyond their broad shoulders, Leonard could see Tokunbo speaking with Raymond Sowell, Governor Thornton's security head. Leonard caught Tokunbo's eye and waved to him. Tokunbo leaned in and whispered something to Sowell who shouted, "You may let Special Agent Farmer through, Mr. Ban."

Leonard strode over and shook each man's hand. "Great to see you, Tokunbo. And nice to finally meet you, Mr. Sowell. I've heard a lot about you."

"There's certainly a lot for Tokunbo to tell. Good, bad *and* ugly. He and I go back more years than I care to remember."

"And you've certainly come a long way," Leonard said. "Both of you."

"Have we really come such a long way, Tokunbo? Have we really changed all that much?"

Tokunbo slapped Sowell on the back. "Our wardrobes, certainly. Beyond that? Who knows?" He waved his hands in a dismissive gesture. "And who cares?"

"Speaking of wardrobes, Mr. Sowell," Leonard said. "Your suit is divine. Ralph Lauren, isn't it?"

Sowell nodded. "Call me Raymond."

"One can't go wrong being on a first-name basis with a man who has the ear of our next President."

Sowell smiled thinly at the comment.

"Mine's Polo, too," Leonard said, flipping his lapel over to show off the tag. "Look."

Tokunbo chuckled. "Mr. Lauren's Savile Row Wide Stripe Suit is Purple Label, Leonard, not Polo."

Thoroughly embarrassed by his *faux pas*, Leonard quickly changed the subject. "Once again I want to express my gratitude for tonight's invitation, Tokunbo."

"You had a satisfactory time then? I was worried when I saw with whom they had you seated."

"Think nothing of it. The man was entertaining if nothing else."

"You lie badly."

Leonard shrugged. "Notwithstanding the seating assignment, I had a splendid time. And that is the truth. The dinner was excellent, as were the speeches. I got to say hello to some old friends, and I made some new ones, too."

"Excellent," Tokunbo said.

Through the men's room door came the sound of running water. "If you'll both excuse me for a moment," Sowell said.

"I guess that's my cue as well," Leonard said. "I have an early day tomorrow. Nice to meet you, Raymond. And thanks again, Tokunbo."

"Glad that you could make it," Tokunbo said. "Just as I am glad that you had an enjoyable time."

Leonard turned to leave then paused. "Oh, and before I forget, it appears that vice may be gearing up for another raid on your club."

"What have you heard?"

"As I'm sure you're aware my slob of a partner used to be on the goon squad before joining the Bureau and he assists them time and again with requests for information and the like."

"I am aware."

"Well yesterday afternoon a call came in on his cell and he took off like a shot. An hour later he's on his computer, perusing the file on your club."

"Although I do appreciate the heads-up, Leonard, it is completely unnecessary. I operate The Colosseum with a keen eye to both the letter and the spirit of the law. As I have told the authorities on numerous occasions, they are not only welcome to visit my club whenever they chose, they are welcome to join. Although our client list is strictly confidential, I am not speaking out of school when I tell you that we have several of Boston's finest on our rolls already."

"I just thought you should know. Intolerance for the gay, lesbian and transgender community in this day and age is simply inexcusable," Leonard said. "If those dinosaurs in vice were to have their way it'd be Stonewall all over again. Why can't they leave us be?"

"Indeed," Tokunbo said. "I cannot believe that his former colleagues are still reaching out to him for assistance. He joined the bureau, what? Ten years ago."

"Twelve," Leonard said. "And that's what was odd about the whole thing. When I checked the call log on his phone, it wasn't even vice who called."

"Oh, really?"

"The call was from Mr. Rourke."

"So it was merely a coincidence then that the file was accessed after he took the call."

"Maybe you're right."

"I am sure that Mr. Rourke was simply looking for an update on any progress you may have made in locating Mr. Buchanan's missing kith and kin."

Leonard nodded. "Once again," he said, "I'm sure you're right."

"Now if you will excuse me, Leonard. All this talk of telephone calls has reminded me of a rather important call that I must make myself."

The door to the bathroom swung open and Governor Thornton rolled into the hallway with Raymond. The governor approached Leonard with his big hand extended. Leonard took it and was subjected to a hearty, bone-crunching handshake.

"I have it on good authority that I am going to be the next president," the governor said, his eyes glinting mischievously.

"With Babs in your corner how can you lose?"

The governor opened his mouth and laughed heartily. "Assuming I escape the nominating convention unscathed, I guess it's no secret how you'll be casting your vote come election night."

"For you, sir."

"If you're on a first name basis with Raymond, you're on a first name basis with me. You got that, son?"

"Of course, Terrence."

The governor spun his wheelchair in the direction of the elevators. "Walk with me, Leonard. I've already said my goodbyes to the room."

"I'd be honored."

They exited through the back of the hotel and headed toward a trio of black SUVs, motors idling, exhausts spewing cyclones of white smoke into the ebony sky. "Like you I also have an early morning, and some of us need our beauty sleep more than others." He gave a self-deprecating laugh. "Make-up can only do so much when a man gets to be my age."

The governor backed his chair onto the motorized lift and was gently raised into his well-appointed SUV.

"Your speech tonight was truly inspiring," Leonard said. "I cycle to work in the spring and summer months and ride the bus the rest of the year."

"My speech was strictly by the numbers, Leonard. It is the actions of uncompromising stewards of the planet like you that are truly inspiring." The governor motioned to Raymond, his driver this evening, to open the front passenger door. "But tonight I hope you'll forego Boston's world class public transportation system and allow me the courtesy of seeing you home."

"That's not necessary, sir."

"Terrence. And just get in the truck, Leonard."

"Thank you, Mr. President."

"Mr. President," the governor said thoughtfully. "Don't tell anyone I said this but I could really get used to the sound of that." He reached between the big bucket seats and clapped Leonard on the shoulder. "It has quite a ring to it, don't you think?"

<u>59</u>

It appeared that the desk clerk had taken Buchanan's threat seriously. They returned to The Rex to find their radiator as cold as a bureaucrat's heart. The only problem was that the city was in the midst of a sub-zero cold snap and the rest of their room wasn't any cozier. The curtains were closed and the television provided the room's only illumination. The Arab news anchor with one of the local networks had an accent so thick that Daniel couldn't make out a single word she was saying. Judging by the troubled look on her brow, however, the news wasn't good and he was probably better off not knowing.

"I'm going to call Terry," Daniel said shortly before midnight. "I want to see what she can dig up on Shabazz."

"What about Galton?" Buchanan said. "He'll help us out."

Daniel looked at Buchanan and grinned at him through chattering teeth.

"Oh," Buchanan said, with only his eyes showing above the covers. "I get it."

Officer Wagner was not at HQ when Daniel called, but dispatch promised to relay a message to call him on his cell ASAP. Daniel's phone rang less than two minutes later.

"You never said goodbye," Terry said. "I'd hoped to see you again before you left."

"I was wondering if you could do me a small favor."

"For you? Anything."

"I need you to scrape up all the dirt you can find on one Tokunbo Shabazz."

"Chairman of the Massachusetts Human Rights Commission? That Tokunbo Shabazz? You don't think he's involved, do you?"

"Acting Chair," Daniel said. "And as a matter of fact, that's exactly what I think."

"Where in hell are you, Rourke?"

Daniel laughed. "It's probably best that you don't know. But I can say this; I'm too frigging cold to be in hell."

"Well, if you want me to send you the info, I'm going to need to know where you're holed up."

"You've got me there."

As Terry read back the address there was no trace of surprise in her voice that he and Buchanan hadn't left town after all.

"When can I expect to hear from you?"

"How does first thing in the morning sound? My shift ends at six. I'll run his name through our database as soon as I get off and print whatever pops up." The line went silent for a moment. "Tokunbo Shabazz? Man, oh, man. You'd better be right. You go after this guy without proof and you're in for a mess of trouble. If you can believe what you see in the news, Shabazz is sky-high connected."

"Unfortunately, I don't have an interpreter on the payroll, so I haven't exactly been following the local news."

"Whatever," Terry said, and then disconnected the call.

Outside their window the blizzard howled as loudly and as forlornly as the hookers in the rooms surrounding them. Curled into the fetal position beneath the scratchy, mismatched sheets, Daniel listened to the desolate sounds and thought of Terry Wagner and managed to chase away most of the chill from his bones.

<u>60</u>

If Terry Wagner hadn't been surprised at hearing that Daniel and Buchanan were still in town and poking around, Daniel was equally nonplussed when Terry showed up on their doorstep at eight o'clock the next morning. She was carrying an inch thick, legal-sized manila envelope and a black leather Samsonite garment bag. Buchanan took her bag and her hooded parka and tossed them onto his unmade bed on top of yesterday's tighty-not-quite-so-whities.

"Nice digs," Terry said to Buchanan, adding when her amused eyes found Daniel. "The mould on the walls really brings out the bruises on your roomie's eyes."

"You should see the other guy's fist," Daniel said.

Terry was wearing blue jeans and a baggy American Eagle hoodie. Her long auburn hair was pulled back in a pony tail and her face had that freshly-scrubbed Noxzema girl look. She was even more stunning than he remembered.

"Has it stopped snowing?" Daniel said.

"Ask me in May or June," Terry said.

"You're not covered with the stuff," Daniel said. "It's why I asked."

"There's a two story garage at the back of the hotel that the whores use when the rooms fill up during tourist season. I parked in there."

"I never noticed a garage," Buchanan said.

"The entrance is through an alley around the other side of the block. And before you start to wonder, I live in Portsmouth now, but I was born and raised in Boston. My buddies and I used to frequent the place in our college pub-crawl days. Cheapest rates in town. Close to the cheapest drinks in town."

"I didn't say anything," Daniel said.

"Me neither," Buchanan said.

"I know," Terry said. "But I didn't want you speculating either."

"What's in the envelope?" Daniel said.

"I think you may be wrong about Shabazz," Terry said. "He had some problems early on, got mixed up with one of the local gangs, the Castlegate Road Gang, but he got out. He hasn't had a run-in with the law since he was sixteen."

Daniel said nothing.

"The man may be a raving homosexual maniac but there's nothing I could find that points to his being a homicidal one. Although . . ."

"Although what?" Daniel said.

"A '57 Mercedes-Benz ragtop registered to Shabazz was issued a parking citation by one of our patrolman less than a mile from the Calhoun home."

"When?" Buchanan said.

"Shortly before the abduction."

No one said a word as the radiator lapsed into a clamorous series of knocks and pings. Buchanan had gone downstairs shortly before Terry's arrival and demanded that their heat be restored. The radiator had been stoking for the last forty-five minutes and the temperature in the room was once more beginning to nudge past the comfort zone.

"The guy's forty, forty-five years old," Daniel said. "What's he been doing since he left the gang?"

Terry opened the envelope and extracted a sheaf of papers. "Enlisted straight out of high school. Navy. Rose to the rank of Petty Officer Second Class. Honorably discharged. Kicked around at various jobs for a few years before enrolling in an arts program at Boston College."

"He never finished, did he?" Daniel said.

"Flunked out of more classes than he passed. Never did graduate. A couple of years later though, he earned a degree from someplace called Columbia Pacific University."

"It's a defunct degree mill," Daniel said. "I looked it up after my meeting with Shabazz."

"What else you got?" Buchanan said.

"He's loaded," Terry said.

"Not a penny earned, I'd bet," Daniel said.

"He made his money through a series of civil rights shakedown lawsuits about a decade back. My favorite was the one where some kid at Taco Bell mixed up his order and gave him an orange pop instead of a Coke. He claimed it was a premeditated racist act. The Associated Press ate it up, ran it every day for weeks."

"What was the outcome?" Daniel said.

"The seventeen year old Hispanic single mom who served him the pop was fired. The parent company settled out of court for just over three mil."

"Anything else of interest?" Daniel said.

"He's been with the Massachusetts Human Rights Commission for the past five years. He's an outspoken advocate of homosexual rights and a media darling because of it."

"The man's gay as the birds," Daniel said. "There's nothing saintly about a gay man crusading for gay rights. It's pure self-interest. It'd be like me taking up the cause of the chronically cool."

Terry rolled her eyes. "Here are some recent Society Page photos showing him and his boyfriend mincing the red carpet at some of the trendier charitable events."

"Lemme see," Buchanan said.

Terry handed Buchanan a grainy photocopy of a black and white newspaper photo.

"The Chicken Dance guy," Buchanan said, tilting the photo toward Daniel.

"Chicken Dance guy?" Terry said.

"Just forget about it," Daniel said.

"If I didn't know it was a guy, I'd swear it was one of the Jessicas. Biel or Alba. I can never keep them straight."

Daniel leaned in. "Yeah," he said. "I can see how he might fool someone."

"Not an eagle eye fella like you though," Buchanan said with a mischievous grin.

"Speaking of chickens," Daniel said.

Terry appeared interested but confused. "What is it with you guys and chickens?"

"What can you tell us about the transvestite?" Daniel said. "Have you got anything in there on him?"

"Given name, Earl Horowitz. Had it legally changed to Earlae when he was emancipated at age fifteen. He started showing up in the local rags with Shabazz about two and a half, three years ago."

"Is that it?" Daniel said.

Terry rifled through the papers. "Born in Bismarck, North Dakota. Mother went AWOL when he was twelve, leaving him with a stepfather who pulled a Michael Jackson. In and out of foster homes until he left for the Big Apple at fifteen." She ran her finger down the left-hand side of the paper. "Two arrests for solicitation. One conviction. No jail time. Some runway work as a model. Paris. Milan. New York. No arrests or warrants since moving to Boston three years ago. He earns a paycheck hosting a kids' show named-" She began to scan her papers.

"Chubby Duck," Daniel said.

Terry nodded. "That's it. According to the critics it's no Barney but it seems to be doing okay."

"What about the step-father?" Buchanan said. "He do any time for what he did?"

"He was charged, but he died of a massive stroke before the matter could get to trial."

"It fits," Buchanan said somberly. "He never had the closure that a trial and a guilty verdict would have brought."

Terry nodded, on Buchanan's wavelength. "He's killing his abuser over and over again, trying to find peace, to put an end to all that's wrong in his life. But the peace doesn't come."

"It never will," Buchanan said.

"In a corny, clichéd kind of way, it fits. And then again it doesn't," Daniel said. "I met with Shabazz and I wouldn't rank altruism high on a list of his character traits. He's all about appearance, status, and what's in it for him."

"Love?" Buchanan said.

"Maybe," Daniel said. "Maybe not. I'm just not convinced."

"So how did Shabazz show up on your radar?" Terry said.

"Do you have an hour or so?" Daniel said.

"For you, I've got all day." She gestured at the garment bag on Buchanan's bed. "All night, if necessary."

"On that happy note," Buchanan said, "I think I'll pop out and see if I can't find a restaurant that doesn't give me the shits. Assuming I strike pay dirt, you guys want me to bring something back?"

"No," Daniel and Terry said in perfect harmony.

Buchanan paused on his way out the door. "And guys," he said. "While I'm gone, as our new friend Custis said, don't do nothin' I wouldn't do. Especially not on my bed, if you get my drift."

"You're not into that whole whips and gerbils scene are you?" Terry said.

"Naw," Buchanan said. "A worldly guy like me doesn't need props to satisfy a lover."

"Then I guess we'll be fine," Terry said, impaling Daniel with her gaze. "Because I don't need them either."

For the next forty five minutes, Daniel told Terry everything they had discovered thus far. He showed her the pictures they'd found at Marshall Thomas's house, and described the video footage. He showed her the copies they had made of the deeds of The Colosseum properties, and of the registration documents pertaining to the numbered corporation that held the titles. Finally, he showed her the cigar that he had found during their search of Shabazz's loft.

"There's certainly more here than meets the eye," Terry said. "Luckily, I'm off duty for the next four days and am prepared to offer my expert service as your faithful sidekick."

"Are you sure you want to do that? If our investigation goes south, you can kiss your career good-bye."

"And if we clear it on the sly, I can write my own ticket in the department."

The bed creaked suggestively beneath them as Terry shifted her weight to remove her hoodie. "Is it getting hot in here, or is it just you?"

Beneath the bulky sweatshirt, she was wearing a black belly-shirt that showed off her flat stomach to full advantage. On the lower right hand side of her periwinkle bellybutton was a small tattoo of the Giza Pyramids.

"Wow, Daniel said.

"Heaven on Earth," Terry said, running her fingers over her bare skin.

"Uh-huh," Daniel said.

"I was talking about the pyramids," Terry said. "Menkaura, Khafra, and Khufu, the great pyramid. There are scholars who believe that they were more than simple tombs, that they were, in fact, a replica of heaven on earth."

Daniel couldn't stop staring at the tattoo. It was like she had just revealed a secret and intimate part of herself to him. "It really is getting hot in here," he said as he spun away and forced the window open another inch. "You feel like going out for a coffee until it cools down some?"

"Is that a date-coffee, or a coffee-coffee?"

"A coffee-coffee." Terry looked quickly down and away and he knew that his latest rejection had stung her. "For now."

When she looked up at him there was fire in her eyes. "I grew up with four older brothers, and a hard-ass, blue collar dad who made damn sure I knew how to take care of myself. I'm tough as nails, and I have a thick skin, but I'm still just a girl underneath."

"I-"

Terry motioned with her hand for him to zip it. "In case you haven't figured it out yet, I like you, and I'm interested in getting to know you better. If that appeals to you, great. If not . . ." She folded her arms. "You can fill in the blank however you like."

"I don't expect you to understand, but things are a little complicated right now. My life. My headspace. Suffice it to say that I'm not . . . uninterested."

"Suffice it to say that I'm not uninterested?"

Daniel offered a sheepish grin and shrugged.

"You sure know how to sweet talk a girl."

"It's a gift."

"You've had it how long?"

"Since puberty."

"Since puberty, huh?"

Daniel nodded.

Terry smiled. "Probably too late to return it then, even with a receipt."

"The receipt's long gone, I'm afraid."

"Too bad."

<u>61</u>

Earlae switched on the flashlight and stepped into the shadowy cell, Sarah Calhoun's drawn, pale face glowing like a full moon at midnight. She was sitting uncommonly still in a rickety wooden chair, back straight, hands in her lap. Dark, heavy bags high on her cheekbones made her equally dark eyes seem Japanimation-large. Unblinking, the old woman was staring hard at her, into her, with an unreadable expression.

Mired in a swamp of conflicting emotions, Earlae slogged to within striking distance, knife held low in her hand, jagged edge up. "I had a mother just like you," she said, backhanding the old woman across the face. "Saw nothing. Didn't care about what went on right under her Noo Noo coke suctioning nose. Didn't care about anyone but herself. Including me."

The old woman brought a shaking, gnarled hand up to touch her wrinkled cheek, crocodile tears forming in her rheumy eyes.

"It took me five years to find her after she took off and left me with *him*. I found her wasting away in a hospital bed with full-blown AIDS. She looked like a scary Halloween skeleton. I had a question I wanted to ask her. Just one. Do you have any idea what it was?"

"Of course, I do."

"And do you know she said to me?"

The old woman's top lip began to quiver.

Earlae screamed the question over again. "Do you know what she said to me?"

"I can't imagine."

"She said she did it because it made her . . . made her wet. And then . . . then she slipped her bony fingers under my skirt and . . . and she touched me."

Earlae pressed the blade to the old woman's throat.

"Her words were salt on my soul. And her touch, after so many years, was . . . was even worse."

"Francis finally told me," the old woman said, her Adam's apple bobbing against the razor-sharp blade. "He told me everything."

"Told you what?"

"He told me what William had done to him."

"You knew. Don't try and tell me you didn't know. You're no dumbbunny. You knew it all along."

"It happened only once. While I was out of town at a Red Cross conference. Francis ran away before I'd returned. He never told me. Never told a soul. Not until he came to see me last week." She lowered her eyes, tears streaming into her lap. "If I'd known, I'd have killed him with my cold, bare hands."

Earlae hit the old woman again, this time with the butt end of the knife.

"Liar," she roared.

The blow opened a small cut beside the old woman's left eye. A single drop of blood was trailing, almost in slow motion, down her face. She didn't bother to wipe it away. Instead, she reached out to Earlae, putting her hand on her arm.

"I understand," she whispered.

"What do you understand, old woman?"

"Why we're here. All of us. Why you're doing what you're doing. Francis told me what he's had to live with since that night. And no matter what happens between us, no matter what you do to William, to the others, to me - I understand."

Earlae raised her knife to strike the killing blow, but something wasn't right. She had seen something in the other that she wasn't expecting. Regret. Compassion. The familiar self-loathing. And when the old woman mouthed, "I'm so sorry, child," she couldn't bring herself to do it. Not now. Not in a million years. She opened her fingers and the knife clattered to the floor.

A tiny smile appeared at the corners of the old woman's mouth. "If you feel like talking," she said, lifting one of her withered matchstick legs from the seat of her chair and dropping it back down, "I'm not going anywhere."

Earlae sat down beside the old woman, drew her knees up into her chest, and her autobiographical version of a Grimm's tale just seemed to tumble out.

<u>62</u>

It was approaching three o'clock in the morning and Daniel, Buchanan and Terry were sprawled on the floor scouring the files for patterns, leads, clues, something, anything they had missed that might break the case open. They were four hours and two dozen bottles of beer into the brainstorming process, and had discovered nothing new. The high point of their evening had come when Terry figured out how to maintain the room at a constant, comfortable temperature by making frequent adjustments to the aperture of the window.

Buchanan was the first to vent his frustration, tossing the color crime scene photographs of Eric Murray's anally eviscerated corpse into the air. "I've said it before, but I'm gonna say it again. This is Looney Tunes."

"More like Itchy and Scratchy," Terry said.

What they had in front of them was a puzzle, Daniel knew, with all but the last piece in place. The big picture, that's what was troubling him. He just wasn't seeing it yet.

"We've got enough in here." Daniel tapped two fingers against his temple. "And here." He motioned to the scatter of files. "To solve this thing. We have the edge."

"How do you figure that?" Terry said.

"We're smarter than they are."

"And if we're not?" Buchanan said.

"I have to believe that we are. Otherwise, what's the point? What hope would we ever have for seeing justice done?"

Buchanan twisted off another bottle cap. "This is about revenge," he said. "End of story."

"I wasn't the most talented fighter in my weight class," Daniel said, getting up and shadow boxing, throwing punches in bunches, "but I was able to capture a Golden Gloves title on my first attempt. I won because I had a gift." He ducked and parried a flurry of phantom blows then returned fire, left jab, left jab, right cross. "When I was in the ring I could see a punch coming before it was thrown. I knew when a feint was a feint, and I knew when it wasn't."

"What are you trying to say?" Terry said, standing up and stretching out the kinks. "That life is a boxing metaphor?"

"Isn't it?" Daniel sat down on the corner of his bed. "No doubt you've heard of the low blow and the double-cross. How about toeing the line, throwing in the towel, going for the knockout, letting down your guard? I could go on."

"Your point?" Terry said.

"What we are seeing, what we're focusing all our attention on is the killer's feints. We're only seeing what he wants us to see."

Buchanan let out a loud belch. "So lay it out for us punch drunk folk."

"This really is about vengeance, Frank. There's no denying that. And that's what makes the setup so sweet. But there's something else going on beneath the surface. I can feel it."

"Ninety percent voodoo," Buchanan said.

"Exactly," Daniel said.

"Run with it," Buchanan said.

"Remember there are two distinct minds at work here. That much we can agree on, right?"

"Of course," Buchanan said.

"There's Earlae, the tortured, emotional mind, the mind that maims and ultimately destroys. And then there's Shabazz, the calculating mind, the mind that takes the time to flip the mirrors, to prepare and arrange the artfully mutilated bodies so very meticulously for discovery."

"I'm with you so far," Buchanan said.

"So what if this whole setup isn't crazy? What if the calculating mind is also the controlling mind? And what if the primary mind he is controlling is that of his partner?"

"Keep going," Terry said.

"What has always bothered me about this whole scenario is the selection of the victims. If the emotional mind was the controlling or alpha mind, you'd expect the choice of victims to be more . . . random. Bottom-feeding molesters who'd made the evening news most likely. But they're not. With the exception of your aunt, Frank, each of the victims was a part of the same twisted cabal, and we have the photographic evidence to prove it."

Daniel leaned over and opened the window another inch, letting in a rush of cool air. Although there was no traffic and the Poontang Palace was closed for the evening, the hookers were still out in force, trudging relentlessly through the frigid squall in quest of their Holy Grail, a twenty-dollar blow job.

"What if the primary purpose of these murders was to eliminate these people, not for revenge *per se*, but for some other reason?"

"What reason?" Terry said, turning and bending over to return her empty bottle to the box.

Daniel's gaze wandered covertly over Terry's backside. Her low-cut jeans were well-fitted and hugged all the right curves nicely.

"I don't know," he finally admitted.

At this point in the evening, he decided, tired as hell and buzzed from a half-dozen beer, the only thing he knew for certain was that Buchanan had been right about what he'd said the other night. Terry's butt really was pure poetry.

"What about Big Bobby?" Buchanan said. "You think it's worth taking another run at him?"

"No way," Daniel said. "He's too scared. He knows what they'd do to his daughter if they ever found out he ratted them out. He's seen their handiwork first-hand. There's no way he's going to talk."

"Who's Big Bobby?" Terry said.

Daniel and Buchanan looked at each other. "In for a penny," Buchanan said, and then he told her the story of Big Bobby Crudup, complete with blow-by-blow commentary and a Rorschach-style analysis of the spattered blood.

"So he's the traitor who wiped the hard drive at Craven's condo," Terry said. "Galton mentioned he had a couple of possible suspects, but he didn't want to name any names until he had enough on them to nail their ass." She sat down on the bed beside Daniel and slapped her hand on his knee. "I wonder if this Big Bobby character even knew what was on it."

Outside the window a mixture of rain and snow began to fall, sending the hookers stampeding for the squalid shelter of The Rex. The room brightened momentarily as a streak of lightening split the starless sky, followed a split second later by the unmistakable peal of thunder.

Daniel jumped to his feet as the final, unifying piece of the puzzle slipped neatly into place.

The answer was indeed in the files.

<u>63</u>

Tokunbo found Blake on the sitting room couch munching microwave popcorn and watching Vittorio De Sica's neo-realist masterpiece *The Bicycle Thief.*

"It's time?"

Tokunbo nodded.

"I am overjoyed. I can hardly believe it."

Blake followed Tokunbo over to a stainless steel instrument table covered with a pair of sky-blue mechanics coveralls. Tokunbo shook out the coveralls then pulled them over his Juicy Couture jeans and John Richmond black knit sweater. "In case it gets messy," he said.

"Will I see? You promised that I would see."

"You shall see," Tokunbo said.

"And will I feel it, too?"

"I promised you the most exquisite agony imaginable, and that is precisely what I intend to deliver."

Blake crossed himself. "*Culpae poenae par esto,*" he said.

"And then some," Tokunbo said.

"I am literally tingling with anticipation." Blake held out his bare forearm. "Look," he said. "Swaddled in gooseflesh."

"Our gentleman's agreement stands then?" Tokunbo said.

"Despite the many terrible things I have done in my life, I am nothing if not a man of my word."

"If you would be so kind as to disrobe."

With the exception of Blake's paparazzi-prized face, his sleekly muscled body was a patchwork of scabs and scars of every size and design. Standing no more than a hot breath away, Tokunbo was unable to spy a single plug of flesh that hadn't been pierced, slashed or burned.

"Give me your hands," Tokunbo said.

Blake held out his hands to which Tokunbo secured a pair of suspension cuffs attached to a BDSM spreader bar. He hooked a heavy-gauge chain to the eye of each cuff and then attached the chain to the electric winch and pulley system he had rigged up earlier in the day. When Blake had been elevated to the desired height, toes dangling an inch from the ground, Tokunbo attached a second spreader bar to his ankles.

"I must look like DiVinci's Vitruvian Man," Blake said.

"It is an uncanny resemblance."

Tokunbo wheeled the instrument table around behind the filmmaker, and picked up two eighteen-gauge Tuohy needles. "In the interest of expediency, I shall forego the usual local anesthetic. Forgive me if it stings."

He inserted the needles into Blake's interspinous ligament, one in the cervical region, the other mid-lumbar, and then he simultaneously breached the ligimentum flavum, locating the filmmaker's epidural space with the ease of a surgeon. Following a loading dose of ropivicaine and fentanyl to initiate the nerve block, he administered sufficient volume of the solution to deaden the pain for the desired duration.

To test the efficacy of the procedure, Tokunbo cuffed Blake's scrotum, crushing his testicles to paste.

"Did you feel anything? Anything at all?"

Blake smiled wistfully. "I felt nothing. My flesh is numb from scalp to sole."

"S'wonderful," Tokunbo said.

"I am intrigued," Blake said. "What manner of torture is it that allows the victim to suffer no pain?"

"The analgesic effect has been calculated to dissipate shortly after your . . . your corrupted soul's formal unveiling."

"S'marvelous," Blake said.

Tokunbo selected a scalpel from the wide array of surgical tools and faced the suspended man. "I will be using a Swann-Morton #10 sterile surgical blade. It has been modified with an adjustable guard to breach only the epidermis." He held the scalpel in front of Blake's wide coffee-colored eyes. "One does not want to slice any deeper as it would rupture the delicate protective membrane that separates the skin from the underlying structures. Assuming my cuts have been properly executed the hide should peel from your body along these membranes-"

"As though you were removing my favorite dressing gown," Blake said.

"Chinese silk?"

"Hand-embroidered taffeta."

"Vintage?"

"Circa 1872."

"Magnificent?"

"Beyond compare."

Tokunbo positioned the blade mid-line at the crown of Blake's head then paused. "The most common mistake is in attempting to facilitate the removal of the hide with the blade."

"One can only imagine the mess."

Tokunbo began by tracing a shallow mid-line posterior cut from the crown of Blake's head to his anus. Then he cut around the circumference of the right wrist, up the arm, across the shoulders and down the opposite arm. He repeated the process for the lower extremities from right calve to left.

"How goes it back there?" Blake said. "If you'll pardon the pun, I can't see a bloody thing.

"Minimal bleeding actually." Tokunbo stepped back around to face the man. "Exactly as I had anticipated."

"No danger of a quick death then?"

"I would not worry about that if I were you."

"What's next?"

Tokunbo returned the scalpel to the instrument table. "I use my hands and the full weight of my body to yank, pull and pry the hide from your body."

"Chop, chop," Blake said. "Interest of expediency and all that."

Standing on his tip-toes, Tokunbo used his fingertips and thumb to locate the flaps of scalp that his blade had opened. He gripped the edges tightly and with a quick, downward snap of the wrists detached the filmmaker's face from his skull.

With the whites of his eyes stained red by a steady seepage of blood that he was no longer capable of blinking away, Blake was staring intently at Tokunbo. "Other than the effort of your exertion, I didn't feel a thing." His eyes rolled down to look at his dangling, distorted face, then returned to Tokunbo. "Pity."

"Patience is a bitter plant."

"But it has sweet fruit."

"The sweetest."

The work on the torso went strictly by-the-numbers until Tokunbo encountered a particularly stubborn section of hide near Blake's umbilicus that required nearly a minute, and some rather aggressive thumb and fist manipulation, to extricate.

"Now for the legs," Tokunbo said.

Aside from having to use his fists and elbows to detach the skin at the droop of Blake's buttocks, the lower half came away even quicker than the top half did.

"Finished?"

"Not quite."

Whistling Snoop Dogg's *Gin and Juice* through his teeth, Tokunbo picked up the BernzOmatic plumber's torch from the tray. He sparked it up with a flint striker and ran the hissing blue flame over the filmmaker's torso to cauterize the meat. To inhibit blood loss in the half-dozen or so remaining problem areas, he used an absorbable collagen-based hemostatic agent, pressing it directly to the wounds. Three minutes later, when the hemorrhaging had slowed to an acceptable trickle, he took two steps back and put his hands on his hips.

"I have finished."

"How do I look?"

Blake's head was a glistening crimson sphere, his body a gruesome diorama of pulsing veins and arteries, exposed cartilage, and randomly twitching muscle.

Tokunbo smiled.

"Open my eyes," Blake said, "that I may see."

Tokunbo snatched up the mottled, misshapen hide from the floor and held it aloft.

"Not that," Blake said. "I am tired of looking at that ratty old thing. I want to see what they saw." His tongue flicked out and licked his porcelain veneers momentarily white. "Show me as I really am."

Tokunbo dropped the hide. "The mirror is in the master bedroom."

"Get it, man. And be quick about it."

Tokunbo ducked into the bedroom and returned in short order with a full-length, splay-legged George IV mahogany cheval mirror. He rolled it into position, directly in front of Blake.

Blake jerked his chin at Tokunbo. "You make a better door than a window."

Tokunbo stepped aside to allow the other an unfettered view of his handiwork. The filmmaker stared at his reflection for a long time without speaking, the pious silence of the sitting room broken only by the syncopated pitter-patter of blood on the harlequin tiled floor.

"You approve?" Tokunbo said.

"Finally," Blake said, "I can see the truth."

"You are a travesty of humanity, of life itself".

"But it's all for naught if I do not feel the pain," Blake said. "Pain is penance. It will expiate my sins."

Tokunbo glanced at his watch. "Soon," he said. "I assure you."

The muscles in Blake's cheeks jumped, coaxing a smile from phantom lips. "You're right. It's approaching as we speak. Distant, but closing fast. Like a runaway locomotive." He stiffened then cried out in full bore agony, a howl of torment that was barely human. "Hurry with your questions, Tokunbo. It is inside me now. Hurry. Before I am . . . overwhelmed by searing . . . joyful . . . pain."

Before Tokunbo could begin the inquisition, Blake took a shuddering series of rapid breaths, and murmured, "Come closer. As close as you dare. Just don't . . . block . . . my . . . view."

Tokunbo drew nearer, so as to not miss a single syllable of the dying man's confession. In between the jolts and spasms of Blake's penance he posed his questions. Although Blake's words were particularly troubling, the mystery as yet unsolved, he knew at least where his quest would take him next.

<u>64</u>

Daniel waited for the final echo of thunder to fade into oblivion before speaking. "We've spent so much time dwelling on what they wanted us to see that we've completely ignored the one thing they didn't want us to see."

"The computer files," Buchanan said.

"But the files were wiped," Terry said. "You said so yourself."

"What if they weren't? What if they survived?"

"I'm listening," Terry said.

"Thumb through the Blake's FBI file and tell me what you see."

"The computer's clean," Buchanan said. "Galton's expert took it apart chip by chip. He said the deleted information was irretrievable. Said whoever wipe it knew what he was doing."

Daniel smiled. "Humor me. Take a look at that fluff magazine piece and tell me what leaps out at you."

"Where's the file?" Buchanan said.

"On the floor," Daniel said. "Next to the hot plate."

Buchanan scooped up the file. He located the photocopied article and tore it off the brad for a better view. His lips moved as he silently read the text. "I still don't see," he began, then trailed into silence.

"Do you see it now?"

Buchanan snapped his fingers and pointed at Daniel. "The electronic notebook," he said. "The fucking thing was staring us in the face the whole time." He flipped the picture around to show it to Terry.

"It wasn't in the inventory. That's for damn sure," Terry said. "Maybe the perps took it."

"What if they didn't take it?" Daniel said. "The article says Blake enjoyed the solitude and isolation of his country retreat. It also says he found his inspiration there. If that was the case it would follow then, would it not, that he wrote his screenplays there."

"And maybe hid the notebook there," Terry said.

"It's certainly worth a look," Daniel said. "Don't you think?"

"You're a goddamned genius," Buchanan said.

"There's no mention of the cabin in the file," Terry said.

"Which means it wasn't searched by the cops or the feds," Daniel said.

"And if they missed it," Terry said, "maybe the perps missed it, too."

"First thing in the morning I'll call the magazine, see if I can't get a line on the broad that wrote the article," Buchanan said. "See if she can't steer us in the right direction."

<u>65</u>

David Blake's country retreat was a ramshackle cabin tucked in a scraggly evergreen forest two hours west of Boston. It had a covered porch that sagged in the middle and a cedar shake roof that sagged on both sides. Filthy gingham curtains hung crookedly in the darkened divided-light windows on either side of the door.

"Quaint," Terry said as she slowed her concourse-condition Datsun 280Z to a walking pace.

"If you mean that as a euphemism for total dump," Daniel said, "I'm inclined to agree."

"I can't believe he found his inspiration here. He's hot, and he's worth millions. I would've pegged him as more of the Martha's Vineyard type."

"The million dollar condo was his public persona, his super-ego. This place was the man. His id. The part of him that the tabloids, and the adoring public, never saw."

"You think he did more than write here then?"

"Yeah."

"You think he brought the kids here?"

"Oh, yeah."

"You believe in the death penalty?"

"Of the cruel and unusual variety."

"Me, too."

Terry rolled past the cabin and parked out of sight around a sharp curve in the icy, pothole-filled road. She killed the lights in the instant that a cluster of low-hanging clouds scudded over the full moon and deepened the darkness around them. Aside from the occasional rollicking deer, they hadn't seen a house, a car, or anything other than trees since exiting the highway twenty minutes earlier.

"Expecting company?" Daniel said.

Terry pulled a flashlight out of the glove box. "A girl can never be too careful."

With Terry holding her fingers over the reflector to limit the glow to the bare minimum required, they got out of the car and stumbled into the congested, gully-filled woods. Daniel was wearing an unlined leather car coat over a t-shirt and jeans, no gloves, and he was really beginning to notice the cutting wind. As he walked, he blew into his cupped hands in an effort to ward away the numbness that had taken hold in his fingertips.

"Do you want a turn with the gloves?"

Terry was wearing a hooded Helly-Hansen parka, ski pants, navy watch cap and a pair of lined waterproof gloves.

Daniel cast a covetous glance at her toasty digits.

"No," he said. "I'm okay."

Eventually, they reached the edge of the woods bordering the cabin, and stopped. The windows were still dark, and there were no footprints in the calf-high snow approaching the structure from the rear or either side. By all appearances, they were alone.

"Let's go," Daniel said.

"You realize that what we're about to do is against the law," Terry said.

"Do you want to wait here while I check it out?"

"Are you kidding me?"

The cabin was unlocked, unwired, unplumbed and consisted of three sparsely furnished rooms, a kitchen/living room and two bedrooms. Small toys, the kind that come *gratis* in kid's meals from the various fast food joints, were scattered over the rough plank floor between a pair of overstuffed couches, and the kitchen cupboards were filled with coloring books and ice cream tubs overflowing with crayons of every hue imaginable. Some of the pages in the books were simple scribbles without recourse to the lines, while others were veritable works of art. All of the pages were colored using blacks and grays and browns. No rainbows. No green fields. No happy-faced, rosy-cheeked nuclear families.

"What's that smell?" Terry said.

The odor in question was coming from a wafer-thin foam mattress resting directly on the floor in the larger bedroom. There were no sheets on the mattress, and its surface was a duplicate of the one that Daniel had seen in Blake's condo, mottled with stains the origins of which he still had no intention of contemplating.

"Those streaks there are blood," Terry said, pointing. "The others look like-"

Daniel held up his hand.

To the right of the mattress was a small louvered door. Daniel opened it to reveal a closet filled with Blake's vivacious, designer-brand clothes. He was about to shut the door when he noticed, partially covered by a pair of silk, paisley-patterned pajama pants, what appeared to be a loose plank in the floor. Using the key to his Malibu home, he wedged the board out while Terry aimed her flashlight into the hole.

"Is it . . . ?"

"It's a metal box."

Daniel set the insulated, fire-proof box on the floor and opened it carefully, just enough to peek inside.

"Got it," he said.

He removed the electronic notebook from the box, powered it on and was immediately greeted with a request for a password. He tapped a couple keys at random and when nothing interesting happened he turned to Terry.

"Do you know anything about computers?"

"About as much as you do, by the look of it."

"Remind me again why I brought you along?"

Terry looked at him and her face was tender and open.

"You needed a ride," she said, holding his eyes with hers, "and I happen to own a pretty sweet set of wheels."

Daniel was surprised by the sudden realization that he really liked, even trusted, this girl, as a friend, and maybe more. The epiphany caught him off guard, causing him to break the connection, and look quickly away.

"Let's get this thing back to the Rex to let Frank have a crack at it. Maybe he can-"

Terry's fingers closed on his arm. "Shhh," she said. "Do you hear that?"

"I do."

"It sounds like thunder."

The sound was almost on top of them now, loud enough to rattle the windows.

"Not thunder," Daniel said.

"What is it then?"

"Tupac Shakur. If I'm not mistaken."

Daniel was about to suggest they beat a hasty retreat back to the Z when a smoke-filled, banana-yellow, mid-seventies El Dorado with low-profile, fifty-series tires slid to a stop in front of the cabin.

"Swing Low, Sweet Cadillac," Terry said.

A black man sucking on a joint got out. He had wavy, henna-colored hair and was wearing a black G-Unit warm-up suit, black fingerless gloves, and enough gold around his neck to bury a pharaoh. He was tall and bony but strong looking.

"You notice any hookers on the drive in?" Daniel said.

Terry shook her head.

"So what's a pimp doing in this neck of the woods?"

"Surreal, isn't it?"

"Slightly."

"You think he's alone? That's a lot of smoke for just one guy."

"Could be he's Jamaican."

The pimp walked around to the back of the car and popped the trunk. He took a final hit off the joint before hefting out a five gallon can of gasoline. The can nicked the paint job on the way out and he said, "Shit," stretching the word into two distinct syllables.

"Shee-it is right," Terry said.

"How's that?"

"In case you've forgotten, there's no back door or window in this joint."

The pimp carried the can over to the cabin and began to slosh the gasoline over the porch and the wooden foundation. Luckily, his powers of deductive had been dulled by years of substance abuse and he failed to register the import of the tracks in the snow that Daniel and Terry had made on their trek inside.

"When he moves around to the back," Daniel said, "we'll make a break for it. It's best if we can sneak away without being seen."

Unfortunately, the pimp had no intention of subjecting his lily-white Nikes to the deep drifts that had collected around the sides of the cabin. Instead, he continued sloshing the gasoline out front until the can was empty. He tossed the can onto the roof then patted down his clothes for matches. Finding none, he headed back to his car, cursing loudly along the way.

A Shih Tzu with a pink bow on its head appeared in a puff of smoke as soon as the driver door was opened. Head lowered, tail wagging tentatively, the little dog began snuffling around on the ground. The pimp started walking back to the cabin, matches in hand, when he shouted, "Muthafucka," and made a lunge for the Shih Tzu that was in the process of relieving itself on one of the El Dorado's mag wheels.

"How many times I told you not to piss on my ride, Biggie? How many muthafuckin' times I told you that?"

The pimp scooped the Shih Tzu up into his arms and stared at it with his black-pebble eyes. Unintimidated, the little dog began to lick its master's face. The pimp giggled, tickled the dog under the chin, then placed it gently back inside the car.

"Shit, Biggie," the pimp said. "What am I goin' to do wit' you?"

The compact disc was between tracks and the next sound they heard was that of a paper match being struck, followed hard upon by a loud whooshing sound. In a matter of seconds licks of orange flame engulfed the front wall, streaking blue across the dry pine plank ceiling. A thick, acrid smoke soon filled the air, making it difficult to breathe. Then Tupac was back on the stereo, waxing poetic about murdering whites with his nine millimeter.

"Where is he?" Daniel said.

"I can't see a thing. My eyes are burning out of my head."

"Is he gone? Has he left yet?"

Terry squinted through a crack in the curtains and shook her head. "This guy's hipper than shit," she said. "You wouldn't believe what he's doing."

"What do you mean? What's he doing?"

"Dancing."

"Dancing?"

"The Running Man, I think."

"Let me see."

Daniel put an eye to the crack. Bathed in the raging red and rippling incandescent yellow light of the fire, the pimp was indeed getting down and funky on the snowy lawn.

"Shoot him."

"I'm off duty. No gun."

"Whatever happened to a girl can never be too careful?"

Terry shrugged demurely.

"We can't stay here much longer. What if Huggy Bear is packing?"

"Then we're S-O-L."

Daniel only needed a second to come up with a plan. "I'll go first and draw him away. You count out five Mississippis then run like hell. Head straight for your car and pick me up a half-mile down the road."

With the licks of flame dancing all around them, the pimp dancing out front, Terry reached out and patted Daniel's hand, giving him a fast disarming smile.

"Keys are in the ignition," she said.

Then she reached for the door handle, threw open the door and charged outside.

<u>66</u>

Daniel heard the pimp shout, "Stop," then heard the sound of feet crashing into the wild at the back of the cabin. He tucked the notebook under his arm and bolted from the flaming structure after Terry. He had barely taken up the chase when he heard a car door open. Still running, he glanced back at the caddy. That's when he saw them. The pimp hadn't come alone, after all. *Could be he's Jamaican?* What an asshole comment. He took a second glance back. They seemed to be in no hurry, casually unzipping their parkas to bust out the nines and the sawed-off shot guns. There were five of them. They were young, but all battle-hardened gang bangers judging by the look of them.

Daniel ducked into a grove of pines for cover and immediately picked up his pace. In short order, he heard the gang bangers reach the edge of the woods. Branches slapped at his face as he entered a labyrinth of fragrant spruce. He made a lightening quick series of lefts and rights, stepping on exposed roots and rocks to avoid leaving a telltale trail. Eventually, he reached the edge of the grove. Ahead of him was a circular meadow, a hundred yards in diameter. In the wan moonlight he could make out Terry's footprints a dozen feet to his right, bisecting the open meadow to the shelter of the woods opposite him.

Daniel listened. Quiet. He didn't like quiet. Where were the gang bangers? How close were they? He let loose a silent curse in his head. He could reach the other side of the meadow by weaving in and out of its thickly forested perimeter, hopefully evading his hunters in the process, but that would waste too much time.

He glanced up at the sky and saw that luck was finally with him. In a few moments a dragon-shaped patch of cloud would obscure the moon long enough for him to navigate the meadow under the cloak of darkness.

Daniel tensed, getting ready to make the sprint, when a pistol shot rang out and bark exploded on the tree next to his head, spraying his face with sticky sap. He dropped to his chest and rolled quickly to his left as two more shots struck the ground near him. He rolled again, taking refuge behind a thick trunk and peered out. There was no sound, no movement other than the swaying trees, no signs of life. Then something moved in the distant trees – a momentary shadow amongst the shadows. He muttered his second curse aloud when he heard the sound of running feet and breaking branches in the grove of spruce behind him. Think, he reminded himself. Every problem has a solution. But his heart was pumping so furiously that it was difficult for his mind to focus

And then the moonlight was smothered by the cloud.

Daniel didn't think anymore; he simply acted. He scrambled to his feet and sprinted through the inky blackness onto the meadow.

He had legged out a dozen strides when the edge of the moon began to peek over the dragon's outstretched wings. He sensed a presence off his left as the darkness began to recede. He turned just as a silhouette raised its arm and a shot rang out. He felt a thump in his chest and stumbled over backwards.

Momentarily, the cloud cleared the moon and the dreadlock-framed face of his would-be executioner came into view, posturing threateningly over him. He was wearing droopy jeans and an unzipped down-filled parka over an evening gown-length basketball jersey. He was still a kid, fifteen years old, tops. On his classic, though largely underappreciated, *A Man Alone* album, Sinatra said 'empty is the eyes of animals in cages.' Emptier still, Daniel knew, is the eyes of animals uncaged. His rambling thoughts were interrupted by the trash-talking arrival of the other four gang bangers. They approached him with a rhythmic strut, surrounding him, teeth bared in a garish display of yellow gold and flawless, near colorless diamonds.

Daniel felt his chest. There was no blood, no bullet hole. The notebook computer, sitting on top of the snow beside him, had saved his life.

Or had it merely granted him a reprieve?

"I'm with a cop. People know we're here."

As one of the gang bangers raised his sawed-off shot gun in reply, Daniel saw the shadowed movement a second time, in the trees beyond the group, maybe fifty yards distant. He was dressed completely in black, and was sighting along a rifle equipped with a large suppressor.

Before the gang banger could get off his shot there was an innocuous *Fffft* sound and his body twisted then pitched violently forward. *Fffft. Fffft. Fffft. Fffft.* The last thing Daniel saw before the corpse landed on top of him was the bling-filled smiles being wiped from the faces of the remaining gang bangers.

Despite his previous admonition to Buchanan about Greeks and their gifts, Daniel rolled one corpse aside, leaped over another, and tore into the woods after Terry.

Clouds were approaching the face of the moon once more and the sky grew darker. To his left, he could hear the roar of a river churning along its banks.

Keeping Terry's and the pimp's tracks in sight as best he could, he vaulted a fallen tree, the trunk two feet in diameter and chest high, the root ball ripped completely from the ground. A hundred yards in, the river appeared through the screen of trees, its flow too furious to freeze, the water frothing and swirling over the ice-capped rocks.

"Hold it," the pimp shouted from the darkness ahead of Daniel, out of breath, his voice hoarse. "Hold it right there or, I fuckin' swear, I'll bust a cap in your bony ass."

"Don't shoot," Terry said in a calm voice. "I'm unarmed and I'm stopping now."

Rounding a bend in the river, Daniel spotted them as the moon reappeared. The pimp was a couple of inches taller than Daniel, and had the typical build of a crack addict, weighing in at a scrawny one-thirty or one-forty. He was a mean-looking son-of-a-bitch and had a large nickel-plated six-shooter trained on Terry's chest. He was holding the gun sideways, the way that the thugs do in all the critically lauded boyz in the 'hood movies, so that the sights were useless.

Daniel looked quickly around for something he could use as a weapon. Should have picked up a shot gun when he had the chance. Stupid. Stupid. Stupid. He set the notebook down on a rock and located a heavy, four-foot-long hardwood branch on the forest floor. It was all he could find in the short time that he had and it would have to do. He gripped it on the narrow end with both hands and set it on one shoulder as though it were a Louisville Slugger.

Although the river, not to mention the Caddy's subwoofer, helped to mask the sound of his approach, Daniel still had to be careful. The element of surprise was all that he had going for him, and a single twig snapped underfoot could very easily give him away, get the two of them killed.

If Terry noticed him approaching, she never let on. Her eyes never once lit on him. Daniel had heard it said that the most beautiful things in the world were among the most useless. Surely, Terry Wagner was the exception to that rule. She was fire under ice, and ice under fire. Positively amazing.

"The fuck are you?" the pimp said to Terry, his quickened breath steaming around him.

"My name's Wagner. I'm a cop. Who are you?"

The pimp closed the gap with Terry. He loomed over her, but she didn't take a step backward. He began sliding his head back and forth to the bass-heavy beat of the music.

"You a dick?" He chuckled. "Look more like a pussy to me."

"Funny," Terry said, "I was thinking the same thing about you."

"You got a real smart mouth on you," the man said, reaching out to stroke her cheek, "for such a fine brick shithouse bitch."

"You really ought to pick up some Cool Mint Listerine," Terry said. "Quit blowing your dough on GeriKurl and costume jewelry."

It was a fine line that Terry was walking, Daniel knew. She was getting wise with the pimp to keep him distracted, to buy Daniel a little more time. But if she kept it up, didn't tone it down some, the pimp might just shoot her for spite.

The pimp gave the cylinder of his gun a spin while he processed the insult. "You a lezzie or somethin'?"

"As far as you're concerned."

The pimp backhanded Terry across the face with his empty hand. When she didn't fall at his feet, he kicked her legs out from under her.

"You don' wanna give it up for Dark Davis that be your loss. 'Cos soon as you tell me what I gots to know, I'm gon' put a hole in your head the size of the Big Dig and take it anyway." He chuckled again. "So long as the pussy's still warm, it don' make no difference to me. Dead or alive, it don' make no difference. Know'm sayin'?"

Terry was sitting down with her arms around her drawn up knees. "How much are you getting paid? I'm curious to know what the going rate for killing a cop is these days."

"It ain't about the bread, man. You pigs are way the fuck off, that what you been thinkin'. Shit."

"So what's it about then? Enlighten me."

Although Daniel couldn't see the pimp's face, he could hear the smile in his voice. "Power," he said.

"Who's behind the killings? Who are you protecting?"

Daniel was maybe two dozen steps away and closing.

The pimp pressed the six-shooter to the center of Terry's forehead. "Are you afraid to die," he said, his words perfectly synchronized with Tupac's, "or do you want to live forever?" He pulled the trigger.

<u>67</u>

Earlae was sitting cross-legged on the Victorian fainting couch, watching Bo perform his intricate katas, her four fowl friends perched on the plush, silk cushions on either side of her, Edogiawarie snuggled in her lap. Bo was wearing the white kung fu pants with the peace symbol patch sewn over the tear in the seat. He was topless and his fine muscles rippled with each balletic movement.

"M-O-B," Earlae shouted over the music, and the roosters crowed loudly.

Bo was working out to vintage hip-hop, their million-dollar loft reverberating to the coarse sounds of the black man's struggle for respect and equality in white America.

"I have a question?" Earlae said.

Bo descended effortlessly into the splits, going flat to the floor, a towel looped around his neck as he began the cool-down phase of his workout.

"Am I a racist if I rap along with the bros? I mean, if I'm bustin' rhymes with the Wu Tang Clan, and I happen to say the 'N' word, does that make me a racist?"

Bo said nothing.

Earlae was about to press him for an answer when Edogiawarie groaned.

"Are you sure?" she said.

She looked down at the tiny boy in her lap. Despite a steady diet of greasy KFC, his limbless, meter-long form was scrawny, with numerous ribs and vertebrae poking through his slick brown skin. His nose was two pulsing slits above his wide, lipless mouth, like the nose of a seal. Only his exquisite, almond-shaped eyes, gazing forlornly up at her in obvious distress, were unquestionably human.

"All righty then," she cooed.

Earlae picked him up and toted him over to the tole-painted litter box behind the fountain. Lying inert on his belly, a feeble, intermittent stream of yellow darkening the mound of kitty-litter beneath him, he twisted his lumpen head away from her, embarrassed.

"Don't worry, sweetie. I won't peek."

The lights were low, and the drapes on the bank of surrounding windows were open. The snow was swirling, blowing in mournful gusts against the thick, insulated glass.

"I have another question," she said to Bo. "It's about something I came across on the web the other night."

He was standing now, toweling off his moist, hairless chest. He didn't say a word. Didn't even look at her.

"I read that the government in China has scientists working twenty-four-seven to prove its people aren't human. I know that what they're really attempting to show is that they're somehow better than the rest of us poor schmoes. But it got me to thinking. If they ever did succeed in proving they're not human-

"Hold on," she said.

Behind her, Edogiawarie had begun making a small, syncopated whimper, to let her know that he was done, and wanted uppy. She stooped and brushed off the deodorized granules sticking to his skin before picking him up. Safe in her arms once more, she hugged him in tightly against her, and ticked him under the chin.

"Where was I? Oh, yeah." She smiled devilishly. "I was thinking that if they ever did succeed we could sell them on E-Bay as pets. If they're not human, then the various human rights laws wouldn't apply to them, right? Even if we only got a nickel a head, we'd be gazillionaires."

For the first time all day, Bo looked straight at her, his gaze intense, his silence eerie.

"Aren't you going to chastise me for being silly?" She thrust out her backside and gave it a sensuous Shakira-like shake. "You know, a little spanking before giving me a tongue lashing I won't soon forget."

"The remaining captives will be put down by 1PM tomorrow."

"Excuse me?"

"I have been advised by a credible, inside source that the FBI is closing in on you. We must get rid of the evidence. To protect you, of course."

"But-"

"We have broadcast our message to the masses, Earlae."

"But the kids, Bo? What about the kids who are still out there and in danger?"

"We cannot save the world."

"But-"

"Do you want to go to prison for the rest of your life?"

"It's just that-"

"Do you?"

"It's just-"

"Do you have any idea what the criminal element would do to someone like you in prison? The things your stepfather did to you would seem like romantic foreplay in comparison."

Earlae began to pace around the room, trying to make sense of the thoughts and suspicions that were spiraling through her skull with the breakneck intensity of the Tasmanian Devil.

"It will all be over soon."

Earlae stopped dead in her tracks, looked Bo dead in the eyes. "It'll never be over. I'll never forget the things we've done. The things I've done."

"Stop being such a drama queen," Bo said, almost smirking. "With the exception of Mrs. Calhoun, I knew them all. They were my associates. Not yours. My friends. Not yours. I gutted them, skinned and filleted them, but I did not let it affect me. I refused to."

"Maybe I'm not strong like you."

"Then you certainly would not want to go to jail. You would not survive it. Am I right?"

For the first time, Earlae hesitated. "You're such a smarty pants. You're right," she said. "You're always right."

"Maybe we did not save the world, but we did our part. Which is more than most people can say. Tomorrow it will be done with and we can get on with the rest of our lives together." He turned and began walking toward the bedroom. "Oh, and before I forget. I want you to call Lloyd while I am attending to my bath. Tell him to meet us at the club at precisely ten o'clock in the morning."

"I don't think-"

"No, you do not, do you?" Bo said, without stopping.

"But Ace is-"

"Going to meet us at the club at precisely ten o'clock in the morning. Do you understand?"

She looked out the windows again, and it was like she was inside one of those novelty globes, the kind that you shake and the plastic snowflakes swirl around the idyllic family home. Nothing more than an illusion, she knew. All of it.

"I'm certainly beginning to," Earlae said.

<u>68</u>

There was a sharp click as the hammer of the pimp's gun dropped on an empty cylinder.

Still a dozen steps away, Daniel remained helpless.

"Shit," the pimp said, laughing heartily. "I know there's a slug in there some place." He pressed the six-shooter to his own head and pulled the trigger. Another sharp click.

"Do you know what I would have asked me if I were you?" Terry said.

Eight steps.

The pimp gave the cylinder another spin. "What would you have axed, bitch?"

"I would have asked whether I'd come here all by my lonesome."

"I'da axed the same thing I was you. I'da told you I brought five a my niggas wit me. You heard the shots. The Cavalry's dead, baby. Ain't nobody left to save you."

"Are you sure about that?"

The pimp said nothing.

Terry winked at Daniel.

The pimp chuckled. "You think an old hood nigga like me don't know the score? I looks behind me and whatta you do? Plant a boot in my nuts and do the fade into the great outdoors. Shit."

Terry looked up at the pimp and shrugged. "I guess you're a whole lot smarter than you look."

"You gots that right."

The pimp thumbed back the hammer and was in the process of returning the barrel to Terry's forehead when Daniel finally stepped into the batter's box. He knew they needed the pimp alive to cut a deal, and answer their numerous questions. He just didn't care.

Swinging from his heels, he went yard on the base of the pimp's skull, sending the pimp and his nickel-plated six-shooter spiraling through the air in opposite directions. The gun landed on a stump, discharging harmlessly into the woods, while the pimp landed on the riverbank, one blindingly white sneaker skipping playfully over the rushing white water. There was blood running from his mouth and both of his ears. Aside from the foot with the soaker, he wasn't moving.

Daniel turned his hand over and clasped Terry's wrist, hauling her to her feet. The momentum carried her straight into his arms and he clutched onto her with the urgency of a drowning man being hauled from the drink.

He could smell her hair, her skin. Even through the stench of the fire, she somehow managed to smell freshly scrubbed, intoxicating.

"Is he dead?" Terry said.

Her lips were close to his. There was wintergreen on her breath. Her eyes were all pupils, and their attraction, their almost lunar pull on him, was irresistible.

"I . . . I don't know. I took a first aid course back in college but never actually learned how to check for a pulse."

"Feel for it on his neck," Terry said.

Their foreheads were touching now. There was a drought in Daniel's mouth. "It's covered with blood. You feel for it." When he spoke his face was close enough to Terry's that his lips brushed softly against hers. They were moist and yielding and had parted ever-so-slightly in response to his touch.

Terry kicked the downed man a few times in the ribs. He neither budged nor grunted. She didn't look down; her wide, inviting eyes never once left Daniel's.

"He's dead," she said.

Daniel extricated himself from Terry's physical hold on him and staggered a step backward. For long seconds, no one moved. He couldn't stop his heart from racing. It was beating faster now than when he'd been charging through the forest after her, faster even than when he'd feared he might not reach her in time.

"What did you think you were doing running out like that?"

"I'm a cop. I was doing my job."

"Well, I happen to be a male chauvinist pig, and for future reference, that takes precedence over your being a cop."

Tupac was rapping in the distance about what he wouldn't do for love. There was a smirk on Terry's face. She was really enjoying the situation.

"Sure it does," she said.

For a while, Daniel said nothing. Eventually, he let out a long breath, and said, "I was afraid he was going to . . . to hurt you, that's all."

"I haven't known you for long," Terry said, "but I'm a pretty good judge of character. My feminine intuition told me that if anything went wrong, you'd turn up to save your lady fair."

"Are you cool with what just happened?"

"If you hadn't come along, that would've been me down there," Terry said. "I'm definitely cool with it."

Moonlight shimmering on her hair, radiant on her face, she smiled at him sweetly. She was fiery and frisky, confident and strong. But she was also pig-headed, smart-mouthed and, at times, a royal pain-in-the-rump. She was an enigma that he was only beginning to appreciate the meaning of, and utterly compelling because of it. Despite the dead man cooling at his heels, Daniel couldn't help himself. He smiled back at her.

Terry gave him a playful bump with her hip.

"What?" she said.

Daniel looked down at the pimp. His black-pebble eyes looked much the same as they did when he was alive and hipper than shit. "The countdown has begun," he said. "As soon as the bodies are discovered-"

"Bodies?"

"Mr. Davis wasn't lying about his backup."

"Oh, my god. Those gunshots . . . With all that happened, I completely forgot about them. You're okay? They didn't hurt you did they?"

"I'm fine."

"And Mr. Davis' . . . ?"

"His quote-unquote niggas?"

Terry nodded.

"Dead. All five of them."

"You . . . you killed five armed-"

"To get back to the matter at hand," Daniel said. "As soon as the bodies are discovered, they're going to assume we have possession of whatever's on this thing that's worth killing for and cover their tracks. Beginning with the elimination of the remaining hostages. At least that's what I'd do."

"Me, too."

"I figure we've got ten maybe twelve hours to solve this thing before that happens."

Terry used her foot to roll the pimp's body the rest of the way over the bank and into the river.

"Make that twenty-four," she said. "Now about those other bodies?"

"What a devious little mind you possess."

"I'll have you know that interfering with a crime scene is a serious offense. What happened with Mr. Davis was an unfortunate accident, I assure you.

"Sure, it was," Daniel said. "And I'll tell you all about the others after they've met with similar, ah . . . accidents."

<u>69</u>

Biggie leaped out of Terry's arms as soon as the hotel door was opened, yipping and yapping and running through the cluttered room in ever tightening circles.

"What the fuck is that?" Buchanan said.

He was sitting Indian-style on his bed surrounded by a half-dozen open file folders. He was bare-chested and had on a pair of cut-off jeans that were so short they could only be described as Daisy Dukes. Surgical tubing ran the length of one leg from his sock to disappear beneath the frayed edge of his Wrangler cut-offs. Hurriedly, he picked up a file folder and used it to conceal his foreskin reclamation contraption from Terry.

Daniel smiled. "You said you thinking of getting a dog for your daughter, so . . ."

"What the fuck has my wanting a dog for my baby girl got to do with that thing?"

Biggie hopped up on Daniel's bed and sat down, motionless, her moist nose pointed at Buchanan. The pink ribbon in her hair had come undone and was dangling off-kilter over one eye.

"That thing happens to be your new pooch." Daniel winked at Terry. "The guy at the pet store said the man/dog relationship works best when you match type and personality. So I asked him-"

"I know where you're going with this, and I suggest you quit while you're ahead."

"So I asked him for-"

"I'm fucking warning you, Rourke."

"-the fruitiest dog he had."

"His name is Biggie," Terry said, attempting to suppress a grin and failing miserably. "He's a Shih Tzu."

"Figures," Buchanan said.

"Oh, yeah, and before I forget," Daniel said, taking the electronic notebook from out of his jacket. "While we were out we also picked this up." He set the notebook down on the spindly laminate coffee table.

"Any problems?" Buchanan raised an eyebrow as he caught sight of the damage. "Is that a bullet hole?"

"It still works," Terry said. "We tried it in the car."

"Lucky thing," Buchanan said.

"Unfortunately, it's password protected," Daniel said. "And I had to kill a hipper-than-shit pimp named Dark Davis to get it here."

"After escaping from a raging inferno," Terry said. "And after Daniel's butt was saved from five, armed-to-the-teeth gang bangers by a mystery man in black with a silenced sniper rifle."

"Password schmassword," Buchanan said.

"Did you hear what we just said, Frank?"

"Yeah," Buchanan said. "I heard you."

"And?"

"And you know how to take care of yourself," Buchanan said. "Not to mention you had a cop with you, which kinda-sorta made everything legal."

"This is still America," Terry said. "Not Somalia."

"Was it self-defense?"

"The pimp had a gun pressed to my head," Terry said. "It most certainly was."

"So unbunch your thong, lady."

"Well, we didn't report the incident," Terry said. "And that presents one or two small problems."

"No, it doesn't," Buchanan said.

"How do you figure that?"

"Who do you report it to? On one level or other the authorities are involved. Besides it's all just a matter of semantics. You're not really not reporting it. You're merely delaying it."

Terry looked at Daniel. "You know in a warped kind of way, he's right."

"What about the guy with the sniper rifle?" Daniel said.

"He whacked five guys who were threatening you with death?"

Daniel nodded.

"Could he have whacked you, too?"

"In a heartbeat."

"Is there a downside I'm missing?"

"Who the hell is he?"

"Galton?" Terry said.

"He's old school, and a bit of a cowboy," Buchanan said. "But I don't make him for it. It's not his style."

Daniel shrugged it off for a later time. "Can you get through the password, Frank?" he said.

"Child's play."

As Buchanan rolled off the bed to pick up the computer his feet hit the floor and the surgical tubing tightened, tugging his dick out from under the frayed lip of his shorts. Terry screamed, Daniel doubled over in laughter, and Biggie once more began to bark and run around the room in ever tightening circles. The hooker in the room above them stomped a stiletto heel for quiet.

Red-faced, Buchanan tucked his little-fella back into his shorts.

"Sorry about the scream, Frank," Terry said. "It's just that I haven't been on a date in over a year. And it's been even longer than that since I've seen . . . one of those."

"Forget about it," Buchanan said.

"Come to think of it," Terry said, "I can't remember ever having seen one that looked quite like-"

"When I say forget about it," Buchanan said, "I mean forget about it."

"If you're about done flaunting the family jewels," Daniel said, "maybe you could spare a moment for the computer."

Buchanan opened the notebook and switched it on. "Just gimme one minute."

While he waited for Buchanan to work his magic, Daniel picked up the latest edition of The Ring magazine and flipped through its pages while making idle chit-chat with Terry. They discussed movies, music, philosophy, politics, and time seemed to just fly by.

Twenty minutes later, Buchanan muttered, "Stupid piece of shit," then slammed the notebook closed.

"Child's play?" Terry said.

"I look like a fucking kid to you," Buchanan said.

"It'll be light soon," Terry said. "The smoke from the fire has probably been spotted by now, which means it's only a matter of time before the bodies are found."

"You hide the car?"

"Daniel ran it into the woods a couple miles away," Terry said.

"Bodies visible from the cabin?"

"No," Terry said.

"Then we've still got some time to find out what's on this thing that's worth killing for."

"I have a question," Daniel said.

"Shoot."

Daniel waved his magazine in front of Buchanan's face. "Why are half the pages missing, Frank? I haven't even had a chance to read it yet."

"There's a high school I remember seeing a couple of blocks from here," Buchanan said. "After breakfast I want you guys to haul-ass over there, grab the first geek with glasses you see and get him to crack the password."

"What are you going to do?" Daniel said.

"Keep an eye on The Colosseum. I have the sinking feeling that this thing's about to come to a head."

"Now about the magazine?"

"Housekeeping hasn't been by in two days."

"So?"

"So we ran out of toilet paper. You need me to spell it out for you, Einstein?"

Daniel slam-dunked the magazine into the garbage can. "Frank," he said, "if we don't solve this case soon, and I mean soon, I really am going to pitch your screaming carcass out the window."

<u>70</u>

Buchanan was three bitter cups of coffee into The Colosseum stakeout and his back teeth were floating. He hopped up and down on the spot, even tried pinching it off, before reluctantly giving in to nature's call, stealing into a nearby alley to relieve himself behind a dumpster within sight of the club's main entrance.

He had just started to let it rip when he heard a noise coming from the cluttered, trash-filled shadows behind him. He spun and saw a three-legged dog hunched jackal-like over a discarded pizza box, alternatively snuffling and licking the grease-stained cardboard.

"What the fuck?" Buchanan hissed when he turned back around and caught sight of a dumpster diver's face not six inches from his own.

The man was in his late thirties with long matted hair and a patchy beard. Where his arms should have been was a pair of three-fingered talons facing palms-up in a perpetual 'beats me' gesture. He was holding the half-eaten remains of a large brown rat in his left talon. He started to chuckle and then to laugh.

"What's so funny?" Buchanan said.

"I didn't see a goddamned thing. Not me."

The man laughed until his face turned purple and one eyeball audibly popped from its socket. He snatched the glass orb from mid-air and quickly pressed it back into place, white side out. Smiling broadly, he exposed a mouth full of the glistening, webby strands of raw meat. "Don't you hate it when that happens?"

The man pocketed the rat and tumbled out of the dumpster. He was wearing a sleeveless, burnt-orange leisure suit, green polyester shirt and a pair of badly scuffed white leather duty shoes. He tilted his head to the side as he studied Buchanan.

"Ain't nothin' wrong with a man pleasurin' hisself now and again," he said.

"I am not pleasuring myself," Buchanan said.

The man bent at the waist until his head nearly touched his knees, looked up at Buchanan, and made a frenzied whacking-off motion with his right talon.

"Last week I was lookin' in the front window of that Chink negligee shop 'round the corner, mindin' my own business, givin' myself a little pleasure, when this pack of mullahs swarmed over me and-"

"For the last time," Buchanan said. "I am not pleasuring myself."

"You know the type. Scraggly beards. Sandals. Painted toenails. Intolerant as hell. So they start layin' all this shit on me in some spastic, foreign tongue, tuggin' at my cock, and grabbin' at my balls with their crooked, ringed fingers. All because I-"

"I'm taking a leak. Okay?"

The man straightened up. "Takin' a leak, eh? I've always been of a mind that a man's cock is like a six-shooter."

Out of sheer morbid curiosity, Buchanan blurted, "How's that?" and immediately regretted it.

"Shootin' blanks or no, if you ain't prepared to use it as the Good Lord intended, you leave it in the holster."

"Then how the fuck you supposed to go to the can?" Again there was regret.

The man closed his eyes and fell silent. Buchanan thought that perhaps he had simply chosen to ignore the question when he noticed the urine stain spreading outwards from the crotch of the man's slacks, heard the wet farting sounds, and saw the stream of green-grey effluence pouring over his duty shoes from underneath his flared pant leg. The smell was truly noxious. Evidently rat smelled worse the morning after than even Semper Fi Sausage did.

"Got a smoke?" the man said as he continued to shit and piss his pants. "Some herb, maybe? A little spice for the mind."

Buchanan shook his head.

"Could I interest you in a little sexual pleasure then? I'm good to go. Nothin' like a good, wet shit to lube a man up." He tossed back his greasy locks with a flick of his head and his good eye narrowed vampishly. "Five bucks and you can do with me what you will. Don't even got to cuddle afterwards, you don't want to."

It was the best offer Buchanan had had since arriving in Boston. He fished through his pockets with his free hand and found some cash.

"Here's a ten."

Buchanan waited until the man had plucked the bill from his hand then pulled back his fist and knocked him cold.

"Keep the change."

He was still relieving himself when a classy, silver-blue S-Type Jaguar rolled to a stop in front of The Colosseum. It was a little after ten in the morning and the club was not yet open for business. Wearing a black leather overcoat, Raymond Sowell got out of the car and beat a tattoo on the club's steel door.

"Holy shit," Buchanan muttered.

The door was opened by Shabazz himself, and heated words were immediately exchanged.

While there was enough natural cover that Buchanan stood a good chance of getting close enough to overhear their conversation, he simply could not do so in his present condition. Unfortunately, a dozen young Asian secretary types, their colorful scarves and raven-black hair riled by the wind, were braving the weather for a smoke on the nearby sidewalk. While intermingling with the public with a spurting dick in your hand might not draw so much as a second glance in flakey LA, Buchanan had a feeling that the same could not be said of tight-jawed Boston.

Still, he had to get closer.

From his current location, he could hear snatches of sound, but he couldn't make out any words. An echo from the alley's brick walls was scrambling and distorting their voices. Did he just hear his aunt's name mentioned, or was it all in his head? He tried to empty his bladder faster by pushing harder but that only seemed to inhibit the flow.

Goddamned prostate.

Buchanan turned when he heard a low, rumbling sound coming from behind him.

The dog had finished with the pizza box and was walking stiff-legged toward him, hackles raised. It stopped at his side, motionless, staring intently across the street at Shabazz and Sowell, ears back, growling softly.

Buchanan looked up in time to see Sowell push Shabazz backwards with his open hand. Shabazz retaliated with some kind of spinning back kick which Sowell caught neatly in his hand. Holding Shabazz's leg aloft, Sowell leaned in and said something else that Buchanan could not hear.

"Fuck, fuck, fuck," Buchanan mouthed.

Finally, he shook away the last drop of piss and zipped up. Keeping mostly to the shadows, he stole to the edge of the sidewalk. Unfortunately, the show appeared to be winding down.

Sowell let go of Shabazz' leg and then, without another word, climbed into his car and pealed away. Shabazz scowled up and down the street for nearly a minute after the secret service agent had gone, challenging several bystanders with his eyes before disappearing back inside the club.

A foghorn moaned from somewhere out in the harbor as Buchanan groped his pockets for his phone. It was one of the loneliest sounds he had ever heard, and his heart ached with missing Charlotte. He flipped his phone open and punched out a number. Galton answered on the first ring.

"It's me," Buchanan said.

"Where are you?"

"I need a favor."

"What is it?"

"I wanna see Raymond Sowell's file."

Buchanan felt something brush his pant leg and looked down. The three-legged dog was gazing up at him with warm, taffy-colored eyes, its nose pulsing and twitching, its long, crooked tail wagging tentatively. Unlike the countless other street dwellers that he had seen in his life, there was still a glimmer of hope in this animal's eyes.

"Secret Service golden boy? Thornton's security head? That Raymond Sowell?"

"One and the same."

"You don't think he's involved in this mess do you? I've had recent meetings with him and-"

"I know all about your meetings with the governor. Just get me the info. I'll explain it all later."

"What you're asking me is gonna raise some serious red flags in some serious places." The line went silent while Galton considered the pros and cons of acceding to Buchanan's request. "Although I probably should know better at my age, I'll get back to you within the hour."

"Thanks, man."

Buchanan kneeled down and patted the dog on the head. Whimpering softly, it pressed its bony, shivering body into Buchanan's thigh. As he hugged the dog in against him, the poor creature licked his face hungrily, and he couldn't help but think of the morning he had literally stumbled upon Charlotte, and the wonky words of Yogi Berra; it really was *deja vu* all over again.

"How close are you to wrapping things up?"

"Real close," Buchanan said.

"Good. And in case I haven't said it already, you've got my word – so long as you end this thing quickly - I'll personally clean up any mess you guys make."

Buchanan laughed. "You might want to start with this fucked-up little alley in Chinatown

"You gimme the address, I'll be there in five."

"But seriously folks," Buchanan said. "If they've harmed so much as a single hair on my aunt's head, I'll be taking you up on that offer. 'Cos things are gonna get Katrina-messy before the day is through."

"You wanna give me some names?"

"You want names, read tomorrow's obits."

"Now about that alley you mentioned."

"It was a joke."

"I don't get it."

"You get back to me in thirty with the Sowell background and I'll explain it to you over a beer some time."

The wind began to gust, whirling and tumultuous, as it tugged a shroud of smoky grey clouds over the sky. Buchanan could taste salt in the thickening air.

"Whiskey?"

"Whatever wets your whistle."
"Old lady, too?"
"The more the merrier."
"Thirty it is."

71

Leonard strolled twice around blustery block before settling into a recessed, awning covered doorway directly across the street from The Colosseum. For all intents and purposes, he was The Invisible Man. The collar of his Aquascutum trench coat was up and his eagle eyes were masked by a pair of wraparound Vuarnet sunglasses. To play it safe, he decided he would watch the club for a minimum of thirty minutes before making his move. Behind the shades, his eyes were in constant motion. Left, right, near, far. The consummate professional. He didn't miss much. He never missed much. The wait passed uneventfully as a steady flow of pedestrians traversed the sidewalk in both directions. He studied everybody, everything, but no one, and nothing, caught his eye. No feds. No locals. No marked or unmarked vehicles patrolling the street either. Apparently the club wasn't under surveillance. Yet. Two steps out of the doorway, he collided with a large, exceedingly rumpled homeless man coming out of the adjacent alley.

"Sorry," Leonard said.

The man's hat was pulled down low. He didn't respond to Leonard's apology. Didn't even look up. His reaction, or lack thereof, wasn't rudeness, or a slight, Leonard knew. The man was obviously down on his luck, and it was his shame that had silenced him.

Leonard pulled out his monogrammed Gucci money clip, another graduation gift from his mother, and peeled off twenty dollars in fives. He passed the bills to the man. "For cigarettes," he said.

"Don't smoke," the homeless man mumbled.

"Do you drink coffee?"

The homeless man nodded.

"Get a coffee then. Someplace warm before the rain starts."

Under the rumbling, charcoal sky, Leonard crossed the street to a pair of unmarked metal doors. He paused and took a final furtive glance over his shoulder before swiping the passkey that Tokunbo had given to him shortly after the club's grand opening. There was a series of clicking sounds as the electronic lock disengaged. Inside, the park-like vestibule was deserted. He crossed the bridge and entered the main room.

"Tokunbo," he called out through cupped hands. "It's Leonard." Although the club wasn't yet open, Leonard's visit couldn't wait. From a rather greasy payphone a block from the office, he'd tried his friend on his home phone, and on his cell, but was unceremoniously dumped into voicemail each time. He hadn't left a message. He couldn't. Couldn't leave evidence of any kind that he'd interfered in an open investigation, local or otherwise. "I need to speak with you."

Tokunbo was an early riser, a workaholic, and a perfectionist. He had already been to the office, and with less than an hour to go until lunch, Leonard had no doubt that he was here, somewhere, seeing to it that everything was in order before the club opened its doors to the public.

Leonard dusted off his high school Spanish and interrogated the cleaning crew and the kitchen staff. He'd just missed him, he was told. Tokunbo had answered the door not ten minutes earlier before storming back to the loft in a rage. Leonard jogged to the elevator and was about to press the call button when a voice murmured behind him in broken English, "No, senor. Is forbidden."

Leonard turned. It was one of the cleaners. Short. Curly black hair. Bushy black mustache and an even bushier unibrow. His eyes were wide and his raised hands were shaking.

Leonard showed the man his credentials. "*Policia*," he said.

"*El Diablo*," the cleaner said.

"It's okay," Leonard said. "FBI. Not ICE. I'm Tokunbo's friend. *Amigo.*"

The cleaner crossed himself and ambled away on bowed legs, muttering ominously to himself in his native tongue.

Leonard called for the elevator and stepped inside. Seconds later the door opened onto what Tokunbo coyly termed the games rooms. He approached the sparkling stainless steel stairwell to the loft and began to ascend. Three strides up, he heard a muffled sound coming from beneath the stairs.

He leaned over the railing. "Tokunbo? Is that you?"

There was no reply.

Leonard turned and headed back down the stairs. The short wooden door beneath the stairwell was open a crack. His nostrils pulsed reflexively. He pulled the door open and sniffed. Most of the smells were familiar. He sniffed again. But there was something else. Something he couldn't quite place.

"Tokunbo? It's Leonard. Are you down there?"

Again there was no reply.

Leonard headed down the stairs. In the large, candle lit chamber at the bottom, he was about to call out again when he sensed a presence behind him. He whirled around and came face to face with Tokunbo Shabazz.

"I've come to warn you," Leonard said.

"I already know."

"You do?"

"But of course."

Leonard laughed. "Why am I not surprised? You never cease to amaze me."

Tokunbo reached up and stroked his cheek. "And you, me." His long, bony fingers lingered on the grafted skin.

"I'm afraid the nerve endings never properly took root," Leonard said. "Although I know you're touching me, I don't feel a thing."

"Head to toe, heart to soul, I am the same way, Leonard. Except when I am with Earlae. With Earlae I can feel."

"You really love her, don't you?"

Tokunbo closed his eyes. "I am getting out," he said as he opened his eyes. "For her. Today."

"You can't just close up shop."

"I can. And I will."

"But-"

"Do not worry, my friend. If nothing else, I am a practical man. There is another, highly lucrative, iron in the fire, I assure you."

"Governor Thornton," Leonard blurted.

Although Tokunbo said nothing, Leonard could read the truth in his eyes.

"I watched you and Sowell together the other night. Plotting rebellion, weren't you?"

Tokunbo smiled mischievously.

"I want in."

"Do you now?"

"I do."

Tokunbo considered his request in the amount of time it took him to blink. "Okay," he said. "If that is what you really want."

"It is."

Leonard's nostrils pulsed again. He walked over to the nearest wall sconce, where the thin flame of a handmade beeswax candle danced merrily beneath a reservoir of expertly blended essential oils. "Jasmine, Rose, and Ylang-ylang. All aphrodisiacs." He took a deep whiff. "Sandlewood. Another aphrodisiac. And Basil. For concentration. But there's something else in the air. Something I can't quite place. Earthy. Almost primal."

Tokunbo smiled.

"What is it, Tokunbo? Tell me. I simply have to know."

"Walk with me, Leonard."

"You're not going to tell me?"

"Better than that," Tokunbo said. "I will show you."

72

The principal was standing on her credenza watering a hanging fern when Daniel and Terry entered her office. She was in her mid-thirties and great to look at, shimmering blue-black hair, a barely street-legal skirt, red silk with gold embroidery, long, well-toned legs, stiletto heels. Noticing that she had visitors, she hopped nimbly down and took a seat behind her desk. A thin trail of smoke was rising from a small brass incense holder on the desktop nearest Daniel.

"I'm Kelly Chen." She flashed Daniel a smile that was more than friendly. "Miss Chen," she added, leaning heavily on the word *Miss*. "How may I assist you?"

"That smells great," Daniel said. "What is it?"

"It's a synergy of forty-one natural ingredients, herbs mostly." Miss Chen used her hands to fan some of the smoke toward her and inhaled deeply. "The practitioner at the herbal shop said it's an ancient formula designed to turbo-charge a woman's libido."

"Does it work?"

The tone of her voice was a purr and more suggestive than mere words could ever be. "At the moment," she said, "it seems to be working quite well."

"Anyway," Terry broke in loudly. "We need you to direct us to your computer science department."

"If you're looking for someone in particular, I'd be happy to page them for you."

"We're just looking for some help. We need to speak with-"

"I am sorry, but I'm afraid, I-"

"My name's Wagner. I'm a cop." She flashed her shield. "My associate's name is Rourke. We're here on official business. And we're in a hurry."

Miss Chen's composure never faltered. "Is one of our students in trouble again? If you'll give me a name, I'm sure we can-"

"What you can do," Terry said, perhaps a little too sternly, "is provide us with directions."

The principal slid out from behind her desk. "Come," she said. "I'll take you there personally."

Her shapely hips swung with a rhythmic, prideful motion as she strolled down the high school's narrow, locker-lined hallway. Through the thin and clingy material of the skirt, Daniel couldn't detect a single panty line. Terry shot Daniel a look over her shoulder when she noticed where his sight was focused. Daniel blushed hotly.

Busted.

"Hussy," Terry mouthed.

Daniel smiled diplomatically.

The computer science department was located on the back corner of the school's third and topmost floor. Inside the room a dozen students were hunched over personal computers and pecking wildly at the keyboards. All of them were of Asian descent. None of them wore corrective eyewear or looked like geeks in any way, shape or form. Pornographic images - girl on girl mostly - were visible on most of the monitors that Daniel could see.

Miss Chen gave Daniel another suggestive smile. "If you need anything else - anything at all - you know where to find me."

"We have some technical questions concerning a computer in our possession," Terry said. "Is there anyone in particular we should ask for?"

She pointed. "Joey Kwan. The muscle man at the back. If anyone can answer your questions, it would be him." She shouted something to the boy in Cantonese and he nodded. "Joey will speak with you."

Joey Kwan was five feet tall and weighed at least two hundred pounds, none of it fat. The skin-tight white t-shirt he was wearing had the word Freakatoid emblazoned across his swollen pectorals in bold red letters. His oversized jaw muscles said that he was heavy into the juice and had been for quite some time.

"Joey Kwan?" Daniel said.

The kid looked up from his monitor with mixed amusement and suspicion. "Who wants to know?"

"We have need of your talents. We heard you were the resident hacker."

Joey smirked. "If you're looking for a hacker, check out the grammar school down the road."

"I believe the term you were looking for is cracker," Terry said.

"Two points for the hottie," Joey said.

Terry showed Joey her shield. "We have a notebook computer that's password protected. Is that a problem for you?"

"The password, or the fact that you're a cop?"

"Either one."

"Hotties with handcuffs have always been a turn-on for me, you know?"

This time it was Terry's turn to blush.

"So you can get us in?" Daniel said.

"Child's play."

"Where have we heard that before?" Daniel said.

"Just give him the notebook," Terry said.

Daniel handed it over.

"Your computer's been shot. Nine mil by the looks of it. You are aware of that, right?""

"Just get us in," Daniel said.

In mere seconds, Joey announced, "Done."

"What's that?" Terry said as a second request for a password appeared. "What's happening?"

"Nothing I can't handle," Joey said. The password screen disappeared with the first key stoke. "That's strange."

"Is that it? We're in?"

Joey shrugged. "It would seem so. You looking for anything in particular?"

"Pictures, videos, e-mail," Daniel said.

Joey scrolled through the directory. "One video file. No pictures. No e-mail."

"Does it look like anyone tried to wipe the disk, or tamper with it?"

"Looks okay to me."

"Open the video," Daniel said.

A moment later, Joey let out a low whistle. "This is some seriously twisted shit. What kind of fucked-up shit are you guys into?"

Daniel felt a cold ripple along his skin. "What is it? I can't see over your traps."

A strobe burst of lightening lit the nearby window, and thunder roared.

Joey shifted his chair to the side. "Home grown porn by the looks of it. Some real sick shit." He moved his face closer to the screen and squinted. "That asshole at the back looks familiar. You know him?"

Between thunderclaps Daniel said, "Yeah. And his faithful side-kick, too."

"You get a look at his face?" Terry said.

"Like a kid on Christmas morning," Daniel said.

Joey said, "What's his n- Hey."

The screen flared brightly, throbbed for a moment then faded to black.

"What happened?" Daniel said.

"Jeez, I . . . I don't know," Joey said, clicking wildly away at the keyboard.

"Dead battery?"

"Power light's still on. Battery's fine."

"What is it then?" Daniel said.

Joey cycled the notebook off and on. The screen remained black. "The frickin hard disc is fried," he said. "That's what."

"Why? How?" Daniel's stomach tightened as he considered the full ramifications of the loss. Without the video who would believe them? No one, he knew.

"That second request for a password must have been some kind of security failsafe," Joey said. "Not surprising given what was on it, huh? Should have kicked in sooner though."

"The slug must have messed with the timing," Daniel said.

The kid's wide shoulders slumped. "I should have known better."

Daniel put his hand on one bowling ball-sized delt. "We only got in, however briefly, thanks to you. We're lucky we saw anything at all."

"Yeah, lucky," Terry mumbled.

There were tears in her eyes. Daniel wrapped his arms around her and hugged her tightly.

"Joey's right," she said. "This is some seriously fucked-up shit."

And Dark Davis had been right, too. It wasn't about money or vengeance after all. It appeared it really was about power.

Although the contents of the notebook had been banished to the great cyber-beyond, the images continued to linger in Daniel's mind, and he suspected they would do so for quite some time.

<u>73</u>

The ceaseless rain was falling fast when Daniel and Terry hailed a cab outside the high school. Under storm clouds lurid with lightening, they were empathetically silent on their stop-and-go journey to The Colosseum, digesting the full import of the images they had briefly seen, and then lost. Eventually, the cab reached the club.

"Do you see him?" Daniel said.

Terry pointed. "Over there."

Buchanan was standing under a wind-billowed awning on the other side of the street as the rain lashed him, and the wind gusted at him, Red Sox cap pulled low over his face. Terry opened the door and dashed through the slicing quicksilver sheets to join him under the awning. Daniel paid the cabbie then did the same.

"Is it open for business?" Daniel had to shout to be heard over the din of the storm.

Buchanan lifted his sodden sleeve and squinted at his watch. "They opened the doors about five minutes ago."

Daniel jerked his thumb toward the club. "Inside," he said.

The lights in the main room were dimmed and the large projection screen opposite the dance floor bar was lit up with one picture morphing into another at ten second intervals. Each picture in the series was an extreme close-up of an old person's mouth, pouted and wrinkled and joyless.

"They look like anuses," Daniel said.

"How many times you see an asshole smoke a cigarette?" Buchanan said.

"I see assholes smoking every day. On the other hand, if you're asking me how many times have I seen an actual anus smoke a cigarette, there was this nimble little minx at a bachelor party in Vegas a few years back who could do the most amazing things with her-"

"We get the picture," Terry said.

"No, no," Daniel said. "I don't think you do. Picture this, the girl's flat on her back, with her long, tattooed legs flipped up and over her head-"

"Enough," Terry said.

After taking a seat at a table on the club's upper tier, Buchanan filled Daniel and Terry in on the events of the morning.

"So Galton was right to be concerned about Farmer," Terry said.

Buchanan nodded. "What a dipshit. He looked like something straight out of an old Bogie flick. Trench coat with the collar up, sunglasses-"

"In this weather?" Daniel said. "It's like dusk out there."

"Oh, yeah. All he needed to complete the picture was a toothpick to worry in his mouth-"

"And a busker Dooley Wilson to provide the soundtrack," Daniel said.

"So get this," Buchanan said. "I come out of the alley after talking to Galton and actually run smack into the guy."

"You do?" Terry said.

"Guess what he does?"

Daniel and Terry shook their heads.

"He gives me twenty bucks."

"He didn't recognize you?" Daniel said.

"Why'd he give you the cash?" Terry said.

"For coffee. The dumb shit didn't have a clue who I was. Thought I was some starving homeless guy."

Daniel patted Buchanan on the tummy. "An empty stomach would've been my last guess."

"Fuck you."

"So the guy's dumber than Paris Hilton," Terry said. "Nothing to worry about."

"He's got a gun," Daniel said. "Guns and dumb can make for a pretty lethal combination."

"Speaking of lethal," Buchanan said. "You couldn't see Shabazz's leg it moved so fast, yet Sowell catches it like it was . . . was some second string little leaguer's off-speed pitch. Now that's someone we gotta worry about."

"Interesting," Daniel said.

"Speak of the devil," Buchanan muttered.

Daniel hunched lower in his seat. "Where?"

Buchanan motioned with his eyes toward the handsome black man in the tailored charcoal suit who had just entered the circular room through an arched doorway thirty feet to their left.

Sowell rolled through the crowded club like a juggernaut, ignoring the whistles and the cat calls of its patrons, heading straight for the elevator. Halfway there, he was intercepted by Tourettes, who did his utmost to stop him, walking backwards, hands raised, knocking down a transvestite in a blue gingham dress in the process. Finally, Sowell stopped, assisting the transvestite to his feet. Tourettes took the opportunity to clutch and tug the secret service agent to a seat at the nearest vacant table. For several minutes Sowell did all the talking while Tourettes just twitched, blinked and nodded. Eventually, Tourettes let loose with a stuttering, particularly venomous burst of ethnic slurs and had to cover his mouth with both hands to allow the other to continue. When Sowell had said his piece, he rolled back out the way he had come, and Tourettes scurried unimpeded past the bouncers and into the elevator.

While Daniel processed what he had just seen, his eyes fell on the transvestite, who was dusting off his backside while chatting to a group of mustachioed, leather clad men at a nearby table.

"Check out the tranny," Daniel said.

"What about him?" Terry said.

"His butt's covered in dust."

"So what," Buchanan said.

"We've got to get into the elevator," Daniel said, toppling his chair as he stood. "Now."

"What for?" Buchanan said. "There's nothing back there but a bunch of perverts with more dough than sense. And we've already searched Shabazz' loft. It was empty, too."

"They're back there, Frank," Daniel said. "Aunt Sarah's back there."

"But where?" Buchanan said.

"When we snuck in the other night Earlae entered the room from a door beneath the stairs to her loft. Remember?"

"I remember," Buchanan said. "And at the risk of repeating myself, so what?"

"Something about the logistics of her entrance has been bothering me ever since."

"What do you mean?"

"She came up, Frank. Up a series of cut stone steps."

"The pervert room is already in the basement," Buchanan said, joining Daniel on his feet. "So where exactly do the steps lead?"

"That's the sixty-four thousand dollar question."

"And you have the answer, don't you?"

"Watching that transvestite dusting off his Dorothy from The Wizard of Oz getup it hits me."

"Out with it, man."

"Do you remember what each of the forensic reports noted finding trace amounts of on the bodies?"

"Dust," Buchanan said.

"Stone dust," Terry said.

"Limestone and granite to be precise," Daniel said.

"Good work," Buchanan said.

"There are tunnels beneath this building," Daniel said. "It's the only way to account for the forensic findings."

"And it's also how Shabazz was able to stash, execute, and mutilate his captives without being seen or heard by anyone," Buchanan said.

"It's certainly plausible," Terry said. "These buildings have been around since prohibition. Hidden rooms and tunnels were commonplace in this part of town back then. Bootleggers used them to transport their booze, and to provide their customers with a relaxed, cop free environment."

Buchanan glanced at his watch. "When is Galton gonna get back to me with the Sowell info? I should have heard from him twenty minutes ago."

"The information is irrelevant," Daniel said. "We've seen what was on the notebook. We know the identity of the man who's been pulling Shabazz' strings. And we know what's really been going on."

"Christ almighty," Buchanan said. "In all the excitement I completely forgot about the notebook. What did you see? Tell me."

"Later," Daniel said.

"But-"

"Later, Frank. We'll tell you everything later, I promise. After we rescue your aunt."

Buchanan picked up an empty beer bottle from a nearby table. "You want I should lure the bouncers away?"

Daniel shook his head and looked at Terry. "You still have your badge handy?"

Terry nodded.

"Use it."

<u>74</u>

Earlae slipped into Sarah Calhoun's cell and gave her head a sad, slow shake. The regal lady in the rickety wooden chair smiled bravely up at her, very nearly breaking her heart. There was no way to sugar-coat the news, so she simply spit it out.

"Tokunbo wants me to kill you. He said he didn't care how I did it, other than it should involve a great deal of . . . pain."

"It's Francis, isn't it? He's got a stubborn streak in him a mile wide, just like his old auntie. I knew he wouldn't leave town."

"Maybe. I don't know. Tokunbo doesn't talk to me anymore. Not in a long, long time."

"If it's not Francis, what else could it be?"

"I told you, Aunt Sarah, Tokunbo doesn't talk to me. All I know is that everything went kinda wonky after he heard Blake's confessional. He says he's doing it for me, but I don't believe him. The big fat liar."

"What are you going to do?"

"I wouldn't harm a hair on your chinny-chin-chin if that's what you're asking. I could never hurt you, Aunt Sarah." She stamped a foot. "I can't do this anymore. I can't. And I won't."

"You're a good person, Earlae. I knew you'd see the light eventually."

"I just don't know what's up with Bo. He's so different now. I don't understand. It's . . . it's like I don't know him anymore."

"Maybe you never did. Like me with William. Maybe we never knew them at all."

Earlae nodded somberly. "I tried to reason with him, last night, and again this morning. But he wouldn't listen to a single word I had to say."

"CUNT-EYED NIPS," Ace shrieked as he poked his head into the cell, almost giving Earlae a coronary.

"What are you doing here?"

Ace was supposed to be upstairs in the loft, out of harms way, waiting for her to find Bo and make one last ditch effort to sort things out. They could turn themselves in to the authorities. When the truth came out about the men and women they'd killed there wasn't a jury around that'd convict them.

"They've found the tunnels." Spittle flew from his mouth which was twisted in rage. "A minute behind me. Maybe less."

"Calm down, Ace. What's happening?"

"Haven't you been listening? They're coming. Let's gut the old bat while we still have the chance."

"Who's coming? The police? The FBI? The Boy Scouts?"

"The old bat's nephew and his pretty boy friend."

"But I thought-"

"They'd split town? COCK SUCKIN MACACAS. Well, they didn't."

"What are you doing here? I told you to wait for me upstairs."

Ace's squinting eyes fixed on Aunt Sarah. "Let me do it, Earlae. I wanna do it."

"No way."

"Let's do it together then. I want that nosey cop to suffer for spoiling my fun."

"Get out of here, Ace," Earlae said, pushing him toward the door. "Lickety-split. If you stay they'll catch you. I don't care what happens to me, I really don't. But it's not too late for you."

God, she hoped it wasn't. For both their sakes.

Ace pulled a dollar store pocket knife from his maroon Members Only jacket and fumbled open the wavy chrome-plated blade. "The nephew's a cop. He won't hurt me. He can't. I've had diversity training at work, you know. I'm gay as the birds, and I'm sick. That makes me untouchable. He so much as looks at me the wrong way and I'll charge him with a hate crime, sue him for every penny he's worth." His voice was barely human and as he spoke twin trails of blood gushed from his nostrils, streaming over his lips to drip from his pointy chin. "So he'll arrest me - politely if he knows what's good for him - and my lawyer'll have me back in my Santa suit by dinner."

Earlae's heart was pounding and she felt suddenly dizzy. It was all her fault, she knew. So many lives ruined. So many dead. And all because of her.

No more, she vowed. No more.

Ace was moving his blade toward Sarah Calhoun's throat when he suddenly stopped. His eye slits went wide as he turned and caught sight of the E-Z-Out Knife in Earlae's hand. He stumbled into her and she caught him in her arms. He was shaking all over, close to death. He started to cry, then mumble incoherently, something about frying fish and burning beans.

"I can't make you out," Earlae said.

One of Ace's hands began tap-tapping on her backside as he raised his tear-filled eyes to hers. The timbre of his voice rose enough for her to make out the words, and the familiar tune of *The Jeffersons* theme song. ". . . *we finally got out piece of the pie.*" And then the tapping stopped.

Ace left a long smear of red down the front of her white cotton parka as he slid lifelessly to the floor.

"Are you okay?" Aunt Sarah said.

"I couldn't let him hurt you. You're my best friend in the whole wide world."

"Thank you, Earlae. I-"

"There's no time for small talk. When the dust settles we'll have a girl's night out, manis and pettis, a few too many drinks, and shoot the poop then. Okay?"

Earlae lifted the old woman out of the chair and placed her gently on the floor.

"It's a date," Aunt Sarah said.

"You were right about Francis. He really is here, and I'm going to find him. He's a policeman. He'll know what to do." Earlae took two steps then paused in the doorway. "While I'm gone I want you to be as quiet as a mouse. Bo's still skulking around here someplace. If you hear anyone coming shut your eyes and lay still. If Bo thinks you're dead, he'll pass you by."

"Be careful, Earlae."

In her best Terminator voice, Earlae said, "I'll be Beethoven."

75

Inside the club's restricted area, after searching Shabazz's apartment and finding it empty, Daniel handed Terry his phone. "Buzz Galton and tell him to get here ASAP with the storm troopers."

Terry put her hand on Daniel's shoulder and gave it a gentle squeeze. "Be careful," she said.

"*Que sera, sera*," Daniel said.

Buchanan removed his back up piece, a tarnished .38, from his ankle holster and offered it to Daniel. "Take this, Doris Day," he said. "You might need-"

"I don't-"

"Yeah, you do."

Daniel unzipped his jacket and flashed Dark Davis' nickel-plated six-shooter. "Already got one." He glanced at Terry out of the corner of his eyes and smirked. "And for the record, I want it noted that mine's considerably larger than his."

"I should certainly hope so," Terry said.

A red-faced Buchanan quickly steered the conversation back to topic. "Smith & Wesson's classic 629," he said. "Forty-four Magnum. Fully loaded?"

"Two shots."

"Last count there were four bad guys down here. Five if Sowell comes back."

"So I'll make sure they're standing in a line before I shoot."

"Speaking of which," Buchanan said. "You know how to use that thing, right?"

"Point and shoot. Like a Polaroid."

"Just keep in mind it ain't your dick, so don't go pulling on it. You wanna hit someone, aim center mass and squeeze the trigger gently." Buchanan re-holstered the .38 and drew his 9mm from the shoulder harness.

"I don't see those guns," Terry said. "Anyone asks, I didn't see them."

Buchanan jacked a round into the firing chamber. "What guns?"

Beyond the oak-plank door, the passage angled sharply into the earth, lit by a pair of energy saving, full spectrum incandescent bulbs.

"Let's go get her, Frank," Daniel said as he ducked through the low doorway.

<u>76</u>

Daniel and Buchanan reached the bottom of the stairs to find an eerie, candlelit chamber from which a series of tunnels rolled outward in all directions.

"This is the place, alright," Buchanan said. "Beneath the girly incense smell, there's death in the air."

Daniel knelt down. "Footprints. Two sets."

"Heading in opposite directions," Buchanan said. "One uphill. One down."

"Two roads diverged in a wood," Daniel said.

"I don't like it, but time is of the essence," Buchanan said. "We gotta split up."

"High road or low?" Daniel said.

"Low road. Why should I change now?"

"I'll shout if I find anyone."

Buchanan looked hard at Daniel. "Don't waste your breath. As far as I'm concerned, it's seek-and-destroy. Time for justice to be done. Your kind of justice. You find any of 'em, Shabazz, Farmer, the transvestite, the spaz, take the killshot. I'll read 'em their rights at the funeral."

"Works for me."

With his six-shooter extended in front of him, an extremely itchy finger on the trigger, Daniel tracked the footprints up one tunnel and into another. At the tunnel's end was a ladder. He climbed the ladder and passed through a hatch into a cavernous garage. He stood and gaped in astonishment, his eyes bedazzled by the blazing fluorescent light glinting off a veritable sea of chrome and highly polished lacquer paint.

Lined up on the pristine concrete floor, like some teenage boy's wet dream, were more than a dozen prestige vehicles, both modern and classic. The collection included a post-BMW Rolls Royce Phantom, sporting low profile, aftermarket alloy wheels, a Mercedes-Benz SL Roadster, mid- to late-fifties, a Cadillac ESV with 22-inch, seven spoke chromed aluminum wheels, an Indian Bonneville Sport Scout motorcycle, 1930s, with custom pin-striping and a suicide shift, and a cherry-red '61 Chevrolet Impala SS convertible, top down.

Daniel ran his hands reverently over the Impala, the first true American muscle car. His dad had owned one in the early eighties, and he remembered fondly touring The Five Boroughs in it as a child, his hair billowing in the wind as he watched the speedometer climb ever higher. 'Liftoff,' he used to scream over the throaty roar of the dual header exhaust as the needle swept into the triple digits.

"Giddy-up, giddy-up, 409."

Tucked away in the far corner of the garage was the odd vehicle out. Using the same logic that had broken the case after the Ira Banks abduction, he decided it merited a closer look.

It was a nondescript Ford panel van, windowless, with white factory paint, and factory wheels. On the street it would have been the next best thing to being invisible. Obviously, it was what Shabazz had used to transport his victims.

Had he located Sarah Calhoun? Was she still alive? Or was he too late?

Daniel threw open the rear cargo doors.

The interior walls were covered with soundproofing baffles, and an elaborate series of leather S and M-style restraints were bolted to the floor. Sadly, the restraints were empty.

"Damn," he said.

It appeared he's chosen the wrong path. The action, it seemed, was all down below. With Frank.

Daniel leaped down the hatch and raced back through the tunnels. He was approaching the chamber where he and Buchanan had begun their subterranean quest when he spotted something crucial that he had missed on his journey topside. Mounted to one of the rough-hewn lintels at the intersection of three tunnels was a wireless surveillance camera. *Oh, shit.* If the tunnels were wired for sight and sound, Shabazz could very well know they were here, and Frank could be walking into a trap.

Daniel broke into an Olympic-style sprint.

77

Daniel was charging full-speed-ahead down the tunnel that Buchanan had taken when Terry pulled up beside him, her long strides seemingly effortless, gazelle-like.

"Where's Frank?" she said in a conversational tone.

Daniel lifted an arm and gestured ahead of him.

"In trouble?" she said.

He sucked in a breath before responding. "Maybe."

"Galton's 10-17. I'm coming with you."

"But-"

"He's on his way. I gave him detailed instructions on where to find us. Don't argue with me, you'll lose. I'm coming."

Daniel sucked in another breath. "Thanks," he said. "I can use all the help I can get."

Above them, just as there had been on the way to the garage, surveillance cameras were mounted in the supporting beams of the ceiling. Daniel couldn't help but wonder it Shabazz was watching them right now. The man was cunning, he knew, and ruthless, and left very little to chance.

Were they heading into a trap? Probably.

Was Frank okay? Hopefully.

At the end of the twisting tunnel they entered a large, fully furnished room. If Daniel hadn't known he was beneath the streets of Boston he might well have been on the threshold of a nineteenth century London gentleman's club. There was a pair of green leather wingback chairs, oversized, tufted, and a matching sofa. Between the chairs was a pedestal cigar ashtray, Deco, with a reclining nude for a handle. Floor to ceiling bookshelves spanned two of the lengthy walls. The shelves were full, and the spines of the several hundred hardcover, leather-bound volumes appeared never to have been cracked. In the corner opposite the chairs was a low stage complete with age-faded velvet curtains.

Terry tapped him on the arm and gestured for silence.

Voices could be heard on the other side of a partially open door on the left hand side of the stage.

"I'll go first," Daniel whispered.

Terry looked down at the cannon in his hand and then at her own empty hands. "No argument here," she said. "This time."

They exited stage left to enter a long hallway. Along its length were a series of wood-plank doors with heavy gauge dead-bolt locks.

They located Buchanan in the farthest room on the right. He had captured the transvestite and was in the process of reading him the riot act, a look of unrestrained rage contorting his face.

"Shabazz took Aunt Sarah," he said when he saw Daniel.

"Took her where?" Daniel said.

Buchanan gestured at Terry. "What's she doing here?"

"She's done her part. Galton's 10-something or other."

"Seventeen," Terry said.

"We missed her by two minutes, five tops," Buchanan said.

"Where is she?" Daniel said to their prisoner.

The transvestite raised his hand.

"What did I tell you?" Buchanan said. "You don't have to do that. This ain't the fucking third grade, and I ain't your fucking teacher. So you got something to say, fucking say it."

"I know where he's taking her. It's where he's taken them all."

"Was this her cell? Daniel said.

The transvestite looked shamefully down at his feet.

"Was it?"

"Yes. Everyone was kept here. Everyone but Blake. Blake was Bo's special project."

"What is this place? These tunnels? These rooms?" Daniel said.

"It used to be a speakeasy," Terry said.

"A speakeasy? What's that?" Buchanan said.

"An illegal club where the mob sold liquor during prohibition."

"How do you know?" Daniel said.

"I have a masters degree in American history," Terry said. "In some cities, New York, Chicago, San Francisco, they were actually quite elaborate affairs, offering food, live bands and, in some cases, female companionship."

"That's probably what these rooms were for," Daniel said. "Turning tricks. These locks are too new to be prohibition-era."

"Bo installed them," the transvestite said.

Terry spun the transvestite around and pushed him face-first into the wall. "You have the right to remain silen-"

"Wait," Buchanan said. "The transvestite's changed teams. He's batting cleanup for the good guys now."

"Earlae," the transvestite said. "My name is Earlae. And I'm a girl."

"Earlae's with us," Buchanan said. "He- She's gonna take us to Aunt Sarah. Aren't you, Earlae?"

"This way," Earlae said, grabbing Buchanan's hand, leading him into the hallway.

Beyond the cell block was an iron door with multiple locks. The door was ajar and through it was an unlit corridor. On a shelf beside the door were four MagLite flashlights, which Earlae distributed to each member of their group. The corridor was constructed of stone block and smelled of must and decay. Rodents of considerable size, eyes blazing red, darted in all directions through their perpetually sweeping beams.

"This was probably an escape tunnel," Terry said. "Something the owner could use to make a quick exit should the cops come calling."

"I wonder who owned the place," Daniel said.

"Back then the Boston underworld was run by the Gustin Gang, the Irish mob," Terry said. "Although Frank Wallace headed the gang, the day-to-day management of the speakeasies was probably left to one of his lieutenants. Bernie McLean, maybe, or Sean Malloy."

"Sean Malloy," Earlae said. "Bo found some old ledgers. He said Malloy ran this place. We're on our way to his apartment right now. It's in an abandoned building about ten minutes away."

Ahead the corridor angled sharply downward. Earlae stopped and raised her light from the floor. A hundred and fifty feet distant the corridor dead-ended at a stone block wall.

"What is this?" Buchanan growled.

"Come and see," Earlae said as she began to skip down the slope with a skeptical Buchanan in tow. "It's really neato."

"Secret passage?" Terry said when they had reached the end of the line.

Earlae nodded.

Terry grinned over at Daniel. "I'd read about them in school, but I never thought I'd get to see one first hand. It really is . . . neato."

Daniel gave Terry a look.

"Well, it is."

Earlae passed Buchanan her flashlight then ran her hands over the rough cut granite masonry. Shortly her probing fingers found a smaller than usual stone that appeared to be floating in the spongy mortar surrounding it. She pressed down firmly and there was a loud clicking sound. She put her shoulder to the wall and pushed with her legs. Creaking and groaning under its monstrous weight, a great slab of wall swung slowly outward.

"Neato," Daniel said.

"We told you so," Terry and Earlae said.

78

Earlae was lowering a leg into the hole when Buchanan stopped her. "What's wrong?" She jerked her leg quickly back.

"Don't you hear it?" Buchanan said.

The group fell silent. The babble of water could be heard through the opening. Buchanan shone his light into the tunnel beyond and took a long look around. When he turned to face the others his expression was severe.

"It's an old storm drain," he said.

"So?" Earlae said.

"It's still in use."

"And?"

"I dated this UCLA frat brat in the late nineties. He was part of a group of urban explorers that traveled the globe exploring abandoned buildings, sewers, storm drains. You name it." He took another pensive look through the doorway. "And they had a saying, 'If it rains, no drains.'"

Daniel nudged forward and shone his light inside. "It doesn't look deep."

"Yet," Buchanan said.

"Bo and I have been inside a gazillion times," Earlae said. "Once or twice, we've even made – you know – down there. Safe for ages three and up. No kidding."

Anger, or maybe frustration, edged Buchanan's voice. "Have you ever gone down when it's pouring rain out? Have you?"

"Maybe." Earlae scrunched her face up, thinking back. "I don't know. Maybe not."

"So where does this leave us?" Terry said.

"I'm heading in regardless," Buchanan said. "Anyone cares to join me I just wanna make sure they know the risk. Quite a few explorers, seasoned ones at that, have bought the farm in places like this. They can fill up pretty fast in a downpour."

"How fast are we talking about?" Daniel said.

"A hundred, two hundred years ago, when the sky let loose, where'd all the rain go?"

"Into the ground," Daniel said. "It soaked into the ground."

"Problem is, in a big city like Boston, there ain't no ground anymore. It's all shingles and brick and concrete and asphalt. So when the rain comes down now, where's it go?"

"It evaporates?" Earlae said tentatively.

Buchanan made a loud buzzing sound. "Wrong," he said. "It runs off the roofs, over the sidewalks, onto the streets and down the drains, every blessed drop. Millions upon millions of gallons. Billions maybe. Do you understand the magnitude of the problem now?"

"We get it," Daniel said.

"In or out?" Buchanan said.

"Count me in," Daniel said. "If Shabazz can do it . . ."

Terry and Earlae nodded in agreement.

Buchanan dropped into the opening first, followed by Earlae, Terry, and Daniel. The coffin-shaped tunnel was made of red brick, its walls covered in a thick, monkey-shit-yellow slime. The curved ceiling was high enough that they were able to stand without ducking or hunching. The flowing water was ankle deep and ice-cold.

"Which way?" Buchanan said. There was no echo as he spoke. The yellow slime on the walls seemed to absorb his words even as they were spoken.

Earlae looped her arm through Buchanan's and started walking. "We just go with the flow."

They walked for a time in silence. The system was more expansive than Daniel had hoped, with numerous splits and turns. North? South? East? West? He had long ago lost any sense of direction. Buchanan must have been voicing the very same thoughts as he suddenly blurted to Earlae, "Are you sure you remember the way?"

Earlae affected a pout. "Just a few more minutes."

"What should we be looking out for?" Terry said to Buchanan.

"The water level first of all. It's not too bad at the moment but that can change. The biggest danger is a flash flood, having your feet washed out from under you and hitting your head, getting knocked unconscious, and drowning. Or having your body broken and mangled going over a waterfall."

"Underground waterfalls?" Daniel said. "You can't be serious."

"They exist, believe me. Some are only a few feet high. But I've seen falls with fifteen, twenty foot drops."

"Earlae piped in, "The waterfall up ahead is even bigger than that. Not Niagara Falls big. But it's still pretty as a postcard."

Buchanan stopped. "You neglected to mention anything about a waterfall."

"Because we don't go over it. The ladder to Bo's fortress is *beside* the falls. And if you really must know, it's not the waterfall you should be scared of."

"What do you mean?" Buchanan said. "What else is down here?"

Earlae placed the flashlight under her chin and affected a scary laugh. "Vampires."

"Vampires?" Terry said.

Earlae puffed out her ample chest. "Not to worry," she said. "You'll be okay when they see you're with me. Bo taught them a lesson in manners they won't soon forget."

Daniel decided it was time to change the subject, before Buchanan blew a gasket. "You've done this before, Frank?" he said. "Gone underground like this?"

Buchanan chuckled bitterly. "Just once. It was supposed to be a romantic getaway with the brat. Paris. His treat."

"Of course," Daniel said.

"Before we left all he talked about was Les Mis. Here I was thinking we'd be taking in the play at the Palais des Sports, front row center, and instead we spend it-"

"Traipsing the conscience of the city," Daniel said.

"Huh?"

"It's what Victor Hugo, the man who wrote *Les Miserables*, called the sewers. I read the novel in high school. A good fifty pages or more take place underground."

"Don't I know it," Buchanan said. "Now. We spent the whole fucking week slogging through the city's drains and sewers, knee deep in French shit and piss and God knows what else. Haven't spoken to him since."

"Speaking of knee deep," Terry said. "Has anyone else noticed that the water level is rising?"

Daniel looked down. Indeed it had risen. It was now up to their calves.

Buchanan grunted. "Let's bust a move."

Seconds later something bumped into the back of Daniel's legs, heavy enough to almost knock him down. He turned and shone his flashlight behind him. "Hey, guys," he said. "We've got company."

It was the body of a man, floating face down in the murky water, the flaps of his filth-mottled overcoat spread out on either side of him like the wings of a fallen angel.

"Anyone we know?" Buchanan said.

Daniel flipped the body over with his foot. The man was Hispanic, middle-aged, unshaven, his clothes threadbare and ill-fitting. It didn't take an ME to determine the cause of death. His throat had been slit from ear to ear.

Daniel shook his head.

"Let him go," Buchanan said. "Nothing we can do for the poor bastard now."

Daniel moved his leg let the corpse drift peacefully past.

A hundred yards farther, Buchanan stopped. He motioned the others for silence, and tilted his head, listening. "Waterfall," he muttered.

"The waterfall is farther in," Earlae said. "What you're hearing is the sound of the water entering *the vampire's lair*."

"Will you knock it off with that vampire shit," Buchanan said. "It's really starting to piss me off."

"Alrighty then," Earlae said. "But don't say I didn't warn you."

They rounded a bend and saw an orangey-red light flickering in the distance. Buchanan motioned for silence, and they continued on. The tunnel opened ten feet up the wall of an arched, cathedral-like room into which five drains similar to their own gaped. The water from each of the drains flowed down slides into the room where it was funneled toward a concrete pipe large enough to accommodate a runaway locomotive. Torches sputtered from brackets mounted on the walls which were covered in masterful graffiti depicting life on the streets, horrific, soul-numbing scenes of hell on earth that would have made the Dutch painter Hieronymus Bosch envious.

Earlae tapped Daniel's arm, pointed, and mouthed the word, 'Vampires.'

Standing in the swirling waist deep water in one corner of the chamber were a half dozen kids dressed completely in black. They were rifling through the pockets of the floater that had struck Daniel moments earlier.

"Which way?" Buchanan said.

Earlae gasped when one of the kids turned and hissed a warning to the others. They let the body go and sloshed through the water to scale a trio of iron rungs set into the far wall.

They were Goths, Daniel saw, with pierced faces, dyed jet-black hair, and paper-white complexions that told of a life spent in shadow and darkness.

"Runaways," Terry said. "Nothing to be concerned with."

"Which way?" Buchanan said again, smacking Earlae on the backside to get her attention.

"There's a narrow flight of stairs around the corner," Earlae said. "We go down them and follow that big pipe to the waterfall."

A rat suddenly appeared from a hole in the bricks beside Daniel's head and leaped into the water. A second rat poked its twitching nose out of the same hole, had a quick look around then also took the leap. Soon dozens more rats appeared all around them, squeaking and squealing as they belly-flopped and cannon-balled into the swiftly moving current.

"Oh, shit," Buchanan said.

"What?" Daniel said.

"My friend said that rats were like the canaries the old time miners used to keep. They act like a kind of early warn-"

The unmistakable roar of rushing water suddenly rose from the darkened void at their backs.

"Down the stairs to the ladders," Buchanan shouted. "Climb as high as you can and hold on for dear life. It's our only chance."

Beside Daniel, Earlae screamed. He turned in time to see a tsunami-like wall of water barreling down on them.

<u>79</u>

Tokunbo placed the valiantly struggling lady onto the lace-draped canopy bed in the guest bedroom. She might have been dead from the waist down for more than a decade but she'd put up one hell of a fight.

"Handicapable. That is what you are."

"Francis is coming for me."

"Of course, he is coming. He and his merry band of do-gooders. I saw them on the monitors on our way in."

"You're going to be sorry."

Tokunbo frowned. "Do you honestly believe that he can best me?"

"I don't just believe it. I know it."

"Although a part of me respects your spunk, another part, the larger part by far, actually pities you."

"Finally, we can agree on something. Because I pity you, too."

Tokunbo was through with storm drains. Back inside the master bedroom, he shucked his chest waders and slipped on his Lanvin low-top sneakers. He checked his watch, a Rising White Casio, and headed into the sitting room. He nodded a casual hello to special agent Farmer, who was quietly hovering nearby. At the period mahogany dry bar he poured himself a snifter of Cognac, Remy Martin Louis XIII, and took a seat to await his guests.

No matter how he played it in his mind, it was going to be a massacre. Killing the old lady's nephew and the female police officer would be strictly business but doing Rourke was another matter. Pressed for time or not, the manner of that smart-mouthed racist's death was going to be . . .

He paused in his thoughts to swirl the amber liquid around in his palm before taking a sip of the 100-year-old ambrosia.

"Inspired."

<u>80</u>

Before Daniel could take a single step he was engulfed, washed down the slide into the macabre chamber. Carried by the momentum of the drop, he went down under the choppy surface, inhaling a mouthful of water, tasting the grit and the grime of Boston's streets, the bile of its overflowing sewers. He kicked to the surface, and immediately began to cast about the room for the others. The force of the runoff gushing from the sextet of feeder pipes was dismaying, generating numerous, conflicting currents. The din was overwhelming. All around him, the tumultuous water was covered with squealing, panic-stricken rats. It was pure and unadulterated chaos, and it took him more than a moment to get his bearings.

Finally, he saw the others' blurred forms.

Terry and Earlae were caught in a vortex a dozen feet to his left, clutching tightly onto each other, and spinning slowly around in a counterclockwise direction. Buchanan was nearest to the wall with the ladders. He was reaching out to a kid, who was reaching out to him. Their fingers touched but they couldn't get a grip and he spiraled helplessly past. Luckily, his arm was snagged by the next kid down.

' Rescued by vampires, Daniel thought. What a story this would make for the grandkids. He reached out for a kid, the one who'd initially missed Buchanan, and shouted for the others to do the same. He kicked hard, bobbing closer, closer. Almost there now.

What Daniel witnessed next was beyond comprehension. "Frank," he shouted. "What the hell are you doing?"

Buchanan had turned on his rescuer and was flailing at him with both legs.

Seconds later, a scissor-kick landed high on the kid's arm and his grip was broken. Daniel watched in horror as his wildly thrashing friend, fighting the current and losing badly, was dragged kicking and screaming down the massive exit pipe.

Finally, Daniel moved into range of an outstretched arm, and the kid, mostly toothless, with a port-of-wine birthmark on one side of his face, caught his wrist. But instead of pulling him into the safety of the ladder, the kid kept him at arm's length, fumbling with the clasp of his watch. It was a '67 Doxa Submariner. The world's first orange face dive watch. It had been his dad's. No way was he going to lose it now. Especially not to this social misfit. Daniel reached into his waistband and drew his revolver which he leveled at the kid's expressionless, remorseless face. The kid let go.

Daniel lost sight and sound of the others as he followed Buchanan down the concrete pipe. Face first, and on his stomach, he reached for something, anything, to stop him, but there was nothing at all to grab hold of.

On a long straightaway the current became less topsy-turvy. Daniel tucked and rolled, on his back now, feet in front, in case a wall or other obstruction should appear. Two rats were on his chest. He brushed at them. One dropped off, but the other, clamped onto his jacket by its razor-sharp teeth, didn't budge. In the distance he could see the beam of Buchanan's flashlight bopping over the grey concrete walls. He returned the revolver to his waistband and pulled out his own flashlight.

And then Buchanan's light was gone.

Suddenly, the aperture of the pipe narrowed. Daniel just managed sneak a breath before he was thrust underwater. In Australia a few years back, while snorkeling off the Great Barrier Reef, he had managed to hold his breath for more than three minutes. Now, shivering with cold, his heart racing uncontrollably, he doubted he could hold it for a quarter of that time. If the pipe didn't soon end, he would surely drown.

There was no sense of up, down, right or left as he spiraled at breakneck speed through the drain's numerous twists and turns. On the verge of losing consciousness, imaginary stars twinkling before his eyes, the pipe finally opened up. The beam of Buchanan's light flashed again, maybe forty yards in front of him, and then disappeared.

Left, right, left again.

Then he heard it. *The waterfall.* Over the steady roar of the rushing water, he could hear it. While it wasn't Niagara Falls loud, his instincts warned him it was just as deadly.

The walls of the pipe were too wide for him to spread his arms and generate the necessary friction to reduce his rate of speed. There had to be some other way? Wasn't there always? But it was as if his higher reasoning skills had been placed on standby. There was only one thought in his head: In a matter of seconds he'd be heading over the falls without a barrel.

A corner appeared out of nowhere. Daniel's boots rammed into it, and he was filled with a sense of weightlessness as his body, arms flailing, was sent arcing through the air into an immense mist-filled chamber. He slammed into a wall and his head snapped back, striking the hard surface. He dropped to the ground. Felt the water pouring over his face. Then he felt someone's arms encircle him, picking him up, and holding him steady.

"Frank," he managed to say. "What . . . ? How . . . ?"

"The others," Buchanan said. "Where are-"

As if on cue, Terry slammed into the nearby wall with an audible grunt, and seconds later, Earlae appeared, cast out of the water to land in a sopping heap beside her.

"Go to them, Frank," Daniel said. "I'm alright. Check the others." He was woozy from the blow he'd taken to the head, and numb from the cold, but he could still stand on his own.

While he waited for the cobwebs to clear, he took stock of the surroundings. The water had deposited them in a structure that bore more than a passing resemblance to a New York City subway terminal. The group had washed up on what would have been the boarding platform, with the flood of water coursing through the ten foot groove that the train would have occupied. Aside from where the water crested and broke into the wall thirty feet down, the slosh of water on the platform was only ankle deep. Ten feet away a waist-high railing marked the outer edge of the platform. Daniel stutter-stepped to the railing and looked down. It was easily a thirty foot drop. Luck had certainly been with them. He wondered darkly whether it would hold.

Shortly, Terry joined him at the railing. She wrapped an arm around his waist. Her lips were blue and her jaw was quivering uncontrollably. "Who's your furry friend?"

Daniel looked down at his jacket. In all the excitement he had completely forgotten about the rat, which was still clinging to him tooth and nail. "I haven't named him yet," he said. "What do you think of Harvey?"

At that moment the rat let go, splashed into the shallow water at their feet, and was quickly carried over the edge.

"I'd say he didn't like it," Terry said.

"You think?"

"Inventory," Buchanan barked. "Guns, lights, who's got what?"

Daniel's flashlight was firmly in hand. He lifted his jacket to reveal the gun in his pants. "I'm good."

Buchanan shone his beam on Earlae. "Where's your light?"

"I . . . I must've dropped it."

Buchanan swung the beam to Terry. "You?"

Terry pulled the flashlight out of her pants pocket and shone it back at Buchanan. "You still have the .38?"

Buchanan nodded.

"Give it to me."

"Are we fucked?" Buchanan said to Earlae.

She shook her head.

"So how do we get out of here?"

Earlae pointed over the falls. "That way."

The bottom rung of an iron ladder could be seen within reach of where they stood. Daniel leaned over the railing and glanced up. Five rungs up it disappeared into the swirling mist.

Terry said, "Do you think they made it?"

"Yeah," Buchanan said. "They had enough of a head start. Aunt Sarah weighs a buck, a buck five. She wouldn't have slowed a big, strong guy like Shabazz down any. They made it."

"Let's get going then," Terry said. "We stand around much longer we'll drop dead from hypothermia."

Buchanan grabbed the ladder and gave it a shake. It was rusty, but appeared solid enough. "I'll go first," he said. "Daniel brings up the rear."

The ladder led through the mist to a narrow metal catwalk. On one end was another ladder, which scaled the heights to a manhole cover through which the rain still poured. On the other end was a doorway through a crumbling concrete wall.

"Which way?" Buchanan said.

Earlae pointed the way. "Just one more, teeny-tiny, tunnel to go."

Daniel stole a wistful glance up the ladder at the other end of the catwalk before ducking into the tunnel ahead of the others.

<u>81</u>

The doorway was an access point to an old utility tunnel. Lined with aluminum-jacketed wires, conduits, and pipes, there was just enough room for single file, hunched human passage. Municipal addresses were stenciled in black at various exit points along the tunnel. Three addresses along, Earlae pointed, "In there."

With Daniel still in the lead, they headed into a crawlspace approximately sixty feet in length. At the end was a round, heavily corroded metal door reminiscent of a submarine hatch.

Daniel pushed down on the door's lever. Nothing happened. He pushed down harder. Still nothing happened.

"Frank," Daniel said. "I could sure use your weight up here."

"I hope that's not a crack," Buchanan said as he crawled over Terry and Earlae to join Daniel at the door. "I'm tired, and cold, and on the verge of a murderous rage. I'm just not in the mood."

"Jeez," Daniel said. "I thought you guys were supposed to be jolly."

Although the quarters were cramped, Daniel twisted far enough to one side to allow Buchanan a grip on the latch.

"On three," Daniel said. "One. Two. *Three.*"

The pair pushed down hard, and with the sound of metal grating on metal, the latch grudgingly gave way.

Breathing heavily from the exertion, Buchanan looked back at Earlae. "Shabazz got through here by himself?"

"With a crowbar. He must've taken it up with him."

Daniel tugged the door open enough to admit even Buchanan's recently expanded girth. He shone his light through the doorway to reveal a large mechanical room. Inside were the corroded hulks of an ancient furnace and half a dozen boilers. One wall was filled with a multitude of rusting and unworkable controls, dials and switches and levers.

"I'm going in," Daniel said.

He entered the room and took a cautious look around, shining his light into every crook and crevice.

"Empty," he called out.

"I told you already," Earlae said, her angel face appearing in the high doorway beside Buchanan's. "Bo's Fortress is upstairs. Top floor." She pointed to a door. "We're in the basement. The stairs are through there."

"Shabazz could be anywhere," Buchanan said. "From here on in we're in ninja mode."

Terry made a show of looking down at the gun in her hands. "Silent," she said, "but deadly."

"Shoot to kill," Buchanan said.

With his own gun firmly in hand, Daniel opened the door and stepped cautiously out into a wide hallway piled high with garbage and upended, mould-covered furniture. The smell of rot and mildew was caustic, as was the stench of urine. Forty feet to his left were the stairs Earlae had mentioned.

"I see the way up," he said.

With Daniel maintaining the lead, the group hiked over the refuse. At the top of the stairs was a pair of swinging wooden doors with dusty porthole windows. They opened with a mournful groan.

The building's first floor had been completely gutted. Even the interior walls were gone. The twenty foot ceiling, stripped down to its structural planks and timbers, was held aloft by a series of exposed load-bearing columns. The windows and the front and rear exits were boarded up tight. In the center of the room, between tarnished brass banisters, a sweeping staircase descending from the second floor ended abruptly in mid-air, its base sheared completely off.

"Is that the only way up?" Buchanan said.

Earlae nodded. "It wasn't like this before," she said. "There were cracked plaster walls, tons of furniture, a chandelier covered with creepy spider webs, and a staircase that came all the way down."

"When were you here last?" Daniel said.

"I only came once. Nine or ten months ago. Just after Bo discovered it. This place was his. Way too spooky for me. I told him he could keep it."

Earlae shone her light onto an empty wall near the front door. "The check-in counter was over there. The little bell still worked, if you can believe it."

Daniel took a couple of steps into the room. Something crunched underfoot. "This was a hotel then? It wasn't an apartment building."

"Yeah, it was a hotel. Bo said it was called-"

"The Malloy." Daniel shone his light around his feet to reveal a tangle of red and yellow cords that snaked across the floor to coil up each of the supporting columns.

"I don't remember seeing those things," Earlae said. "What are they?"

"They're detonating cords," Terry said. "They lead to holes drilled into the columns which have been packed tight with dynamite. They're held in place with-"

"A glob of insulating foam," Daniel said,

Terry looked at Daniel, and they simultaneously blurted, "Discovery Channel."

Buchanan rolled his eyes. "Man, you guys gotta get out more."

Terry continued to look at Daniel. "If you mean that as a euphemism for getting laid, I hear you."

"The Malloy," Buchanan said solemnly. "Isn't that the name of the hotel-"

"Scheduled for demolition," Daniel broke in. "It sure as hell is."

"Oh, shit," Buchanan said. "When?"

"Today," Daniel said.

"What time you got?" Buchanan said.

Terry shone her light on her wrist. "Twenty-two minutes to one."

"As I recall it, the detonation's scheduled for one," Daniel said. "That doesn't give us much breathing room."

"Anything else I should know?" Buchanan said.

"They'll fire three warning horns," Daniel said. Ten minutes, five minutes, and one minute prior to detonation."

Terry nodded.

"Won't somebody do a final search of the building before the blast?" Buchanan said.

"This close to detonation? It's already been done," Daniel said.

Terry patted down her pockets then waggled her fingers at Daniel. "Give me your phone. I lost mine."

"What are you doing?" Buchanan said.

"Calling Galton to stop the countdown."

"Smart thinking," Buchanan said.

Terry's mouth tightened. "Phone's dead."

"Water damage," Daniel said.

"Lemme try mine." Buchanan pushed the power button on his phone. His mouth tightened.

"Dead?" Daniel said.

"Yeah."

"Try yours. Maybe it's-"

"It's at The Rex."

Terry walked over to the boarded-up front door and pushed. "Well we're not getting out that way. Not without a battering ram."

"It's your call, Frank," Daniel said.

"She's my aunt," Buchanan said. "Whoever wants out can split back the way we came. No hard feelings."

"I'm in," Daniel said.

"Me, too," Terry said.

"Me, three," Earlae said.

Buchanan gave Daniel a boost to the bottom-most tread of the emasculated staircase. Daniel stood and tested the structure for strength. Although it creaked and groaned ominously, he was satisfied that it would hold their weight. He shone his light upward. Thankfully, the remainder of the staircase, following a central open column all the way to the top, appeared to be intact. He dropped to his belly and assisted the others up one at a time.

Grouped together on the second floor landing, they probed the darkness with their lights. On either side were rows of doors with tarnished brass numbers on them. The constant motion of the beams created a shadowy illusion that the doors were being cracked open and then quickly closed again. Although Daniel knew it was all in his head, he couldn't quite shake the feeling that they were being watched. More cameras? He performed a quick scan of the ceiling's perimeter. Nothing. No cameras. No chewing gum, pencils or toaster ovens either.

"Damn smell of piss is even worse up here," Buchanan said.

Terry shone her light onto the floor. "That's why." The red, rotting Persian-style runner, probably glorious in its day, was all but obscured by years of accumulated waste, both animal and human.

"Chop, chop," Buchanan said.

"Single file," Daniel said. "Keep at least three steps apart to distribute the weight. And stay close to the edge. The stairs feel solid enough now, but we don't know what to expect ahead."

Forming a line, Daniel in front, Terry at the rear, they headed upward through the gloom. Each time there was a creak underfoot, Daniel tensed, stopping and testing the next tread with his foot before proceeding.

All went smoothly until Daniel was midway between the sixth and seventh floors. There was a slow creaking sound and he felt a tremor underfoot. He raised a hand and motioned the others to a halt.

"What is it?" Buchanan said. "You see something?"

"Didn't you feel that?"

"Feel what?"

Daniel shrugged it off to his imagination, and took another hesitant step. There was another creak, and the stairs shifted beneath his feet.

"Don't move a muscle," Daniel said.

"Can't stop now," Buchanan said. "Tick-tock."

Daniel had just begun to lift his foot when the staircase started to wobble, tossing him backward against the banister. He shone his light upward and saw the problem. One of the bolts that anchored the staircase to the topmost floor had let go. "Just a few more feet." He gripped the banister tightly, transferring as much of his weight to it as he dared, and moved another step higher.

Four more steps and Daniel was standing on the upper landing. He looked down at the anxious faces below him. "Use the hand rail to support your weight. Move slowly and steadily. No herky-jerky motions."

Terry, who had just rounded the sixth floor landing, poked her head around Earlae. "The movement is getting worse."

She was right, Daniel saw. It was like he was standing on a wharf, watching his friends bobbing in a boat on a tempest sea. Something clicked in his head from his high school science days.

"Wave forms," he called out.

"What?" Buchanan said.

"You've got to time your steps to go against the rhythm of the oscillation."

"Go against the what?" Buchanan shouted back.

"It's like pushing a kid on a swing. If you move with it, you'll only add to its energy. Move against it. When the stairs move up, step down. All of you at the same time. And don't forget to use the hand rail like I told you. It's your only chance."

They continued slowly upward.

Creak.

Another bolt let go and the staircase lurched sickeningly.

"Pull me up," Buchanan shouted, reaching out.

Daniel caught his hand and hauled him onto the landing. Hopefully, the reduction in weight would buy the others the time they needed.

"Keep going," Daniel shouted.

Frozen with fear, Earlae was staring up at him with wide eyes, her thin body trembling. "I . . . I can't move," she muttered.

Terry slipped in close behind Earlae, whispering something in her ear that caused her to start climbing again.

Creak.

Three steps later Earlae was within reach. Daniel hoisted her to safety. He turned back for Terry. "Two down, one to-"

With a thundering whoosh the massive staircase let go, crashing all the way down to the main floor. A rolling cloud of dust ascended, enveloping them.

"Terry," Daniel shouted.

He felt a tap on his shoulder and turned. A rather dusty Terry Wagner was standing behind him with a huge shit-eating grin on her face. "I made a leap for it when you were helping Earlae up. Lucky thing, huh?"

"So much for all that silent as ninja crap," Buchanan muttered.

"Silence is overrated," Terry said. "Going after a scumbag like Shabazz, I'll take deadly any day."

They were standing in a furniture strewn sitting area. Unlike on each of the lower floors there were no corridors rolling outward, only a single door. The doorknob was missing and the door was ajar, the space beyond shrouded in darkness. From inside could be heard the sound of falling water, and a strange, almost feral keening.

"That it?" Buchanan said to Earlae. "They're in there?"

The fear that had taken hold of Earlae on the stairs still had its grip on her. Still wild eyed. Still shaking. Daniel couldn't help but wonder if it was in response to all they had been through to reach this point, or was it the fear of what lay ahead?

"They're in there?" Buchanan said again.

Her answer to Buchanan's question eventually came in the form of three slow-mo nods of the head.

"I'll go first, and alone, just to check things out," Buchanan said. "Anything comes out that isn't me or Aunt Sarah, shoot it between the eyes." Holding his flashlight alongside his gun barrel, he swept its beam into the room then ducked inside.

"Clear," he shouted less than a minute later.

Daniel, Terry and Earlae entered the room and converged on Buchanan who was standing over the eviscerated form of Ira Banks. Somehow Banks was still alive. He was making the unnatural sound that they had heard from the sitting room, fumbling with bloody fingers to stuff his unfurled intestines back into the foot-long gash that had been opened in his belly.

"Karma," Daniel said. "You gotta love it."

The apartment's spacious living room was covered with a mildewed carpet of indeterminate color. The walls were paneled in a peeling oak veneer. Through a broken skylight, a wash of rain spilled onto a threadbare, red velvet sofa. The smell of mold and age permeated the chilly air. Five doors opened off the room.

"Did you check those?" Daniel said.

"Kitchen, bathroom, two bedrooms, and a den," Buchanan said. "All of 'em empty."

"So where's Shabazz?"

"Already split by the looks of things," Buchanan said.

"We would have passed him in the tunnels, or on the stairway," Daniel said.

"Unless he saw our lights on the way down and ducked into one of the rooms on a lower floor," Terry said.

"Well there's no way we can search any of them now," Daniel said.

"Thirteen minutes to one," Terry said. "Time to find a way out and pronto."

Buchanan shone his light on Earlae's face. "You said you could lead us to Aunt Sarah?" he said with a snarl, shoving her roughly into a wall. "Were you lying? Were you setting us up, you sick, suicidal fuck?"

Buchanan's reaction seemed to wake Earlae from her stupor. She began to cry. "If I were you, I'd hate me, too. For what it's worth, I didn't lie. To myself, maybe. But not to you guys."

Daniel watched the veins swell in Buchanan's head and neck in the seconds before he hollered, "So where the fuck is she?" He threw a knockout punch at the wall beside her head, drew back his injured hand, and began to shake it violently.

Earlae brushed away the tears and gave the wall a tap. "Steel plating. Bo said the gangster's hideout was designed to be Tommy Gun proof." She pressed a knot in the wood paneling and Daniel heard a metallic click. A shaft of electric light cut a pyramidal swath over the floor as a six foot wide segment of wall nudged open. "Bo's special place." She slid the pocket door all the way back to reveal a second apartment that was, in layout at least, the mirror image of the first.

"Outta the way," Buchanan shouted, knocking Earlae aside as he drew down on the lone figure silhouetted inside.

<u>82</u>

"Don't shoot," Terry shouted. "Wait, Frank."

A shirtless man, head lolling, was suspended off the ground by a series of surgical steel hooks piercing the skin of his shoulders and upper back, stretching it grotesquely. A noose was fastened around his neck. The hooks and the noose were secured by thick cables attached to the exposed pickled-oak beams of the ceiling.

"Looks like someone forgot his safeword," Daniel said.

Buchanan grabbed hold of the man's hair and lifted his head. "It's Farmer."

"Dead or alive?" Daniel said.

"Unconscious," Buchanan said. "There's not enough tension on the noose to choke him out."

"Leave him," Daniel said.

Buchanan didn't argue the point. "Let's check the other rooms. We gotta find Aunt Sarah pronto."

Daniel opened a door to reveal the well-appointed master bedroom suite. No Sarah Calhoun. No Tokunbo Shabazz. Mounted in the wall above a Chippendale desk was a bank of twelve LCD monitors. Each Hi-Def screen was showing a revolving live feed from Shabazz's numerous surveillance cameras. The storm troopers had finally arrived, Daniel noted. Men and women in navy windbreakers with FBI emblazoned on the back were swarming through the club, Shabazz's apartment, the garage, and the subterranean cells. He looked quickly around the room for a telephone, a two-way radio, an Aldis lamp, something, anything, he could use to contact Galton and have the countdown halted. But he found nothing.

"In here," Terry shouted.

Daniel, Buchanan and Earlae rushed into the second bedroom. Sarah Calhoun was sprawled on a four-poster bed. "I heard a ruckus then I heard voices," she was saying. "I thought it was that awful man coming back to finish what he'd started."

Buchanan picked up his aunt and kissed her on the forehead. "I'm taking you home," he said.

"I knew you wouldn't leave me. And I told him so."

"Where is he?" Daniel said. "Where's Shabazz?"

"I don't know."

"Probably watching the show from the street," Terry said. "Which is where we should be." She checked her watch. "Twelve minutes to one."

"Uncle Billy?" Buchanan said.

"He's here. Somewhere. I heard him bawling like a colicky baby when we arrived."

"No one's in the master bedroom," Daniel said.

"Or the kitchen," Buchanan said. "Which leaves the shitter or the den."

They located William Calhoun in the bathroom, curled into the fetal position on the floor. One ankle was shackled to David Blake's skinless corpse. It was rancid smelling and alive with creepy crawlers. The meat, where it rested on the floor, had rotted open, oozing a pulpy pus-like fluid that had dried to a yellow crust around the corpse's edges. When the old man saw Buchanan standing with Sarah in his arms he looked quickly away.

"Save me," the old man whimpered.

Buchanan looked down on him, and said nothing.

"Tick-tock," Terry said.

Daniel glanced at William Calhoun, almost pitying the man. Almost. "He comes. He stays. We put a dozen bullets in his head. It's your call, Frank."

"He's made his bed. Like the Indian." Buchanan turned and headed back the way they had come, into the dilapidated apartment. "Buildings like these had exterior fire exits. If we can kick the boards off the windows we should have more than enough time to climb down."

"I do not think so," Shabazz said as he stepped into the threshold between the two apartments.

"Fuck," Frank said.

"Francis," Sarah said.

"Put down your weapons," Shabazz said. "Now."

"Go to hell." Buchanan passed his aunt to Earlae and began to back slowly away, gun pointed center-mass at Shabazz.

Buchanan was trying to open the distance between the three of them. Doing this, Daniel knew, would make it less likely that Shabazz could shoot more than one of them before the other two could cut him down. Between Daniel and Buchanan, Terry also began to move.

"Put them down," Shabazz said, seemingly unfazed with the ploy, "or I'll execute the old lady."

"You will not," Earlae said, turning and shielding Sarah with her body.

"Earlae," Shabazz barked. "Put Mrs. Calhoun back to bed."

"No!"

"Do as I say. Now. I will deal with your shenanigans at a more opportune time."

"Like you dealt with your partner?" Daniel said.

Shabazz walked over to Farmer. "Partner? Do not make me laugh. He was a tool in every sense of the word. A white-guilt-ridden tool to be used as I saw fit. He thought he was *helpin' a po' brother out*. His arrogance was astounding." He pursed his lips. "Personally, I found his opinion of me, of my kind, to be even more insulting than yours, Mr. Rourke."

Shabazz did a double-take at Earlae. "Why are you still standing there? Put Mrs. Calhoun back to bed this instant."

Earlae looked at Daniel, who nodded that it was okay. It was best to get the two of them out of the room in case a full-fledged firefight should erupt.

"We're at an impasse," Daniel said, hoping he could reason with the man. "If we don't-"

"An impasse?" Shabazz took three cautious steps in Buchanan's direction, causing Buchanan to take three steps backward to maintain his distance. "I hardly think so."

"How do you figure that?" Terry said.

Shabazz took another two steps, as did Buchanan. He placed a cupped hand to his ear. "Listen, watch, and learn."

Buchanan said, "What the fuck are you talking-"

Fifteen feet to Daniel's right there was an unsettling groan. One moment Buchanan was there, and the next he was not.

Terry tried to dance away from the yawning crevice Buchanan had opened in the water-logged floorboards, but moved just a split second too late, screaming as she dropped through to her knees. Her gun went spiraling through the air to land behind Shabazz. She began clutching at the splintering planks in front of her, but each time she found something to grip onto, another piece would break away, and she would slip farther down.

"Daniel, help," she cried.

He was the only one with a gun still trained on Shabazz. If he made a move to save Terry, it was over for all of them.

"Daniel," Terry called out again.

Oh, Hell. "Earlae," Daniel hollered. "Attack." He leaped toward Terry, landing on his belly, legs spread wide to distribute his weight. Behind him he could hear a scuffle. *Atta girl, Earlae.* No gun shots. So far, so-

Another plank splintered. Terry lost her grip and screamed again. As she fell, her arms shot up, and Daniel caught a wrist. The downward force of her momentum dragged him close enough to the edge that he could look into the abyss.

Buchanan was lying motionless on the next floor down. His eyes were open and blinking.

"Frank," Daniel called. "Get up."

Behind him the sounds of the battle intensified. Earlae was making piercing, primitive noises the likes of which Daniel had never heard. Twice Shabazz cried out in pain. If she could only keep him occupied for a few more-

The floor groaned again, and the red velvet sofa began to slide over the wet carpet.

"Hurry, Frank."

Daniel was helpless to do anything but watch as the sofa jack-knifed over the edge to land with a hollow thump on top of Buchanan, causing that floor to give way. A cascading effect could be heard as Buchanan crashed through each successive floor.

"No-o-o-o-o," Daniel called out hoarsely.

The first warning horn sounded its death knell.

Ten minutes to detonation.

Daniel felt sick to his stomach over the loss of his friend. They had been through so much together, had come so close, to have it end this way. Daniel made a vow to himself that Buchanan's death would not be vain. He would finish what they'd started. He was going to save Sarah Calhoun. Right after he saved Terry.

"Don't squirm." His arm was aching, his grip slipping. "It's only making things worse."

"Pull," Terry said.

"No good," Daniel said. "I can't lift you at this angle. Not with only one arm."

Daniel turned for a quick look behind him. Earlae was charging at Tokunbo with her head down. Tokunbo caught her by the hair with one hand and pistol whipped her with the other. Then he let go, and she fell. He turned back to Terry just as Earlae was grabbing hold of Tokunbo's leg, her mouth wide-open for a bite.

"Roll away from the hole," Terry said. "The momentum should raise me high enough to get my other arm over the side."

"Here goes." Daniel rolled onto his left side, using his legs for leverage. Terry's advice was good. Her head slowly came into view.

"Can you get your elbow over the edge?"

"I think so."

Terry's elbow appeared, and the strain on his arm lessened. He shifted his position and grabbed the back of her coat with his free hand.

"Excellent. Now swing a leg up."

"I'll try."

"Don't just try. Do it. Hurry."

A flailing leg caught the floor on her third attempt. Daniel tugged on her coat, and she rolled away from the edge.

"How touching," Shabazz said. His pantleg was soaked with blood, and his face and throat were riddled with scratches. Earlae was crumpled on the floor, eyes closed, unmoving. He took exaggerated aim at Terry. "Too bad it was all for naught."

Daniel lunged to his feet, shielding Terry with his body. He saw the flash from the barrel, felt the jackhammer blow in his shoulder before he heard the report. The slug spun him completely around and drove him backward. He landed with a thud on top of Terry.

"An heroic gesture," Shabazz said. "But it changes nothing."

Daniel could hear Terry struggling for air beneath him. She began to hack and cough as she tried to catch her breath. "Shoot . . . him . . ."

"Gun," he said. "It fell into the hole."

"Let me . . . up. I'll-"

"No," Daniel roared. "Chauvinist pig trumps cop. Stay down."

It was all up to him, he knew.

If he didn't stop Shabazz, Terry would die.

Like Julie had died. And Buchanan.

Besides, he wasn't about to lose his undefeated record to that psycho son-of-

He staggered to his feet and took a lurching step forward, grinning madly at Shabazz. He took another step, and his grin widened. Shabazz was a dead man. In killing Frank and taking a potshot at Terry, he'd jumped off a bridge. He hadn't gone splat yet. But he was falling fast. Suicide imminent.

Behind Shabazz, Farmer's head snapped up. His eyes opened.

"Say goodnight, Mr. Rourke," Shabazz said.

"Daniel," Terry cried out.

The second slug hit him in the chest. He rocked backward a step but remained on his feet. Almost immediately an intense burning sensation began to radiate outward from the wound and time slowed down.

Before Shabazz could squeeze the trigger a third time Farmer wrapped his arms around him and squeezed. The gun went off, but the bullet missed its mark. Shabazz went berserk, roaring and snorting like an animal, smashing Farmer in the face with the back of his head as he twisted and lunged to break free. The hooks tore through Farmer's flesh, but he didn't let go. Even as the noose tightened around his neck, he held on for a long as there was life.

All Daniel could do was stumble forward. His legs were leaden. Shabazz was only ten feet away but it felt like ten miles. He reached Shabazz before he could cast off Farmer's lifeless grip and take the kill shot.

Daniel threw a left hook. It connected with the point of Shabazz's chin. He had given it all he had, but in his weakened state it wasn't nearly enough. He threw another hook, which missed badly. He fell headfirst to the floor, splitting his skull open. Blood oozed from the gash above his eyebrow. Above him, a gloating Shabazz smiled while Farmer's corpse, with bulging eyes and twisted mouth, twirled lazily on the noose beside him. "Look at your pretty lady friend," he said. "Hurry, before you lose consciousness. I want you to watch while I kill her."

Daniel tried to rise, but Shabazz planted a toe in the bullet hole in his shoulder and ground it down. Daniel's body began to thrash as if a thousand volts had been unleashed upon his nerves.

"No need to get up," Shabazz said. "Just watch."

There was a gunshot, a mere pop, and the smile melted from Shabazz' face. He fell to his knees, an uncomprehending look on his face. Slowly, he turned his head.

"Earlae . . . ?"

She was holding Terry's .38 tightly in both hands. "They told me the whole story on the way here. I know what you did to those kids. My precious babies. Edogiawarie, too. How could you, Bo? How could you?"

"I did it . . . did it all for-"

"You."

Earlae kicked Shabazz in the face. He teetered forward, landing on top of Daniel. On his back, in the open guard position, Daniel morphed into a triangle choke. He lifted a leg up to encircle Shabazz' neck and shoulder then used his foot to lock it at the knee. Shabazz began to struggle, but the choke was set hard and deep, and there was nowhere for him to go. Daniel pulled his legs together, cutting off the blood flow from the carotid arteries to the brain. In a matter of seconds, no more than a half-dozen, the struggling slowed as he brought Shabazz to the edge of consciousness.

"You grew up poor. You never knew your father. Your mother was a drug addicted whore. But that didn't give you the right. For any of what you did. It just didn't."

Shabazz' sleepy eyes found Daniel. "White devil muthafuck-"

Daniel increased the pressure until he felt a soul satisfying pop.

The second horn sounded.

Five minutes to detonation.

Daniel unlocked his legs. Still the champ. Still undefeated.

<u>83</u>

Terry kicked the bobble-headed Shabazz aside then gently assisted Daniel to his feet. "Can you make it?" she said, one arm around his waist, holding him steady.

Sweat was pouring down his face, and the already searing pain was intensifying, rolling outward from the wheezing hole in his chest in tsunami-like waves. "Yeah," he said.

"Which way?" Terry said to Earlae, who by now had Sarah Calhoun draped over her shoulder in a fireman's carry. The old lady was crying, whimpering, calling out the name 'Francis' over and over again.

"I don't know."

"There's got to be some other way out," Terry said. "Shabazz never mentioned another exit?"

"Bo and I used the same stairs we did. But they're gone."

"If Malloy went through the expense of bulletproofing his hideout," Terry said, "you can bet he didn't cut corners when it came to another way out. A hidden way. In case the cops discovered where he was hiding." She glanced around in all directions. "It's why we didn't find Shabazz when we searched the apartments. And it's also why he wasn't stressed about the countdown. He'd used it before. So he knew how much time he needed."

"Are you saying we can still make it out of here?" Earlae said.

Terry nodded. "But where to look? Shabazz just sort of . . . appeared."

"Master bedroom," Daniel said. "If I were Malloy, it's where I'd have put it. Close to where I . . . where I laid my head."

A second sliding door was built into the back wall of the clothes closet. Luckily, they wasted no time searching for it as Shabazz had left it ajar to facilitate his escape. Beyond the door was a wrought-iron stairwell that zig-zagged downward into ebony darkness.

Terry switched her flashlight on. "Go, Earlae, go. Daniel and I will be right behind you." Earlae started down the stairs. "And no matter what happens, keep moving. Get Sarah the hell out of here."

"For . . . Frank," Daniel said.

"For Frank," Terry said.

Daniel was slowing Terry down, but there was nothing he could do about it. He considered digging in his heels and telling her to go on without him, but he knew all about Terry's pig-headedness, and precious time would be lost while she tried to talk him out of it. So he soldiered on, with Terry's help, as best as he could.

"Sixth floor," Terry shouted.

Something in Daniel's mind seemed to tilt and whirl. Terry's face was no longer beside his, but above. And for one dismaying moment, her intense eyes and determined but sensual mouth made him think he was looking at . . .

"Julie," he said.

No, he thought. *Not Julie.*

His mind was playing cruel tricks on him. Julie was gone. It was Terry he was looking at. She was alive. And she needed him. He thought back to the day they had met. A white cop named Black had been reading a magazine with Cassius Clay on the cover. Or was it a black cop named White? Clay was there, of that much he was certain. He remembered the beating the mouthy old man had taken at the hands of a young and hungry fighter named Larry Holmes. Remembered what Clay had said in an interview shortly after the fight.

"My face is still pretty," Daniel said.

Terry looked up at him – she was below him now – and smiled. "It's beautiful," she said.

The darkness that surrounded them was alive, a ravenous beast held at bay by the fragile yellow beam of Terry's flashlight, just waiting for him to close his eyes and quit. Can't let her die, Daniel thought. If he passed out now, she would stop to pick him up, and precious seconds would be lost. If that happened, she would be done for. Daniel concentrated. Left foot, right foot, left foot, right foot. Kept moving forward. She thought she was the one rescuing him, but she really wasn't.

"Fifth floor," Terry yelled.

Daniel stumbled. Somehow Terry kept him from upright. Somehow he kept going. Somehow they were going to make it. They just had to. Somehow.

Terry had just shouted, "Fourth floor," when the one-minute horn sounded. He felt Terry's grip on him tighten, her pace quicken.

"Going. To. Beat. The. Clock," she said through gritted teeth with a certainty that almost made Daniel a believer.

At the top of the final flight a thick cast-iron door lay open in front of them. Ten steps, and no more than half as many seconds remaining, Daniel figured. Ahead of them, Earlae reached the bottom and slipped through the narrow aperture with Aunt Sarah. Three steps away, Terry shifted her grip and tossed Daniel in after them. He landed hard on his side.

"Hurry," Earlae shouted.

BANG-BANG . . . BANG-BANG-BANG . . . BANG . . .

The detonating charges were ignited in a staggered pattern, a process, Daniel knew, used to control the speed and direction of the building's collapse. He struggled to keep his eyes open, trying to stay in the light as the darkness of the void closed in on him.

Had to remain conscious.

Had to be certain that she was okay.

For a moment nothing momentous happened. Time just seemed to hang as Terry leaped into the air. Then, with a thunderous whoosh, the building collapsed, brought down by its own mass. Terry rolled when she hit the ground beside Daniel, tugging the heavy door closed in the same fluid motion.

Cracks began to appear in the reinforced concrete of the tunnel as a series of bone-rattling aftershocks rippled the earth. Although dust and minor debris rained down on them, the structure somehow maintained its integrity.

Somehow . . .

Somehow they really had made it.

The crippling pain was gone. Daniel was numb all over. He had worked the tail end of enough gunshot cases to know what that meant. Not that it mattered. He looked over at Terry, who smiled at him again. All that mattered was that this time - this time at least - he had saved her. He closed his eyes, free-falling into the infinite, impatient darkness.

84

Julie stepped out of the darkness and reached out for him. They began to dance, moving in slow, small circles on the large seascape balcony outside Daniel's bedroom. Etta James was singing *Fool That I Am*. The stars were twinkling. The moon was full, positively aglow. The scent of her perfume, her very presence, was making his head spin.

"You really are a boy scout, aren't you?"

"So I've heard," Daniel said.

"Be prepared, isn't that their motto?"

Julie stepped back, still moving to the music, and looked at him, her emerald eyes filled with wonder. "Are you prepared, Daniel?"

"Prepared for what?"

She lifted her hair up off her neck. "Helping me undress, for starters."

The dress slid down her long, lithe body and dropped to the cedar decking. Her black lace bra matched her stockings and garter belt. She wasn't wearing panties.

"In case you're wondering," she said, "the clasp is in the front."

The bra slid down her arms to the floor behind her.

"Do you have a preference," she said, "what I should do with the stockings?"

"Keep them," Daniel said. "The heels, too."

Julie started to work on his belt. "Now how did I know you were going to say that?"

When she had Daniel fully undressed, she ran her hands over his chest and shoulders. "You're bigger than he is," she said, meaning Paul Watson. "Not as tall, but definitely more muscular." She squeezed his arm and affected a giggle. "Flex."

"No problemo," Daniel said. "How's that?"

"I never felt a thing. Do it again."

Daniel raised an eyebrow. "You want to feel this particular piece of my anatomy flex, you're going to have to squeeze somewhat farther to the south than my biceps."

Julie joined her hands at the small of Daniel's back and pulled him in against her. He could feel her heartbeat. He could feel her breath going urgently in and out.

"Are you going to chit-chat all night," she said, blinking once, twice, "or are you going to kiss me?"

Daniel gave a large, put-upon sigh.

"If I must," he said.

And then he did. With his eyes closed. For a very, very, very long time.

***

Inside the bedroom, the muted-ochre light of the flickering fire was all that held the darkness at bay. Daniel poured the champagne carefully, so that it wouldn't foam over the rim of the fluted glasses. On the California beach-stone hearth beside them sat a bowl of freshly harvested blue and green grapes.

Julie reclined to the floor, and raised one knee. "I'm ready," she said.

Daniel glanced between his legs and smiled. "Ditto."

"I mean I'm ready for a grape. Peel me a grape, handsome love-slave."

Daniel plucked a pair of grapes from the bowl, and kneeled over her supine form. "Actually," he said, "I can do one better than that."

"Please, do."

Placing a grape on the tip of his erect penis, he levered it downward, then let it fly. The grape arced high into the air to land neatly inside his open mouth.

"Sa-wish."

He reloaded.

"Now you."

"Disgusting," Julie said.

"You want disgusting? I can do disgusting."

He dropped down beside her and whispered in her ear. The logs in the fireplace settled with a flare, brightening the room for just an instant.

Julie giggled. "That's beyond disgusting. But I'm game if you are."

***

Despite the fact that the morgue's meat room was refrigerated, the stench of death was heavy in the air. On the Rectum Magnitude Scale it was a definite eight, falling somewhere between a sick man's fart and Rosie O'Donnell's bathroom the morning after two-for-one burrito night at her local tacqueria. Seemingly oblivious, Buchanan took a large bite out of his heavily buttered croissant, chewing loudly with an open mouth.

"Christ," Daniel said. "How can you eat with this retch-inducing smell?"

"This is nothing. You ever changed a diaper you'd know what I mean."

Munching blissfully away, Buchanan walked over to the wall of stainless-steel drawers, opening one up to reveal a cadaver in a black vinyl body bag. He unzipped the bag enough to expose former gang-banger Hebrew Ben Judas's torso, or rather what remained of it.

"You did that?" Daniel said.

Buchanan shook his head. "Not that it didn't cross my fucked-up mind."

Daniel's stomach churned as he looked this most gruesome death in the eye.

"What happened to him?"

"Beautiful craftsmanship, don't you think? It's called a Sicilian necktie. Used to be quite popular in the old country. Still is in some quarters. Although," Buchanan said, obviously giving it some thought, "I haven't seen one in years. As you can see, an incision is made through the windpipe and the tongue is pulled out through the hole so that it dangles down the chest-"

"Like a necktie."

Buchanan bit another hunk out of the croissant. "A messy, messy business," he said. "And slow. Sometimes they bleed to death. Sometimes they suffocate. All depends on how the incision is made."

"What about the arms, and the chest?" Those particular wounds were what Daniel had meant all along. "What could possibly do that to a man?"

Buchanan took another bite. "Not what, who."

"What do you mean?"

"Let's just say, you're living on the street and you get the munchies, you eat what's handy."

"Tastes like chicken, right? Anything else I need to know?"

Buchanan unzipped the bag the rest of the way, and smiled. Daniel's eyes were immediately drawn to the genitals. Although he'd been dead for days, the guy still had the most spectacular piece of wood that Daniel had ever seen. The rest of the body had already begun to shrivel, but not the penis.

"Implant," Buchanan said.

"No way. Seriously?"

Buchanan put the pastry between his teeth, and lifted the humungous phallus up in his hands.

"Put it down, Frank. You're beginning to frighten me."

Buchanan mumbled through the mouthful of pastry, "Cheap bastard. Coroner said it's the economy model - like a pipe cleaner - you just bend it out of the way when you're done doing the wild thing. Check it out." He bent the dead man's penis into the shape of a question mark. "Ta-da."

"And I've been told I have a warped sense of humor."

Wiping his hands on his pants, Buchanan said, "You ask me, we're both pretty fucking twisted."

Daniel slammed the drawer shut. "You're probably right," he said.

***

"You must leave us now," Julie said in an even voice as she returned from the cellar. Clasped tightly in her hands was a large butcher knife. Try as he might, he could not take his eyes from the blade, wicked and glinting in the purple light of the toppled mushroom-shaped table lamp.

"It's the one that he raped me with." Her eyes were clear and peaceful. "If this isn't justice, I don't know what is."

"Downright poetic," Daniel said, a frown cutting deep lines in his face.

Police sirens purred softly in the distance, just minutes away.

"Go," Julie said. "Before I change my mind."

Daniel looked at Watson's ruined face, bloodied, the pupil of one eye dilated, a slow-moving river of snot stretching from his nose to his lacerated mouth - and he knew that she was right. He made a little choking noise, and said, "I love you."

Julie rushed over and hugged him, laid a soft chain of kisses around his neck.

"And I love you. Never forget that. Believe me, if there was any other way . . ."

"There's always-"

"Not this time." A beautiful smile found her lips. "You would've made one helluva husband," she said, her voice husky with conflicting emotions that not even such a smile could conceal.

She tried to step away, but Daniel couldn't let her go.

The sirens were a block closer and closing fast.

"You have to leave," she said softly, almost seductively.

Daniel nodded and then, in an act of monumental will, he did.

Over his shoulder, on the way to the front door, he paused and watched Julie approach the near-catatonic Watson. Watched as she curled his fingers around the well-worn bone handle of the butcher knife then cover them with her own. Then he could watch no more.

***

Buchanan nodded. "While we're on the subject of Julie," he said. "How did your meeting with her mom go?"

"She's easily the most self-absorbed, self-deluded person I've ever met, and I've never loved Julie more than I do at this moment."

"Because she could grow up around that - despite that - and become the person she did."

"She inherited her mom's looks, but the meat and potatoes of her character she got from her dad."

"He's dead, right?"

"Car accident. Shortly after she was born."

"It's tough for a kid to lose a parent."

"Like you, she got through it okay. She lived life on her own terms, and she died the same way. I'd always known why she made the choice she did, intellectually, at least, but I'd never really accepted it."

"Emotionally."

Daniel nodded.

"You about ready to move on then?"

Daniel considered the question carefully before answering. "Maybe it's time," he said. "Time I turned my boat against the current and started paddling like hell."

"Whatchu talkin' 'bout, Willis?"

Daniel smiled. "Am I ready to move on? I've certainly been mulling the possibility."

"With a certain Portsmouth cop and her buns of steel?"

"I wouldn't know about that. Her buns, I mean."

"Pure poetry," Buchanan said. "Take a gander the next time you see her, you don't believe me."

"What about you and Miss Thomas with the nice pins?"

"Maybe we're both ready."

***

"Remind me again why I brought you along?"

Terry looked at him and her face was tender and open.

"You needed a ride," she said, holding his eyes with hers, "and I happen to own a pretty sweet set of wheels."

Daniel was surprised by the sudden realization that he really liked, even trusted, this girl, as a friend, and maybe more. The epiphany caught him off guard, causing him to break the connection, and look quickly away.

"Let's get this thing back to the Rex to let Frank have a crack at it. Maybe he can-"

Terry's fingers closed on his arm. "Shhh," she said. "Do you hear that?"

***

"Hold me," Julie whispered, her body a hot shadow pressed against him.

"I am holding you," Daniel said. "I'm right here."

"Tighter," she said. "I need to know that I'm not alone."

"For as long as you can stand me, you'll never be alone again."

He tightened his grip and she purred.

"Julie?"

"Yes, Daniel?"

He swallowed, and before he knew it, the three little words that he had kept under lock and key for the entirety of his adult life were released . . .

85

"I love you," Daniel murmured, opening his eyes and blinking back the blinding light to reveal Frank Buchanan's craggy, whiskered face. *What the . . . ?* There was a San Francisco fog in his head, and some pain, and the pounding of his pulse was loud in the gleaming white room.

"Feeling's mutual," Buchanan said.

"What the heck did you do to him?" Terry said, simultaneously leaning into Daniel's line of sight and punching Buchanan hard on the shoulder. "He spends a couple nights alone with you at The Rex and the next thing I know he's a full-fledged gay pride recruit."

"Homophobic bullshit," Buchanan said. "Gays don't recruit."

"You don't?" Terry said.

Buchanan winked at Daniel while making a pumping gesture with his hand. "No need to," he said. "We multiply by masturbation."

"Weirdo," Terry said.

"Enough already with the stand-up," Daniel said weakly, smiling through the pain. "You're Abbott and Costello banter, however well-intentioned, is making my head spin."

"You had us worried," Terry said.

"Where am I?"

"Hospital," Buchanan said. "Mass General."

"I'm still dreaming."

"No," Buchanan said.

"I have to be. You're dead, Frank. I watched you die."

Buchanan smiled. "It'd take more than a seven story swan dive to take out a big, tough guy like me."

"What happened?"

"The water-logged floorboards took most of the *oomph* from the fall. Still knocked me out though. Came to just as the final warning horn was sounding. I knew I didn't have time to get back up top to help you, but that didn't matter. I knew you'd see things through for me. So I dug myself out of the rubble and headed out the way we came in."

"Were you hurt?"

"Broken leg. Two broken ribs. It coulda been worse."

Daniel's throat was killing him. He took a drink of water from a plastic cup with a straw in it that was sitting on the bedside table. "How long has it been?"

"Merry Christmas," Buchanan said.

"Christmas? I've been out for . . . ?" He tried to do the math in his head, but couldn't.

"For six day," Terry said.

"Six days?"

"Be thankful you're here at all," Buchanan said. "You were stone-cold dead when they brought you in. No pulse. No brain activity. If it wasn't for the fact that Terry here administered CPR until the paramedics arrived, kept the blood flowing through your fucked-up system, you'd have been a vegetable. Had you pulled through at all."

Daniel turned to Terry. "Thanks," he said.

"Now you owe me two," Terry said.

"So which one am I?" Buchanan said solemnly. "Abbott or Costello?"

Terry patted Buchanan on the belly. "What do you think?"

Daniel laughed, and the next thing he knew . . .

***

. . . he was staring into the kindly face of a black man in his late fifties. The man was nattily dressed in a white turtleneck sweater under a charcoal mohair-and-wool pin-striped suit. His hair was close-cropped with grey highlights at the temples. There was a stethoscope around his neck. Buchanan and Terry were nowhere in sight.

"Lordy, lordy," the man said with a smile. "I just had to see it for myself." His melodic, resonant voice suggested a Caribbean upbringing.

"See what?"

"That you're really alive."

"I hope that's not an unusual occurrence," Daniel said, "this being a hospital and all.

The man had a rich, infectious laugh. "No, no, no," he said, "of course not. It's just that you had lost most of your blood by the time you arrived in my OR. Off the record, I really didn't think you were going to make it." He took Daniel's hand and checked his pulse, comparing his own reading with that of the incessantly beeping monitor on the wall beside the bed. "Your friends told me what happened. The way they tell the story, it seemed as though you were just looking for an excuse to give up the ghost."

Daniel attempted a chuckle and felt a wave of nausea overtake him. "I think I'll take the fifth on that one, Dr. . . . ?"

"Where are my manners? My name is Precious, Dr. Ezekiel Precious, and I'm the sawbones who plugged your holes. I'd like to take credit for you being here, but the surgery was strictly by the numbers. The hardest part was up to you. You had to want to come back. Had to fight for it, in fact." He shrugged and grinned broadly. "And here you are."

"Step number eleven," Daniel said.

"I don't understand."

"Private joke," Daniel said.

The doctor shrugged again. "Although miracles like yours may happen daily on Oprah's wonderful show, they do not happen in this place quite so often. Unfortunately." He took a moment before continuing. "You were gone from this world for quite some time - clinically dead they call it - so I must take advantage of the opportunity to ask you something."

"Ask away, doc."

"Is there a heaven, Mr. Rourke?"

"Call me Daniel."

"Is there a heaven, Daniel? You don't strike me as the type of man who would ever have to worry about going to that other nasty place."

Daniel closed his eyes and the image of Julie looking back at him made him lightheaded. The darkness was gone and he remembered it all. The nights they had spent together. The feel of her skin against his. The smell of her perfume. Her taste. Then he considered the promise of similar nights spent alone with Terry Wagner. "Yes," he said when he finally opened his eyes, "there most certainly is."

Dr. Precious nodded. "Quite frankly, Daniel, only one of your friends thought you would pull it off."

"Which one?" Daniel said.

He could see the doctor's lips start to move, but he never heard a sound, and the next thing he knew . . .

***

. . . Terry was sitting on the edge of his bed and gazing at him with a nurturing look of concern. "I always knew you'd make it." She smiled and it was like the sun coming out.

"Where's Costello?" Daniel said.

"I knew it," Buchanan boomed, moving into view from behind Terry. "You think I'm fat, don't you?"

"Sarah," Daniel said. "How is she?"

"Physically? She's doing just fine," Buchanan said.

"Emotionally?"

"She really had no idea about the perverted shit Uncle Billy was into. She told me if Shabazz hadn't beaten her to it, she would've killed him herself. Funny thing is I believe her. She's one tough old broad. A lot tougher than I ever gave her credit for. Maybe I should have trusted her back when it woulda done us both some good."

"You were just a boy," Terry said. "You did what you thought was right. There's no shame in that. What you did took courage."

"And Earlae?" Daniel said.

"After we got you and Aunt Sarah safely back to the surface, she just up and disappeared. With all of Shabazz's money, too."

"Cleaned out his bank accounts to the tune of six million dollars," Buchanan said.

"Are you serious?"

"Yeah."

"Nice."

"Any other developments? Has anyone else gone down?"

"The computer was the only concrete connection to the top, so the buck stopped at Shabazz."

Daniel broke into a grin. "Maybe not."

"What do you mean? Why do I get the feeling there's something you haven't bothered to tell me?"

"I've been in and out of unconsciousness for the better part of a week-"

"Eleven days."

"So cut me some slack."

Buchanan made a cutting motion with two fingers. "Done," he said. "Now out with it."

Daniel shook his head. "When I'm well enough to enjoy it."

"But he'll get-"

"He's going nowhere."

86

Daniel was parked with Buchanan in Terry's Z across the street from Raymond Sowell's dingy South End apartment. It was a modest-sized building with a stoop straight out of Sesame Street. A half-dozen crack heads, all black, were sprawled on its stairs like casualties of war, as if Big Bird, or Gordon Robinson, had found the wrong religion and gone jihad on their asses. The Z rocked gently in the wind as they watched Sowell's windows for signs of activity. There had been no movement whatsoever in the fifteen minutes they'd been parked, crack heads included.

"You sure about this?" Buchanan said.

"Pretty sure," Daniel said.

Buchanan took out his gun, and flicked the safety off.

"If he's home-"

"He's not."

"I'm just saying, if he is home, and if you're right, that Sowell really was the prick who set this whole sorry mess in motion, then he'd better say his prayers. 'Cos if he tries anything, even breathes the wrong way, I'm gonna empty my clip into his heart."

"No," Daniel said.

"Yeah," Buchanan said. "You've seen his file. He may have started out as a surveillance geek, but he was a NOC for the bulk of his career. A sniper. A trained assassin. I know you. I know what you're thinking. But you're wrong. Even on your best day, if you weren't still recuperating from a pair of near fatal gunshots, he'd kick your ass."

Daniel bit down hard. "Let's go," he said.

Buchanan took another look at his watch. "Six forty-five," he said. "You really think he's up and at 'em this early?"

"According to Galton, the governor's a notorious early riser. Up at five. Knee deep in paperwork at six. He's gone."

Buchanan pulled out his gun and covered it in his unzipped jacket. "You're wrong, and a part of me hopes you are, I'm shooting him dead."

"It's not going to happen, Frank. So get over it."

***

With Buchanan leaning heavily on his crutch beside him, Daniel went to work on the lock on Sowell's second floor apartment. He could hardly wait to get a look inside. He was curious to see how close the picture he had in his head jibed with reality. Eventually, the lock turned, and Daniel opened the door.

"Let's go," Buchanan whispered.

The walls and ceiling were egg-shell white, and the floor was wood parquet, shiny, like that of a freshly waxed school gymnasium. There were no photos in frames, no trinkets of any kind scattered over the sparse IKEA-style, build-it-yourself furniture. To Daniel's mind the unit had all the warmth of a Midwestern Days Inn.

Buchanan made a loud *humph* sound in his throat over by the twenty or so volume bookshelf.

"What?" Daniel said.

"He's our guy alright."

"What did you find?"

"*Catcher in the Rye.*"

"So?"

"That proves it."

"What are you talking about?"

"Chapman read it," Buchanan said, waving his gun as he spoke. "The nut-job that murdered Lennon. And Hinkley, Jr.. Reagan's would-be assassin. He read it, too."

"Put the gun away, Frank."

Daniel gave Buchanan the thousand yard stare until he re-holstered his gun.

Daniel approached the bookcase with his head tilted, taking a good look at the titles. Unlike the volumes in Shabazz's subterranean library, these weren't mere ornaments. The spines were broken, and the pages were dog-eared. *Don Quixote. In Search of Lost Time. The Great Gatsby. Dead Souls. Atlas Shrugged.*

"It's just as I'd imagined it."

"What is?" Buchanan said.

"Sowell's apartment."

When Buchanan hobbled into the bedroom to begin the search, Daniel headed for the den. The room was modest in size and had been converted into a no-frills gym. One wall, adjacent to a tiny, curtainless window, was covered with mirrored tiles. A Smith Machine was butted against the opposite wall, with a motorized treadmill and a beat-to-shit, freestanding heavy bag on either side of it. Daniel walked past the treadmill and felt the kiss of warm air on his cheek. He touched the motor housing. It was still hot.

"Frank," he called.

"Get in here," Buchanan said, no longer in the bedroom. "Now."

Daniel found Buchanan in the bathroom. "Check it out," he said, gesturing toward the bathroom mirror. The glass was opaque with steam. "What do you make of it?"

Daniel turned and headed back into the living room. "My guess is that we're-"

"Not alone," Raymond Sowell said.

He was standing to the left of the bathroom door wearing only a towel. Beside Daniel, Buchanan went for his gun. But before he could clear the holster, they were staring down the barrel of Sowell's gun. Like Dark Davis's six-shooter, Sowell's piece was also considerably larger than Buchanan's.

"*Put the gun away, Frank,*" Buchanan said in an angry, sarcastic tone.

On the off chance that Buchanan might try something stupid, Daniel stepped between the two men and approached Sowell.

"Don't," Buchanan began.

Daniel held out his hand. Sowell looked at it, but didn't otherwise react.

"I just wanted to say thank you."

"For what?" Sowell said.

"For what you did at Blake's cabin. You saved my life. And Terry's."

"You knew?"

"I suspected. I didn't know for sure until I got a look at your file."

Sowell set his gun down on a side table, and took Daniel's hand, giving it a hearty shake. "About what Mr. Buchanan said before you came inside. If you were healthy, I'd put the odds at six to four."

"My favor," Daniel said.

Sowell just smiled.

"You bugged our car?" Buchanan said.

Sowell shrugged. "Old habits," he said.

"You knew we were coming, heard my threat, yet you still found time for-"

"A quick shower," Sowell said. "I'd just finished my workout and had a real stink on."

"You know why we're here," Daniel said.

"I do."

"Where is it?" Daniel said.

"What the hell are you two talking about?" Buchanan said.

Sowell turned and headed toward the bedroom.

Buchanan drew his gun. Aimed it at the man's back. "Stop right there," he shouted.

Daniel pushed Buchanan's arm aside. "It's okay, Frank."

"But he's-"

"On our side."

"He's what?"

"On our side."

"But you said he was behind it all."

"He was. Is."

"Then why-"

Sowell came out of the bedroom carrying a notebook computer. It was the same make and model as the one they'd 'found' at Blake's country retreat. "For what it's worth, it's the original." He passed it to Daniel. "When I wired Tokunbo's little shop of horrors for sight and sound, I dropped in a few extras. Everything he saw, I saw. Everything he heard, I heard."

"So that's why you were at the cabin that night."

"Blake told him where he could find the computer with his dying breath. I already knew it was there, of course, having dipped into its hard drive to set the whole farce in motion, but I couldn't wait any longer for the good guys to find it. And I couldn't let Tokunbo destroy it. I needed to keep the threat alive in his mind. To keep the chain of custody Kosher, I had a squash buddy, a sitting judge, issue a warrant that allowed me to retrieve it. Luckily, the switcheroo went down just before you and the baby Crips showed up."

"But there were no footprints in the snow."

Sowell shrugged and grinned. "Once a spook."

"Well, thanks," Daniel said. "Again."

"Don't mention it again, if you get my drift."

"Mention what?" Daniel said.

Sowell tapped the notebook. "I added an e-mail, and a couple of old snapshots that should prove enlightening."

"Doesn't that present one or two minor chain of custody issues?" Buchanan said.

Sowell placed an index finger to his lips, and said, "*Shhh*."

"Password?" Daniel said.

"It's been removed."

"Let's go, Frank," Daniel said.

Buchanan no longer even tried to hide his confusion. "Go where?"

"To the Batmobile. I'll tell you what I know, and what I think I know, on the way."

"To where?"

"To open your eyes."

"What about Sowell?" Buchanan said. "We're just gonna let him go?"

"Yep."

<u>87</u>

A pair of secret service agents, one black, one Arab, intercepted Daniel and Buchanan on the sidewalk outside the governor's mansion. From the grim expression on their faces Daniel was expecting a knock-down, drag-out confrontation, something he had hoped to avoid, hopped up on painkillers, his wounds nowhere close to healed, his back-up muscle bumbling around on a crutch. What he got instead was an escort.

On the second floor landing, Thornton's harridan secretary spotted them and charged out from behind her desk. But before she could spit a single venomous word, the Arab agent unbuttoned his blazer and gave her a suggestive glimpse of his gun, stopping her in her tracks. Hands raised, she retreated back to her seat and began to peck at the computer's keyboard with a manic intensity.

"He's waiting inside for you," the black agent said.

"You won't be disturbed," the Arab agent said.

Daniel opened the study door and gestured a sullen Buchanan in before him. His friend had been uncharacteristically silent on the ride over. Aside from the painful sound of grinding teeth as he'd powered on the notebook and scrolled through its contents, he hadn't made a single peep.

Inside Daniel was pleasantly surprised to see Ray Sowell, fully dressed, and immaculately groomed. The governor was sitting behind his desk with a quizzical half-smile on his face, unaware of the Category Five shit-storm that was heading his way.

"Worm hole?" Daniel said to Sowell.

"Lead foot," Sowell said.

Buchanan slammed the notebook computer down on the desk, and punched the power key. While it booted, he tossed his crutch and shucked his pea coat, tossing it over the back of a guest chair. Looking hard at Thornton, he unbuttoned his cuffs then rolled his sleeves up to the elbows.

"I want you to put an end to this shit. Right now."

"I'm sorry?"

"I want you to confess. Now."

"Confess to what, Frank? I don't understand."

"You make me watch fucked-up video again, *Terrence*, and I'm gonna bust you in the nose."

The governor looked at Sowell. "Tokunbo assured me-"

"That Blake's computer was lost in a fire?" Daniel said.

Still looking at Sowell, Thornton nodded slowly.

"Shabazz was mistaken," Daniel said.

"You knew about this?" Thornton said.

"I know everything. *Everything.*"

Thornton lowered his head. "Then fall, Caesar!"

Buchanan opened the requisite file and hit play.

The opening scene was a bewildering circus of perversions as the camera panned around the overly bright room. Daniel saw a child's face, numb with shock. A twisted limb of another child, red with bite marks. A row of perfect adult teeth, grinning madly. The gleam of a cool blue eye set deep under an arched grey eyebrow. Eric Murray snorting a line of coke. Ira Banks laughing. A half-dozen children. Maybe more. None of them were laughing.

The camera paused on Marshall Thomas. He was drenched in sweat, and grunting like an ape. A chubby Mongoloid boy was thrashing beneath him, his stubby arms reaching out for a savior who would never come. The boy's face was partially visible over the dripping man's massive shoulders, his eyes like empty black holes staring blankly outward.

The camera zoomed out. On the upper edge of the screen a familiar goodspeak banner was visible on the wall of an equally familiar room. *Diversity: It Includes Us All.* The pedophilic orgy had been held at The Colosseum.

The camera tracked left and zoomed in as it found its next victim.

A boy of about ten with Forrest Gump braces on his legs, dark skin, dark hair, and dark forsaken eyes, sat slumped against a wall. His tiny hands were clawing at his face and throat, as though the pain, or the blood loss, would end the nightmare. Looming over him, George Taylor was masturbating, obviously moved to fever pitch by the sight the boy's blood, his madness, or maybe both. Marie, George's dutiful wife, was sitting on a folding lawn chair just off to the side. She was knitting a brightly colored scarf, head nodding to the unheard beat of the iPod in her ears. Garry Glitter, perhaps. *Rock and Roll (Parts 1 and 2).* As George came, with two spurts, a dribble, and nary a whimper, the camera moved on.

Daniel tasted bile as the camera swept the carnage, gliding over a stack of queer stroke books, grotesque, bull-sized dildos, and broken children, to capture a face made famous in all the celebrity tabloids.

At first glance, David Blake resembled a nihilistic manifestation of Michelangelo's David. Flowing black hair. Ridiculously handsome face. A lean muscular frame pocked with scabs and scars. With his lips pulled back in a baboon's smile, he was grinding his hips into a severely handicapped child with no arms or legs, the child's guppy mouth widened in silent O's of pain and betrayal.

"What's Blake humping?" Buchanan said to Daniel. "Some kind of mechanized sex toy? I couldn't get a good enough look at it on the way over. You drive like shit by the way." It took him no more than a moment to fully comprehend what he was looking at. "Jesus Christ," he eventually gasped.

What Blake was humping was the sausage with eyes that they had seen on the Chubby Duck poster in Blake's condo. In the tunnels beneath The Colosseum Earlae had told them that the child's name was Edogiawarie. He lived with her and Shabazz in the loft and she loved him like he was her own child.

As the filmmaker's climax neared, the muscles in his arms tensed and bulged, and the boy's mouth opened wider than Daniel would have thought possible, howling without relent. Following a final flurry of merciless thrusts, Blake closed his eyes, threw his head back, and let out a howl of his own. Fully spent, he tossed the boy to the floor and staggered out of the frame. Raucous, adult laughter rose above the deep, heartrending sobs of the other children as the camera moved in to capture the poor deformed child flapping over the bare concrete like a broken-back mutt, still howling wildly.

On camera there was movement at the door. Two men entered, a large black man pushing an elderly white, wheelchair-bound man. *Sowell and Thornton*. The governor looked around the room for a moment, his face barely able to contain his emotions. Seconds later he tapped Sowell on the shoulder and they quickly backed out the way they had entered.

What had struck Daniel the first time he'd seen the movie, at the high school with Terry, was Sowell's reaction. Initially, his hand had gone for his gun, like he was ready to gut-shoot every last adult in the room and leave them for dead. But then his arm fell, his hand empty, and he just stared at Thornton. Too bad, Daniel thought, that he hadn't given in to reflex justice. What had stopped him? he wondered. Duty? Someday he would have to ask.

The movie ended shortly after the secret service agent had wheeled his charge out the door.

Sowell leaned over the desk and tapped some computer keys. "The e-mail that started it all," he said.

The phrase 'Out of sight, out of mind' appeared on the page in miniscule font in uncountable repetition. At the bottom was a crude Microsoft Paint drawing of an elephant.

Sowell tapped another series of keys.

On screen was a single photograph, a faded Polaroid, curled on its edges. It depicted a young Terrence Thornton readying himself to deep-throat a gangly preteen Sowell. Behind Thornton, a beanpole that looked an awful lot like Tokunbo Shabazz was looking at Thornton with no discernable expression on his face.

Thornton's head whiplashed as Buchanan hooked him hard on the nose. The governor's face was a mixture of fury, pain, surprise, and embarrassment as his eyes found Buchanan, a fat worm of blood oozing out of one nostril. Then, with the quickness of a rattlesnake, he yanked the top drawer of his desk open and pulled out a .38 Special. Daniel thought he was going to shoot Buchanan in retribution for the sucker punch but that wasn't what he had in mind at all. Instead he pressed the muzzle to his own temple.

But as quick as the old man was, Sowell was even quicker, mongoose quick, grasping hold of the snub-nose barrel and angling it toward the wall a millisecond before the trigger was pulled.

"Sorry," Sowell said. "But it can't be allowed to end that way."

A defeated Thornton snapped the notebook closed and looked up at Sowell with tears pearling at the corner of his eyes. "The elephant," he said. "The one that never forgets. It was you all along."

Sowell face was taut. "Not just me," he said. "All of us. Every child who's ever been touched by the likes of you. We'll never forget. Never."

"But I thought that-"

"You thought wrong."

The governor laid a visibly shaking hand on the computer. "What do you intend to do with this?"

"Pull back the curtain on the great and powerful Terrance Thornton III."

"You don't know what you're doing," Thornton said.

"I do. For the first time in my life."

The governor's eyes moved from one face to another, as though looking for empathy or solace. "There are people out there who believe the physical expression of love between adult and child to be a completely natural act."

"So is murder," Daniel said. "Slavery and cannibalism, too."

Thornton's gaze settled on Daniel. "I'm not one of them, of course. But that won't stop them from making me their poster child."

"For what?" Daniel said. "Legalizing the rape of children?"

Thornton was no longer looking at Daniel. His eyes were focused on a large frame over the fireplace, and the unmistakable glaze over them told Daniel that his mind was somewhere else, somewhere far, far away. Displayed behind the spotless, non-reflective glass were his military service medals. 'I'm no hero,' he had told the students at William Craft. *Damned straight you're not.*

"Society says it's wrong. Today." The thinnest of smiles touched the governor's lips, and then his eyes returned to Daniel. "But not long ago society said miscegenation was wrong. Not long ago, until 1973, society said homosexuality was a form of mental illness. Now it's just another lifestyle choice. As we speak homosexuals are tying the knot in multiple states in ever increasing numbers."

"Get real," Buchanan said. "It's not the same thing and you know it."

"Technically," Daniel said, "it is. All a part of the same slippery slope."

"And with the influx in immigration from Muslim countries," Thornton continued," what do you think is going to happen to the current sanctions against polygamy? Are you aware that incest between consenting adults has already been decriminalized in several European nations? Sweden even allows marriages between siblings who share a parent."

"If Johnny jumped off a bridge, would you? Didn't your mother ever teach you that?"

When the governor spoke again his voice was more distant and more solemn than a fading star. "The times they are a changin', Mr. Rourke. Like marriage. For better, or for worse."

"Not a chance in hell," Daniel said. "Not even in Massachusetts."

"I used to think I was alone, but I'm not. I wish like hell I was, but I'm not."

"You're the guilty conscience of a fringe movement of freaks and perverts," Daniel said. "Nothing I've got to worry about."

"Do you have any idea how many women in this country are estimated to have been sexually abused as children? *One in four.* That translates into millions of women. Tens of millions, actually. Our mothers. Our lovers. Our daughters. And then there are the men. One in five is their estimate. That's millions more. And fully half of them, boys and girls, have suffered multiple abusers."

"Your point?" Daniel said.

Thornton's mouth was smiling, but his eyes frowned. "Has it ever crossed your antiquated *Father Knows Best* mind that you're no longer even part of the majority, Mr. Rourke? Has it ever crossed your mind that you're the real freak? The latest freak *du jour*."

<u>88</u>

Frank Buchanan answered the door before Daniel could knock. He was wearing shorts and a sleeveless, threadbare NRA sweatshirt. Although his right leg remained in a cast, he no longer needed the crutch to get around. He led Daniel through the Portsmouth house to a sitting room with a million dollar view of the becalmed Atlantic Ocean. Biggie and a mangy three-legged pooch were pretzeled together on the pine floor in a twenty-four carat rhomboid of early afternoon sunlight. They pounced on Daniel as soon as he sat down, giving him wet, bitey kisses on the nose and cheeks. Buchanan said, "Down," in a firm tone and the dogs returned to their place in the sun, tails sweeping the floor.

"How's the leg?" Daniel said.

"Doc says I'll be River Dancing in no time."

"My condolences to your family."

Buchanan slapped Daniel heartily on the back. "Gimme a sec," he said and ducked out of the room.

Two minutes later, Buchanan appeared with an urn of coffee and three oversized mugs on a silver service tray. Sarah Calhoun joined them shortly thereafter in what had to be the Aston Martin of motorized wheelchairs. Her hair had been colored and cut and she was wearing makeup. Charlotte, Buchanan's adopted daughter, was fast asleep in her lap.

"You look fantastic," Daniel said.

"I do, don't I?" Sarah said with a smile. "I went out with my new BFF this morning. We had a mani and a pedi. Then we went for coffee and cheesecake, and we gossiped forever." Her laughter verged on a giggle. "I feel like a schoolgirl again."

"How are you doing otherwise, Sarah?" Daniel said.

She kissed Charlotte on the top of her head then looked over at Buchanan. "Better," she said. "Now that I've got my little Francis back."

"Aunt Sarah," Buchanan said.

She winked at Daniel. "Did Francis tell you he had a date?"

"Aunt Sarah!"

"And with a girl, too. Such a sweet young thing. It's about time he had someone special in his life. Don't you think so? He's been a bachelor far too long."

"I've talked to Eunice on the phone a coupla times, and she's been by for a visit. Once. It's not like we're getting married or anything."

"Getting maweed," Charlotte squealed as her cornflower blue eyes popped open. "Dadda's getting maweed."

"I thought you were sleeping," Buchanan said.

Charlotte closed her baby-blues and responded with a rather convincing sample of snores.

"You see what I'm getting myself into living here with these two, ah . . . ladies?" Buchanan said.

Charlotte rolled off Aunt Sarah's lap and lurched across the room toward the dogs. "Kitty," she exclaimed.

"Living here?" Daniel said. "What do you mean?"

"I never told you? I guess I didn't."

"Told me what?"

"I'm thinking of staying on a while. At least until I'm satisfied Aunt Sarah's all right." He took a sip of coffee and looked out over the slick, glassy water. "Maybe longer than that if things work out okay."

"You want to know something?" Daniel said. "Now that we've cleaned the place up some, I kind of like it here myself."

"Been thinking of sticking around yourself, have you?"

"Perhaps."

"That wouldn't have anything to do with a certain lady cop with a terminal case of the hots for you, would it?"

Before Daniel could respond, Biggie began to yap at Charlotte, who was having a tug-of-war with the three-legged dog's tail. "Whee," she said.

Buchanan sprang from the couch. "Charlotte," he said firmly. "Let go. Now."

Charlotte waited until Buchanan had almost reached her, then let go of the tail and toddled off in the opposite direction to take up position behind a large roll top desk.

"Have you spoken to Galton lately?"

Buchanan shook his head. "In case you haven't noticed, things are a little on the chaotic side around here." To Charlotte, he said, "Please come out of there."

Charlotte poked her head out and smiled sweetly up at him.

"There's been some real drama going on with Thornton's prosecution."

"Oh, yeah?"

"After the obligatory not guilty plea, it was the same old same old," Daniel said. "The lawyers buried the prosecution under a tsunami of paper. Motions alleging defects in the institution of the prosecution. Motions alleging defects in the indictment. Motions for change of venue. Motions to suppress-"

"Suppress what?"

"Thornton's lawyers wanted the notebook computer excluded from trial. They claimed it was tainted as it was obtained as part of an unreasonable search and seizure."

"Will it fly?" Buchanan said.

Daniel shrugged. "Might've," he said. "Although the back door Sowell took to get the warrant was sketchy, it was nonetheless legal. Still, it's a potential gray area. Its admissibility would've come down to the politics of the judge they drew."

When Buchanan attempted to squeeze in behind the desk to go after Charlotte, she squirted out the other side like a wet watermelon seed, caroming off an ottoman and a brass floor lamp as she made a giggling-mad dash down the hallway toward the front of the house.

Buchanan snarled, "Enough with the smoke and mirror legal-eagle bullshit-"

"Bowshit," Charlotte said, mimicking perfectly her father's surly tone of voice.

"Enough with the legal-eagle bull*poop*," Buchanan corrected himself as he charged down the hallway after his daughter. "You said it was the same old same old. Past tense. So what's the story now?" He scooped Charlotte up into his arms, her chubby bow legs still pumping, and she blurted, "Oh, *poop*."

"He's changing his plea to guilty."

"What? Why?"

"Initially, Ray Sowell was to be given immunity from prosecution in exchange for his testimony. Well, Ray and I had drinks, and we discussed the trial at length, possible outcomes, *et cetera*, and we both agreed that he should be charged as a co-conspirator."

"Sowell agreed to be charged as a-"

"Co-conspirator."

"Is he nuts?"

"On the contrary," Daniel said. "My first impression of the man was bang-on."

"So Thornton's pleading guilty in order to-"

"To prevent Ray from ever having to see the inside of a prison cell. Early next month, he'll formally change his plea and agree to a Statement of Facts in which the name Raymond Sowell never once appears."

"This is fucked . . . uh, messed up."

"Despite one or two hiccups. It's ingenious."

"Hiccups?"

"That whole you, me, Sarah, and Terry almost dying thing."

Buchanan laughed. "That's a pretty serious case of the hiccups, man."

"It all worked out in the end."

"What really went on? Do you know? Do you really know?"

Daniel nodded. "It wasn't about revenge, or even power. We were all wrong."

"So what was it about?"

"Justice."

"Justice," Buchanan repeated.

Daniel could tell from his friend's tone of voice that he was skeptical. "It all started years and years ago, shortly after Thornton got back from Vietnam. He'd always been attracted to young boys but he'd never acted on the attraction. When he returned stateside, however, messed up on painkillers, not to mention several other popular drugs of the day, the urges grew stronger, and he let his guard down."

"Kind of like Dr. Jekyll and Chester the Molester."

Daniel nodded. "It was with a couple of kids at the shelter he'd founded."

"Peace Brother," Buchanan mumured sadly.

"He'd apparently started it with good intentions, but that soon changed."

"That picture of Thornton and Sowell-"

"Ray was the first," Daniel said. "Then came Shabazz."

"Were there others?"

Daniel shook his head. "He went into counseling, cleaned himself up, and somehow tamped the urges back down. According to Ray, he put his heart and soul into the shelter, and what was left over he put into his work. The guilt over what he'd done plagued him-"

"That's what they all say."

"He really tried to atone. He took in Ray through the Foster Parent program, and tried to do the same with Shabazz. But Shabazz was incorrigible."

"More like a psychopath."

"He gave Ray a family, and the best that life had to offer. Love, stability, the best schools, world travel, you name it."

"A fairy tale ending," Buchanan said sarcastically.

"Almost," Daniel said. "The fairy tale ended the night of the video shoot. Unbeknownst to Thornton, Marshall Thomas, his campaign manager, had tastes similar to his own."

"They're like dogs," Buchanan said. "They can sniff each other's assholes out from a mile away."

"Could be you're right," Daniel said. "Why else would Thomas have invited Thornton to his private soirée at The Colosseum?"

"Where Blake raped that poor wiener-shaped boy."

"One and the same."

"But Thornton didn't touch any of the kids. He left almost as soon as he arrived."

"He did," Daniel said. "But you saw the look on his face, the Mona Lisa smile, the way his eyes just seemed to light up."

"And Sowell saw it, too. On the face of the man who might well have become the next Commander in Chief."

"Thirty-some years of atonement down the drain."

"So that e-mail Thornton received-"

"Was from Ray. He set the whole thing in motion. He thought Thornton had gotten better, had made amends, but he saw that he was wrong. The old habits hadn't died after all."

"Thornton thought he was being blackmailed, and he took steps to put an end to the threat."

"Again all thanks to Ray. He was the one who added Shabazz into the equation, putting just enough spin on the facts to let the monster loose. To take down not only Thornton, but the whole crew. Shabazz included."

"Only one way it could've gone down."

"And it did. Thornton was being manipulated by a master manipulator, and he was desperate, not thinking straight."

"All well that ends well, huh?"

"Justice *was* served."

"We almost died," Buchanan said. "That doesn't mean anything to you? Sowell gets away scot-free and you're okay with that?"

"More than anyone else, Frank, you know what he's been through. Did he really get away scot-free?"

Grudgingly, Buchanan mumbled, "I guess not."

"You remember the morning you saw Ray and Shabazz scuffle outside the club?"

Buchanan nodded.

"Do you know why Ray was there?"

Buchanan shook his head.

"To secure Sarah's release."

"Now why would he agree to something that stupid?"

"Shabazz was afraid of only one man."

"Sowell," Buchanan said.

"Yeah," Daniel said. "So he promised Ray he would release her. He said he would let her go that night."

"He was planning a double-cross."

"Obviously. He was going to try to kill Ray. How? No way of knowing that now." Daniel looked over at Biggie and the three-legged pooch, still curled up in the sunshine. "Are you going to let sleeping dogs lie?"

Buchanan nodded curtly. "What about Earlae? How'd she fit into it all?"

"It was just as we'd thought. Shabazz used the sins of her past to manipulate her into exacting revenge-by-proxy on her dead stepfather."

Buchanan was silent for a moment. "So she was nothing more than a sacrificial lamb."

"More a martyr for the cause," Daniel said.

"His cause."

"Once Shabazz thought he had negated the threat to the Governor, the plan was to have Earlae accept responsibility for the killings via suicide note."

"But Shabazz had second thoughts."

"He really did love her," Daniel said. "And when Earlae introduced Lloyd Mathis into the mix - you remember him, the little man with Tourettes syndrome - Shabazz went to Ray and told him that Mathis, and not Earlae, would be playing the part of the patsy."

"Wouldn't have worked," Buchanan said. "Earlae's DNA was all over the crime scenes."

"Shabazz was a psychopath, remember? Not a rocket scientist."

Buchanan stood and began to pace angrily around the room. "And to think I would've voted for the guy."

Daniel smiled sweetly. "Not me, he said.

Buchanan stopped pacing. "One more question," he said.

"Shoot."

"Does your sudden desire to lollygag in the chilly northeast have anything to do with a certain lady cop with a terminal case of the hots for you?"

Daniel cracked a lopsided grin. "Do you mind if I borrow your phone, Sarah?"

"Step number twelve?" Buchanan said.

"And about friggin' time," Daniel said.

He located Terry at her home number, second ring. "Busy tonight?" he said.

"I was wondering how long it was going to take for you to work up the nerve to call me."

"I'll pick you up at seven. We can grab a bite in the city at this swanky place that Special Agent in Charge Reagan recommended. It's called Palmer's."

"Swanky indeed," Terry said. "Red or black?"

"Excuse me?"

"What color dress do you want me to wear? Keeping in mind that the black Donna Karan is by far the shorter and tighter of the two."

"Black, please."

"Men," Terry said. "You're so predictable."

Daniel looked over at Buchanan, who had pinned his daughter to the floor and was planting loud, wet raspberries all over her roly-poly belly while the dogs lapped gleefully at her face. The little girl was wriggling this way and that as she attempted to avoid death by saliva. Her laughter, like a series of tiny bubbles popping, was quite possibly the sweetest sound that Daniel had ever heard.

"I wouldn't go quite that far," he said.

<u>89</u>

Palmer's was located on Beacon Hill in a Federal-style mansion with high ceilings, richly carpeted floors, and a working fireplace in each of its three private dining rooms. For the occasion of their first date, Daniel had chosen a Dolce & Gabbana navy three-button single breasted wool pinstripe suit, white cotton shirt, Armani black leather lace-ups, and if he didn't look good enough to eat, he hoped he looked at least good enough to nibble on. Terry, on the other hand, wearing the skimpy Donna Karan dress, really did look good enough to eat.

"Why are you staring at me like that?" Terry said shortly after they had been seated and their orders taken.

Daniel grinned wolfishly.

"My father warned me about men like you."

"Your father's a wise man."

"All of a sudden it hits me that I really don't know much about you. So before this . . . this *whatever* between us takes on a life of its own, I'm thinking you should maybe spill one or two of your deepest and darkest secrets."

Daniel did precisely as requested, and as the evening fairly flew by, he was surprised that he was telling her so much more about himself than he had expected to. It was a conversation more about establishing connections than drawing boundaries, which was unusual for Daniel. In his life thus far there had been only a few people with whom he could really open up. His mother and father, certainly. No one else since Julie. It had taken him a long time to figure out that it was the loss of this human connection that had left him empty following her death. He needed to be connected with someone again, he knew, and he had a hunch that Terry might be one of those rarest of individuals.

"This isn't at all what I'd expected," Terry said when Daniel had finally stopped blathering.

"It's not?"

"Me being a cop, you being a former prosecutor, I thought we'd spend the entire dinner talking murder and mayhem, yet here we sit waxing philosophical on love and regret-"

"And hope," Daniel said.

"Especially hope."

"To be honest, it's not what I'd expected either."

What remained of the logs in the fireplace made a kind of wistful sigh as they settled into the glowing pyramid of embers beneath, sending up a shimmering cascade of sparks.

"It was your love for Julie that brought you back."

"It wasn't what she'd have wanted. But, all things considered, it wasn't what I wanted either."

Terry held out her hand, and Daniel took it.

"There was something else?"

"Not something else," Daniel said, his words a whispered confessional. "Someone else."

She was staring hard at Daniel's eyes with a molten gaze. The sense of the future was inevitable and vast in her wide-open, fully dilated eyes. They held onto his and wouldn't let go. "Who?" Her voice was very hoarse.

Daniel smiled. "Are you going to eat that?" He motioned at her dessert plate.

"Some first date you are," Terry said, recovering her composure nicely, her tone playful once more, "won't let a lady have her Black Forest cake and eat it, too."

"I don't want your cake," he said.

"You don't?"

"Unh-unh."

"Then what do you want?"

"I want your cherry."

Terry motioned the waiter over.

"Please bring the gentleman a bowl of your finest cherries. It seems he has his heart set on mine, but he can't have it."

Their waiter, a sixty-something Englishman with a red half-coat and stoic features, said simply, "Pity."

Daniel put his hands on either side of Terry's face and kissed her hard on the mouth.

"On second thought," she said as their lips drew apart, plucking the plump red fruit from the icing and pressing it to his mouth, "you may cancel that order."

"An *excellent* decision, mum," the waiter said.

They looked at each other silently for a moment, recognizing in each other the same special something that they had seen not so long ago at David Blake's cabin. Only this time Daniel did not look away. He ran a hand lightly over her cheek. Other than a hint of lipstick, she wasn't wearing makeup, and didn't need to. Her hair, the same shade as the Vermont autumn that used to take his breath away as a child, felt like spun silk between his fingers.

"You're dazzling," Daniel said. "You . . . you light my way." It sounded like a line, but it was the honest-to-God truth.

"And you . . ." She gazed at him appraisingly as she searched for the right words.

"Look good enough to nibble on?"

She closed her eyes and leaned in and kissed him, her arms pulling him in tight enough that he could feel her incredibly toned body trembling. In time, her lips moved to the hollow in his throat and she nipped him there gently.

"Umm-hmmm," she responded.

"I knew it."

Terry whispered in his ear, "Do you still have your room at The Rex?"

Daniel's throat tightened at the thought of the two of them alone together in the tiny room with the paper-thin walls and the creaking bed, and for one of the few times in his life he found himself at a loss for words. In fact, it was taking his complete concentration just to keep breathing. He nodded vigorously.

"Check please," Terry said.

"I'm afraid your money's no good here," the waiter said. "Patrick Reagan's orders."

Daniel wasn't sure how this 'whatever' between them would progress, whether the future he had glimpsed in her amber eyes would last a lifetime, a year, or a month. He surveyed the naughty Samba of her backside as she excused herself from the table and headed to the cloakroom to collect their things. And if it were to last but a single night?

Daniel scrambled to his feet and rushed to catch up with her.

He could live with that.